the DEMON SOULS series
BOOK TWO

KALIK

JOSH BROOKES

the DEMON SOULS series
BOOK TWO

KALIK

chapter
ONE

⊙ Ψ ℳ

"LUCIKEFER!"

The door was thrown from its hinges as he smashed through it with what remained of his strength. He felt a spike of elation at the sight of the wood splintering into a thousand pieces, scattering across the floor; he still had *some* power left.

But it wouldn't be enough.

His pursuer close behind him, Lucikefer looked left and right, frantically searching for a place to hide.

Noticing a second level to the warehouse he'd just aggressively invaded, the demon quickly decided that some elevation would be to his advantage. He would have a better view of his surroundings up there, something which his pursuer would lack down on the ground.

Lucikefer made for the staircase, his legs too weak to launch him supernaturally, and darted up as fast as he could. He cursed his fatigue as he tripped and almost fell back to the bottom of the stairs.

The shadows of a dark corner were extremely welcome, but Lucikefer only just made it before part of the wall came crashing down, bricks and glass smashing and crumbling across the floor and adding to the mess.

Sunlight streamed in, highlighting the figure that walked through the hole that had just been created.

Lucikefer's infernal chaser.

Zale Hood.

"Go . . . away," Lucikefer panted to himself, speaking quietly so that Hood would not hear him. How long had this been going on? Why couldn't the kid just leave? Lucikefer was *so* tired now.

He was shocked to hear Zale laugh.

Damn. He'd forgotten about the cursed child's super hearing.

The Enthraller raised his auto-rifle and spat to the open warehouse, "Come here so I can kill you!"

With fear clawing his insides, Lucikefer used what little power he had left to throw his voice so that Zale would not locate his position. "You can't kill me! I survived Daemnos. I can survive you!"

Zale wasted no time in roaring back, "I don't know how you survived, Lucikefer. You should have been obliterated by your uncle, you bastard."

From his hiding place, Lucikefer could see the boy spinning in circles, trying to determine where the Royal lay. Lucikefer stopped the flow of air going to his lungs, terrified of the possibility that Zale would hear his breath.

Zale continued to taunt him. "But you know what? I don't care how you did it. All I *do* care about is that you're severely weakened now. The last five months have taken their toll on you. You never got a chance to properly heal after your uncle kicked your arse.

"Right now, you aren't strong enough to fight back. I can kill you and I intend to do just that."

Everything Hood was yelling was true; Lucikefer could barely stand anymore, his physical strength all but gone. He was relying on supernatural energy, and even that was dwindling faster than it could regenerate.

Lucikefer could feel panic rising in his chest.

The end felt frighteningly near.

But the Royal was nothing if not a brilliant liar—a master pretender—and despite the fear sitting in his stomach he managed to mask it with a confident mocking tone. "You are powerful, young one. But can you control your anger? I think not. It will destroy you. You aren't strong enough to fight it. How can you hope to defeat *me*, Lucikefer, the . . . *rightful* prince of demons if you can't even defeat yourself?"

This ramble was not aimless. It was important to keep Zale distracted until Lucikefer found a way out of here. Confuse him with predictions and prophecies.

He just needed time.

Unfortunately, Lucikefer was getting no chances to look around because he was too busy ensuring Zale didn't come his way.

And Zale didn't seem to care about what Lucikefer said. He didn't even appear to be listening.

This was evident in the way he clearly muttered, "Oh yeah?" Before Lucikefer could react, Zale spun on his heel and the next thing he knew his vision was flashing blue. A blast of electricity hit him squarely on his skull inspired visor and Lucikefer screamed as his body convulsed, his limbs jerking from the voltage.

He was thrown back from the sheer force, slamming into the

wall and bouncing off it. He came crashing to the floor, rolling over the side of the staircase and tumbling down painfully.

Groaning, Lucikefer pushed himself to his knees and raised his head to glare at the approaching Zale. "Not even weakened!?" he exclaimed in disbelief, noting the strength in the kid's strides. "*How!?* You should be on your knees after a blast as large as that."

He grunted as Zale kicked him onto his back and struck him on the stomach with the butt of his rifle. "I am far stronger than you give me credit for," Zale snarled.

Lucikefer laughed an irreverent laugh, though it wasn't aimed towards his attacker. "I see," he sighed. "It appears my Enthraller truly was a failure. His own arrogance resulted in his feeding me incorrect information. He believed both you and Badrick to be weak."

"Yes, well—" Zale interrupted his own words to give a shout of fury; Lucikefer had used the distraction of him talking to shimmer out of sight.

He materialised on the rafters hidden in the darkness of the ceiling, which even the strong overhead lights did not illuminate. It reminded Lucikefer of the Daemonium, and how their resident mental had hidden in their ceiling many a time.

Gasping at the exhaustion from the effort of using a power as advanced as a teleport, and trying to stay balanced even with his body screaming in protest, Lucikefer glared down at Zale, hoping beyond hope. He was so weak he'd only been capable of a local teleport.

But if he could just keep quiet enough, Zale might think he'd teleported out of the warehouse.

His hope was brutally extinguished as Zale cackled insanely and bawled, "You don't have enough for another teleport like that! Come out, come out, wherever you are!"

He had to stop himself from shouting the vilest curse he could think of. Hollering insults would not help him right now. Though his heart hammered against his chest in protest, Lucikefer continued using powers. Once again throwing his voice, he spoke to the room.

"Your friend didn't want to die, yet we killed him. We made him suffer."

He didn't say this out of spite. There was cunning in the taunt. If Lucikefer could make Zale angry, he would stand a better chance. A mad Zale was a mistake-making Zale.

It seemed to work, as Zale responded with an enraged shout of, "You can't get away from me!"

The next blast of voltage missed Lucikefer by miles. He chuckled, amused, convinced his plan was working. "Missed!" His voice bounced off the walls chaotically, making it impossible for normal people to determine its source. Hopefully it would fool Zale too. "Don't change the subject, Hood. You can't pretend you aren't hurting from the loss of Badrick."

Lucikefer's smug grin became strained when what he expected to happen didn't at all. Instead of Zale throwing more electricity every which way, the kid simply stopped moving and lowered his arms, allowing his gun to swing idly to his side.

It was then that Lucikefer heard him chuckle.

The Royal bared his teeth. What the hell was so damn funny to the electric bastard?

"I know what you're trying to do," Zale sighed, just loud enough for the demon to hear. "You really think I'm stupid enough to fall for that?" He gazed back up at the room, his blue visor reflecting the sunlight that shone into the warehouse. "You can't make me angry, Lucikefer. Would you like to know why?"

Lucikefer shuddered at the malevolence in Zale's voice. It seemed to reverberate from the walls, bouncing towards him and sending chills down his spine.

He would have replied to Zale's question . . .

Only he never got the chance.

Before he could open his mouth, Zale screamed, "Because I already am!"

The following blast hit Lucikefer dead-on. It knocked him from the rafters and he fell, screaming, back to the ground floor with a bone-breaking shudder.

Thankfully, however weak he got, Lucikefer was still a demon. No manner of fall would ever end him.

Unfortunately, the angry Enthraller just might.

"Just why do you think I'm hunting you to your death?" Lucikefer became aware of Zale's presence above his body, the Enthraller's voice ringing in his already pounding ears. He pointed his weapon at the writhing Lucikefer, taking a moment to watch him squirm pitifully. After a pause the demon felt a painful kick hit him in the side and he rolled onto his back.

Lucikefer breathed heavily and spat black blood onto the inside of his helmet. Struggling to a sitting position, unable to do anything more, he gazed up at Hood, hating him more than he ever had during the last five months.

"I know . . . you, Hood. I've . . . been around you for . . . years. Previous experience . . . shows that you will show mercy to . . . to me."

"Key word in that sentence?" Zale wasted no time in asking. *"Previous."*

A pistol came into view. His auto-rifle slung in expert time, Zale brought it to bear and fired the weapon into Lucikefer's face. At point blank range, the round was just enough to smash the visor and knock him back.

Lucikefer gasped and rolled onto his front, forcing his dwindling reserves into repairing the damage before Zale saw inside.

Even with the threat of death he would never let someone like *him* see his true face.

He took a moment to assess the rest of the damage and was grateful to find he was unwounded. The bullet had disintegrated from the effort of smashing his visor and left his face unspoiled.

Even so, he cursed vilely, turning back to Zale. "It'll take more than a bullet to kill me, Hood," he murmured darkly.

"Oh, I know," Zale responded cheerfully. "But I want you to suffer and feel pain first." Another bullet hit Lucikefer on the chest. "And F-Y-I, it's *Mister Hood* to you!"

With every word he fired a shot, furiously emphasising what he spoke.

When the last bullet left the weapon and Zale was forced to reload, Lucikefer used the respite to roar, "Enough! I grow tired of this. If you are going to kill me, then damn well do it already."

It was a ploy that had worked many times over the centuries.

Infuriatingly, Zale didn't fall for it.

In a voice that parroted Lucikefer's, Zale crooned, "Previous experience tells me that you'll take advantage if I do. You'll counterattack me. And, unlike you with me, I haven't read your intentions wrong."

"Curse you, Hood! It looks like one piece of information from Stefan was correct. Your powers of deduction are frustratingly amazing."

Zale flipped the pistol in his hands boastfully. "I know," he chuckled. "It's my redeeming factor. I'm the detective of the Daemonium family."

Lucikefer's eyes widened and he grinned savagely. *An opening!*

"And what was Badrick?" he cackled.

For the first time in five months, Zale fell for one of his ploys. He started shooting rapidly, angrily, but the bullets weren't properly aimed and they bounced harmlessly off Lucikefer's armour.

He'd been gathering his power since he'd fallen to the ground, waiting for an opportune time. Having created one himself, Lucikefer tapped into the energy he'd gathered and darted forward, charging supernaturally fast at the Enthraller. He brought his fist back, charging it with power, fully intending to smash into Zale's visor, breaking through the blue and reaching his face.

With gleeful anticipation, he awaited the satisfying smash and responding death of the one who had bothered him for so long.

But it never came.

Lucikefer felt a kind of unprecedented frustration he had never before experienced as Zale expertly ducked the fist, yanked out a knife from its sheath with perfect grace and sunk it into Lucikefer's midriff.

Like the bullets, this mortal weapon, despite its blade being constructed from demonic metals, would not kill him.

It didn't even come close to endangering his life.

But it hurt like *hell!*

Zale unstuck the blade and pushed him away. Lucikefer staggered back, gasping in agonising pain, black blood erupting from the wound. With his sense of balance destroyed, Lucikefer almost tripped, stumbling pathetically.

Zale helped him to the floor with another electrical blast.

Choking from uncontrollable spasms, his armour scratching the concrete on the floor, Lucikefer took a minute to get his breathing back under control and allow the blood from his wounds to congeal.

He should have been able to heal instantly, but his strength was at an all time low.

His face was still sore from the bullet. That was how low he'd sunk.

If he couldn't even stop an ache, how could he hope to survive this?

With his breaths calming now, he gazed up and asked, "I have to know. How did you see that coming? I used my powers to attack you. I should have been too fast."

Zale laughed in his face as Lucikefer tried to stand, though he only managed it as far as his knees. "One," he said, "I didn't fall for your stupid ploy. I knew what you intended. Two, I have electro-synapses. I can sense anything coming. I'm friggin' *Spider-Man*."

Lucikefer frowned; this name did not ring any bells in his memory. He tried to think back over his centuries of living, but to no avail. "Who?" he snapped impatiently.

Zale scoffed rudely. "You don't know who *Spider-Man* is?"

"Should I?" he sighed tiredly. "Is he a powerful demon?"

Zale did not respond for a moment. He didn't even move. For the first time ever he appeared genuinely stunned.

Lucikefer was going to question his sudden unresponsive behaviour when, for no reason at all, Zale simply shot him again. Through pained chokes, the demon screamed, "What was that for?"

The Enthraller ejected his magazine and slotted in a new one. As the clip clicked into place, he sighed. "I've had enough. Enough of your stupidity. Enough of your poison. Enough of *you!*" He snarled like a vicious animal. "I'm going to kill you now."

"Like hell you are!" Lucikefer bellowed in response. Summoning energy from sheer force of will, he jumped up and pulled out his secret weapon; the one he'd been preparing to spring on Zale when the time was right.

A perfect moment had never presented itself and he knew he was close to the end.

It was now or never.

He flicked the object twice and an electric blue blade emerged as if from nowhere, slicing through the air with a sizzle. Lucikefer gave a wild, hopeful lunge, aiming for Zale's neck with the intent of lopping his head clean off.

His hopes were shattered when his enemy dodged the strike with lightning reflexes that even Lucikefer would have struggled to match at full strength.

Zale laughed hysterically and hollered, "Do you really think you can beat me with my own sword? I can't believe you still have that." He holstered his pistol and appeared to leer at Lucikefer mockingly. "They're not allowed in the field," he drawled.

Lucikefer allowed himself a small chuckle. "Still playing by the rules, Hood? That is why you will always lose. Those who play by the rules are no danger."

A fresh idea already forming in his quick-thinking mind, Lucikefer opened his mouth to speak.

Then immediately shut it again.

He took a step back, feeling a fresh pang of alarm despite his sense of elation at having achieved what he'd intended without any effort whatsoever.

Though, truthfully, he didn't know what to do now.

His hand shook as he studied the changed visor in front of him, the familiar blue vanished without a trace.

Zale's visor was now black.

Neither spoke for a moment, only staring at each other.

Then, quite unexpectedly, Zale reached for something strapped to his lower back that Lucikefer had not noticed before. With the speed of a cheetah, he unstrapped it and flicked it twice.

Lucikefer's eyes widened when he saw that Zale's blade was different to any of the others he'd seen.

All of those before had straight blades, but this new weapon was different. The blade was curved, like some kind of scimitar. Lucikefer had been alive for many, many years. He'd travelled to all four corners of Hell and across the furthest reaches of the human Universe. His knowledge of human history was extensive, and so he instantly recognised the inspiration behind the design of this new weapon as from the Saracen culture, from when the Holy Land was besieged by King Richard's Crusaders.

The fact that the blade was curved defied Lucikefer's understanding of the science behind the weapons Hood had created. A blade such as this was impossible!

He couldn't help his curiosity over it.

Nevertheless, he kept his mind clear. Questioning something as menial as a curved sword at this moment would have been careless and stupid. Besides, Lucikefer's final, desperate tactic might just have worked. The blackness was on Zale's visor, and he'd just rebelled against the rules by using a sword out in the field.

I knew it, he thought quickly, swinging his own blade to distract Zale's attention and giving himself time to think. Zale's black visor followed it like a puppy tracking a hunk of chicken. *Maybe I can bring out that* black *rage. If I don't he may just kill me. I need to keep encouraging rebellious behaviour.*

His mind made up, Lucikefer snarled, "Come on then, Hood. Be a rebel. Play against the rules. Use your sword here and now. Fight me."

Zale didn't move.

He didn't even twitch.

The only movement coming from him at all was the swirling electrical energy in his blade.

The stillness—the silence—made Lucikefer's skin tingle, and he felt a coldness crawl up his spine. He gazed at Zale in confusion, trying to figure out what was going on.

What is he doing?

But then the black faded. The electric blue consumed the darkness and Zale returned to normal.

Lucikefer was so engrossed watching the transformation happen that he utterly failed to react to Zale's next move.

He darted forward, swinging his sword up in a calculated strike, one devoid of thoughtless anger despite Lucikefer's manipulations.

The curved blade sliced a huge gash in Lucikefer's chestplate and he staggered back, fresh black blood spewing from his body. Lucikefer screamed in agony, dropping his own sword. Desperate and panicked that all his plans had failed, he tried to turn and run.

Zale struck him on the back with his foot and kicked him to the floor, halting his escape.

Lucikefer writhed where he lay, screaming unintelligibly. Every single time he tried to trick Zale, or taunt him, or anger him, force him to make a blunder, the Enthraller outfoxed him.

Every.

Single.

Time.

He screeched in barely contained fury, hating Zale so much he felt like his head and chest were going to burst from the rage. As he bawled at the top of his lungs, Zale deactivated his sword and strapped it to his body. Then, pulling his auto-rifle from his back, he stepped forward and aimed it at Lucikefer's head.

"I'll charge this bullet with my power." His voice was nothing more than a hiss, but the menace contained within was enough to silence the demon, who fell into terrified quiet. "I reckon I can just about do it. When it hits you . . . that will be the end."

Lucikefer could do nothing to prevent it. He wanted to—*of course* he wanted to. What awaited a demon after death was far worse than anything humans had to deal with on Earth or in Hell.

Damn, even Hell was Heaven compared to a demon's '*afterlife*'.

He glared up at Zale, terror flowing through his veins. He began to shake from his fear, like a common mortal. He couldn't help it.

He didn't want to die.

He was *Lucikefer!* The almighty son of the Demonic Royal Family.

He couldn't just *die*.

But Zale didn't care that he was a Royal.

Didn't care that he didn't want to die.

Zale *was* the end.

Lucikefer knew it.

This was the end.

He closed his eyes, whimpering stupidly, humiliated and terrified all at the same moment. He awaited the bullet and the all-consuming darkness that would follow, leading him into everlasting torment.

Counting the seconds before it came.

One . . .

Two . . .

Three . . .

He kept going, counting automatically, half worrying he was already dead and would be forced to forever count towards a death that already occurred.

But after he hit twenty, Lucikefer realised the bullet had not come. The darkness had not claimed him.

It was then that he heard Zale cry out in alarm and his eyes shot open to see the Enthraller staggering backwards, staring at his arms.

They were electrified, voltage travelling up and down, zapping, sparking. Zale exclaimed again, and Lucikefer realised this was not of the boy's own making.

Staring in confusion himself, he called out to the Enthraller, "What's happening?"

He never got an answer. The electricity flowing through Zale's body exploded, shooting into the air and smashing into the ceiling.

What must have been ten thousand volts electrified the warehouse walls. The whole room lit up a vibrant blue and white by the disturbance.

Left-over tools and machinery either exploded or danced about the place. The windows yet to be smashed did just that, littering the place with shattered glass. Lucikefer's dropped sword was struck by a rogue volt. It jumped into the air and exploded, the power trapped within it escaping and adding to the voltage ravaging the warehouse.

In the midst of this chaos, Lucikefer was blinded by a sudden flash of red light. He clenched his eyes against the glare, snapping angrily, but the wind was knocked out of him as he felt his body leave the concrete and smash into the wall far behind.

Whatever the red light was had thrown him back.

When he was able to stand—not to mention see—Lucikefer's eyes fell upon something he never believed he would glimpse again.

In the middle of the warehouse, ignoring the voltage that was now dying out, standing between him and Zale . . .

His armour fresh, clean, untarnished as if newer than a newborn baby, he clicked his fingers and aimed them at Zale, who was stumbling to his feet—having been thrown back himself— and staring at the new arrival with disbelief.

And in a nonchalant voice that really did not fit the situation, the Badrick asked, "You miss me?"

chapter
TWO

Scorch marks lined every nearby wall, not to mention the floor. Black and angry, some still fizzled with orange flames. The devastation was so great that even Lucikefer's stolen sword lay in pieces some distance away.

Zale spotted the Royal fleeing as fast as he could, frantically stumbling away. Lucikefer smashed open a back door and disappeared into the sun that shone through the open threshold.

But Zale didn't go after him.

He didn't even care about the chaos all around.

He was too stunned.

Only one thing mattered to him.

Standing before him, as if nothing had happened, was his old partner—Badrick Varner himself.

Several moments passed after Badrick spoke, in which Zale could only stare. Now he stumbled to his feet, using the wall he'd been thrown against to stabilise his weak legs.

But after that he had no idea how to proceed, though he *was* dimly aware that he should say something, or at least shoot whatever was standing in front of him.

From the moment Zale saw him, disbelief filled his chest. Because there wasn't a single moment when he believed that the real Badrick was alive and well.

It had been five months; his body should have been decayed and rotten and atrociously malodorous . . . But here he was, fresh as the day he was born.

It *wasn't* Badrick.

Badrick was dead.

"Hello?" the thing pretending to be his partner said. "Anyone in there?" It waved a hand in the air as if to get Zale's attention.

These words spurred Zale into action. In a flash he retrieved his auto-rifle, jumped to his feet and advanced, weapon cocked and raised in the direction of the creature that had stolen Badrick's image.

"Who are you!?" he roared, spit flying from his mouth and specking the inside of his visor. "*What* are you?"

'*Badrick*' took a wary step back and put his hands in the air. "Careful, buddy," he said slowly. "I just got this body back."

"Don't you *dare* talk with his voice!" Zale screamed, his arms shaking angrily. "Use your own, you coward! Show me who you are!"

The green armoured figure sighed, but did as he was ordered. His hands found his helmet and, with a twist, he slid it from his head.

Revealing Badrick's face.

Zale's limbs lost their strength. He felt his arms go limp and fall to his sides. His mouth gaped stupidly as he stared at the perfectly fresh features of his partner. His mind raced noisily inside his skull; he knew nothing less than a Royal demon could perfectly replicate another sapient being, so there was no way this was any Ordinarius or Singularis.

Unless Daemnos himself was standing before him—and that was surely impossible—this truly was Badrick.

Badrick spoke again before Zale could. "It's me, dude. Swear down."

"But . . . " Zale choked. He coughed to clear his throat and tried again. "How can it be you? You died."

Badrick lowered his hands, the wary look vanishing from his eyes. It was quickly replaced by immense sadness; the look, Zale recognised, of a man who was recollecting deep, dark memories. "How long has it been?" he asked softly.

"Five months!" Zale screeched, still freaking out.

"Damn!" Badrick exasperated. "Still not eighteen. Close though. I guess that's something."

Zale often rambled in a way similar to this, and knew people got irritated when he did. But this was the first time he'd ended up on the other side, and felt a new feeling of impatience because of it.

He took another step forward and exclaimed, "Dude!" Badrick instantly stopped and looked back up. "If this is really you then start talking."

Badrick half smiled and gazed around the warehouse. "Right now? Wouldn't you rather go somewhere else?"

"Now!"

He sighed and gestured to the closest staircase, indicating for Zale to sit. Zale didn't move, only clicked his fingers again even more impatiently. Badrick gave him a tired look, but conceded nevertheless with, "Fine, if you wanna wear our legs out all day, be my goddamn guest and stand there."

"I'll be fine," Zale muttered. "But I want answers now. How are you standing here?"

Badrick put his hands together and murmured, "In order for you to understand, we need to go back to the beginning."

"When's the beginning?"

"When Daemnos took over and killed Stefan," Badrick informed him, apparently deciding he wasn't going to stand and walking over to the staircase to plonk himself down. When he was comfortable, he continued, "I opened the tenth fissure to get enough power to beat him, but Daemnos had tricked me. Doing this let him loose.

"We both know what happened next. Stefan died. I died. Ten fissures was too much."

"Yeah," Zale scoffed. "I remember."

"Most Enthrallers die when they get to the eighth fissure, but because Daemnos is a Royal demon he doesn't work the same way. His power was enough to keep me going. If I had opened the fissures gradually I would have been fine. Opening them all so quickly is what killed me."

This didn't sound right to Zale and he instantly questioned it, despite knowing it would prolong the conversation; in truth he was getting a little impatient with the back-story. But he just couldn't help himself.

"But wouldn't you have been a walking corpse like Stefan?"

"I don't really know how it works," Badrick sighed, his saddening expression indicating that the mention of Stefan's ordeal was upsetting him, "but Lucikefer is different to the other Royals. I don't know why. No Enthraller can handle him without dying so he needs to constantly keep them alive. But Daemnos is like the other demons. His Enthraller doesn't just *die* from having him in their souls *but* he is powerful enough that his host doesn't collapse when getting to eight fissures.

"But only if they don't open them all at the same time," Badrick laughed. "That was my mistake."

"OK, OK, I get that," Zale half snapped, irritated at himself for asking such an unimportant question. "Get on with it, or I'll shoot you anyway."

Badrick grinned in his direction, unabashed. "Because Daemnos is so powerful he knew my death would only be temporary, which is why he let me do it in the first place. For the last five months Daemnos has been rebuilding my body, cell by cell, atom by atom.

"Of course it's not that simple. In order for the process to work, the Enthraller has to be strong enough to withstand being dragged back to life. As I understand it, it's been tried only three times before in all of history.

"It's not like the Resurrected you deal with usually. What Daemnos did was true life reconstruction. The other two Enthrallers apparently went mad, their consciousnesses and souls torn apart by the strain.

"But Daemnos said I was strong enough. He said my past makes me complex and powerful. It's the same emotional stuff he peddled to make me stop the *dru'dar*."

"The what?"

Badrick sighed tiredly and corrected himself. "The crystals. They were called the *dru'dar*."

Nodding absentmindedly, Zale gifted Badrick a moment to breath. This allowed Zale some time to compose himself after his freak-out. He was calmer now, able to gather the questions he had in order of priority.

Zale studied Badrick as his renewed partner massaged his temples, groaning painfully. Badrick did not explain why his head was hurting and Zale didn't ask him.

Perhaps the resurrection had left its mark. Maybe a headache was a small sacrifice for new life.

New and *improved* life, at that; it amazed Zale to hear Badrick not only talking about detailed and advanced demonology, but also with any kind of comprehension. Apparently being dead for five months was good for him . . . as mental as that sounded.

"OK," Zale finally spoke, continuing the conversation, "you were strong enough and now you're back. You said Daemnos rebuilt your body. Was that from scratch or is this the old one, new and improved?"

"This is my old body," Badrick smiled. "I'm fresh and alive and I'm still an Enthraller, with Daemnos as my demon. I'm also at fissure thirteen."

Zale started and gaped at him. "So it's true? There *are* thirteen . . . Well, are you alright?"

Badrick nodded with a reassuring smile and said, "I'm fine. Daemnos has put me back as I'm supposed to be, as if I'd opened the fissures one at a time."

"Why did he bother?" Zale asked, finding this part hardest to believe. "You were dead. He was free. Why not just let you stay dead?"

To his infuriation, Badrick shrugged. "He would have just been sucked into another human. Stick with what you know, right?"

Zale immediately shook his head, spluttering, "No, no, no, no, *no!* Daemnos is a *Royal.* We know Lucikefer could ignore this force that pulls demons into people. There's no way Daemnos is a victim to this when his nephew wasn't. Whatever the reason he got stuck in you the first time, after you died he could be free forever. So, I ask again, why bother?"

"If I'm being honest, I don't know." Badrick gave him a nervous smile. "I'm sure we'll find out eventually. But Daemnos has been nothing but helpful to me, in his own way, and I believe him when he tells me he's on our side."

"And when exactly did he tell you all this?" Zale queried, his eyebrow raised curiously.

That sad look found its way back onto Badrick's face again. He didn't answer immediately, only stared at the concrete, fiddling with his helmet.

Eventually he spoke. "Daemnos didn't let me go to wherever we go when we die. To bring me back, he couldn't let me pass on. He needed to stash me somewhere else. Somewhere . . . on the other side of the veil."

"What does that mean?"

"It wasn't an afterlife. It was somewhere else. Somewhere for my soul to stay while Daemnos worked on my body. We talked during that time. It helped distract me from the darkness. The loneliness."

Zale could tell talking about this was upsetting to Badrick, but he couldn't stop himself from asking, "What was that like?"

"You don't want to know."

Seeing as that was clearly all he was going to get, Zale did Badrick a favour and changed the subject, moving onto his next question. "OK, I understand all that. But *how* did you actually come back? This is an entirely different type of resurrection than usual. Not even Daemnos has enough power to bring a person back whole; soul, body and mind. I've studied the Old Texts extensively and nothing in them says anything about even Royals having this capability. What did he do? *Jolt* you back to life with a defibrillator?"

"Correct," Badrick grinned like a proud dad. "As always. Yes, we *did* use a jolt. It was you."

At first what Badrick said didn't register in Zale's mind quite as completely as it should have. He nodded along for a moment, 'thinking' on these words.

But then his brain actually started working, and real thoughts kicked in. His eyes grew wide and he gave Badrick a disbelieving glare.

"I'm sorry?" he muttered. "I think I misheard you there," he added sarcastically. "I thought you said I was your external power source."

"Think about it, Zale. Your powers were exactly what we needed. We used you as a supernatural defibrillator. We drained you of electricity and zapped me back to life. Then I teleported here . . . out of the ground you buried me in." He gave Zale a playful glare. "Disgusting, by the way."

Zale ignored the comment. Instead he rewound them back a few seconds with, "You *drained* me? What the hell do you mean?"

Badrick's hands came up in an apologetic gesture. "Sorry," he said quickly. "Wrong choice of words. It wasn't like that. You still have all your power, still have Horas, still at fissure eight—"

Badrick comically jumped in fright when Zale made a piercing squawk of surprise. "Fissure eight!?!"

Badrick seemed shocked at Zale's surprise. He reached out and steadied Zale's shaking limbs, asking, "Didn't you know you were at the eighth?"

Zale shook his head roughly. "I . . . don't . . . I didn't . . . " He couldn't continue. *Now* he took a seat, stumbling over to the staircase and falling roughly onto the bottom step. Staring at the opposite wall—the scorch marks, the shattered glass, the dislodged bricks—he managed to open his mouth and murmur, "I . . . haven't been getting exhausted every time I use a high voltage blast."

He felt a vibration on his shoulder and knew Badrick had placed his hand on his pauldron in some kind of attempt at comfort. "You're OK, dude. I promise. You're not in danger."

Zale turned back to him and looked him in the eye. "How can

you be sure? I'm at the eighth fissure. No one but you has survived that."

"I watched through the veil. I saw you. You're fine, I promise. Horas is healthy. You're healthy." Badrick chuckled and threw his hands into the air. "You're the best damn agent in the Daemonium. Is it really so surprising you can handle eight fissures? You're powerful, Zale. You and Horas are amazing."

He was certainly glad to hear he wasn't going to collapse and die, but Zale couldn't help the numb feeling in his chest.

Eight fissures?

And not dead.

He never thought . . .

He never imagined he'd be strong enough to do what others could not.

Zale couldn't even recall opening the other fissures. Not a single symbol appeared in his mind at any moment in the last five months.

When had it happened?

A familiar sensation began in his head—like an engine starting up—and he knew that, given a few more minutes, he would start obsessing over this. Would not stop pondering on this confusing turn of events until he understood it entirely.

But with the timing of a pro, Badrick refused him this chance by speaking. "You told me emotions are key to our powers. You've been *very* angry recently. That could have something to do with it."

"Maybe," Zale uttered softly. "All I've been focused on is finishing the job your bastard demon failed to do."

"Yes." Badrick's tone of voice went surprisingly dark surprisingly quickly. He turned his attention away from Zale and looked over to the far end of the warehouse, checking out the backdoor Lucikefer annihilated so fervently in his desperation to flee. "Speaking of Lucikefer . . . how about we continue this conversation another time and stop him for good?"

24

chapter
THREE

It took everything he had to use the dash ability. It was a simple power and it was humiliating how hard it proved. But Lucikefer managed it, feeling the final dregs of his strength vanish as he reached as far as he could go.

He'd held on for so long—pulled power from the darkest recesses of his form—but it was over now. He was spent.

But he'd managed to get far; thirty miles with one thirty second dash. That was pretty good for a demon on his last legs.

It proved he was still the almighty Lucikefer, the most powerful entity in existence.

Taking a moment to catch his breath, he studied his surroundings. There was the beginnings of a forest to his right, as well as a large river directly ahead of him.

Useless. There would be no sanctuary within those trees.

However, on his left was a massive, naturally formed rock archway.

It was perfect! With his powers gone he would need a place to hide and rest, regain his strength until his powers fizzled back into existence. It would take a long time—years maybe—and he would need to get back to Hell in order to fully heal. But if he could just stay hidden long enough to get enough energy to jump back home then he would be fine.

Lucikefer made for the archway, his legs groaning in protest. He forced himself onwards, the thought of getting under the shadow powering him on.

He felt a sense of elation as he drew up to the welcoming darkness of the archway, only inches away . . .

. . . when he felt a surge of power, unholy in its strength, emitting some distance behind him, and his jubilation died.

Knowing he was too far out in the open to hide, Lucikefer chose the only course of action left to him, and stopped running so he could turn to face the new arrivals head on.

He roared in dire rage at the sight of *them*.

Zale and Badrick.

The accursed Enthrallers had somehow teleported all the way from the warehouse to his location. Zale did not have that power, which meant Daemnos was still inside Badrick and had transported them both.

Lucikefer had never been very good at keeping his temper in check, even when his life was in jeopardy. This was what made him shout, "Badrick! It *is* you! How?"

"Hello again, honey-bunch. Miss me?"

"How!?" Lucikefer repeated, even more demanding.

"Daemnos, mate," the kid chuckled cockily. "All Daemnos."

"Curse you!" Lucikefer shouted. "You should be dead!"

Badrick laughed again, cruelty lacing his voice, undoubtedly fuelled by his hatred for Lucikefer. "Oh well. Never mind. Maybe next time."

Zale stepped forward and interjected. "Not that we're giving you a next time, Lucy."

That was the last thing he wanted to hear and Lucikefer took a tentative step back, finally falling under the shade of the archway.

For all the good it would do him.

He studied the pair of them in turn, wondering if he could outrun them.

Not likely; he was practically a human at this point, though it disgusted him to say. He had no access to his powers and was physically weakened.

Not that his tiredness mattered; *prowess* had never been the right word to describe his fitness even at its peak.

He was a demon.

A powerful one.

What need did he have for physical strength?

Right now?

A lot.

His lack of it would be his downfall.

He knew it.

They knew it.

"Lucikefer," Badrick called, "you tried to murder millions of people. You corrupted an innocent boy and turned him into a monster. Stefan was a victim and you destroyed him with your evil and empty promises.

"I'm going to punish you for it. And though I know what you demons have to look forward to when you die, I don't think it's good enough." Badrick tilted his helmeted head and spoke over his shoulder. "How about it, Zale? Does the Void sound painful enough?"

"Oh yes," Zale hissed, such malevolence in his voice that at any other time Lucikefer would have been impressed. "That sounds *beautiful.*"

"No," Lucikefer whispered, the sound escaping his lips involuntarily. He took another step back.

He didn't realise he was literally walking into his own cage until Badrick threw out a hand. A powerful force gripped Lucikefer, halting him in his tracks, trapping him in place.

As he struggled against Badrick's grip, the kid hollered, "I will trap you in the Void between worlds. This arch will serve as the door. It will be your prison."

"No!" Lucikefer roared, practically screeching with terror. With his limbs shaking (or at least they would be if he could move), he attempted one last ditch effort to trick them. "It'll never work. I'll linger! My reach will extend beyond the Void and I'll do damage to this world."

"Perhaps," Badrick agreed. "But not enough to cause real harm. Now stay still, I have to concentrate."

And without further ado, he lifted his head to the sky and began to chant.

Oe gultr kam Monkavil yokr est ak . . .

The ground rumbled and the dirt moved, shaking harder and harder as Badrick's chant went on. Energy fizzled and zapped, surrounding Lucikefer and enveloping him in a cloak of suffocating power.

The Royal attempted to thrash and flail.

But he was unable—he was stuck!

The energy he was putting into his muscles was immense. Any other time, it would have been impressive.

But that didn't matter. A force far stronger than him had taken control and Lucikefer ultimately failed, shouting all manner of curses and threats with the only muscles that would move. He vowed agonising deaths and one way trips to Hell where he would torture them for all eternity.

Neither of them listened.

"Say goodbye, Lucy," Zale cackled over his din. "This is the end for you."

"No! I will kill you!"

"Ah, shut it, bitch!"

. . . Sah pol vi dolke ak wo osteruk. Iu ot milm, ak vi selek an qe iltrruk ormant kam qe Voltr . . .

Lucikefer's mind went fuzzy as madness overwhelmed him, his fear overriding his senses completely.

"I will return!" he hollered. "This isn't over, Hood! I will—"

He never finished the sentence.

As he spoke, Badrick uttered the final words of the chant;

. . . T' loc upa ym mon dak wo ista alk Sola k' T' wovas yta vi hukta voavar!

And with one final flash, Lucikefer was ripped from the world and dumped into the Void.

Zale stared at the empty space his foe once occupied, hardly daring to believe they'd finally done it.

Lucikefer was defeated.

"He's gone," he muttered. "It's finally over." After a moment's pause he added, "It's about damn time!"

"We got our revenge," Badrick muttered in reply.

Badrick wasn't moving a muscle. His hand was lowered now, its captive no longer present, and he was staring at the arch as if in deep contemplation. Zale could hear his teeth grinding together, easily audible with his super hearing despite the sound being muffled beneath Badrick's helmet.

They didn't talk for quite some time, simply standing there, basking in the sunlight.

Though, with a start, Zale realised there was no warmth in the light. It startled Zale to realise this; though his under-suit would always protect his body from the air's bite it was still ridiculous that he'd never spotted the ice on the leaves before this.

Until the moment the object of his obsession had been removed, he'd been oblivious.

Zale checked his environmental readings and was startled to see it was below freezing.

How long had it been this cold?

Zale lost track of which month he was in quite some time ago, but with some quick maths work he deduced they were actually coming up to Christmas, or at the very least it was just after.

If only it snowed in England—ever—he would have been able to keep track.

But when had his life ever been easy?

This strange, unrelated thought on what would make his life simpler sparked something in his mind. He blinked in surprise, but acted on his new thoughts immediately. "I swear to God, this is never going to happen again." He pointed a warning finger at Badrick. "I *will* have a simple life. I'm staying by your side for all eternity and I'm never letting you or anyone else go through this crap again."

Badrick chuckled and put his hand on Zale's pauldron. "Thank you, Zale," he said. "That's . . . er . . . very kind."

Badrick turned his back in order to trudge through the icy grass towards the rock arch. When he was almost underneath he looked up and studied its rough edges.

A moment's pause . . . and then, "Lucikefer is suffering . . . Good," he muttered darkly, turning in Zale's direction. "Come on, man. It's time to go home."

At that, Zale's face dropped.

Remembering what surely awaited him back at the Daemonium caused his stomach to churn. A feeling of anxiety he hadn't experienced in quite a long time. And that wasn't the only sensation he was feeling for the first time since running out on his home. It was strange—stranger than strange—but now that Lucikefer was finally gone he felt . . . *different*.

Calmer.

Docile.

He felt a gratifying sense of relief at not having anger burning through every inch of his body for the first time since Badrick's 'death'.

"You alright?"

He started, realising he'd been stuck in his own thoughts for longer than he'd realised and was standing in silence like an idiot.

"Sorry," he muttered. "But we've got a problem . . . with the Daemonium."

Badrick's next tone of voice gave Zale the impression he was frowning. "What do you mean?"

Zale sighed; never before had he been so irritated at being unable to read expressions because of their helmets—most of the time they were only worn in times of battle and that was no time for feelings—but now he was starting to get immensely frustrated with it.

Zale smiled sheepishly (pointlessly) and said, "I mean . . . I haven't returned since you died." The shame of his actions was flooding through him like a violent, unforgiving deluge now as he explained, "I sort of went . . . AWOL."

"Oh, Zale," Badrick sighed sadly. "You didn't."

"I did," he admitted. "When we return, it might be a somewhat rocky reunion."

There was a moment of silence as Badrick mused over this newest revelation. His head was slightly bowed and he was clearly staring at the grass in thought.

But then he said, "You're one of their most valuable members. That is a fact. I don't think the repercussions for you abandoning them for nearly half a year would be too big. If they're clever, they'll just slap your wrists and leave it at that."

Zale didn't agree in the slightest. Badrick's claims of his importance to the Daemonium were as overstated as Reynolds' had been in the past. "Can't say I'm all too eager to find out if you're right about that."

"We have to go back." Badrick approached him as he spoke. "What the Daemonium does is too important. The world needs us on their side. We have to face the consequences of our actions and return to active duty. Besides, you have to finish my training."

Zale scoffed loudly. "Like you really need training *now?*" It wasn't even a real question; he could see clear as day that there was nothing left to teach Badrick.

Apparently, Daemnos had imparted a substantial amount of knowledge during Badrick's time in the veil.

Besides, technically Badrick already passed his Trials.

The green helmet slid off and Badrick's face was brought back into the sunlight. He smiled kindly and said, "Either way, we've gotta go back. It would not do for us to stop acting altruistically. The human race needs us to stay vigilant."

"When the hell," Zale tutted fractiously, "did you learn to speak so formally?"

Badrick laughed, but otherwise didn't respond. He put his hand on Zale's pauldron, never removing his smile. "It'll be fine, mate. Come on. We're needed."

And with that, he placed his helmet back upon his head and led Zale away from the arch and on to the next difficulty in their never endingly problematic lives.

chapter
FOUR

The Daemonium looked just the same as he left it.

A towering construction.

Futuristic in its design.

Utterly massive.

Zale had always marvelled at the Daemonium's ability to keep their primary base of operations, as well as their endeavours, secret and hidden from the world. They utilised the power of money, threats and fear, and not to mention a hefty element of actual mind control.

It was a system built from the ground up centuries before the first governments. Faced with a dangerous, controlling element far older than itself, the ruling factions of the world had been ill-prepared to combat the influence the Daemonium had over the planet.

It was a necessary evil to combat the monsters of Hell, and though it was awful . . . it worked.

And quite frankly the simple logistics of an operation *that* big and *that* old were just impressive.

But Zale couldn't appreciate that at this very moment; the sickly feeling in his stomach prevented it.

The facility loomed over them as they crossed under its shadow. Mere moments later Zale jumped as voices roared over the wall and the sound of weapons being cocked cut through the silence. "*Halt!*"

Badrick stopped first, his arm shooting out to keep Zale back.

It felt weird, his partner taking the lead on this. Throughout his entire career Zale had been in front, the commander of whoever he'd been partnered with; Carla, Landis, Dylan, Badrick . . . It was an unfamiliar feeling to follow someone else.

Nevertheless he appreciated it. He couldn't think straight right now. If he had to do the talking in this situation they'd probably end up getting shot by the guards hefting guns in their direction.

"Hold your fire!" Badrick shouted up at them.

"Identify yourself immediately!"

Zale knew what was happening. The guards at the Wall Entrance always received information on who was going in or out of the facility, and right now their sudden appearance wasn't corresponding with the information.

Badrick turned to him and laughed, communicating his amusement. "Hail!" he roared in a mocking tone. "It is I, Badrick Varner, with my partner Zale Hood. We have returned from our mission to defuse the crystals Lucikefer armed, successful in our efforts."

He fell silent and waited for the guards to reply.

Confused silence followed for quite some time. It ensued for so long that Zale started to wonder if they'd simply walked away.

But then there was a call of, "Hood is there?"

"Uh oh," he muttered, immediately picking up on their desire to identify him specifically.

There was another moment of silence before a loud, grinding din drowned out any and all other sounds. The gate blocking their path began to crawl open and two red armoured soldiers charged out. "Enter!" one of them bawled minimally.

"Well," Badrick said, excitement lining his voice, "here we are."

Zale did not share his enthusiasm, but nevertheless followed as he traipsed across the threshold. As they passed, the door cranked closed behind them.

They were escorted through the grounds across the beautiful yet battle scarred grass. A few dirty holes pockmarked the area, reminiscent of the Apos raid over half a year ago.

Zale frowned disapprovingly. The Daemonium was really slacking in the cleanup operations these days. Usually they were quite quick with the supernatural repairs to their gorgeous grounds.

Before they could reach the Gate they were accosted by the door guards, who questioned their escort. After a short conversation they were admitted. Zale was forced to part with his weapons and they were instructed to head through the halls until they found the HQ.

Free of their escort, this time Zale led the way through the familiar halls. They passed the firing ranges, the duelling arena and the obstacle courses until eventually they found the right door and emerged into the incredible HQ.

The familiar walkways spread over their heads, the walls they stretched between taller than four houses atop one another. Agents and soldiers ran around fervently, performing whatever task they'd been assigned—missions, battle reports, debriefings—

everything that came with life at the Daemonium.

It was definitely strange to be back among them, walking the halls and rooms Zale had long called home, but despite his anxiety he felt a great relief to be back.

As they walked in, both of them drinking in the sights, Zale realised they were being observed. Three men and one woman, lurking on the lowest walkway, staring at them as they ventured inside.

Council Members.

Zale didn't like the way they were eyeing him up. He had no doubt the guards radioed in their arrival and the men and woman's presence was no coincidence. He knew his return would spark up a lot of activity after everything he'd done.

But still . . . they were being creepy.

So distracted by these eerie members of the Command Council, Zale didn't realise someone was standing in his way until he'd walked right into a body. He jumped back, opening his mouth to apologise . . .

Then stopped when he realised who it was.

"Well . . . well . . . well," the body said slowly.

Zale couldn't speak; the anxiety had increased tenfold. Fortunately Badrick undertook the responsibility of replying. "Reynolds," he smiled, his voice warm. He removed his helmet and grinned at Reynolds. "It's good to see you."

"It is good to see you as well," Reynolds said. "Alive," he added. "We found your grave." He glanced at the squirming Zale.

"My demon rebuilt me," Badrick told him, "and brought me back."

"You're going to have to tell me how." Reynolds was just as wary of Badrick as Zale had been. This could be discerned by the distrusting look he gave the olive-armoured recruit, and the way his fingers twitched. "But I imagine Daemnos has been keeping secret many of his skills."

"You knew all along, didn't you?" Badrick said after a moment's hesitation, a little accusingly. "About Daemnos being my demon."

"No," Reynolds said. "Not so much. Only after the fourth Trial. But it *was* one of the Command Council's theories."

"Yes . . . well . . . " That was all Badrick said on the matter.

Apparently he was still a little miffed at all the cloak and dagger that had surrounded his training and wanted to avoid talking about it.

Reynolds didn't pursue the matter. Instead he turned his attention back to Zale. "It's good to see you," he said softly. "It's been . . . months."

"Yes . . . well . . . " Zale parroted his partner, unsure of how to proceed.

"You understand what must be done now?"

Zale knew full well what the protocols dictated had to happen now and he guessed Reynolds would rather avoid speaking it aloud just as much as he. Giving the sergeant the consideration he deserved, Zale simply nodded.

"I shall . . . " He hesitated, the pit in his stomach growing deeper and darker. "I shall report to the Council immediately."

Badrick watched Zale depart, heading up one of the ramps, up which he knew was the door to the BCR. Further on would be the never ending staircase to the conference room. That was probably where Zale was headed.

"What's going on?" he asked, unsure of what was happening.

"Zale must go to the Council and answer for what he has done," Reynolds said simply. "As for you, Badrick, you must follow me. Some of the Council wish to talk to you."

He was ushered along without being given any time to answer, Reynolds moving with the speed of a cheetah. As always the Daemonium gave him not a moment to think, no time to process.

With five members of the Council now staring at him and making him uncomfortable, Badrick spent the next two hours describing everything that had happened; finding the *dru'dar* in London and the surrounding areas, how he'd disarmed them, absorbing so much power that the fissures were forced open, and not to mention the chaos caused by their destruction.

He described how Daemnos had taken over to defeat Lucikefer, and how Stefan refused to allow his demon to fight the battle himself.

Despite wanting nothing more than to forget the ordeal, at the Council's pressing he also did his best to explain what he experienced during the five months he'd been dead, tried and clearly failed to accurately communicate what it was like.

The constantly interrupting questions didn't help.

But what the Council wanted to know the most—what they *kept* coming back to—was whether or not Daemnos could be trusted.

"Royals are, by their very nature, untrustworthy creatures," one of them told him. "Our dealings with them in the past resulted in catastrophe. How can we be sure Daemnos is any different?"

Badrick momentarily forgot himself and scoffed derisively. "From what I heard, you've encountered *one* of them, not including Lucikefer." Understanding that he was being rude, he took a moment to breathe and relax. This mocking attitude would have to go—it'd been too long since he'd had to answer to authority, but he would have to get back in the habit of respecting his commanders. "I'm not going to lie," he said calmly, "Daemnos is still a demon. That means he's tricky and evil. But . . . I really believe he's with us. Despite the secrets he is still keeping, the effort he put into bringing me back and staying inside my soul, I think, proves he is on our side."

"That is the part I don't get the most," someone said. "If he felt obliged to give you life again, I could perhaps understand. Some demons have been known to get attached to their hosts. But why would he jump back inside you?"

Badrick shrugged at them. "Like I said, there are still some secrets. I won't lie about that. But even so, he wouldn't have been able to resurrect me and stay out."

This drew frowns from everyone present, especially Reynolds. "What do you mean?" Badrick was asked.

"When an Enthraller is brought back to life, their demon is dragged back to them, even if they have a new Enthraller. Reconstructing me forced him back into my soul."

The look of alarm on the faces before him was disconcerting, but not surprising. Badrick knew they had never encountered anything like this.

"Are you certain of this?"

"We were not aware of this."

"That is troubling."

Badrick nodded his agreement. "I thought you should know." It was true, although he wasn't without his ulterior motives. Badrick wasn't sure what they were going to do with him after this debriefing was over, but he knew what he wanted. He hoped that by giving this little titbit he'd picked up during his death he would prove his usefulness and improve his chances of a good result.

"What would happen to the new Enthraller?"

"They would die," Badrick told them.

"Does this apply only to true resurrection?" a woman asked over horrified gasps. "Or would a . . ." She shuddered into silence, her eyes wide.

Knowing where this was going, Badrick said truthfully, "I have no idea. Daemnos doesn't have a lot of experience with the Resurrected. I can only tell you what he knows, but I think it would."

Worried glances were shared. Hurried mutters were swapped.

Eventually the Council turned back to him and in a shaky voice one of them said, "Thank you for telling us this.

"But back on topic . . . You're sure about Daemnos?"

Sighing irritably, Badrick said, "Yes. I said he can be trusted. Until you find evidence to prove me wrong, I wouldn't look this gift horse in the mouth."

"That's good enough for me," Reynolds interjected before the Council could repeat their question *yet again*. "I say we count our blessings. A Royal on the side of the Daemonium? We never even believed it possible. We were so scared to come across one that we never considered any might want to help us."

"It's highly unlikely . . . " the woman tried again, but trailed off at a gesture from the man to her left.

"I agree with Sergeant Reynolds. He is the only Council Member who has faced a Royal. His opinions are sound." At a look of distrust from the rest of the Council, he added, "Imagine the benefits of having Daemnos under our control."

A sharp pain stung Badrick's chest and he quickly interrupted them. "You don't control Daemnos. He's a willing helper. Try to remember that."

Happy? he snarled, rubbing his chest.

A voice inside his head laughed and replied, *Aye.*

His comment got him some heated glares but he utterly ignored them. Chest pain aside, there was no point humouring their arrogance by engaging in an argument that any human, Enthraller or not, could *control* a Royal to any degree.

They would just have to accept what Badrick was telling them, whether they liked it or not.

To his great relief, the Council declared that their time on the subject was up and they had to move this session along. Within minutes they were on a totally new topic—one that gave him some anxiety; what to do with Badrick now he had returned.

They questioned him on his readiness, to which he replied favourably. They tested him, asking questions only those proficient in demonology could answer.

And then they made him demonstrate his mastery over his powers and his physical prowess. This wasn't a difficult request to fulfil and by the end of his impressive exhibition no one present could deny that, not only was he further ahead than any of their recruits, but he was capable of more than most initiated SpecOps operatives.

The Council left him alone after that, moving into a private room to discuss the matter. Reynolds gave him a confident smile as he closed the door and joined the conversation.

Not that this simple wooden barrier made much difference; Badrick could still hear them talking.

Having a Royal in his soul meant he had every demonic power imaginable, and he'd quickly picked up on the super hearing trick that Zale favoured.

Though fuzzy at first, as if he were tuning into a radio station, the Councils' voices became clear in his ears.

"He's clearly capable," Reynolds was telling them. "Think about what you just saw. Clearly Daemnos wants him ready. He hasn't just rebuilt him, he's improved him."

"Can we really trust that what the demon wants will benefit us at all?" a man's voice said.

"Does it even matter what Daemnos wants?" Reynolds laughed. "By giving Badrick everything he's condemned himself to a life of servitude. Even he now has to obey the rules of Enthrallment. Daemnos won't be able to manipulate Badrick anymore, not like he has in the past."

"He's right," another voice concurred. "Think about what this means for us."

"We have the most powerful Enthraller *ever* recorded willing to serve the Daemonium," Reynolds chuckled.

"Badrick's intentions are unclear at this—"

"Oh, for God's sake!" Reynolds snapped. "Just for once can the Council not be so . . . *British Parliament?* Don't manipulate this. Don't make this something it isn't. Be thankful. Badrick returned, didn't he? He came back the moment the Lucikefer threat was resolved. Doesn't that speak volumes? It tells us everything we need to know."

Reynolds continued to argue in Badrick's favour for several minutes with only one other person aiding him until, eventually, the rest were slowly convinced to at least put aside their worries.

With the last disagreeable member silenced, the door opened and the group returned, all looking strangely pleased with themselves. When they next spoke they did so with the air of people having had the greatest idea.

"We have decided, Varner," one of them said, "that there is no point returning you to the training program. You are clearly ready to be instated as a SpecOps operative."

They had no idea that he knew their confidence was a farce. He'd heard everything and their words angered him; they used the fake tones of people attempting to hide the fact that they were not the ones to arrive at the correct decision, but knowing that they should have been.

Badrick didn't call them on it.

There was no point.

"The only problem," the woman muttered, "is who to partner him with."

Badrick's brow creased with confusion. "I'm sorry," he spoke over them, "but I don't think it's a problem. I have a partner."

A murmur of angry voices ensued and, with a frown of her own, the woman firmly stated, "Operative Hood was registered as AWOL many months ago. He has spent the time dodging our scanning devices and avoiding our agents, all the while wreaking havoc across the country chasing down a Royal on some kind of revenge mission. He abandoned the Daemonium. His crimes must be punished."

"What are you going to do?"

"It is likely the presiding judge will sentence him to imprisonment. His actions were unacceptable."

The Council jumped in fright when Badrick stepped forward and shouted, "Don't you dare!"

"Remember your station, Varner!" the woman snarled back. "Just because you have a Royal in your soul does not give you the authority to override the Council's decisions. You—"

Her voice cracked and she fell silent, her face whitening, as Badrick raised his hand and ignited it. He let the flames dance menacingly, the lights flickering in his eyes. "Just try to stop me!"

Spinning on his heel, Badrick charged away, bursting through the door.

"Badrick!" Reynolds called after him. "There's nothing you can do!"

He didn't listen.

He didn't stop.

There was no way he'd let the Council get away with this.

chapter
FIVE

Zale glared at the agent sitting on the highest seat, sighing every time he spoke, already sick of looking at the man's face.

It was absolutely typical that Jonathon *bloody* Carver would be the presiding judge over his courtroom trial, as well as the jury consisting of only those inside the Council who really hated him.

He wished the current leader of the Council was around. He'd never personally met the woman but he knew, unlike this sordid lot, that she wasn't *all* bad. Maybe she would have been fairer to him here.

Frankly, the whole affair was inequitable. What chance did he have at a fair trial with these guys in charge of proceedings?

He'd been sent to this courtroom within minutes of arriving at the Council's lair, given only enough time to strip down to his under-suit.

There was a brief mention of not wanting to waste time being the reason, but Zale had the sneaky suspicion that they simply wanted to imprison him as fast as they could. But not, apparently, without having some fun first, and for what had to have been over an hour now, they'd rambled on and on and on.

"You know our laws," Carver was blabbering as Zale pretended he was *anywhere* else. "You do not abandon the Daemonium for your own agendas. As a SpecOps operative, your actions are all the more severe. You are expected to provide an example to the more basic castes in our society."

Zale tutted and rolled his eyes. *For the love of God*, he thought. *There they go again with the caste system.*

It was a stupid ideology among some of the highest ranking Enthrallers that there was some kind of hierarchy dividing the ranks. Frankly, he considered it a disgusting idea.

Sure, there was a chain of command. The agents, soldiers and operatives answered to their Command Groups, who answered to the Council, who answered to the Hierarch . . . when he cared enough to involve himself in affairs.

But everyone was supposed to be equal. Every member was just as important as the rest. There was no *'caste system'*, even if half of those in charge wished there to be.

The fact alone that Jonathon agreed with this ideology proved that he was the wrong person to be a presiding judge. He was an opinionated idiot. The same went for every single one of those present that nodded their heads at Carver's words, glaring at Zale as they did so.

"I'm sorry," Zale spoke up in response to the accusations, "but I'm pretty sure I ended the greatest threat of the decade."

"No, *Badrick* ended the threat," Carver retorted, enjoying this a little too much. "He is being debriefed at this moment. The reports I'm receiving on my port-pad tell me everything I need to know. So not only was your five month obsession unacceptable, it was utterly fruitless. Someone else succeeded where you failed.

"Badrick will be honoured for his actions. You, on the other hand, will face the consequences of *your* actions."

Zale sat back in his chair, arms crossed, deciding to keep his rejoinders on this to himself. He could read Carver completely. The man was totally transparent. He was only praising Badrick to stamp down on Zale as much as he could. Once he was done with this court, he would go back to trying to get Badrick in trouble.

Carver was cruel and stupid like that.

"You have shown complete disregard for our laws," the agent continued. "You are charged with desertion, a crime equal to betrayal, and you know as well as I what the protocols dictate must now happen."

"The protocols say *nothing* about what must happen now!" Zale responded with a scoff. "We are currently doing what they tell us to do. What happens next is down to you. You're not following any laws, so stop pretending you're being loyal to the Daemonium. It's pathetic."

Carver's responding angry expression didn't faze Zale in the slightest. The fury of this *little man* was nothing compared to what he himself experienced recently. The thought of his own rage—how dangerous he really was—scared him far more that Carver's hissy fits.

The idiot was nothing compared.

"We will not stand idly by and allow you to get away with what you have done to us," Carver snarled maliciously.

"I'm sorry," Zale laughed, "unless I'm mistaken, Badrick and I put our lives on the line to save your sorry arses from not only being revealed to the public, but also having to deal with Lucikefer yourselves."

Carver tried to interrupt, but Zale spoke louder, allowing him no chance to be heard.

"You talk about my actions as though they were terrible, but exactly what were you doing during the whole thing? Your inability to find me has nothing to do with me abandoning anyone. You couldn't find me because *you* weren't anywhere to be found.

"*You* were supposed to stop Lucikefer while we stopped the crystals. Where were you? I'll tell you where; cowering from the crystals, only coming out of your holes when the threat was eliminated. Badrick and I were smack-bang in the middle of the blast radius. But you lot were nowhere to be seen even *after* we did our part of the job."

Carver's face suddenly flushed angrily and he quickly said, "There was . . . a complication."

"No, no, no, no!" Zale cracked up, forcefully throwing his derisive laugh at them. "I've got the word. You were *tricked*. You lost the energy signature, didn't you? Lucikefer hid himself from your scanners as always and you were too dumb to learn from that lesson. Badrick was left to fight him all on his own because *you* can't do your jobs."

"Enough!" Carver roared, a vein on his head popping from his ire. "Zale Hood, you stand accused of desertion, endangering the lives of innocents, risking the exposure of the Daemonium . . . "

Zale tuned him out. He didn't have to ask anyone to realise he had left Carver stuck for words. With no intelligent comeback, with no real ground to stand on, with no way to deny Zale's accusations, he had simply reverted to repeating himself, as if no one could see right through his ineptitude.

Zale was also not surprised to hear whole new charges being thrown his way.

Especially not those last two.

Of course the Council would condemn him for an action they themselves would have been forced to do if put in his position.

'*Endangering the lives of innocents*'—as if allowing the crystals to explode would have been better. This option, balanced against losing only a small portion of real estate, was obviously not acceptable. Any five year old could see that.

'*Risking the exposure of the Daemonium*'—as though it would have been better to let London be utterly levelled instead of racing out in full armour to ensure they succeeded.

Ridiculous, manipulative politics. That was all this was.

But it didn't matter. His argument of logic would change nothing. He could not easily change the minds of the jury, even if his words proved Carver to be an idiot.

The problem was that everyone present was too like-minded. They all agreed with Carver. They seemed to believe Zale should be punished severely, even if that required a few fabricated charges to be slapped upon his person.

"Do you realise just how long it took to cover up your actions?" Carver said. "Explosions of demonic power in London, destruction of real estate, armed, armoured figures riding recklessly on the streets. The money we have had to spend, and the threats to Government issued, not to mention the mind-control . . . It was a bad clean up and we almost lost everything. This is because of you and you weren't even here to aid us in the efforts."

His cruel grin had returned and Carver was leering at Zale with unrepressed glee. Zale bit the inside of his cheek; he sensed a shift in the proceedings, guessing that Carver was seconds from declaring his final sentence.

His lips parted and Zale sensed the end coming.

And it probably would have if not for the sudden violent slamming of the ornate wooden doors and the dramatic entrance of an olive green figure.

Still clad in his armour, with only his helmet missing, Badrick barged into the hall, power literally crackling around his form, his expression livid. Following in his wake, Reynolds appeared in the doorway, looking worn out. He pulled at Badrick's arm in a fruitless attempt to make him turn back.

Badrick wasted no time. When he was by Zale's chair, he glared up at Carver and shouted, "What the hell are you doing!?!"

"Sergeant Reynolds," Carver snapped, ignoring the recruit, "please escort trainee Varner from the courtroom. We are in session."

"I'm trying," Reynolds muttered angrily.

"Not hard enough, clearly."

"Have you ever tried to force the Enthraller of a Royal to do anything?" He glared at Carver, communicating intense distaste at his colleague treating him like he was a lower rank.

"I ask again," Badrick stopped Carver from retorting. "What do you think you're doing? You're going to imprison my partner?"

Carver bristled angrily. "Operative Hood must be held accountab—"

"Don't give me that crap!" Badrick hollered, startling the agent. "Slap him on the wrist and be done with it. Give him a goddamn medal. He stopped Lucikefer from healing after Daemnos was finished with Stefan. If Lucikefer had been given the time to rest then the danger he presented would have gone on much longer. I wouldn't have been able to imprison him. He would still be at large."

"That is hardly the poin—"

"No, that *is* the point, because as always Zale saved your arses. *Again.* And you want to punish him for it?"

For the second time Carver was argued into silence. He gaped stupidly for a few moments, his lips opening then closing like some kind of ugly fish-man.

When no new words came to him, he simply repeated himself yet again. "Hood stands accused of desertion, a crime as serious as betrayal."

"Don't bother," Zale sighed as Carver ranted on and on. "He won't listen. You can't convince him."

A look of desperation flashed in Badrick's eyes. He clenched his fists angrily.

But then divine inspiration apparently struck and he shouted over Carver, "In that case, how about I refuse to stay?"

That shut Carver right up. His mouth clamped shut as his eyes popped with surprise at what he'd just heard.

"What?" he snarled.

His enemy subdued and paying him his full attention, Badrick grinned savagely, victoriously, and bawled into the stunned silence of the courtroom. "If you imprison Zale, I'll leave. You won't get any help from me or Daemnos."

Carver sneered in an attempt to undermine Badrick's threat, though he could not hide the uncertainty tainting the look in his eyes. "The Daemonium has survived untold centuries without you. It will not suffer any in the future if you leave. We wouldn't like it, and though we wouldn't have the power to stop you, with all your strength, we don't need you."

From the looks on the juror's faces, none of them agreed with this claim.

But none spoke up.

Badrick looked desperately from one to the other, but not one met his eye. His gaze fell back upon Zale and they stared at each other for a moment.

Badrick's face went stony. His eyes stern, his mouth a thin line, he turned upon Carver and, in a voice barely audible, he muttered, "Then maybe I should just blow us all up."

Zale jumped up as flames ignited in Badrick's left hand, his fingers menacingly curled. The flames danced between them, flickering and licking the table closest. The wood darkened from the heat, proving just how devastating these flames really were.

"Badrick, what are you doing?" he said, grabbing him on the arm.

"What I have to."

"Stop this, you'll make it worse."

"Get off me, Zale."

Badrick's voice was so dark that Zale instantly reeled back, shocked.

His partner looked totally changed. Not evil, but darker than usual, royally pissed off and overly determined to get his way.

This new level of confidence in Badrick was not comforting. In fact nothing about Badrick's resurrection had been very reassuring so far.

He'd been nothing short of vengeful and volatile, and although Badrick was always somewhat angry, these were not traits Zale would have attributed to him before.

More than anything else, Zale wanted to study him.

Watch him and figure out what was wrong.

Because obviously there was *something*.

But he didn't even get enough time to plan because Carver suddenly shouted, "You wouldn't dare!"

"Oh, you wouldn't believe what I'd dare to do these days," Badrick cackled. "You have no idea what I've seen and done since we last met. I'm a different guy, fellas, and I need my partner with me.

"Removing Zale from duty would be your biggest mistake to date and I've been told of some of your greatest. You *need* him. What have you actually managed to do yourselves without using him recently? Think about it."

The jury's silence was answer enough.

Amidst the silence, Reynolds spoke up. "I think you should listen to the boy, Carver."

"Your attachment to the accused blinds your judgement, Reynolds," Jonathon muttered softly, his rage deflated in the face of this fiery threat.

"Completely," Reynolds admitted. "But I can recognise the threat of a Royal clear enough. Take my advice and do the right thing."

The jury fell into hushed whispers, talking amongst themselves and hilariously excluding Carver. The Council Member glared hatefully at them as they traded words and Zale couldn't help but feel elated at the sight of it.

After what felt like endless hours—though it had to have been only a few minutes—the jury silenced and one of their number stood. "We agree with Sergeant Reynolds and . . . Master Varner."

Zale knew without a doubt that their only reason for this declaration was due to their fear of Daemnos. None of them wanted Zale to get away from this trial favourably, but the fact that they were ants compared to the ultimate power in the room was all too clear to them.

"However," another spoke up bravely, "there is still the matter of the illegal usage of the Trial swords in the field."

"Ah yes." Carver snatched up this new topic immediately, using it to fuel his plan to get Zale as badly punished as possible. He picked up a sheet from his papers and studied it carefully. "It has come to our attention that you have designed and built an unregistered sword which you used in the field. What say you to these accusations?"

"I admit to them," Zale sighed, "but only 'cause it's awesome."

Carver bristled angrily in the face of his mockery and retorted, "You *know* our laws, yet it is another you have broken. The jury and I find this unacceptable. We—"

He was cut off by the jury. "Actually, we are not of that mind." Zale's eyebrows shot up in surprise and he practically gaped at the speaker. "If you've seen the weapon specified, and have any understanding of the sciences involved, you would recognise the impossibility of its design. A curved blade, as far as we are aware, is not possible. Its structure would be too unstable. It would fall apart.

"Yet somehow Operative Hood has constructed a perfect model. We're going to skip the unnecessary debate, as we already know that Master Hood would refuse to construct any more of them."

They were certainly right about that. Zale smiled to himself, envisioning the argument that would occur if they tried to force him.

"Now," a new speaker on the jury said, "we have come to our verdict. The jury has ruled to put Zale Hood on one year probation. If he succeeds in adhering to our laws it will be removed after the year is up. If he breaks even one rule during the next year, he will be immediately imprisoned.

"As for the sword, we will confiscate it. The wonder of its existence is of great interest to us. The science guys would love to get their hands on it."

"You aren't touching it!" Zale roared.

"Do not argue with us, Operative. You are being let off easy. Accept our verdict or be imprisoned. It's your choice."

Zale growled lividly, cursing the days the jury members were born. Nevertheless he bit his tongue, understanding that there was no way he could argue the point. They'd already pushed their luck and, frankly, he didn't want Badrick to threaten the Council again.

He didn't like Badrick's new behaviour. It was probably best to avoid it if possible.

"Fine," Carver sighed. His body was screaming defeat, but in his eyes Zale could see unmatched irritation.

His anger was beautiful.

Zale wasn't proud of taking such enjoyment in the misery of others, but with people like Carver he couldn't help but feel total delight.

Carver gathered his papers and organised them, tapping them on the desk to sort them together. "It is the ruling of the court that Operative Zale Hood be placed under one year's probation. He shall return to his regular duties in two days alongside his partner, Badrick Varner, once he has been instated as a full operative."

Carver stood, brushing off his blue uniform and glaring at them one last time. He about faced and hurriedly left the room, exiting through a door behind the jury.

"I don't like this," Badrick muttered, allowing the flames in his hand to die.

"Leave it," Zale sighed. "It's better than we could have hoped."

"Perhaps, but I still don't like it."

Badrick pulled open the wooden door that shut Zale into his defendant cubicle and allowed him to step out. As he closed it again, Reynolds squeezed past the departing agents and soldiers and drew up closer to them.

"Don't do that again," he said sternly, poking Badrick on the chestplate. "That was dangerous and stupid."

"Sorry, sir," Badrick said, bowing his head slightly in apology.

Reynolds sucked on his tongue for a moment, then chuckled lightly. "Why, despite my better judgement, do I gain amusement from seeing you two piss everybody off?"

It had been a long time since Zale heard Reynolds speak so informally. Hearing it made him smile, allowing the strain of the last day to gratifyingly lift.

"I'm serious, though. I would try not to make a habit of embarrassing the Council, you two. I know you love doing it but there's only a certain amount of times they'll allow it to pass before they retaliate."

"They can tr—"

"No, Badrick," Zale stopped him. "Reynolds is right. We've been dissident a lot recently, and not every Council Member deserves our disrespect." He glanced pointedly at Reynolds. "It *is* good to see you, sir," he added.

"Stop calling me, sir," Reynolds sighed. "At this point it just feels weird coming from either of you." He stepped forward and slapped both of their shoulders. Zale felt it more than Badrick, his under-suit providing far less protection than the recruit's metal pauldron. "Now . . . get to your rooms and rest. I think you both deserve it."

"I've slept enough," Badrick laughed.

"Screw you!" Zale spat unsmilingly. "I'm going to *sodding* bed right this second." He nodded to each of them in turn. "Badrick. Sergeant. I'll see you later."

With that he left the courtroom, eagerly seeking the comfort of the only place that was truly his and his alone.

chapter
SIX

The familiar orange/brown walls greeted him as the lift doors dinged open. Zale hurried out, pushing past the staring Enthrallers and doing his best to ignore their hurried whispers as he brushed through their ranks.

He felt a distressing sense of desperation as he drew closer to his room and found that arriving couldn't happen quickly enough. By the time he fell through its door Zale suspected he was on the verge of a panic attack.

The click of the latch closing signalled the arrival of satisfying relief as silence surrounded him. He took several deep breaths and cast his eyes over the welcome sight of his belongings.

His armour had been returned to its container. He could tell because of the glowing green light, signalling its presence inside.

Zale chuckled lightly at the sight of it, somewhat surprised it was here. He thought they might try to finally force him to store his armour in the armoury, where he was supposed to keep it, but it seemed the higher-ups had not thought of this amongst the rest of the day's issues.

As his eyes panned across the room, they fell upon the open box just sticking out from underneath his bed. The stab of regret in his stomach was unbearable. He'd made a last minute call to bring his secret personal sword when they'd left to deal with the crystals.

It had been the *wrong* call.

He utterly loathed the idea that not only did everyone now know of its existence, but they had taken it from him for study.

What they were probably doing to it made him sick to his stomach.

A rebellious plot to steal it back formed unwelcomingly in his head. That was bad; he should have shaken the thoughts away the instant they formed, but he just couldn't.

Zale wanted his sword back so much he was seriously considering the idea.

He closed the box and gently slid it back under his bed, empty and alone now without its usual occupant. After that he sat down upon his mattress, moaning aloud with the sensation of feeling soft materials beneath him.

He got to enjoy it for less than ten seconds before a soft surge of power shot through his chest. Recognising the commotion within him immediately, Zale closed his eyes and said, "Hello, Horas. You haven't appeared to me in a while."

A deep, powerful voice replied, "I have been watching you, though."

Zale opened his eyes, glancing at his demon and smiling at the sound. Horas sounded nothing like what other Enthrallers had documented with their hellspawn. He wasn't all . . . how did they put it? *Growly* and *snarly?*

No. Horas was more eloquent than that.

Of course, when concentrating, Zale could still hear himself in the demon's voice. That aspect was the same as every Enthraller in history.

His chosen visage was just the same as other demons too. Horas used a variation of Zale's own armour to portray his body, the only difference being the shoulders. They were thick, massive, almost like smaller, flat versions of roman shields that covered the entire upper arm.

"Oh, I expect you have, you old *electrobuzzer*, you," Zale chortled in reply to Horas' statement.

Horas sighed, his deep voice rumbling intensely. "I am only here to tell you not to doubt yourself."

Zale was surprised to hear him say this. He wasn't aware that Horas had any knowledge of what stubbornly coursed through his mind since he left the courtroom. "How—" he began.

"We share the same body, Zale. I know everything about you. As I should."

Neither spoke for a moment. They stared at one another, Zale's electric blue eyes boring into the visor of the one responsible for their strangeness.

When he finally did speak it was with a tired sigh. "I'm glad everything worked out," he said. "I'm happy Badrick's alive and well. It's just . . . "

"You are no longer the senior."

"Yeah," Zale admitted shamefully. "I know it's wrong, but I like being the one to help people. But now he's more powerful and probably more savvy than I at everything we do."

Horas quickly shook his head. "It is not wrong. Being the one to help others learn and grow is never something to be ashamed of. As for Badrick, his new . . . improvement does not mean he no longer needs you. I suspect Badrick requires your presence still. Just because Daemnos has imparted a millennia of demonology upon him does not mean he has the same experience as you.

"Remember what you promised at the arch. *Do not* abandon him."

"I would never do that," Zale tutted.

"Doubting yourself is abandoning him. Feel confident and we shall all persevere."

Zale figured that was Horas' insane way of saying that no good would come from his solemn mood.

A laugh escaped from his lips. "You speak so weird," he muttered.

He could sense Horas smiling at his grin. The demon saluted him crisply and said, "I shall return to your soul. If you need me, you know where to find me."

"You're going already?"

Horas actually laughed; something he had never done before. It was a little alarming. "There is someone who has not, for five months now, been able to do what she wants most with the *only* one she wants to drag into her room and do it with. This person is about to come through that door. I think I shall give what happens next a miss. Better strap in, Master Hood. You are in for an . . . interesting night."

He vanished, leaving these somewhat cryptic words floating in the air for a surprised Zale to decipher.

But he was gone only seconds before there was a loud, furious rapping on the door. Zale quickly jumped up and pulled it open, not wanting to give whoever was on the other side another reason to sound irritated.

He was immediately assault by a bundle of gorgeously styled, long, blonde hair and choked as two strong arms crushed his ribs.

"Carla!" he wheezed.

His oldest friend released him, spent half a second smiling happily in his direction, then punched him on the shoulder so hard that he fell against the wall from the sheer force of it.

Stabilizing himself against the closest chair, he rubbed his wounded limb and winced as the pain refused to subside.

"You left!" Carla hollered stridently. "You left for five months and you didn't come back! You didn't come back at all!" She went to swing at him again, but he managed to dodge the attack. He grabbed her arm and fended her off as she tried over and over to bruise him.

Eventually she lost her balance and fell into his chest.

He was prepared to keep defending himself, but it proved unnecessary; she didn't resume her strikes. She simply stayed where she was, her face pressed into the leather of his under-suit.

Zale guessed that Carla had just come back from a mission, as she too was wearing nothing but hers. Maybe she had come straight up upon hearing of his return.

"They didn't let me see you," she whispered. "I've been trying for hours, but they said you'd been imprisoned."

"They tried," Zale told her. "Badrick stopped them."

Carla pushed away from him to look into his eyes. "Someone else said you're now on probation. Did you really sneak your sword out?" Zale nodded guiltily. "Idiot," she muttered. "I didn't even see you grab it when you left. How'd you do that?"

"I'm a ninja," he chuckled.

She punched him again, this time on the chest. Thankfully it was only a half-hearted strike and hurt very little.

"Where have you been?" she asked, her voice cracking slightly.

"Chasing Lucikefer," Zale said truthfully. He rubbed his hand over his chin, feeling the hairs that had grown in the two days he'd forgotten to carve them off with a wet dagger. He quickly dived into his story of the past few months, knowing she would want to hear every last detail.

Zale didn't stay idle as he spoke, giving himself his first proper shave in ages as Carla listened to his story. He removed his under-suit and underwear, wrapping himself in a dressing gown and throwing the filthy clothes in the corner.

It had been a long time since he'd been this fresh, even with the odd boxer shorts and socks he stole randomly across the months to keep himself clean. It just wasn't enough, and he was extremely glad to be able to wash himself properly.

"So he's gone?" Carla sighed when he was done talking. "That's good."

"Isn't. It. Just?" he laughed, emphasising each word. He splashed water on his now smooth face and dried himself with a towel.

"But why did you chase him?" Carla queried. "Why didn't you come back for help? Why did you abandon us? Why did you abandon . . . "

"You," he finished. Zale stared at his reflection in the mirror, glaring at his own face in self hatred, his mind haunted by the dead look in his usually bright eyes. "I'm sorry," was all he could say.

"I missed you," she said quietly.

"I wish I could say the same," he muttered. "I should have done. I should have missed you more than anything. So much that I wouldn't have left. That's what scares me."

At first Carla looked extremely hurt. But as he'd continued talking, her expression changed to one of curiosity. Carla knew him better than anyone, and had quickly picked up on his tones. She knew there was some deeper meaning to his words than had originally been clear.

"What do you mean?" she asked.

It took him a moment to answer. When he did, he spoke softly, quietly, as though admitting what he felt too loudly would make him a terrible person. "I don't understand why I chased Lucikefer," he sighed. "Sure, if it had been you who died, I would have chased him to the end of the earth.

"And though I'm fond of Badrick, it's . . . My logical instincts should have kicked in.

"But they didn't and . . . it's not because overly powerful emotions got in the way. Something else happened to me. Something . . . "

"Tell me," Carla pushed when he refused to continue.

"I had this terrible feeling in my chest the whole time. For five months I haven't felt sadness, happiness, or anything regular people feel. I barely ate and thought of nothing but killing Lucikefer. Something else took me over, and it wasn't any human emotion at all. I didn't chase down Lucikefer because of what happened to Badrick. I followed him because I *needed* to kill him. I wanted to kill him for myself, and in the midst of that I felt nothing else which . . . is just not possible. Not to this extent.

"I don't understand how to properly explain it. It was horrible. It was . . . *evil*. There's something wrong with me."

Carla jumped up and put her hands on his shoulders. She pulled him into a tight hug, her arms wrapping around the back of his neck. She didn't speak for a moment, but when she did her voice was soft, comforting, reassuring. It calmed him completely, his anxiety vanishing in an instant.

"You're not evil, Zale. You have a demon inside you, and a powerful one at that. You're bound to act like one sometimes."

Zale didn't agree with that; he didn't believe the force that overcame him had anything to do with Horas.

But he didn't say anything about it. He couldn't talk on the subject anymore.

It hurt too much.

Carla pulled away again, treating him to the kindest smile anyone had ever given him. "You're not evil," she whispered. "You're a good man."

Her arms fell away and reached around her sides, her hands disappearing behind her back.

"Now shut up," she whispered. Zale's eyebrow rose as he heard the distinctive sound of a zip . . . *unzipping*.

Carla's under-suit fell from her form, dropping to the floor with a *thwump*. She stepped out of it and stood there, smiling suggestively. Her arms draped over his neck and she pulled him in closer, whispering in his ear, "We have some catching up to do."

He couldn't help but bare his teeth in a wide, toothy grin as he felt his worries and fears vanish instantly in the face of this inviting offer.

Zale grabbed hold of Carla's bare thighs and lowered her to the bed.

*

Badrick expected a lengthy ceremony for his instatement into the Daemonium, but it turned out this was not the case. The facility was busy twenty four/seven and couldn't expend much time instating new members, so these rituals were often short and sweet.

He was glad of it; he never liked being the centre of attention, always preferring to stay in the corner where people couldn't stare at him.

Due to their close working relationship in the past, Reynolds headed the ceremony, standing at the head of the ornately decorated room with torches lit behind him, the flames casting an eerie glow over the stone walls and pillars. The red banners that ordained the back of the room looked brighter than they were in the dancing light.

Reynolds began the ceremony by asking Badrick if he was truly ready to take on *'the burden'*. When Badrick affirmed his preparedness, Reynolds followed up with a question on his ability to take *'the burden'*.

"Daemnos has, in your own words, gifted you with everything you need, including physical prowess, absolute control of your powers, of which you possess an unprecedented amount, as well as knowledge of everything he knows. Being one of the Royals, this is expected to be a great deal."

Tell me about it, Badrick thought privately. Ever since he'd gasped his first new breath, so much non-native information had been racing through his mind that he'd had trouble assimilating it into his own brainwaves. He was finding it difficult to concentrate, his mind constantly fuzzy with noise.

He would sort himself out eventually, but that didn't make it fun to have millions of years' worth of knowledge attacking his brain.

"Is everything I have said the truth?" Reynolds asked him.

"Yes," Badrick said. "I am ready," he added formally. He glanced around at the onlookers as he did so. He could just about see a proud looking Zale and Carla standing at the back, half hidden behind the crowd next to one of the pillars that loomed above them.

Reynolds nodded, communicating his agreement. He turned his back and fiddled with something behind him. When he next faced Badrick he was holding the black uniform of the SpecOps division, with a pistol and what Badrick recognised as a port-pad resting atop the folded material. "I hereby entitle you Operative Badrick Varner," he said, speaking loudly to the entire room, "until the moment your status changes or until your death in the service of the Daemonium. Do you accept?"

Getting a little tired of the formality of this party, Badrick simply nodded.

Reynolds smiled wider than ever, like some kind of proud father. "Welcome to the Daemonium, Badrick Varner." The uniform was passed to Badrick, who took it excitedly, anxious to try it on. "You are now entitled to a standard-issue sidearm, the uniform of a SpecOps operative, a port-pad and access to the highest level areas. Congratulations."

A deafening round of applause vibrated the walls as the attending Enthrallers clapped as loud as they could, wolf-whistling and cheering boisterously.

Reynolds stepped closer and spoke quietly, so that only Badrick could hear him. "Your service starts tomorrow. I wish you all the luck in the world." He placed a hand on his shoulder. "Just remember what I told you before the duel. Don't let it get to you"

Badrick didn't frown in confusion at Reynolds' words, but he felt the strain of his muscles trying to make him.

What was the man talking about?

The sergeant had said many things to him during the conversation he was referring to—opinions regarding nature versus choices, the morality of those surrounding him and what he could do to change it—but Badrick now knew that none of it mattered. He didn't need to change a thing. Five months trapped in an otherworldly veil helped him understand the desperate need for the Daemonium.

What they did.

And why they did it.

Badrick wanted to be a part of it all.

He was good.

So why was Reynolds talking like this now? Surely the sergeant understood that Badrick had wised up.

Badrick felt a slap on his back as Enthrallers jostled him in congratulations on their way out. Some of them were so hard that, were this happening six months ago, he would have lost his balance. But he was stronger now and withstood the impacts without effort.

His friends were waiting for him outside. As he joined them they too slapped him as hard as they could, their palms bouncing off his shoulders. They laughed joyfully and Badrick joined in, feeling happier than he had in a long time.

"Everything sorted?" Zale asked rhetorically, smacking him on the shoulder one more time. He grinned at Carla, then Badrick. "Well, then," he winked. "Ready to get back to work?"

chapter
SEVEN

Badrick reported for duty at 10AM sharp. He arrived at the BCR to the welcoming introductions of the Agent Commanders and took a seat near the corner, awaiting his partner's arrival.

He'd spent about an hour that morning staring at his reflection in the mirror, studying the folds and creaseless perfection of his uniform. Because of his armour, whenever he'd imagined getting his official uniform he couldn't help but always picture it olive green. Seeing himself in clothes as black as Zale's confused him every time he saw himself.

It was amusing, to say the least. But he very much liked the way he looked, all officious and important.

As he waited for Zale to turn up, his fingers traced the pistol holstered to his right leg and he played with the port-pad strapped to his arm obsessively, exploring the machine's features and capabilities.

It was a marvel of technology. There was no denying that.

At 10:15 a similarly dressed Enthraller sauntered in, a wide grin spread across his annoyingly handsome face. "*Ay oop!*" he called cheerfully. "Reynolds knocking about in here, or is he where he's supposed to be for once?"

"Sergeant Reynolds is caught up with Council business," a commander grunted, rolling his eyes dramatically. Zale laughed and grasped the man's outreached hand. "Good to have you back, Hood."

Within minutes of their settling in, Badrick and Zale were dropped on scan detail. Zale provided a much required explanation; this job involved watching the monitors for signs of demonic activity in a specific region. Anything the demonic-energy readers positioned on their many satellites and outposts detected, they would see. If anything popped up in their region they would go out and investigate.

As it was Badrick's first day on duty, they were given only the local area. As it was pointed out, it wouldn't have been very wise for him to suddenly be sent out all the way to a forbidding, unfamiliar country for his first mission.

Besides, Zale was on probation. He'd been told yesterday that this meant he couldn't leave the country. Any mission they received that led them out of English borders, he would have to pass onto someone else.

"Not that it makes any difference," Zale muttered as they sat there, feet up on the consoles lazily and staring blankly at the screens. "I've only got about four to five months in graduated active duty anyway, not including the last half a year, so I never actually went further than Scotland."

"I thought you'd done loads," Badrick countered. "I've heard loads of stories."

"I have," Zale tutted, "during my training. They wouldn't leave me alone. Half my time was spent investigating stuff. They *did* try to bring forward my Trials, in a manner similar to Stefan, but I refused. I didn't want any special treatment, and though Carla and I had been un-partnered by that time I still wanted to graduate with her."

"That was when she changed her division, right?"

"No, actually, we were separated about a year before she changed. The Council did it. They apparently wanted to see how good we were without each other. I got lumbered with other partners, but none of them were anywhere near as good as Carla. I connected with her in a way I've never done since." Zale's expression lit up and he laughed, adding, "There was this time in our third year where we took down, like, thirty or so Kalik together without so much as a scratch on our armour.

"That was a good day."

Badrick smiled along with his partner, glad to see his face finally lighting up. Through the confusion of the veil Badrick tried to keep as close an eye as possible on his partner and it had saddened him to see Zale so full of rage, so without happiness.

This side of him—the one that enjoyed life—was far better.

Badrick was going to keep the conversation going, to afford his partner more time remembering fond memories. He would have liked that.

Unfortunately, they never got the chance.

This was because a red light flashed on their monitors and a shrill alarm blared horribly in their direction. Zale instantly jumped up and rapidly tapped on the closest keyboard.

"Suck it!" Zale laughed, shooting a playfully rude hand gesture around the BCR at the jealous agents still stuck on *scan detail* to a chorus of light-hearted boos and taunts.

Ignoring the discourteousness of this timing, Badrick sighed and leaned in, focusing on what Zale was up to. He was typing furiously, the display on his screen changing faster than Badrick could keep up with.

From what he could gather, Zale had accessed a camera from one of their satellites and was now zooming in as fast as he could on a specific area. The whole of the United Kingdom appeared, before Scotland was cut from the view.

Wales vanished.

Then Northern England.

Soon Zale had it so close to the land that Badrick could see individual trees.

"Is this a live feed?" he queried.

"Of course." Zale zoomed in a little more and amidst the brown on England's winter grass something grey faded into existence.

"What's that?"

"I'm not sure," Zale replied. He continued working, zeroing in on the grey. As it got larger and larger, Badrick realised they were looking at the top of a building.

It was quite a small structure—smaller than it had looked from afar—but it had been made to appear bigger by the multitude of vehicles surrounding it. Badrick saw cars and motorbikes . . . even a half-constructed helicopter.

And littered between them—scattered like bullet casings, uncaringly dumped as if nothing but trash—were bodies.

Badrick recognised them immediately. He would never forget the ones that'd attacked them so soon after his joining the Daemonium.

"Apostaticus," he voiced.

Zale didn't say anything; he was staring at the monitor, rubbing his lower lip with his thumb.

"Zale?" Badrick prompted him.

"I think this is a base," Zale started as if he'd never hesitated. "But I don't understand. We surveyed this area. I'm pretty sure Reynolds did this sector himself." He paused, closing his eyes and slapping his forehead. "We're so dumb. No offence to Reynolds, but next time the BCR should be put in charge of military scouting."

With the knowledge imparted upon him by Daemnos, Badrick had become pretty quick on the uptake recently. Understanding what Zale meant immediately, he said, "It's the same as what we have, right? Someone told me that we have cloaking from cameras. We're invisible to imaging, or something. This has to be the same thing."

"Has to be," Zale answered. "We never imagined any Apos Enthrallers would have that level of power, but it seems we were wrong. They must have gotten the idea from us."

"So why can we now see it?"

"Because they don't have our scientists," Zale scoffed. "Our cloaks are generated through machinery now. But *they* need the demon with the power to be around." He indicated to the screen. "Look at them all. They're all dead. The Enthraller with the power must be among them and his demon is back in Hell, awaiting his next host."

Badrick cast his eyes over the image, drinking in the chaos of the scene. Now that he was concentrating, he could see the dark crimson of blood staining the icy grass.

"So what do we do?"

"Organise a detail of agents," was the professional reply. "I'll notify an Agent Commander and get the green light. We post guards at every entrance to this building that they can find and have them patrol the perimeter. Then we go in and investigate."

Badrick felt a surge of excitement as he realised his first proper mission had finally begun. He quickly left the BCR, heading to the armoury where his armour was being stored and allowing Zale to organise the necessities.

Inside, he punched his ID code into the little computer situated on the panels before him. It beeped affirmatively and he heard a loud whirring behind the metal wall. After a few seconds, a section opened up and his armour appeared through the gap.

He donned it as fast as he could. With expert speed he stripped to his underwear—not caring who saw him—and zipped his under-suit tight. Then it was on with the armour and out the door towards the HQ exit.

Zale was waiting for him, already suited up. He loaded his auto-rifle as Badrick approached, then reached to his feet and pulled up something Badrick did not expect. His mouth fell open as he recognised the scratched metal, the chink in the trigger, the dulled leather on the grip.

"Is that my actual single-rifle?" Badrick laughed. "How did you—"

"I got some guys to go to your former grave to find it the night we got back." He stuck a hand on his hip and added, "One, how could you forget to bring it with you? Two, they said the earth was undisturbed. Did you literally just teleport out of the ground?"

"One, I'm an idiot," Badrick said sheepishly. "Two, I might have done."

Despite the fact it would have been far simpler to just give him a new rifle, Badrick was immensely pleased to have his original back, despite the dirt clogging up the trigger. He felt a kind of attachment to it. The gun had a special place in his heart which no other weapon would ever replace.

This thing had been down some rocky roads with him. He felt complete with it in his hands.

As totally schizo as that sounds, he thought to himself on his way into the garages, following Zale into his car.

As per his custom, Zale drove so fast Badrick felt like he was going to throw up. He greatly preferred teleporting—much faster—but even a slow speed would have been better than Zale behind the wheel.

"Who could kill all those Apos?" Zale mused as he drove his car over brown country dirt, tearing the crisp grass with the rubber of his spinning wheels. "Whoever it was must be mega powerful."

"Who says it was just one person?"

"Good point," Zale congratulated him, but Badrick wasn't fooled; Zale had of course already thought of that.

He probably already had a list of suspects.

"Maybe we have a new faction in town," Zale offered one of his theories.

"I hope not," Badrick replied. "Apos are bad enough."

Thankfully, the drive didn't last long, as their speed meant they arrived at their destination without too long a stomach-churning journey. The car stopped with a shudder, the wheels slipping on the icy grass, and the pair of them clambered out, approaching the scene that greeted them.

Many agents were already present, armour shining in the sun, weapons at the ready, watching the horizons for any signs of movement. Two stood sentry by what appeared to be the only doors leading into the structure. Badrick could already see over the threshold; the doors themselves had been ripped from their hinges.

Many of the vehicles were in bits, but not because of whatever had attacked this place. They had been altered, built upon to include mismatched weaponry, machine guns on the bikes and unstable looking turrets on the cars.

"Don't you just love Apos design?" Zale cackled as they made their way through the makeshift auto-shop. He put his hand on a bike's gun and it instantly snapped free. Badrick laughed as Zale chucked it away.

"This is worse than that tank they had," Badrick commented, directing his hands towards some of the worse off vehicles.

"Ugh, that bloody tank."

They were greeted by the agents guarding the entrance. Zale took the time to garner as much information as he could, enquiring on what they would find inside. Badrick surmised quickly that the situation didn't sound too different than out here; mostly bodies, fire and destruction, with a side order of blood.

Except, according to the guards, it was all underground.

"It's a subterranean complex?" Zale asked, surprised.

One of the guards nodded. "It's much larger that it looks from up here."

"Fascinating." Zale turned to Badrick. "After you."

Inside looked exactly as Badrick had expected. Making their way deeper into the complex, they came across dozens of eviscerated bodies, scattered unceremoniously across staircases and inside hallways, some of them missing limbs, others without their heads.

"Someone did a number on this place," Badrick whispered, almost slipping on the gore.

Eventually, after much skidding and sliding down never ending steps, they reached what appeared to be some kind of control room. Zale beckoned him in and they entered, having to push overturned chairs out of their way.

This place wasn't dissimilar to the BCR, except it looked as though it had been architecturally designed by an idiot. The aesthetic was further ruined by the fact that everything was in pieces. Smashed computers lay everywhere—the glass from their screens creating a dangerous labyrinth of painful footing—tables and chairs were split in half and the walls were marred by deep gouges.

Luckily their metal boots crushed any glass they stepped on, removing the chances of being cut.

"Does this mean the Apos are gone entirely?" Badrick asked. "Are they done?"

"Nah," Zale muttered in return. "This looks like a big base, but it's only one. How many bodies do you think we've seen so far?"

Badrick cast his mind back, counting rapidly from nothing but memory. "Sixty seven," he said confidently.

Zale didn't question how he could possibly have kept count. Accepting this as the truth, he simply nodded and said, "Right, plus the ones we haven't found yet. The Apos are usually a thousand strong at full strength, so this will be quite a hit for them, especially as it appears to be their closest base to us. But trust me, they're still standing strong somewhere out there.

"I'm sure the Apos will stage an attack yet again when they're ready."

With that query answered, Badrick turned his attention to the most pressing question at hand.

"So what did this?"

"I have no idea," Zale laughed. "Isn't that great? I *love* not knowing, it makes it more fun." He climbed onto the black, oval table that dominated the centre of the room and used it to get a better look at the entire space. He spread his arms as he worked, slowly spinning, gazing around at everything in sight.

He wasn't there long before he stopped and dropped down, looming over a corpse that Badrick hadn't noticed before.

"Why are you staring at that dead man?" Badrick asked.

"There's something up with this body," his partner stated. "The others we've seen have been mauled. Deep gashes everywhere. But this guy looks perfectly fine, apart from the fact that he's dead." Zale paused for a second, clearly thinking. "Maybe if I turn him over . . . "

He slung his auto-rifle and gently pushed the body onto its front. The corpse rolled with a sticky wet sound as the Apos' blood drenched clothes unstuck from the floor.

Zale used both of his hands to press down on the spine. "There we go . . . That's a little weird."

Badrick registered his hesitation and quickly called him on it. "What's up?"

"There are two wounds. The first is three gashes on the back of his shoulder. That's where the blood is coming from. But there's another wound, very deep, clearly the killing blow. But it's not bleeding. Not even a little bit."

Badrick tried to think about what this might mean . . . but failed. "OK?"

"It's some kind of dagger," Zale drew closer to the wound and spread the folds of flesh to look inside, "but it's been cauterised. How the heck did they do that?"

"Heated blade?" Badrick suggested.

"A *very* heated blade, if that's the case," Zale laughed nervously. "But I don't know how—" He interrupted himself with a large gasp.

Badrick saw it too; as his partner put his hands closer to the wound, a flash of blue sparked from the inside. This strange tiny surge jumped from the body and touched Zale's finger, absorbing into his hand with rapid speed,

For quite some time after, there was nothing but silence. Badrick's eyes did not move from Zale's finger as his mind whirred in confusion. Somewhere deep down, he felt like he should understand what he'd just witnessed—this was clearly demonic and Daemnos was proficient in demonology—but he was still inexperienced at reading Daemnos' memories. For now, the truth eluded him.

He was going to open his mouth to question Zale, but at that very same moment his partner fell back and started screaming. "No! No, no, no, no! How!? Not this, not now!"

Badrick had no idea what just happened. He didn't understand why Zale had thrown himself to the floor in a panic, appearing as though he was close to tears.

"Zale, what's wrong?" He hurried to his partner's side. "What is it?"

Zale didn't respond to begin with. He only stared at the body, motionless and unresponsive. But then Badrick saw something that made him double-take. For just a moment—a breadth of a second—Zale's visor appeared to get darker. Just around the edges. Black as night.

But when he checked again, the blue was unmarred. There was no sign of black anywhere on his helmet, and Badrick tutted at his own skittishness. It was obviously just a trick of the light from the flickering bulb above them.

Still not responding, it took a swift shake from Badrick to make Zale speak, although when he finally did it was so quiet Badrick strained to hear.

"I recognise this wound . . . It's Kalik."

"This was done by a Kalik blade?" Badrick gasped, surprised.

Zale's last vestiges of strength vanished and he dropped the last few inches to the floor, his back hitting into the wall behind him. He took a moment to breathe, then muttered, "The Kalik are primitive, but they have fashioned weapons in the past."

Badrick's eyebrows rose as he recognised the tone of voice Zale was using. It had been quite a while since he'd heard it; the tone of a lecturer explaining things to a student who hadn't a clue.

At first Badrick was somewhat incensed by this. There was no need to explain anything to him. Through his connection to Daemnos, he was almost certain he knew more than even Zale about the subspecies.

But he didn't say anything, quickly realising Zale was not being condescending or implying he was stupid. From the look of things, Zale had just fallen into mild shock and was operating on habit.

Always having to explain himself to others was a daily occurrence for the genius so this was just what he was used to. Perhaps going through the motions of a thorough explanation gave him comfort during this obviously distressing situation.

Given the circumstances, Badrick decided not to comment, only speaking when Zale needed prompting. "Go on."

"Their most common weapon is a small extendable blade situated above the wrist. It's made from demonic metals with a very basic spring contraption to push it in and out."

"Pretty advanced for monsters," Badrick said. "So the Kalik did this? That's bad. How many must have been here to do all this?"

"That's not even the worst part," Zale sighed. Something in his voice communicated with the honed dread-sensors in Badrick's brain and he recognised that he was about to hear something *very* bad.

"What is it?"

"That discharge," his partner whispered nearly inaudibly. "That's my power. Electricity from Horas. The residue always reacts to my presence."

"So Horas killed these guys," Badrick joked, hoping to lighten the dark mood that seemed to have crept up on them.

Zale's helmeted head was thrown back and he laughed, though it was a hollow chuckle. "If only. That would be delightful." He paused to breathe deeply. "Think about it, Badrick. This is a cauterised blade wound. It's Horas' electricity. Where else have we seen that?"

It didn't take Badrick long to arrive at the answer. "Your swords," he whispered, realisation finally dawning on him.

"Exactly," Zale coughed.

"The Kalik have your swords." Badrick fancied he could actually feel the blood flushing out of his face. "How long have they had those?"

A shrug was all he got in reply. Badrick hit him on the foot impatiently, inciting Zale to sigh dramatically and ask, "Does it matter?"

"What are you talking about? Of course it matters!"

Zale scoffed derisively, growling, "The wound isn't the same shape as my swords. It's Kalik design. The damn creatures have fashioned their own versions of *my* invention. These things are banned in the field for a reason. The Daemonium doesn't want any of our enemies getting their hands on this technology. Well, look, we've failed."

In a sudden display of anger, Zale smashed his fist against the metal floor. An echoing bang reverberated throughout the room.

"Zale, don't be ridiculous," Badrick chided him. "The Kalik haven't made their own versions of your swords."

"The wound is the exact same shape—"

"Then there's something we're missing, because they didn't do it themselves. Calm down!" he added when Zale kicked the nearest chair. "It's OK!"

"It's not *OK!* Think of the damage the Kalik could do with this weapon. They could kill thousands."

Badrick grabbed his partner by the pauldrons and shook him roughly, refusing to stop until the moment he fell into subdued silence. "Not unless we stop them," he spoke as Zale pushed him away.

"How are we going to do that, exactly?" Zale cackled humourlessly. His defeatist attitude caused Badrick distress; he was never like this. It wasn't good. Badrick needed Zale on top form. "The Daemonium isn't going to let this slide," Zale snarled darkly. "They're going to blame me."

"Then we won't let them find out," Badrick snapped. "The Daemonium will expect us to dive right into this when we're done here so it won't look suspicious if you obsess over it. Through sheer luck, we got the mission, remember? Start being positive and remember that. No one else knows yet.

"We can inform the Council after we've solved the mystery. But we have to figure this out before anything else."

Badrick felt a slight tinge of irritation as Zale laughed at him disbelievingly. "Be real, man. We can't keep this hidden from the agents. There are only two of us. Eventually something is going to slip through our fingers. We can't keep the information secret. Something this big will happen again and someone will notice."

Badrick scowled at him. Now Zale was just being stupid. "Have you forgotten everything you can do? You could probably hijack all the evidence before anyone understood what they were looking at.

"And anyway, who would recognise these wounds? The swords have never been used in the field. The Daemonium has no experience with them so they won't be able to figure it out. Not quickly."

Zale refused to listen to him—kept his face turned away—so Badrick hit him once again and continued on.

"This is the only body like this," he said. "I haven't seen any others. If there are more we'll find them, but most look like they've just been clawed to death, so chances are there's only a few out there. That will be *easy* for you to cover up.

"And if you really think we're so bad, then we'll get people to help. Reynolds and Carla. People we can trust. The less who know about this the less likely we'll be found out, but the more people involved in its cover-up the better it can be hidden."

Zale's hands fidgeted nervously, his fingers sliding over one another with agitation. His body language was screaming uncertainty. "Alright," he finally muttered.

"Come on," Badrick pressed. "More enthusiasm than that. Where's that famous Zale Hood bravado?" He got a light-hearted kick for his words, but nevertheless Zale nodded his head.

Pleased with his day's work, Badrick helped Zale to his feet. With his partner calmer, his mind should have started working at top speed again, so Badrick asked him what their next course of action would be.

Zale took a moment to think, then said, "There are cameras behind you and to my right. We need to find the tapes for those cameras and review them back at the Daemonium. We can't let anyone else see what happened inside this base.

"You scour every inch of this place and count the bodies. Look at their wounds and figure out if there are any more like this anywhere."

Badrick tapped him on the arm and nodded his understanding. "What will you do?"

"I'll scour the place too, looking for anything else that might be of interest. When you're done, get the tapes and take them back to the Daemonium. Get an agent to give you a ride."

With their plan of action in place, the pair of them went their separate ways.

After trawling all the way to the bottom of the facility in search of incriminating evidence—and thankfully finding none—Badrick darted back up the staircase and accosted an agent, informing him of what he needed. They spent the next ten minutes locating the security room, eventually finding it inside a filthy quarters chamber, tucked away in a corner.

There were no tapes—this wasn't the 90's—but everything was

recorded digitally. Badrick got the agents to transfer the data to his port-pad and then requested they wipe the computers to ensure that nothing could be salvaged by the Apos.

With everything from the computers transferred to Badrick's port-pad, including documents as well as footage, he about-faced and hurried up the stairs. The sun was blinding when he returned to the surface, so much so that even his visor complained, darkening automatically so as to keep his vision unimpaired.

On the journey home, he let his mind wander over the memories of what he'd seen inside the Apos base. It was a mess, and they were in a dire predicament, but he was positive they would figure it out.

For a while he played with the idea that Lucikefer had given the Kalik one of Zale's swords. The demon had stolen one after all. But he quickly removed that from his list of theories. Why would the Royal do that? It served him no purpose whatsoever, and Lucikefer had only ever done things that profited him alone.

Badrick sighed in defeat. He wasn't great at coming up with theories. Zale's mind was required for the whole detective game.

Badrick was crap at it.

<h1 style="text-align:center">chapter
EIGHT</h1>

Badrick waited impatiently for his partner upon his return to the Daemonium, keeping an eye on the entrance to the HQ from atop one of the walkways to ensure he wouldn't be disturbed.

It didn't work—none other than Reynolds himself found him within minutes.

"Varner," he smiled in greeting. "Been looking for you. How goes the first day?"

"Already got a mission," Badrick told him. "Apos base was attacked."

"What?" Reynolds gave him a confused look. "Did we do that?"

"Nope."

"Who else would want to attack Apos?"

Badrick chuckled humourlessly, tapping his hands on the handrail. "You wouldn't believe me if I told you."

This time Reynolds gifted him with an irritated glare. "Varner, don't annoy me. Who atta—"

"Kalik."

This clearly wasn't what Reynolds was expecting. Immediately, his hand shot out to the handrail to apparently keep his legs from collapsing in shock, and his eyes blinked twice as he tried to process what he'd heard. "Just one?" he finally said. "Or more?"

"Not sure yet," Badrick told him truthfully. "From the scale of the destruction we'd say more. A lot more," he added.

"Well crap," Reynolds sighed simply. "I wonder what brought this on."

The sergeant cast his eyes over the HQ, deep in thought as he chewed his lip. Badrick watched him with absent eyes, buried inside his own head.

Now that Reynolds was standing directly in front of him he no longer felt as confident in his plan as he had back at the Apos base. Truth be told, to tell Reynolds of their larger concerns could potentially be as catastrophic as it would be helpful.

The sergeant was a member of the Command Council after all, and his loyalties to the Daemonium would always come before his emotions. But those loyalties didn't always include the rest of the Council. Maybe not with words, but Badrick felt that Reynolds had often displayed an attitude of disregard for many of them, as though they weren't the Daemonium he served.

Besides, Reynolds was smart. Surely he would see sense. This problem was not down to Zale.

He had to see that.

Taking a blind leap of faith, Badrick spoke up, "There might be another problem," and with that he dived into an explanation, bringing Reynolds up to speed on the situation. As he spoke,

Reynolds listened intently. His eyes narrowed at first, but they quickly widened the further into his story Badrick got. By the time he was done, Reynolds' eyes were practically popping out.

For a time, there was only silence.

Then, with a sigh, "Oh, Varner. Just why?" Reynolds' head fell into his hands, his eyes buried in the palms.

"I need to know where you stand, Reynolds," Badrick said.

He immediately received a glare for his efforts. "Too authoritative, Varner," Reynolds snapped. "Remember who the superior here is."

"Sorry."

Accepting his apology and letting the matter drop, Reynolds sighed once more, rubbing his chin musingly.

"Please don't tell the Council," Badrick pleaded. "They couldn't do anything when Lucikefer stole one of them because we all saw him take it—"

"And the Council issued them out as part of the fight," Reynolds nodded. "There was no way to deny it was their fault."

"But they can manipulate the situation now. Zale would totally be punished for this. We can't let that happen." Reynolds didn't respond, so Badrick continued, "We have to keep it a secret. Will you please help us? This isn't Zale's fault."

"Well, of course it isn't Hood's fault," Reynolds snapped, a little harshly. "The Council confiscated every sword the moment he built them. Their storage is the Council's responsibility, not Zale's.

"But that won't matter," Reynolds sighed sadly. "They will use this against him. I see what you mean, Varner. This *is* a problem."

"Well, maybe," Badrick said. "We're not sure it *was* the Kalik yet. We only have a wound to go on so far."

Zale had been panicking at the base, so he hadn't been in his right mind and Badrick was too busy calming him down. But now he'd had time to think for himself, he realised that in truth they didn't have any real evidence that any Kalik were involved. Maybe it was someone—or something—else entirely.

Someone crafty, trying to pin the blame on the demon subspecies.

Zale would think of this potentiality on his way back, once he'd calmed his mind. Badrick was sure of it.

"You think another player might be involved?" Reynolds asked him.

"I think we live in a world full of devious, blame-shaking sons of bitches," Badrick said as reply. "So yes, I think there could be another explanation."

Reynolds nodded. "Either way, the theft of Zale's sword is a problem." The sergeant closed his eyes and groaned. "Didn't I ask you to stop getting me involved in your Council defying antics, or did I imagine that?"

"We won't drag you into anything," Badrick muttered guiltily. "We'll understand if this is too much."

"Stop, Badrick, for God's sake." Reynolds put his hand up as he spoke, rolling his eyes. "*Of course* I'm going to help you. Zale is already suffering the punishment of a crime he did commit and the Council are looking to snag another charge onto him.

"But I'll be damned if I let them imprison him based on something that was entirely *their* fault. If Zale gets arrested it will be because of something he actually did. No . . . one last time I'm going to help you.

"*One last time!*"

"Thank you, Reynolds!" Badrick breathed, relief flooding through him.

"Don't thank me yet," the sergeant scowled. "This is just beginning. Tell me everything again."

Badrick retold his story, ensuring he didn't leave anything out.

Unfortunately he had never been the greatest storyteller, and kept having to go back a few steps to include something he missed.

Jesus, he thought to himself after the third time. *Count a hundred bodies? No problem. Remember what I did an hour ago . . . Nope, not happening. God sake, Daemnos. Why is your memory ability so unstable?*

Somewhere deep inside, he heard laughing.

"I know full well what the right decision is here," said Reynolds, "despite my deep dislike for the idea of going against the Council . . . *again*." To Badrick's concern, it sounded like he was having second thoughts about helping them and was trying to convince himself a second time. "Badrick, if you find evidence that vast numbers of Kalik possess this upgraded capability, we'll have to bring the entire Daemonium in. It'll be a military matter then, and I won't endanger the world just to keep Zale out of jail.

"However, until we prove that the situation is that dire . . . I can help you. We'll need to work fast. Everything Kalik related goes to Zale until the moment this problem is solved.

"That won't be too hard. If I simply put this order in myself, the Council would wonder why I'm getting involved, but if I talk to one of the agents in the Council, he can get the Agent Commanders to initiate the orders themselves."

"You can do that?"

Reynolds chuckled confidently. "Even without the bigger issue, a massive Kalik attack like this would require major investigation. Zale would have probably ended up the primary investigator no matter what. The Council will worry when they find out about this and the Agent Commanders will want to put their best man on it.

"All I have to do is remind them of that and it'll be simple to get everything sent to you."

"There's still the issue of other people discovering our . . . little problem," Badrick murmured.

"Well, like you said, some hack work will sort that. It'll be difficult. We'll have to think of *everything*." A worried expression replaced Reynolds' tired look. "It's horribly likely that someone will find something before we can get to it."

Badrick beamed at Reynolds despite his fretting. It had turned out miles better than he could have possibly hoped for. Not only had Reynolds agreed to help them, but he'd figured out a way to reduce their need for espionage and have all the information handed to them effortlessly.

"I appreciate it, Serge—"

"Don't thank me," Reynolds snapped. "I will be putting a knife in your leg if this backfires."

Badrick smiled. "Understood."

"Other than that," Reynolds added, "I'll keep an eye out, make sure nobody gets any information we don't want them to have. Otherwise there's not a lot else I can do. Despite the agents constantly using me, I don't have access to the BCR systems. You'll have to get Carla to interfere on that front. I'm sure she'll do anything to help."

Reynolds put his hand to his chin and glanced around at their surroundings. "We're idiots," he muttered. "Talking about this out in the open. We're lucky nobody came this way."

He didn't say anything else. Lost in his head he started walking away, muttering to himself.

Apparently, their conversation was over.

Badrick let go of a breath he had not realised he'd been holding and leaned into the handrail with relief.

So far so good.

As he rocked back and forth on his heels in silence, musing on their situation, life at the Daemonium continued below him as it always did, unaware of his anxiety and worries. Agents and soldiers buzzed around like bees, heading out or coming back from missions, briefings and other such things. Members of every command group flitted between the two control rooms, carrying artefacts and weapons.

All sorts could be observed from his perch on the highest walkway. If he hadn't been so impatient for Zale's return, he might have had fun watching the proceedings taking place.

Especially when, quite suddenly, somebody caterwauled so shrilly from the ground floor Badrick felt anger rise in his chest because of the disturbance. Despite his original lack of interest, he leaned over the railing to get a glimpse of what was occurring.

Thanks to natural powers of recognition gifted to him by Daemnos, Badrick quickly identified an Ordinarius demon, physical and impossibly Enthraller-free, being dragged unwillingly through the HQ.

The hellspawn was kicking and screaming like a petulant child, hurling curses and energy balls alike.

The agents restraining the flailing demon were forced to shoot it in the chest. This wouldn't kill it, but it was enough to knock the demon out cold, much to everyone's relief. As it was unceremoniously dragged away, Badrick noticed a strange aura lingering on its form—invisible to all but him—and realised an external power was attached to the Ordinarius. With a jolt, he recognised its signature as belonging to a certain Royal demon.

"Typical," he tutted aloud. "Even after he's gone the problems Lucikefer made stay with us. What did he do, help the Ordinarius manifest on Earth?"

Lucikefer is powering his form, an unusually helpful voice said. *Without it he would be torn apart from the effort of maintaining a physical body on Earth.*

"Well, doesn't matter now," Badrick chuckled. "He's a dead man walking."

Indeeeeeeeed!

Shuddering from the distinct vibes of mental instability that tickled up his spine every time Daemnos bothered to speak, Badrick forgot about the Ordinarius demon and turned his attention back to the entrance.

This turned out to be good timing; Zale had just walked through the door.

Even from this distance, Badrick recognised the tired and jittery movements of a paranoid man. He looked incredibly anxious, his head darting around as if he expected someone to pounce on him at any moment and throw him into the jail without so much as a 'Who goes there?'

Badrick clicked his fingers, purposefully channelling a small surge of electricity through the air particles. Sensing demonic electricity that wasn't his, Zale looked up sharply, his hand going to his weapon, only to realise Badrick was cleverly signalling him without drawing attention.

"Don't do that!" he snapped when he arrived. "I'm already nervous enough about my powers being used by other people."

Badrick didn't respond. Frankly, he didn't want to waste the time. Instead he tapped on his port-pad and linked the footage he'd cropped and prepared in the time he waited for Zale to return.

His partner responded to the beep of his port-pad. Tapping furiously, Badrick saw him nod with understanding. Within seconds they synced up, finding the correct time-stamp, ensuring it was to the second.

Checking to make sure they were still undisturbed on their perch above the rest, Badrick muttered, "Right then, let's see if it really was a Kalik."

An image of the Apos' control room flashed onto their screens. The footage started to play and Badrick had to quickly turn the sound down. His port-pad was set to the highest volume, something that wasn't welcome at that moment in the slightest.

When he'd got it to a manageable level, he was able to concentrate on the footage.

Two Apos, standing by the oval table right where they'd studied the body, were in the middle of a heated discussion, conversing with disagreeing tones.

The one on the left spoke first. He was obviously subservient to his fellow from the way he spoke with the air of a man only just scraping enough courage to question his senior, despite his clear irritation.

"Master Nell, do you really think it's a good idea to attack the Daemonium again? Our previous assault didn't exactly go as planned?"

The second man—Nell—snapped at the other. "It's been months, Rickard, and our ranks have replenished faster than we could have hoped. Kihja, Furia, Loset, Tosra and Cheros have all returned, not to mention the others. We are back at optimal strength."

The skin of Badrick's forehead creased into an angry frown. Those weren't human names; to him it sounded like they were talking about specific demons. Was this evidence that the Apos had particular demon allies that teamed up with them with every new Enthraller? That was news to him.

And, he suspected, to everyone else.

When they were done here it would probably be wise to inform the agents. They would want to know about this new development.

"That's not what worries me, sir," Rickard persisted. "The attack itself was—"

"Our attack strategy was perfect. If only it wasn't for . . . " He trailed off, apparently too angry to finish his sentence.

"The demon Horas," Rickard spat furiously. "His Enthraller is always there, every single time we attack. What's the kid's name again, sir?"

"Something Wood," Nell answered blithely. Badrick smiled when he heard Zale tut. "The Enthraller doesn't matter," Nell continued, "but Horas is starting to become a problem. He's one of the most powerful demons we know of."

"One of the most well known too," Rickard commented.

"What are they talking about?" Badrick asked Zale.

"Maybe Horas is as much a stud as I am."

"Maybe he's just as arroga—" Before Badrick could finish that sentence, the host of the apparently famous Horas shushed him and turned his attention back to the two Apos.

"That matters not to me," Nell was saying. "We'll deal with him eventually. The plan," he declaimed, as if speaking to a wide audience, "we need to put into action *will* deal with him and all demons like him, powerful or not. Once he and the Daemonium are out of the way, we can focus on D—"

He was interrupted by the lout *rattatat!* of machinegun fire. The sound levels on Badrick's port-pad went into the red as the piercing taps disrupted the video, creating a horrible, flicking, buzzing sound.

Nell and Rickard jumped in surprise, bawling unintelligible questions at each other.

Eventually Master Nell was able to regain his composure and he quickly commanded, "Find your squad, Rickard. Find out what is going on!"

Rickard barely had a chance to acknowledge the order before a large shape barged through the door, bowling over chairs with the power of a bull and reaching the pair of Apos within seconds.

Recognising the shape as a hulking Kalik demon, Badrick watched soberly as the monster dug its claws into the screaming Rickard and crushed his skull. The Kalik picked up the corpse and threw it so hard that it sailed straight out the door, answering the question of why Rickard's body hadn't been in the control room.

Nell withdrew a large dagger and sunk it into the Kalik's shoulder. The demon roared at full volume and spun on the spot, smacking its attacker in the face. Because of its loss of balance from the spin, the strike was only a glancing shot however it was still enough to temporarily stun Nell. The Kalik managed to get a grip on his shoulder, digging its claws into his back and throwing him to the floor.

It raised its left hand, fingers curling into a fist, before . . .

Zale cursed as the image of what appeared was blocked by the demon's body.

"Try the other camera," Badrick suggested. "The angle might be right."

"Way ahead of you," Zale muttered absently, his concentration entirely focused on his port-pad.

Another spit of curses escaped his mouth before Badrick could even switch the feed himself.

Ten seconds later, he figured out why; a frustratingly placed chair, one that had been knocked onto the table, concealed what they so desperately needed to see.

"Typical," he muttered. "That's just typical."

He watched Zale study the footage in the hopes of catching a glimpse of another person present—one that might've falsified evidence—but the cameras had been damaged from that point on. They were neither able to definitively confirm or rule out the possibility.

Badrick didn't quite know what to make of what they'd just witnessed. They hadn't been able to confirm the use of some kind of Kalik-made version of the sword, but at the same time they couldn't dispute it.

The Kalik had killed Nell. That was clear as day.

And it had done it with a wrist blade. That was clear from the way it attacked.

There was no blue glow on the walls, Badrick realised, but he didn't feel much elation at this realisation. If the Kalik truly owned a wrist blade that was made like Zale's weapons, then Badrick calculated that the voltage of such a small weapon would be so low that the brightness was probably dimmed exponentially.

It wouldn't glow as strongly as an original.

And the wound on Nell had been cauterised. The Kalik had been the one to put that wound in Nell. That must surely mean that what they feared was true.

Although, on the other hand . . . maybe not.

Zale lost track of his thoughts as Badrick coughed to get his attention. He turned and stared into his face, thankful that his own was still obscured by his helmet.

He didn't want Badrick seeing his despairing expression.

"I've been thinking," Badrick said, "about something in Daemnos' memories."

"OK," said Zale. "What?"

"It's something from centuries ago. A Singularis demon went on a killing spree, but left an infection identical to another demon's powers all over the wounds he inflicted. He'd bottled it somehow. As a result the Daemonium concluded that the killing spree was this other demon's doing. She was hunted down instead of the actual killer.

"Before we go blaming Kalik for everything, especially now we haven't actually seen your sword on the arm of the suspect, I think we should consider this could be happening again."

"You think that someone else might be cauterising Kalik wounds to shed suspicion onto them?" Zale asked dubiously.

"It's worth consideration," Badrick said stubbornly. "We've

been totally tricked before. Twice in the same day by two of the same damn family."

Zale nodded his head. Funny thing was, a similar theory had actually already walked into his brain on the way home, borne mainly from his desperation to discover that the Kalik *did not* have a hold of his weapons, especially ones they'd forged themselves.

He put his hands on the rail and leaned into it. "I've already thought of it, though I never heard that story before. That's quite interesting."

Whatever the true answer was, he had no doubt his invention was involved in some way. They'd both seen the discharge.

If I were preparing to get up to no good with this weapon, he said in his head, talking to nobody but himself, *I would use the Kalik as a diversion. It's actually perfect. Say I needed to kill a bunch of people, but knew my actions would alert the Daemonium. I'd find a Kalik hunting ground and create false evidence.*

As a result, every time the agents turned up at one of my crime scenes they would chase after the Kalik instead of me.

But considering what is being used . . . how the heck would that even work? Would you trace the Kalik wound with the sword? That would take skill beyond that of a human to not mutate the wound but also making it so realistic we couldn't tell the difference.

It sounded impossible.

But he was forgetting his original concern; that the Kalik had altered his swords to look like their blades. What if someone else had actually done that? It would take a lot less effort to plunge one into a wound that was the exact same size.

But that left the question of 'who the bloody hell had the savvy to alter his weapons?'

"Wanna share your thoughts with me?"

Zale snapped out of his reverie and addressed his partner. "Sorry, man. Got lost in my head." He proceeded to enlighten

Badrick on his theories, speaking quietly so that no one would hear them.

"I'm not so sure about that last one," Badrick shook his head. "A lot of effort to make your own blade identical to a Kalik's. But I guess anything's possible."

"Stop debating it," Zale laughed humourlessly. "Think about it. Would you prefer a dude with my weapon or the Kalik? A Kalik would no doubt share the design with its clan, meaning hundreds of them gaining this power. But people—and regular demons—are selfish. I bet they'd keep it to themselves.

"An army of Kalik is our worst nightmare come true, but one dude with a sword we can handle."

"Don't base your investigation on what you hope to be true," Badrick warned him.

Zale glared at him, annoyed at being told this as if he needed to be. However he never got an opportunity to express his distaste as Badrick very quickly brought up the second world-ending problem—the topic Zale had been fretting over but wanted to avoid because of what he feared it entailed.

"Why would the Kalik attack an Apos base anyway? I don't think just one could do that, and you saw the video. The gunfire continued even when the Kalik killed Nell and Rickard. There were others savaging the rest of the base."

"Why would an army of Kalik gather to kill Apos?" Zale repeated the question. "A matter for another time, trust me."

He felt a pang of guilt at hiding his true thoughts on this matter.

But he just *didn't* want to focus on it yet. Not until he had absolute proof. The chances of his first theory happening were nigh impossible. In his entire Daemonium career he had only ever brought it up with Carla in theory, to which her response was a high pitched laugh.

She was right to mock him at the time. It had sounded ridiculous.

But now . . .

No!

Not until it was proven.

There was no point frightening his partner when it had no place in their investigation . . . *yet.*

In response to his claim, his olive green partner exasperated yieldingly and raised his hands in submission. "OK," he said. "So what do we do next?"

Zale already had his answer. "Our most pressing need is to find out whether the Kalik have got my swords and are using them. First, we scan the crime scene for demonic energy. If some other unseen player was in the vicinity and somehow avoided the cameras while he falsified evidence, his energy signature will hopefully still be present."

"If it was a demon or Enthraller," Badrick said.

"It wasn't a bloody human," Zale scoffed. "No way can a regular person get anywhere near Kalik and avoid getting torn apart.

"Anyway," he continued, as if he hadn't been interrupted, "after that, if we pick up energy, we work on discovering who it belongs to. If not, then our next step is to catch a Kalik in the act . . . " He trailed off, hating himself for what he was about to suggest. "But therein lies our big problem."

"Let me guess," Badrick sighed. "Kalik don't reveal their wrist blade until right before they strike. It's a hunting tradition of theirs. The only way to find out if a Kalik has your invention is to either capture one, allow it to strike, or kill it straight up."

"I don't like it, but we'll have to choose one of those options. " Zale groaned into his hands. "I dread to think which the best one is."

Badrick walked closer to stand next to Zale, fingers wrapping around the handrail. "If you want my opinion, I say the second option. It's the only way to find out if they have your weapons. With the other options there's always something that could be used against us. If we capture or kill one, we *might* find it in possession of your weapon, but what if it was planted on the creature?

"Besides, we don't even know if the stupid things can use such advanced technology. No, we need to see a Kalik use a sword before we choose them as our prime suspects."

The sheer coldness of this suggestion startled Zale. He stared at his partner uncertainly, confused by Badrick's attitude.

What Badrick was suggesting with the air of someone proposing they pop down to Tesco's would place someone in grave danger. If they followed through with the second option there was a risk that the prey the Kalik chose to attack would be murdered.

It wasn't too long ago that Badrick was preaching morality above all else and chastising the Daemonium for their lack of it. He would never have allowed Zale to make a suggestion like the one he'd just put forward.

So why was he making it himself now?

And why was he so damn calm about it!?

The niggling worry in Zale's stomach that followed his belief that Badrick was broken returned for the umpteenth time. Squirming uncomfortably, Zale did his best to ignore it so he could respond calmly.

"We can't let a Kalik kill anyone," he said slowly, controlling his voice with great care, thankful for the helmet obscuring his distrusting expression. "We'll take one down and search it."

Badrick shrugged a little too nonchalantly. "If you think that's best."

Christ! The need to throw Badrick under a microscope and study him extensively was starting to overwhelm him.

But Zale *had* to ignore it. There were far more pressing matters at hand. Badrick's uncharacteristic lack of empathy would have to wait.

"It's going to take a long time to find a Kalik," Zale notified his partner. "It won't be easy. Any suggestions on how to do it?"

"I'll think of one."

Zale decided that would have to do for now. It wasn't great, but at the very least they had a new plan of action.

Which was at least something.

He just hoped it would lead somewhere.

chapter
NINE

Their scan of the savage crime scene, as well as the local area, yielded absolutely nothing. Regardless, Zale tried endlessly, reinitialising the scan over and over again, working his magic on the demonic-energy readers with such skill Badrick couldn't help but watch in awe.

It took Zale two whole days to truly give up. When the machinery failed him, he moved on to what they found at the scene. He studied *everything*; not a single thing went unchecked by the scrutinising eyes of Zale Hood.

He claimed responsibility for the autopsies and, with the help of Reynolds, buried the results in the case files so deep Badrick had concerns that even they wouldn't be able to get back in to the data.

No one questioned Zale's command. Keeping his promise, Reynolds pulled through and, before they knew it, the Agent Commanders had dumped everything Kalik related upon the pair of them. From this point on no one else would intervene.

Unless of course matters got completely out of control.

Now and then new data would trickle in as other agents encountered the beasts, but they were quickly able to recognise that no evidence of Zale's swords was present at any of the occurrences.

The increase in Kalik activity did not go unnoticed by either of them. The Apos attack wasn't an isolated incident. It was just the beginning.

Of what, neither of them knew.

Eventually, after exhausting absolutely every possible angle, Zale had to surrender to the truth; apart from the slaughtered residents, there was no trace of anyone but Kalik within ten miles of the Apos base.

If someone else had been there, they either weren't a demon/Enthraller or were *very* good at hiding themselves.

Badrick had resigned himself hours before Zale, believing the lack of evidence proved no one else had been present. The Kalik were the ones they had to go after, no doubt about it.

There was no way a normal human was involved in these affairs, and Badrick could see no demon in Daemnos' memories capable of masking their presence so expertly.

Of course, Zale disagreed—he never took anything for granted until he had absolute proof.

Or at least that was what he said, though Badrick felt this was somewhat of a lie. He was pretty sure Zale did that nonstop.

With their scanning failed, talk turned to their other options. However, they got no further than two sentences before the doors to the BCR whizzed open and in walked Carla.

Badrick's jaw almost fell open when he saw she was dressed in nothing but her figure hugging under-suit. Within seconds she had spotted them, strutting over as if she owned the place. Clearly understanding she was interrupting, she began draping herself over Zale, sliding her legs over his and bending her back so far that her chest pushed into his face.

"Can you concentrate when I do this?" she chuckled.

Badrick hadn't seen her properly since before his death. The Council had taken all his time since his return and they'd only seen one another for a few minutes at his ceremony.

Seeing her now, gloriously presented in her body-hugging leather, which highlighted absolutely every beautiful detail and making him wonder how the zips didn't snap off, reminded Badrick just why he actually liked this place.

"I *defo* can't," he muttered in reply to her question, even though it hadn't been directed to him. Zale only tutted and did his best to push her off but she fought his efforts, refusing to budge.

"Well," she huffed playfully, turning her eyes onto Badrick, "maybe I'll let *you* have a grope seeing as this one seems so unappreciative." She dramatically leapt to her feet, pretending to be insulted.

For a quick moment it looked like Badrick was about to lose his partner to uncontrollable lust for the next week, but at the last moment the misty-eyed Zale roughly shook his head and yanked the laughing Carla onto a chair.

He quietened her with a solemn look. Through shared instincts the pair must have honed through years of partnership, Carla immediately sobered, picking up on his subtle expressions. In hushed whispers, they brought her up to speed. As she listened, her reactions took a similar journey to Reynolds', going from shocked worry to downright paranoia.

"This is bad," she muttered thoughtfully when they were done.

"But we were lucky you guys got this case, and now everything Kalik related goes to you. That will help. Then again, there's still the problem of people finding out. It's only a matter of time before another agent sees the Kalik using the things."

"There's no real evidence that they have them yet," Zale said, going back over their study of the security tapes.

"Still," Carla sighed, "we will have to be careful. Anything that doesn't get sent to you, we need to make sure we nab first."

"People might start to notice if their mission reports go missing," Zale said. "They'll trace it to our system."

"Pfft!" Carla huffed. "I can cover that easily, just like you taught me. Besides it's not like the higher-ups micromanage us. They won't go peeking into your case files."

"They might now," Badrick voiced, knowing it was exactly what Zale was thinking. "After all that's happened."

Carla shook her head and waved her hand dismissively. "Like those prats could get into Zale's case files. He's always been overly protective of his data, so it won't seem suspicious if he puts it under insane lock and key again."

"Already done," Zale muttered.

It didn't take them long to get a plan sorted and Carla left extremely confident in their success.

"With us and Reynolds on the case, what could go wrong?"

Zale gave her a thankful hug, communicating his gratitude in the way he held her.

"Don't worry," she whispered in his ear. "I won't let anyone get to you."

She was gone before he could reply.

He returned to the waiting Badrick, throwing himself into his chair and sulking against the desk.

"Annoyed the scanning didn't work?" his partner queried insightfully.

"Like you wouldn't believe," Zale mumbled darkly.

More than anything, he'd hoped nothing else would be necessary. More than anything, he'd begged this was all they had to do to sort this problem out.

Because the only course of action that stood before them now made him sick to his stomach.

It pained him to admit that it was necessary, in lieu of being able to come up with anything better. As Badrick had mentioned, just because the Kalik *might* have the weapon on their person didn't prove they could use it.

If they killed a Kalik and found it in possession of a sword, there would be no way to know for sure if it had been left as a patsy—and that was a definite possibility if what he feared was really happening.

And if they simply captured one, the same problem would haunt them. No matter what they tried they ran the possibility of falling into their enemy's trap. If the Kalik were just patsies and on the off chance the real culprit outsmarted them, the Daemonium would end up chasing Kalik for no reason.

There was only one thing they could do. Only one thing that would leave all doubt banished.

To truly know whether or not the Kalik that killed Nell had used one of his swords was to witness another use the weapon again. They had no choice but to discover definitively whether or not a Kalik had the brain power to use such a sophisticated weapon.

Kalik were strict with their blades. They were only permitted to extend the things during a hunt and only at the moment of the kill. To defend themselves against attack, they used their claws and fangs only, which meant that simply attacking a Kalik would prove nothing.

The only way to know to prove their theory was to interrupt a hunt.

As Badrick already pointed out, a Kalik never revealed its weapon until the moment of the killing blow.

They would have a maximum of a second to see whether or not a Kalik was using the weapon before saving its intended target.

To pull this off would take a kind of competence Zale wasn't entirely confident he possessed.

He wasn't sure if they could manage this at all.

And was it even worth it?

Was solving this problem worth potentially putting someone in that much danger?

Badrick seemed to think so. He'd already made his position clear.

Zale's partner was sitting back in his chair now, whistling gently to himself, apparently giving Zale space to consider a plan of action. He was rubbing the fingers of his right hand together absently, apparently lost in thought. However, his peaceful expression suggested he was calm as could be.

Zale got the squirming worry that Badrick was simply waiting for Zale to overcome his moral concerns.

He frowned as he studied his partner. Was Zale just being paranoid? Or was there *really* something wrong with Badrick?

He quickly purged his mind of these thoughts before they took precedence. He could worry about Badrick later.

They had a far more pressing matter at hand.

Cursing his ability to understand the direness of his situation—and deeply wishing he was a simpleton—Zale begrudgingly made up his mind.

He leaned forward and smacked Badrick on the shoe to gain his attention. "Alright," he said, "we have no choice. We have to go through with our second option."

His partner nodded affirmatively. "Find a Kalik and prove it can use the weapon."

Zale huffed derisively at his conciseness; it was far easier said than done!

After all there was no definitive way to find Kalik demons. They were unique among demon-kind in their shared ability to cross over to Earth from deep within their domicile Hell pits whenever they willed it—a feat the Daemonium had yet to understand—and had a habit of doing so at totally random moments.

They couldn't even predict *where* they might cross as their favourite crossing locations appeared to change more frequently than Zale's sex partners, and once they were out they registered so little on the energy scales that finding them was near impossible.

The only two moments their levels spiked large enough to be detectable was the actual moment of crossing and the instance they made a kill.

Sure, you could find those locations, but by the time you located them the Kalik would have moved on and almost immediately afterwards their energy would diminish, making it impossible to track their current real-time location.

The only way anyone ever achieved tracking a Kalik was by luck; the satellites were pointing directly at the place a Kalik crossed. With quick reflexes the satellite cameras would be set to track its physical movements as opposed to its energy levels.

The chances of that happening *now* were more than slim.

Zale explained their limitations to Badrick, who at first didn't understand the problem. Although Daemnos had gifted him with an extensive knowledge of demonology, the Royal wasn't savvy on the Daemonium's equipment.

Therefore Badrick would have to rely on what he himself

learned.

As of yet he had actually studied very little, which was painfully obvious as Zale reiterated for the third time until Badrick finally understood how their satellites worked.

Clearly, the newly appointed operative still needed to be taught a great deal.

But the Council obviously wasn't concerned about that.

Zale couldn't help but roll his eyes a little.

Badrick's response to learning the extent of their issues was just as Zale expected. He displayed a rather large level of frustration, not to mention a hefty element of anger.

"Tell me about it," Zale exhaled, laughing a little despite himself. "We can do loads and our tech is way beyond regular people. But even we have our limits."

"Can't you jiggy it to be better like you did with everything else?"

Jiggy? Zale repeated in his head, frowning. *What kind of word is tha—* Deciding he didn't care, he moved on. "I can't make the impossible possible. Kalik aren't regular demons so we can't track them like regular demons."

Badrick chewed his lip. His eyes misted over as he delved into his mind, becoming oblivious to the outside world. He looked to be very deep in thought, though Zale had a sneaky suspicion that he had absolutely no idea how to help.

"If only we had a tracking device," Badrick sighed. "We need to make a way to track the Kalik."

"We have tracking devices," Zale tutted.

"Well, why don't we use one of those?"

Zale sighed impatiently, wishing that Badrick knew *anything* about the Daemonium. "Because they are designed to attach to the target. We'd have to find a Kalik to use one and what would be the point after that? At that moment we'd just found one."

Badrick grumbled darkly, "I was just trying to help. You don't have to get snippy—"

He jumped as Zale leapt to his feet, his eyes widening, his face lighting up. His hands flapped spastically with excitement, making Badrick flinch away from the flailing limbs.

"What!?"

Zale didn't speak at first; he was thinking too hard.

A single, simple idea—enlarging—splintering into a multifaceted plan—becoming clearer—flashing brightly in his mind.

Within moments a fully formed scheme settled into his head and Zale turned his wide grin upon his partner. With more excitement than he'd felt recently, he beamed, "We *can* track a Kalik."

"Eh?"

Zale laughed with the air of someone realising the answer had been within their grasp the entire time. "Kalik are clan creatures," he said. "They live in massive packs."

"Yeah, I know," Badrick said plainly, apparently not picking up on Zale's proposal with only these words to go on.

Zale tutted, wishing everyone else was as fast as he was. "They strive to stay together," he continued. "Despite the fact that separate clans often war with each other, when one Kalik is separated from their clan they find the first group they can and are accepted straight away, even if it is a clan they've fought with for centuries. They take care of each other, in the strangest way.

"So, with that in mind, dear Badrick, tell me, which group of Kalik is most likely to be nearest to us?"

Badrick shrugged, prompting Zale's eyes to roll.

"The clan that has my weapon," Zale sighed.

"I'm not so sure you're right there," Badrick countered. "How can we be sure the specific clan we're worried have your swords will be close to us at all?"

"The location of the Apos base attack, first of all," Zale said. "In a global consideration, it was right next door to us. Kalik don't share hunting grounds and the landmass of the UK is too small for more than one clan.

"The clan with my swords is the dominant clan that hunts in this country. I'm sure of it."

"If you say so," Badrick said. "So how does this help us?"

Truly impatient now, Zale threw out, "We have a Kalik prisoner, Badrick. We let him go and track him until he finds a Kalik on a hunt. We then follow the hunter."

Badrick's eyes lit up a little as Zale's words finally hit him, but it vanished beneath a frown almost instantly. He gave Zale a considering glance. Chewing his lip, he sighed and said, "It's a good idea but it could go badly."

Zale had to agree there were *some* risks—his plan potentially put civilians in harm's way—but he was certain that the benefits outweighed them tremendously.

"We'll be vigilant," he told his partner. "Together, you and I can stop anything bad from happening." Zale had to fight to keep his face straight as he spoke; he didn't entirely believe his own words.

"But still . . . " Badrick said, "the chances we find a hunting Kalik . . . "

"Or even a Kalik *with* my damn sword, I know, I know. It's a stupidly long shot. But . . . it's a start. We can try other things if we fail but this is what I have."

"Zale, come on!" Badrick exclaimed. "We don't know how many of them might have one. Maybe all thousand of the UK's clan has a sword, but maybe it's just five of them. Maybe even just the one that killed Nell. The chances of this working . . . well, they don't exist, man."

Exasperated that Badrick was repeating his worries, but knowing this was what people did when their concerns were this dire, Zale took a calming breath and tried again.

"You think I don't know all that?" he almost snapped. "But on the off chance it works, I am going to try. I'm going to try any idea I get if I think it *might* yield results."

Badrick nodded his approval of this promise, saying, "OK, so we do this first and hope to find the thieving Kalik that way."

This time it was Zale's turn to frown. "Believe me, I hope it's not the case," he sighed. "I hope we're barking up the wrong tree and either some random demon we *can* catch is the culprit or there's some variable we both missed."

Zale wasn't certain which of those would be better for them . . . but in the end it didn't matter. There was a horrible niggling sensation—accompanied by a dull headache—that told him he was correct in assuming the Kalik were the ones they wanted.

That the Kalik were behind it all.

It horrified him to think about.

They conversed on these shared concerns for a while, both nervous and afraid of what their investigation might reveal. A short talk on the ways their new plan could backfire quickly followed. They both understood the hazards and they would have to make sure they came up with contingencies for absolutely everything that could go wrong.

That was the only way the Agent Commanders would green-light the mission.

"Oh God," Badrick grumbled. "We'll have to get their permission."

"If we're unlucky," Zale scoffed, "we'll have to go to the Command Council as well."

Badrick made a loud, aggressive moaning sound which drew

the irritated attentions of the nearest Enthrallers.

Lowering his decibel, Badrick asked, "Can't we just . . . you know . . . get Reynolds to sanction the mission?"

"I think we've given him enough stress for one lifetime," Zale shot him down. "I'd like to save him more." He took a moment to rub his thumb along his lip. "No . . . We'll do this legit. I just hope someone goes for it."

Which wasn't necessarily all that likely. Unfortunately, not everyone in the BCR was a fan of Zale. And not all of them were all that bright either; their feelings often clouded their judgement.

To get his mission green-lit, he would need to petition to an Agent Commander who, not only didn't hate him, but was also intelligent enough to understand the need for their mission.

But was also not bright enough to see through all the lies they'd have to come up with in order to conceal their true purpose.

"It'll be tricky," he finally voiced. "We can't tell them everything and I don't think they'd buy the idea that we simply want to find a clan. They'll want a reason."

"To find the killers isn't enough of a reason?" Badrick scoffed.

Zale gifted him an amused glance. "This isn't like a murder," he chuckled humourlessly. "Treating this like one would be stupid. It's the same kind of situation as an animal attack." He stretched his arms, working out the knots caused by his tension.

Besides, no one ever stopped a vicious animal by releasing a second.

"Then what do we do?" Badrick almost yelled in response, throwing his arms up in the air.

Zale closed his eyes and did his best to think, but his headache was starting to get worse. "Brain's gone to sleep," he muttered. Rubbing his eyes, he added, "Don't worry . . . I'll think of something."

Zale could only hope he wasn't lying to himself.

chapter
TEN

⊙ Ψ ⋂

Agent Commander Quill cast his eyes over Zale as he made his case. Zale could see the uncertainty in the green globes. His superior appeared to fully understand the severity of their problem, but also comprehended the potential dangers, unfortunately better than most.

Zale half wished he'd chosen a less intelligent Commander, but he had to remind himself that he'd selected Quill for this very reason.

"I know it's just Kalik," Zale was saying softly. "It's not like a demon murder. Or even a Forsaken. They're an animalistic species and they're going to do what they're going to do. We can only limit the damage.

"Until now, sir. This was an organised attack. An assault

carried out by a dedicated strike force. Apos may be Apos, but they're still Enthrallers. They're still a military force. They can fight off a Kalik. Probably even twenty Kalik.

"So think about how many there had to have been. How well disciplined they would have *had* to have been to take out an entire Apos facility."

Quill's eyebrows rose questioningly. "Are you saying you believe they were being . . . *controlled?*"

Zale wasn't sure if he was glad that Quill had asked this question or not.

Because he was right on the money—the man truly was sharp.

He felt guilt stab at his chest; while Zale had always suspected a puppeteer behind this attack, he had yet to confide in Badrick. Even though Zale planned all along to use this theory to get his green-light, he hadn't been able to bring himself to say it aloud. To do so would've made it real.

As far as Zale's partner was concerned the Kalik slaughtered the Apos of their own accord.

Knowing he no longer had any choice, Zale forced himself to whisper, "I haven't voiced this concern as of yet, not even to my partner . . . But between you and me, sir, it's the only way they could get this organised. Someone is pulling the strings."

There . . .

He'd said it.

It was real.

Quill was silent for a moment. He stroked his chin thoughtfully, his expression one of worry.

"I trust your instincts, Hood," he finally said, "though I'd be lying if I said I didn't wish you were an idiot." He took a second to peruse the files Zale provided him at the start of the meeting. "How many dead at the base?"

"Over a hundred," Zale replied. "Badrick said he counted a

total of a hundred and fifty six.”

“You trust that count?”

Zale almost laughed. “It’s Badrick, sir. If Daemnos helped him count a hundred and fifty six, then he counted a hundred and fifty six.”

A smile played at Quill’s face. “You’re right about that,” he murmured.

He said no more, so Zale continued. “Tell me, sir, how many Enthrallers have we ever recorded dying at the hands of a Kalik?”

Quill closed the folder. “Four thousand and twenty eight, not including the attack of 1995.”

At this prompt, Zale’s mind wandered slightly into his knowledge about this incident. Back during the harrowing days of the Devil’s ascension to earth, the resulting burst of power drove the nearby Kalik mad. As a horde, they attacked the nearest population—the Daemonium itself—and killed more than a few soldiers.

But that incident had nothing to do with Zale’s current investigation. That was an isolated assault, and the Kalik had not attacked with any organisation. The scene, so he’d heard, had been utterly chaotic, so Zale hadn’t even once considered studying the reports of the attack.

Continuing his conversation with Quill, Zale asked, “Over how long a time frame?”

“Since the beginning.”

Zale scoffed. “So several *thousand* years?”

“Aye.”

Laughing, Zale threw his hand into the air. “That’s nothing. That’s, like, one death every ten years.” He leaned forward and put his hands onto the desk before him so that he could be at the same eye level as Quill, a technique he’d picked up long ago for psychologically manipulating the emotions of his targets.

If Quill was filled with fear on this topic, he would be more likely to agree with Zale.

"This was different, sir. Run the numbers yourself. This was way bigger than we've ever seen. We have to learn how they did it. We have to find out *who* is controlling them."

"You believe that letting our captive free will lead you to the right Kalik? They live in clans, Hood. They aren't united. One clan has nothing to do with the actions of another."

"I believe our resident will lead us right. He'll go to the closest clan and that *has* to be the one that carried out the attack. The hunting grounds are chosen with purpose and they mostly stay as far away from each other as possible.

"You've read the work of Ivan Sokolov. He discovered that only one clan operates in the entirety of the UK. He also realised how powerful they were. No other clan would dare encroach on their hunting territory. No other clan will come anywhere near this place until the current one leaves.

"If we let our Kalik go, he *will* lead us to the UK clan, and being the only ones nearby they will be the Kalik who attacked the Apos."

"But," Quill began, "if they *are* being controlled, someone capable of such a feat might also be able to convince a foreign clan to attack this territory."

"You speak words of wisdom, sir, but if that is true shouldn't we still make efforts to scratch the UK clan off our list of suspects?"

Quill nodded, but still said, "How do you know they haven't already returned to Hell? The clans don't operate on Earth twenty/four seven. It might take days for them to return."

Zale knew Quill already comprehended the answer to this question. He was testing Zale, ensuring he had thought of everything himself. If he hadn't there would be no way Quill would green-light his plan.

"Kalik generate energy at only two moments; when they cross worlds and when they kill. We detected them coming at the attack. Have we detected any Kalik jumps since?"

"A few isolated crossings, but nothing in this country, and no more than one or two at a time."

"So the attackers are still on the planet somewhere," Zale stated. "Also our captive will wander until he finds a fellow Kalik to be accepted by. I won't stop following him until that happens."

"What do you hope to learn by doing this, Hood?" Quill asked him.

"Do you remember my paper on the Kalik in my third year of training?" Zale said.

"I do. You tried convincing the instructors that the ramblings of Mark Tippen had actual credit."

"I stand by what I said in that paper. That's what I believe to be happening here."

"How can you be sure?"

"I'm confident in my theory, sir. Whoever is controlling them will be on Earth, not in Hell. I will follow our captive until he finds another of his kind. I will then tail the new Kalik in the hope of finding whoever is commanding them. If my theory is correct, and God is with us, the Kalik will report to his commander before going back home."

"That's quite a chance you're taking there."

Right on cue, Quill said the words Zale was waiting for. The entire conversation rested on this moment. If he could get what he needed to say next absolutely correct, done and dusted, they would be.

OK, Zale found himself thinking. *Now I show just a* little *bit of desperation.*

He lifted his hands to the air, controlling carefully the amount of sadness on his face. "In the face of this horrifying danger . . . it's the best idea I can come up with, sir. If it fails, I'll take full responsibility."

Quill nodded slowly, his fingers linked together.

"What if you're wrong, Hood? This could all be the work of the Kalik Overlord."

"The Overlord is trapped in Hell, sir. The Royals caged him eons ago and none of them would ever reopen the door."

He knew Quill wouldn't be able to argue that point. Only a Royal could free the most dangerous Kalik in all of creation and none of them would ever dare to unlock the cage they'd jammed him into.

The repercussions would be immense.

"I trust I don't have to remind you of the potential dangers of what you are proposing," Quill said sternly.

"A tracking device will be planted on our captive. When we release him, we won't be watching on a camera. Badrick and I will be right behind it. If innocents come to danger we will intervene, despite our lead being lost in the process."

"What if the captive jumps back to Hell?"

"I promise you a Kalik lost in our world will find another here first to establish his place in the clan," Zale explained. "This is the way they've worked forever."

The folder slapped against the wood as Quill threw it upon his desk. It skidded a little from the force of his throw, sliding almost off the table. Zale quickly picked up on the action. If he wasn't mistaken, on an emotional level, Quill was exactly where Zale needed him to be.

"Let this go on the record, Hood . . . I trust your judgement. I always have." He provided Zale with a small smile. "You appear to have thought through everything that I, at least, can think of but I won't pretend there's no danger in what you are proposing, and results are far from guaranteed.

"However if this is the best plan *you've* got, I doubt we'll be hearing a better one from anyone else."

"Thank you, sir," Zale said.

A sterner look was thrown his way. "Is there anything else you wish to tell me before we proceed? Anything that could jeopardise the mission?"

With the skill of a pro, Zale refused his expression to betray his emotions and said, "No, sir. I have apprised you of the entire situation."

He felt bad about lying to Quill. The commander was an honourable man and didn't deserve to be played about, but he couldn't learn about the true problem. If he did, Quill would *have* to tell the Council, whether he wanted to or not.

He didn't have the same loyalty to Zale that Reynolds did.

"I agree that this is a real problem," Quill said. "There's no question this was an organised attack. If one clan can organise in such a way, then maybe others will. Maybe they'll unite and create an army we haven't a hope of defeating.

"Alright, Hood," Quill bobbed his head. "I give you the green light. But be warned, Operative, this is a delicate matter. I don't want a single mistake. Let's *not* have the Council calling for our heads, aye?"

"Aye," Zale nodded, saluting Quill.

Badrick sat opposite the door to Quill's office, fidgeting anxiously, wondering how well their fabricated plan was being received. It had sounded legit to Badrick's ears, so much so that he couldn't help but wonder whether or not they should be undertaking the proposed mission instead.

It was selfish, what they were doing.

Discovering how the Kalik were able to organise an army was a priority. They should have been focusing on that.

But Badrick didn't want to have Zale imprisoned forever.

The only way to stop that was to go through with their true plan.

The sound of the door zipping open dragged him out of his head and back to reality. Zale emerged across the threshold, looking downtrodden. As the door shut behind him, he turned to watch its descent, chewing his lip apprehensively.

Badrick's face fell. "He didn't give us the go?"

Zale chuckled humourlessly. "Oh, no, he did."

He brushed past Badrick, hurrying through the BCR. Badrick caught up with him just as he exited the room.

"So what did Quill say?"

"Not much," Zale replied. "I emphasised just how dangerous an organised force of Kalik actually was and he agreed the problem is dire."

Badrick nodded his concurrence. "If they make an army we won't stand a chance."

"That's what I told Quill." Zale slotted his folder under his arm and pointed in the direction of Lab Two. "Get the tranquiliser. I'll get the tracker from the armoury. Meet me at the door to the prison."

Badrick was stunned; he hadn't expected to get the job underway so quickly. "We're doing this now?"

"Of course we're doing this now," Zale spluttered. "Why would we wait?"

"Alright, don't have an aneurysm," Badrick exhaled sharply, pulling ahead of his partner and darting up the ramp to Lab Two. "See you in a second."

He didn't take long acquiring the tranquiliser solution. He utilised the aid of a helpful medic, who provided him with enough of the right cocktail to knock out a Kalik instantaneously. With the solution in one hand and a rifle in the other, he made his way to the prison, meeting Zale at the door.

His partner seemed anxious to proceed and ushered him over the prison threshold impatiently.

Malcolm the jailor was flicking through a *Nuts* magazine when they arrived, his legs propped up on the desk of his office. He was so engrossed in the pages that he didn't notice their arrival until Zale pointed at the cover and said, "Pretty sure I shagged that one once."

Malcolm face lit up when he realised who his visitors were. "Badrick," he said warmly. "Zale. Welcome, welcome. Good to see you again."

"You too" Badrick smiled back.

Zale simply saluted casually.

They didn't waste time. Shutting the door behind them they informed him of their intent.

Malcolm responded exactly as Badrick had expected. He didn't seem too excited at the prospect of releasing a Kalik back into the wild.

"Aside from the fact that after all this time I'm attached to him," he said, "it's not the greatest idea to allow a Kalik that's been cooped up for half a decade, having tests performed on him every week, back into the world. He'll be overly vicious."

"We know the dangers," Zale assured him. "We're taking precautions."

Malcolm sighed and shrugged. "You'd better be a good shot. He'll smell us coming and will be pounding the walls by the time we get there, so there's no chance of surprising him. I'll need to take down his forcefield and you have to get him a second after. Can you do that?"

"I can," Badrick affirmed. "Trust me, I got this."

Reluctant, but willing, Malcolm led the way down the corridor until they reached the correct cell. True enough, the jailor hadn't lied. Just as Badrick remembered, the demon was already smashing its fists against the forcefield, roaring viciously and thrusting its claws.

It glared at them with soulless eyes, the only emotion inside a deep desire to slaughter and feed. It kept flexing its right hand, almost as if it remembered it should have possessed an extendable blade and was instinctively trying to hunt them.

"Ready?" Malcolm gave Badrick a questioning look, his hand raised to the level of his eye.

Badrick hefted the tranquiliser rifle, gave the weapon a quick once-over, and loaded the dart into the barrel. He put his eye to the sights and aimed it at the Kalik.

"You will have less than a second," Malcolm warned him.

"Just do it."

The jailor nodded, counting, "One . . . two . . . three . . . Go!"

He flicked his hand and the forcefield vanished, dissipating in the space of a nanosecond. Less than a heartbeat later, the Kalik lunged for the closest meat—Zale. Its claws flashed dangerously, glinting under the glare of artificial light, the points perilously sharp.

Malcolm's hand flitted to his pistol, his nerve faltering.

Zale didn't flinch, didn't even move.

He stared challengingly as the demon's claws came to within an inch of his eyes.

Moments before they pierced the globes, the claws shuddered to a stop half a millimetre away, the Kalik's middle finger threateningly close. Badrick lowered his rifle with a satisfied smile, eyeing the dart protruding from the beast's neck.

A strange, uncharacteristic whimper sounded from its throat and it stumbled drowsily, toppling into the wall behind. The impact caused it to lose balance and it crashed to the floor, finally unconscious.

"Oh thee of no faith," Badrick smiled cockily. "Or however you say it."

Malcolm breathed a sigh of relief and closed his holster, giving Badrick a furious glare. "You left that a little close."

"More fun that way."

"I was almost blinded," Zale quipped with the inappropriate air of someone commenting on a new kitchen table. "Don't let that happen again," he added, a little more seriously.

Badrick didn't bother responding. He couldn't think of a good rejoinder anyway. Instead he watched with interest as Zale and Malcolm made a small incision in the Kalik's shoulder and inserted the tracker, which was nothing more than a simple, red-coloured disc that throbbed with light, beeping faintly as it vanished from sight.

Malcolm kept his dagger in the wound as they worked. When they were done, Badrick saw why. Once the weapon was removed, the wound healed almost instantly, the flesh knitting together perfectly.

"Small wounds heal so quickly," Zale commented.

"OK," Malcolm said, paying him no attention due to his obvious desire to get this over and done with. "We have to get Susan into the forest, way out of sight of the base. He can't see this place when he wakes up. Finding a clan needs to be the first thing on his mind, or else he'll just attack the walls with rage."

Neither Badrick nor Zale continued this train of conversation. As Badrick stared at Malcolm in stunned silence, Zale's hand went to his forehead and Badrick saw him repressing a laugh. "Susan?" Zale grinned. "*He?*"

Malcolm pouted. "I told him if he didn't behave I'd give him a girl's name." He crossed his arms and glared at the Kalik. "He didn't behave. I gave him a girl's name."

"How'd he take it?" Badrick grinned.

"Well . . . let's just say he never attacked the forcefield until I christened him."

They employed the help of several Enthrallers to transport the Kalik to the grounds. Badrick was one of the porters, taking responsibility of the torso while others took charge of the limbs and the head. It was quite the effort, and he was especially glad when they were able to dump the unconscious creature onto the grass outside.

They were greeted by an armoured combat helicopter. Its blades were already cutting the air, the engine having been started pre-emptively. The pilot helped the porters tie straps to the Kalik's arms and legs before attaching it to a length of wire, which was hooked to the base of the helicopter. Having checked the status of his aircraft, the pilot gave them a thumbs-up, communicating his readiness.

"We'll get our armour on," Zale shouted over the chopping helicopter blades. "Don't go without us. We'll be back soon."

The pilot saluted him and leapt back into the cockpit.

"I just hope it doesn't go into a crowded place," Badrick muttered as they made their way back inside. "We'll be boned if we have to go after it. A bunch 'a civilians would see our armour . . . again."

"I'm more concerned about the people in that situation, Badrick," Zale chided him confusingly. Badrick frowned; why was Zale being so snippy?

Whatever the reason, Badrick decided to put it aside for now. They had more pressing concerns, and even he was feeling some apprehension. What they had riding on this mission was very important, and success was far from definitive. Their chances of getting the results they needed were slim, at best.

He spent the ten minutes it took him to suit up dwelling on their task and its potential problems, unable to stop wishing there was a better way.

But if there was one, Zale would surely have thought of it.

Along with his partner, they linked their port-pads to one of the Daemonium's satellites, which would be following the Kalik's movements. This was to ensure that, should they fall behind the demon, they would be able to use their equipment to keep track of it.

When they were finally ready, they boarded the helicopter and transported the vicious creature to the designated site Malcolm provided. Looking back, Badrick watched the Daemonium shrink and vanish under the glaring winter sunlight as they soared through the sky towards the closest heavily wooded area.

An agent helped them lower the Kalik beneath the branches and to the leaf-coated grass as the pilot kept the helicopter hovering. Badrick and Zale gave their thanks, before leaping from the aircraft, falling through the leaves and landing perfectly on the ground with metallic thuds.

As the noise of the helicopter's blades faded into the distance, the pair checked the direction of the wind. They backtracked a few metres before scaling the trees to take a position hidden within the cover of the frosted branches. From this vantage point they could observe the Kalik without the risk of it seeing or scenting them.

"Careful with your footing," Zale told him. "Make sure you get a strong branch."

He was certainly right about that. Although their armour was supernaturally light, the added weight could still snap a thin branch like a pencil.

"How long will it be knocked out?" Badrick asked, unsure of the effects of the tranquiliser they'd used. He leaned forward to take a closer look and heard the distinctive sounds of wood cracking.

He jumped back before he plummeted to the ground.

"Like I just said," Zale berated him, "stay on the thicker branches." In answer to Badrick's question, he murmured, "Depends on how much you drugged him with." He turned questioningly to Badrick.

"The medics gave me a bottle."

"Then we'd better keep quiet," Zale said, slinking back a few steps and falling into silence. At his words, there was a small rustling sound from below and Badrick spotted the Kalik's bulky arm move groggily.

The sound of ragged, monstrous breathing assailed his ears and with a shaking thrust, the demon threw itself to its feet. Standing stock still for a few seconds, the Kalik swayed as it waited for the bleariness to pass.

Within moments it was back to normal, and Badrick couldn't help but admire the speed of its recovery. Turning left and right with the speed of a mutant cheetah, the Kalik established its surroundings. It sniffed the air, hunting for anything that might be consumable.

Badrick watched with interest as it leaped upon an unsuspecting rabbit and tore it to shreds, devouring the poor animal within a matter of seconds.

When it had its fill of bunny flesh, the demon fell to all fours and gazed around.

With relief Badrick noted the behaviour of a Kalik recognising the fact that it was lost in the wild and was now in need of a new clan. Aside from a quick detour to feed on defenceless woodland creatures, Zale had been correct in his theory that finding a clan would be the beast's first priority.

Eventually, after many tense seconds, the Kalik heaved itself to full height, clenched its fists, raised its snout high in the air and roared into the sky. The din echoed throughout the forest, bouncing off the trees and frightening away any remaining wildlife.

Without warning, the demon bounded off, using both its hands and feet to propel itself forward.

"Go, go, go!" Zale called.

Wasting no time, the pair of them jumped to the opposite tree, aiming for branches strong enough to hold them. With skill years of training—or months of death—had given them, Badrick and Zale landed lightly, repeating the action over and over until they were in full pursuit of the Kalik.

As they expertly traversed the elevated pathway, the Kalik never stopped moving, crashing through the undergrowth, trampling bushes and plants and the occasional animal that failed to evade in time. This pursuit continued for quite some time and Badrick started to wonder if they weren't going in circles.

Was there any end to this goddamn forest?

He was seconds from activating a private call with Zale to ask that very question when, out of nowhere, the trees vanished and only empty space spread before him.

Zale was the only thing that stopped him from falling head first to the dirt. The electric Enthraller grabbed Badrick's hand as he fell and roughly pulled him back to a large branch. Breathing with the adrenaline, Badrick stumbled on landing but thankfully managed to keep his balance.

He breathed a sigh of relief; had he fallen, the Kalik would have heard the thump.

He indicated his thanks to Zale, reprimanding himself for his lack of attention to his surroundings. Deep inside himself, he heard a small, crazy, amused cackle.

He didn't need to ask to know that Daemnos was laughing at him.

"Come on," Zale said quickly, pointing into the distance as the

Kalik continued speeding across the expanse of plain grass that lay ahead. "We need to keep on it." He was now consulting his port-pad, so Badrick quickly imitated him.

The satellite's operator appeared more competent in his job than Badrick was in his; the camera was tracking the Kalik perfectly.

"Damn, that's hot!" Badrick exclaimed when he noticed the colourful blob that was the Kalik on the infrared setting.

"Practically magma blood," Zale agreed.

They descended to the ground and proceeded to sprint across the grass, following the path the Kalik had taken. Zale never stopped conferring with the satellite operator as he ran, confirming the accuracy of his port-pad's readout.

"We've got a problem," he shouted when he was done. "Base says there's a farmhouse about ten miles ahead."

"Is the Kalik going for it?"

"That's the problem."

chapter
ELEVEN

The Kalik stopped by the window of the farmhouse. It threw its fist into the glass, smashing it utterly, and peering hungrily inside. Zale tensed, hefting his auto-rifle, preparing to charge in if the Kalik found an innocent family to slaughter and devour.

Thankfully his readiness proved unnecessary. With a disappointed huff, the Kalik stepped back, evidently finding nothing. The farmhouse must have been abandoned.

Zale and Badrick threw themselves to the ground as the Kalik turned their way in its search for something else—anything else— to do. It was probably trying to sense its closest kin.

For a harrowing moment, Zale believed it had seen them and prepared himself to jump back to his feet and fight. But again, this was superfluous; the Kalik snapped in a different direction and began to amble around aimlessly. Zale frowned. Why was it doing this? It had been so driven before. So determined.

Why was it now just . . . lolling about?

It was only when Zale noticed a large hulk crawling along the ground to the right of their quarry that he finally recognised the behaviour he was seeing—the Kalik was walking in circles, which he knew was a certain ritual of theirs.

And they only did it when they wanted to be accepted into a clan.

And it was usually followed with . . .

Right on cue, the Kalik whirled on the spot and roared dangerously at the hulk. In response, the dark shape rose from the ground, its muscles rippling, jaws grinding, ivory glinting in the sun. As its mass rose above the long grass, the hulk growled back.

A second Kalik.

"That was quick," Badrick breathed beside Zale. "That was *very* quick. We're still close to the base. Are the Kalik watching our home?"

Zale didn't reply at first. His head had started to fuzz. An ill-timed headache was now forming. Wishing he could rub his temples, he sighed and closed his eyes. It was only when Badrick nudged him that he remembered his partner had spoken at all.

"I hope not," Zale said, though he couldn't say the proximity of this Kalik wasn't worrying. Badrick could very well be right; maybe the Kalik *were* scouting the Daemonium.

They watched as the two demons approached each other cautiously. With each step they roared in each other's faces, giving Zale the impression that they were about to engage in vicious combat.

But then *Susan* bowed his head, raising a hand towards his kin. Without hesitation, the other reached forward and clawed a small incision into the back of Susan's hand, growling with genuine affection.

With a deafening crack, Susan shone impossibly and black *light* flashed, engulfing the demon's body.

When the light went out, the Kalik was gone.

"He's been accepted," Zale said. "He's gone back to Hell. Now we follow our new arrival," Zale grinned, pleased with how well their plan was working. He felt a pang of guilt at the memory of the lies he'd told Quill, the shame of his actions haunting him even before he did them.

He *should* be using this Kalik to hunt their commander.

This wouldn't just serve the Daemonium, it would serve the entire world. The threat of someone controlling Kalik was severe to all who lived in this Universe. Annoyingly, Zale felt another stab of remorse at not having shared his theories with Badrick. His partner was still under the impression the Kalik was all they had to worry about.

Zale shook his head roughly. Too much guilt was starting to cloud his mind. He couldn't let that happen. Zale had to clear his head and stay focused on their objective.

But he knew . . . He knew he should prioritise the finding of their commander.

He *knew* it was the right thing to do.

But he just couldn't make himself do it.

If this fails it's not a great loss, his treacherous mind told him. *We have other ways to find the commander . . . surely. This isn't our only option. We can waste this chance because there are always others.*

Whether or not this was true, it didn't matter. As long as there was a way for him to justify his actions, Zale was powerless to deny his selfish desires. A nauseating sense of self-preservation was darkening his soul. He could feel it pressing down on his conscience.

He recognised this feeling. It was the same engulfing presence that had consumed him for five months.

He couldn't ignore its call. Despite his desire to defeat this darkness, he was incapable of fighting its grip, and with shame he knew he would obey its command.

He felt another nudge in his ribs and glanced up just in time to see the new Kalik heading away from them, past the farmhouse and across a country road.

"Let's go," Zale said, feeling his stomach drop as his mind was made up. "The plan remains the same." Ignoring his burning self-hatred, Zale tapped on his port-pad, telling the satellite operator to follow their new quarry.

"When were we going to change it?" Badrick asked, genuinely mystified, unaware of Zale's internal struggle.

He tutted with frustration when Zale didn't reply.

They followed the Kalik the same way they had with Susan, keeping as far back as possible while staying close enough to observe and study the creature's behaviour.

As time wore on, Zale started to recognise certain behavioural attributes and his guilt began to ease in the face of his astonishment that his plan was working. The Kalik was now stopping periodically to sniff the air, and kept digging its claws into the dirt, pulling up small stones and clumps of earth.

This Kalik was on a hunt.

It no longer mattered if they made the choice to use this demon to find their commander; they wouldn't succeed. There was no way Zale was going to stand by and watch the Kalik hunt and kill until it had its fill before wandering off to find someone who may or may not be controlling it.

With the situation as it was, they'd be stupid not to put into action their actual mission.

Sometime during their pursuit, Badrick finally figured out what their quarry was up to. Zale heard him laugh quietly and mutter,

"We're the luckiest guys ever."

"Depends on the way you look at it," Zale replied tightly, stressing on all the things that could go wrong.

"We need to see a Kalik on the hunt, Zale," Badrick rebuked him. "We couldn't have asked for better."

Zale didn't respond.

They followed the hunter for another hour, running after it as it charged across the land. Over time their surroundings altered between grassy plains to wooded hills to small abandoned farmhouses. But no matter what it encountered the beast never faltered except for the instances it stopped to sniff and scratch.

They sprinted for so long that even Badrick, with all his Royal strengths, appeared to be tiring.

Zale was pushing his body past weariness. His muscles were starting to ache, and he estimated they were only half an hour away from screaming with exhaustion. The fear of losing his quarry began to scratch at his confidence. If this endless sprinting continued for much longer they physically wouldn't be able to follow.

Alternatives began to form in his mind. There was no way he was giving up.

He was about to stop running and confer with Badrick on what they should do when he suddenly realised the Kalik had ground to a halt and they were dangerously close.

He grabbed Badrick and threw him to the dirt, diving beside him, instinctively holding his breath. His muscles were tense as he peeked through the long grass that hid them, checking on the Kalik. Beside him, grumbling quietly, Badrick prepared himself for a fight, reaching for his single-rifle and holding it tight.

It was unnecessary. Through great fortune, they remained undetected, though Zale expected by only a sliver.

That had been too close.

Moving extra carefully, Zale took a moment to study their surroundings. They'd emerged into some kind of man-made facility. At first he didn't understand what kind of place this was and he glanced around blankly. But then he started to notice things he recognised—machines, tools, signs—and Zale realised they'd stumbled onto an old, long abandoned mining facility, cranes and equipment dark and dead and looming ominously over them like the Grim Reaper's fingers.

The buildings were incredibly drab, the metallic red paint on the walls peeled and rusted. Most of the windows were shattered, probably from wild animals fighting, foraging or hunting, or maybe even from Daemonium activity in the area.

Old tools and vehicles littered the place. Some of the machines had somehow ended up on their sides. Many were even collapsed in on themselves, rusted with age and warped by curious animals.

"Behold, the frailty of human construction," Zale commented drily.

The Kalik sniffed the air once more. Pausing for the shortest of seconds, it leapt impossibly high, disappearing from sight atop of one of the buildings.

"It's found a hunt," Zale whispered, realising this place apparently wasn't as abandoned as it looked.

Someone was here.

He led the way to a half destroyed security office, which they quickly scaled, using the various pipes and window ledges as foot- and hand-holds.

From this high position, they could see most of the facility.

It truly was a mess. Nothing appeared to be in working order.

"Keep an eye out for the Kalik's target," Zale whispered, un-slinging his auto-rifle and hefting it. "We'll have to shoot the thing just before it strikes."

"Understood."

Badrick brought his single-rifle to bear, ready to fire at a moment's notice. No doubt he knew just as well as Zale that he was better equipped for this situation. His single-rifle was a long range weapon. They would require pinpoint accuracy and timing to kill the Kalik before it savaged its target.

They would have less than a second between that and the revealing of its murder weapon.

Zale didn't know what to feel. The odds that everything would go as they needed were incredibly slim. Least of all, the chances of them actually locating a Kalik with his weapon. *If* what they feared was true, and the subspecies was using a variation of his powerful swords, what was the probability of them finding one?

This Kalik most likely was going to use its own demonic metal blade. This was, without a shadow of a doubt, a waste of time.

It had to be.

There had been no other bodies in the Apos base with that dreadful wound, besides the commander. That meant, had the Kalik used the weapon, it was the only one in the attack to possess it.

How many others might possibly own one?

Probably not many.

The chances of finding another with this one attempt . . . Badrick was right. Those chances didn't exist. It would more than likely take a considerable amount of time, and many of these missions, to prove anything for sure.

Zale closed his eyes tightly and counted to ten, doing his best to purge everything in his head and envision a white screen.

His mind was a jumble recently. He was barely able to think straight.

He greatly feared that it was affecting his judgement—that he wasn't on top form. He was terrified that this wasn't the smartest plan of action and that, under normal circumstances, he would have been able to recognise that.

Nevertheless, it was too late now. They were out here, with a Kalik on the hunt and the climax of their mission closer than ever before.

This was the moment they'd either find out the truth . . . or they wouldn't.

Now and then Zale caught glimpses of a shadowy bulk moving across the roofs and knew the Kalik was still hunting for its prey. Thankfully, nestled in their hiding place they were not only safe from its view but would also be able to see it coming way before it spotted them.

They didn't have to worry about the Kalik discovering their presence.

"Who would be *here?*" Badrick voiced quietly, interrupting Zale's concentration.

Truth be told, Zale was wondering the same thing. What possible reason would anyone have for stepping foot in this desolate place?

"I was just thinking that," he replied softly. "Kids, maybe?"

"You think kids would come here?"

"Of course they would," Zale almost laughed. "Kids are *fecking* idio—"

The sound of scrabbling interrupted him. Instantly recognising the noise as *not* being the Kalik, he turned sharply to discern the source. Climbing out of the large mining hole in the middle of the facility, using the ropes left behind on the massive cranes that loomed above it, was a tall figure.

It wasn't a kid.

And at the exact same moment that Zale saw who it was, his radio fizzled and, with the panic of someone finding out something *far* too late, a terrified voice bawled, "Hood! There's an agent there!"

"Crap!" Zale exclaimed, jumping to his feet, his eyes widening at the sight of the blue armour.

"He must be on a mission," Badrick stated.

Zale pushed aside the debris that acted as their hiding place. "Abort the mission. Get to that agent!" He leapt from the roof and landed heavily on the dirt.

Darting forward as fast as he could, he noticed a large bulk, silhouetted against the sun, descending upon the agent.

He was about to shout a warning . . .

When he heard a cry of alarm behind him.

Badrick was about to follow his partner when something hit him hard on the back. He was whacked so hard he lost his footing, tumbling over the side of the security office and crying out in surprise.

He coughed as he hit the ground, the air being knocked from his lungs upon impact.

Zale heard the commotion and turned to provide aid, but before he could do anything remotely helpful something massive plummeted from above and knocked him to the ground.

The force that pushed Badrick from the roof descended upon him and through the dirt kicked up in his fall he recognised the unmistakable shape of a second Kalik.

Wasting no time he lifted his legs, putting his feet on the monster's chest. With all his might, he pushed, and the beast flew back into the corrugated steel of the security office. Badrick leapt to his feet, scrabbling for his gun, intending to shoot the Kalik before it could regain its footing.

Everything that transpired thereafter seemed to happen in slow motion.

Zale rolled onto his back to see what pushed him. His alarm at seeing a third Kalik was obvious.

Before he could do anything, the agent, who had observed the commotion and was now speeding towards them to lend his aid, was also knocked to the ground. Their original quarry rolled him over and pushed down, pressing its clawed foot into his chest.

Wasting no time at all, it raised its right arm and clenched its fist tightly.

The seconds appeared to drag. The Kalik's arm crawled through the air with the slowness of a snail. Everything seemed to silence—snarls, scratches, cries . . . all hushed—and in the midst of nothingness Badrick sensed the tiniest spark of demonic electricity.

And in that next second, despite his total disbelief—despite the paralysing numbness now coursing through his veins—Badrick made a choice.

He closed his fingers, built power within his fist and threw it up into the air. The energy left his hand with the speed of a bullet and rocketed into the sky. Somewhere out there, orbiting the planet in the dark of space, every satellite in the region would now be freaking out. For a split second any camera that *might* be pointing in their direction would no longer work.

Badrick did it just in time.

Barely a second after his power disrupted the satellites, a sizzling electrical zap cut through the air particles and Badrick saw what he already knew to be true, but deeply wished it wasn't.

Impossibly shaped exactly like a Kalik blade—a long triangle, hole in the middle, forked at the end—the weapon sparked violently. The structure of the blade was extremely unstable, the blade barely formed.

But it was enough.

Badrick had no chance to stop it; he'd used the time available to him to avoid anyone watching from the satellites seeing the weapon.

The blade plunged into the agent's chest. He choked, gripping the Kalik's arm and trying to push the monster away, but his failing strength was unable to do such a thing. His arms quickly fell to his side.

The Kalik removed the blade and deactivated it, roaring victoriously.

Time sped up for Badrick, so quickly it was almost as though someone had hit a fast forward button. Having witnessed the event through the legs of his own attacker, Zale roared in total fury. He jumped to his feet, unveiling a dagger as he did so.

Plunging it in the neck of his assailant, he pushed its writhing body away.

Badrick aimed his weapon at the Kalik he'd fought off. He'd wasted precious seconds disabling the satellites and the monster was now descending upon him with rapid speed.

At the last second, before it could cause any harm—even before Badrick could open fire—Zale's knife spun into the demon's neck

The Kalik was dead before it hit the ground.

A short burst of auto-rifle fire echoed throughout the mining facility and the murderous first Kalik dropped dead atop its victim.

Zale hurried up and pushed it off the agent. He bent down and tore away the leather and armour around the man's arm. Pressing his own fingers into the flesh, he checked for a pulse.

A dejected shake of his head indicated the lack of one.

Badrick limped up to him, his leg hurting every time he applied pressure. Surviving never ending heights was easy for any Enthraller if landing on their feet, but if you tumbled onto your thigh the way Badrick had, even falling off the sofa would hurt.

And his leg *did* hurt.

"He died with honour," he stated as he drew up close. "And

we achieved what we set out to do. Despite all odds, we got proof that the Kalik have your swords, have their own versions, and can use them."

Badrick got the strange feeling that Zale was glaring at him. He wasn't sure why—for God's sake, they'd succeeded. He should have been happy.

But his body language was communicating anger in tidal waves.

Zale stood up, turning away from Badrick. He tapped on his port-pad, waited a few seconds and then spoke to empty space. "This is Operative Zale Hood, requesting a rescue helicopter at our current position. We have an agent K.I.A. Require transport for the body."

Badrick heard a saddened voice on his own comm. reply, "Roger, Hood. E.T.A.—thirty minutes."

They stood in silence after that, awaiting extraction. As they lingered, Badrick kept an eye on their perimeter, ensuring that no other hunting Kalik was about to spring an ambush.

Thankfully, it seemed these three were the only ones in the vicinity.

The relief of this knowledge left room in Badrick's stomach for other, entirely different feelings; a sense of excitement mixed with apprehension was already building.

They'd succeeded in their mission.

That was good.

Best news all day.

But now that they had . . . what was their next step?

chapter
TWELVE

Traipsing back into the HQ, the pair of them sombrely followed the stretcher bearing the deceased agent. Zale watched it pull ahead of them as the stretcher-bearers hurried away, eager to get the body to the Medical Wing, and from there the Morgue.

Zale acted quickly. He issued orders on his port-pad for the body to be set aside away from any medics and doctors who may have wished to perform an autopsy, leaving it just for him. Because this was such a disruptive request, a command for approval from the Council flashed onto his screen. Zale redirected the message to Reynolds, knowing the sergeant would make good on his promise to help.

"So what do we do now?" Badrick's voice punctured his thoughts. "What's our next plan of action?"

Zale gazed down at the Kalik equipment he'd sawn off the beast's arm, glaring at it hatefully. Despite every failure he'd made today, somewhere inside this contraption was an answer to their problems . . . hopefully.

The shape of the weapon's design was utterly mental. Most people would refuse to believe it was possible, what this sword could do. Anyone who studied Zale's science would state the physics didn't allow for the shape to exist.

But they were wrong.

It wasn't impossible.

After all, Zale himself had made a model that defied logic.

No Kalik could have done this—further enforcing Zale's belief the demons now had a commander.

"We need to get a sword," he answered Badrick's query. "I need to get an older model sword so I can go through the upgrades I implemented to create the current versions."

"What for?"

"I want to cross-reference everything against this design," Zale explained. "I need to see at what point in the timeline of my work an alteration in the machinery was possible."

He could tell Badrick didn't understand, but that hardly mattered. Badrick's comprehension was not necessary, only his help.

"I'll go," Badrick said, despite his bemusement. "You go sort out the agent. Where can I find an older one?"

"Antiquated Storage."

Badrick laughed heartily. "There's a place called *Antiquated Storage?*" He gave Zale a quick salute before turning away, following the directions given to him.

Zale allowed his partner to wander off towards the storage rooms, watching him leave as he mused on the past few hours and his partner's seemingly decreasing concern for people's wellbeing.

The olive and white armour vanished from sight and Zale sighed tiredly, dreading what might be coming next.

Right then, all he wanted to do was fall asleep where he was and lose himself to the wonders of dreams.

Unfortunately, he had a duty to fulfil. He couldn't just go unconscious.

And he couldn't stand there mulling over things forever either.

The discovery that their greatest fear was real did not bring him joy. In fact he was feeling worse than ever before. He couldn't remember the last time his stomach felt so empty.

What sent anxiety coursing through him wasn't even the thought of what would happen to *him* if the Council discovered this terrible truth. His selfish self-preservation had evaporated the moment he'd seen the Kalik kill the agent.

No . . . it was more than that now. If the Kalik were organising into an army, having an arsenal of his weapons could turn a catastrophic state of affairs into a world-ending event.

This needed to be dealt with.

The gravity of their situation weighed upon him with an unforgiving pressure and he had to take a few deep breaths before continuing.

It was bad—the simple fact their mission was successful was the worst possible outcome. The chances of their triumph had been resting in the minuses and yet . . .

There were three possible reasons.

One; they were extremely lucky.

Two; a vast number of Kalik owned his weapons, which naturally increased the mission's chances of success.

Or . . .

Three; they were being messed with—someone knew they were coming and gifted a weapon to that specific Kalik to scare them. To show them what they feared was true.

As far as Zale was concerned, this final option was the most likely. After all, what were the chances that the Kalik's first use of *his* weapon had occurred in the area he and Badrick just so happened to be surveying?

Though this thought made him shudder, Zale did his best to gather his composure. When he was sure he was calmed, he trudged after the stretcher-bearers. He found them depositing the body in the corner of the Medical Wing, an army of medics ushering them away from the table as they moaned and complained about the Council interfering in their affairs.

Zale breathed a sigh of relief. Reynolds must have sanctioned his order before the medics could have a chance to study the body.

Zale wandered up to it, ignoring the glares of the medical staff as they passed him by. As he neared the corpse he reached out his hand to begin removing the man's armour.

But before he could even start he heard a familiar voice shout in exasperation. "Can we *ever* go on a mission without you being wounded? I mean, come on!"

Smiling with genuine gladness, he spotted Carla shaking her partner roughly, cuffing him on the forehead as she did so.

"It's not my fault!" John hollered defensively.

"You suck," Carla laughed, punching him on the shoulder.

"Ow! Not there!"

"That's where I punch. You should know that by now. If you get hit there that doesn't mean I'm going to change where I punch you."

"Zale!" John shouted suddenly, noticing him watching from afar. "Get this crazy bitch off me!"

"You want to see crazy, you should get me in bed," Carla spat his way as Zale took the opportunity to forget all his worries for a brief moment and wandered over. "Oh wait, you never will." At that she turned and gave Zale a tight hug, the metal of their armours banging together. "You, on the other hand . . ."

"Hugging like this is difficult," Zale wheezed.

"You'll get over it." She withdrew, tutted at the sight of his obscuring visor and gently pulled his helmet from his head. Hers was already lying on the floor by her feet, so he was able to look into her eyes as they bore pointedly into his. "I heard about what happened. The stretcher-bearers told me."

"Us," John corrected her.

Giving him an annoyed look, Carla continued. "It sounded horrible. Are you OK?"

"No," he replied honestly. "You don't even know the half of it." He gave her a meaningful look and she nodded understandingly. He was grateful for her competence. They couldn't talk about the swords in John's proximity. Thankfully with Carla all it took was a specific eye twitch to make her understand the nightmare scenario was now confirmed true.

She reached over and took his hand in hers, squeezing it.

"Somebody you *don't* know is killed and you get lovin'. I get stabbed and I get punched."

"Shut up, John," Carla hissed.

Laughing, Zale stepped closer and inspected the grisly wound on the squirming man's arm. It was a long gash across the flesh high above the elbow and was bleeding quite profusely. John's arm piece lay discarded on the floor some distance away, but even from back there Zale could see the tearing in the metal and the blood staining the paint.

"Quite a deep cut. What was it?"

"Kalik," John told him. "They're everywhere at the moment."

The look of alarm Zale gave Carla could have stunned a Royal, but to his great relief she shook her head discreetly yet urgently, communicating that the secret was safe. To ensure John didn't notice their brief exchange, she continued the conversation by saying, "One of those stupid blades the bastards have."

"Sharper than a razor," John whined. He turned his attention solely on Zale. "You're the one working on this Kalik problem, right? I heard that right? . . . Right?"

Zale nodded affirmatively as Carla muttered with irritation, "Stop saying 'right', you freak." As he did so he picked up a damp cloth and pressed it against John's wound. The agent winced, but otherwise smiled his thanks.

Zale proceeded to clean away the blood, dabbing softly until it was time to follow up with disinfection. After that, Carla watched him in attentive silence as he began the process of stitching. John howled in pain as the needle poked through the flesh and yanked on the thread to pull the skin together, kicking his legs like a child.

Halfway through his task a medic Zale didn't know stepped up and demanded that she be allowed to continue. "Don't you think you've taken over enough for one day?" she hissed icily when Zale announced he didn't mind finishing up.

"Ouch," Carla chuckled as they were pushed away from John's bed. "What was that about?"

Her chuckles increased when he told her.

As he led her away from John and onto where the slain agent lay, she clearly picked up on his sombre silence, touching his arm and asking, "Is there something else bothering you? I know it's bad and all but . . . it just seems like there's something else."

Unsure of whether it was wise to voice his concerns, Zale at first hesitated, staring into empty space. He only spoke when Carla gave him a hefty punch on the pauldron.

"It's Badrick," he blurted, glaring at the scratch mark Carla just carved with her armoured fist.

"What about him?"

Zale began removing the armour from the agent, taking a piece at a time and leaving each one on a large table nearby.

"He's not the same. Ever since he came back, he's . . . "

"What?" she prompted him.

"Well, he's lost his morals for a start," he somewhat snapped, a little irritated at being forced to speak. "Do you remember what he was like?" Zale sighed heavily. "So adamant in his beliefs on how people should be. So hating of unnecessary cruelty. He would get very angry about it."

"Yeah, I remember."

"Well . . . he's just *not* anymore. He doesn't seem to care that we lost an agent, only that we succeeded in our mission."

"Did he know the agent?"

"No," Zale sighed again, "but it's more than that. He literally didn't seem fazed in the slightest. It was cold and cruel and he's been acting odd ever since he came back. On *that* day he went from sophisticated and intelligent, to vengeful and cruel, and then on to this weird furious confidence."

"You mean when he threatened to blow us all up?"

"Aye, that!" Zale almost shouted. "I mean, what's he doing!?" He took a moment to breath, realising he actually *had* started yelling, and gazed down wretchedly at the deceased agent. "When this man was attacked, I saw what Badrick did. He had an opening. He'd fended off his attacker and had his weapon in hand. He could have shot the Kalik closest or shot the one attacking the agent.

"But he did neither. Instead he scrambled the satellites above us so that no one would see the weapon. I saw him do it. I *sensed* him do it."

"He was just thinking about you."

"Perhaps," he murmured. "But Badrick wouldn't have made *that* choice. Not before he died."

He reached over and unstrapped the chestplate. Spotting the

wound, Carla turned and pulled a curtain around, obscuring them from the curious, watchful eyes of the nearby medics.

"You're right, he wouldn't have," she told him. "Maybe there *is* something wrong."

"Perhaps," Zale muttered again, then shook his head and spoke up. "I wish I could make sense of it . . . but I need to focus on this now. I might learn more about the blade from the wound."

Carla stepped up and took his hand. "John's going to be a while. Let me help."

Nodding his appreciation, Zale handed her a medical sheet and the pair got to work.

Badrick walked briskly towards the door marked *Antiquated Storage* with a thankful sigh. It had taken him almost twenty whole minutes just to find the right door. This place was annoyingly tucked away at the back of the storage facilities, almost completely out of sight of anyone but omnipotent people.

Badrick wasn't omnipotent.

Nevertheless, he'd finally found the right passageway and, with relief, stepped over the threshold, the door zipping shut behind him and plunging him into almost darkness. The lights inside were so dim he could barely see, and was forced to wait until his eyes adjusted. The only illumination was a tiny light bulb hanging from the ceiling. It was just enough to gently brighten the chaotic interior.

Antiquated Storage was right. Very little care was put into the organisation of this place. Everything was dumped haphazardly, with no cataloguing system obvious at first glance.

Or the second.

Or the third.

It was a total pig sty.

He gazed at everything with despair. How was he ever going to find an old model sword in this *tut?* Removing his helmet and setting it down on a shelf, he took a deep breath and dived further inside.

He immediately jumped back when a loud crash sounded directly ahead of him and a writhing body crawled out between two shelving units, knocking over old and dusty equipment and machinery.

Badrick laughed and focused on calming his hammering heart. He called over the din, "Damn, you gave me a heart attack!"

The body looked up at the sound of his voice, pausing in the act of dusting himself off. He coughed and said, "Badrick, right?" Smacking his clothes one more time, dirt and dust puffed from his form like smoke.

Suddenly recognising who this person was, Badrick blinked and said, "Oh yeah . . . Zach, right? I remember you."

"Yeah, that's me." Zach gave Badrick a once-over, casting his eyes up and down. "Nice armour," he muttered, a little awkwardly.

"Thanks."

An uncomfortable silence ensued.

Then, all discomfited, "You wanna help me out?" Zach indicated to all the rubbish. "I'm trying to find a series four single-rifle."

Badrick moved closer, smiling and thankful for the conversation. "That's . . . like . . . really old. Mine is a series seventeen. When's it from, the dark ages?"

"Near enough," Zach laughed. He picked up and threw away, without care, what looked to have been an old sniper rifle. "The Council has asked me to find one so they can finish some kind of quarterly study on their progression over the centuries and whether or not they need to improve their employees."

"That sounds like B.S. to me."

Zach chuckled drily. "Well, maybe."

Badrick agreed to help Zach find what he was looking for. He figured it wouldn't get in the way of his own task; nothing was organised or separated into categories so it wasn't like searching for a gun lowered his chances of finding a sword

By the look of this place, he was just as likely to find one of the things beneath a *Hungry Hippos* game.

"God forbid they organise anything in here," he voiced unhappily.

"No kidding," Zach said. "Not the Council's best decision, despite their effectiveness. Though I do wish the Hierarch would show his face. He knows what he's doing."

"Never met him," Badrick said.

"Not surprised," Zach sighed. "He vanished into his penthouse just before you arrived."

They searched in silence for a few moments. Rummaging through the stacks of rubbish, Badrick found an assortment of old, unarmed grenades, a bunch of aged helmets, and a large pile of obsolete auto-rifles.

But he found no single-rifles.

Or swords.

About ten minutes in, he glanced over to see if Zach had achieved better luck, but judging by the dust clogging his hair and covering his unhappy face, Badrick surmised he hadn't.

Deciding he didn't want to work in unhappy silence anymore, he cleared his throat and voiced the thoughts that had been playing on his mind since he first recognised Zach.

"So . . . Zach . . . I was wondering something."

"What was that?"

"Zale told me you hate him," Badrick laughed. "I was just wondering why. Did he sleep with your girlfriend, or something?"

Zach coughed dust and gave him an annoyed look. "No,

though that *does* sound like something he would do." He knocked aside a box of rusted gears. "I don't hate him at all. He's a brilliant detective."

Badrick had to suppress his laughter, not wishing to appear contemptuous. He could read Zach like a book; now they were talking he remembered that the man was a detective also, meaning he was probably in competition with Zale.

With Zale being Zale, Badrick didn't need to ask to realise that Zach was jealous.

He was saved having to continue the uneasy conversation—which he was painfully aware he'd started—by the appearance of the subject of their dialogue himself.

Badrick waved to his partner as he entered but didn't stop sifting through the dusty contents of the storage room.

"Oh my God, this place!" Zale cried, dumping his helmet next to Badrick's. "You found one yet?" Badrick shook his head. "No wonder. Look at all this crap!" Zale sighed heavily, rubbing his eyes and banging the metal on his arm against the wall. "Alright, keep looking. I'll try at the back." He walked briskly past Zach, giving only a terse greeting, which was returned just as tightly.

Badrick heard Zale pick something up and mutter, "I have . . . no idea what this is." A crash echoed throughout the room as he chucked it away.

They worked in suffocating silence for a long time after that, the only sounds being the calls and crashes of frustration.

Eventually Zach was the one to break the monotony. "Oh wow!"

Badrick couldn't help but be curious. "What?"

Zach stumbled up to him, tripping over the items they'd dislodged and thrown to the floor. "It's an old stun dust grenade."

Badrick smiled and leaned forward for a closer look. "I read about those in my *month's* training," he grinned, putting emphasis on the word *'month'*. "Didn't it throw dust on you, or something? Special dust that makes you unable to move, right?"

"Yes, that's right," Zach laughed. "I used to love these. They're so old now, though, the dust has probably lost its potency." He fiddled with it, bringing it closer to his face. "I wonder if—oh my, I just armed it."

"It's live!?" Badrick screeched.

Zach juggled it unsurely for a brief few seconds, before throwing it in Badrick's direction. "Here, you have it!"

"*I don't goddamn want it!*" Badrick grabbed it from the air and pulled back his arm. "Zale, fix this!"

Lobbing it as far as he could, he watched it sail through the air, disappearing behind the countless dusty shelves. Having heard their cries of alarm, Zale understood exactly what was coming his way. He had half a second to shout, "No, no, no!" before he screamed in panic. A split second later there was a loud bang, followed by a curious puffing sound.

A tense silence ensued.

"Zale . . . you good?"

An entire shelving unit was thrown angrily aside, its contents cascading across the already chaotically messy floor, and a suddenly very brown Zale pushed his way out of the rubble. "Thanks," he snarled, "for that."

Badrick couldn't stop his laughter; Zale looked hilarious. The dust—cloggy and musty from age—looked sickening. It covered practically his entire body, including his face. Zach chuckled along with Badrick, adding, "Well, he can move. Told you the dust was old."

Their cackling was prematurely interrupted by the recognisable sound of the door zipping open. Badrick instantly stopped laughing, not wanting to appear a slacker, when he realised the newcomer was none other than Reynolds.

He realised just how stupid this thought was the moment he got it; Reynolds didn't even know what they were doing.

"Ah, I was told I could find you here, Zach," the sergeant said pleasantly. "Badrick," he added, spotting him nearby. "What are you doing here? Zale . . . what the hell happened to you?"

Zale gave him a forced confused look. "What are you talking about?"

"You're . . . you're covered in stun dust."

"Am I? Hadn't noticed."

Reynolds stared at him for a moment, clearly curious of what he'd just stumbled upon.

But then his expression changed and he exclaimed, "Never mind! I don't want to know. I'll just get a headache."

Zach stepped forward and shook the sergeant's hand firmly. "What did you want me for, sir?"

Reynolds glanced at Badrick meaningfully, who frowned. What was going on here?

The conspiracy spreads, said a small voice inside his head.

His eyes widened as realisation struck him like a brick. With horror at what Reynolds intended, he bawled, "No, sir, please! You can't. You promised."

"I promised to help," Reynolds hissed, adopting the authoritative tones he used whenever faced with insubordination. "We need to end this investigation *now*. Agent Brenner and his team are very effective detectives. We could use Zach's help."

"Do I even want to know what's going on?" the man in question queried, glancing from Reynolds to Badrick and back again.

"Probably not," Badrick sighed, awaiting the moment Zale learned what they were talking about and exploded.

"There's an issue with the Kalik, Zach," Reynolds said softly. "I'm afraid they've gotten a hold of some of the swor—"

Badrick winced as what he'd predicted came to pass: "Whoa, Reynolds!" Zale screeched. "What are you doing?"

"I'm bringing Zach in on the case," he was told sternly. "You think it's easy for me to help you? You've no idea what influencing the agent commanders entails. Hiding it from the Council is easy. We all work in our own sectors. But I need the help with the BCR, Zale. Now I don't care what rivalry you two have. Button it!"

"Yes, sir," both Zach and Zale muttered heatedly, though the elder of the two was still gazing around questioningly.

Reynolds proceeded to tell Zach of the problem they all faced, informing him of the potential theft of Zale's swords. Badrick updated their information, telling them what they witnessed at the quarry.

"So our fears are confirmed," Reynolds sighed, rubbing his chin agitatedly. "That's bad news, *but* you say only one of the three had one of these blades?" Badrick understood the motive behind this question; the moment it became clear that an entire army possessed the weapon Reynolds would have to blow the whistle.

But with just one, they were still safe.

"Sir, we should tell the Council," Zach piped up after having kept silent for so long. "This is a serious matter."

"Yes, it is, Zach. So we *cannot* tell the Council. We have to deal with this ourselves."

"I don't believe that is the best course of action, sir."

"Zale's freedom depends on the secret being kept," Reynolds growled angrily, the rumbles so deep that Zach trembled slightly.

"Think what the Council will do if they find out," Badrick chipped in, hoping to help the situation.

"All due respect," Zach said slowly, "that is not my fault. The weapon should've been kept under better security."

"Exactly," Badrick tutted. "That's not Zale's fault, it's the Council's. They took the things from him and now *they* own them.

They are in charge of their storage. Not Zale. The theft has nothing to do with him."

"But after everything," Reynolds continued, "they won't care. They'll use it against him and I will not be able to persuade them against the decision." He held his hands up imploringly. "Help us, Zach."

Zach bristled angrily, a response Badrick didn't understand. What was there to be angry about? Was this rivalry really bad enough for wanton emotions to get in the way?

"With all due respect, sir," Zach repeated, "I am an agent, you are army. You can't give me orders."

Now it was Reynolds' turn to bristle. With slow menacing steps, he closed the distance between them, practically drenching his power and authority over the agent. "Actually, *I* am on the Council. *I* can give you orders, and though I don't boast about what I've done, I expect respect because of it. Do you remember what Mawr and I did, son?"

Zach nodded. "Yessir."

"You are a good detective, agent, but you allow your emotions to cloud your judgement too regularly." Reynolds took a step back, allowing Zach breathing room. "You're a clever man. Can you not see the logic in our words? Are you really going to sink so low that you let your ally take the fall for something that is proven not to be his fault?"

Zach was sentry-still. Badrick could barely tell he was breathing and he truly could not predict what Zach would say.

He had a horrible feeling it would be bad.

However, quite suddenly Zach's shoulders sagged, the fight draining from his body, and he sighed, "No, sir. Sorry, sir."

Reynolds beamed and clasped Zach's shoulder. "Thank you."

From the back of the room, Zale's hand rose into the air. "Do I get a say in this?"

"No," Reynolds shot him down. "Work with Zach. This is too important. The same goes for you, Hood. Don't let your ego ruin your life. Understand?"

"Fine!"

Satisfied with his day's work, Reynolds straightened his red uniform jacket. He cast his eyes around the room, for the first time actually noticing the hills of crap occupying the space, and sighed, rubbing his forehead tiredly.

"You OK?" Badrick asked him.

"Just tired." Reynolds tried to smile, but failed; it came out as a grimace. "We lost an Enthraller today. Not one we employ, one we hadn't found yet.

"Some kid down the country. We don't even know what happened. We've figured out who his demon was; Koreath. But we have no idea who could have possibly killed the Enthraller."

His interest in other Enthrallers getting the better of him, Badrick asked, "Singularis or Ordinarius?"

"Singularis."

"Powers?"

"Koreath was mentioned in the Old Texts," Zale inputted. He was sulking at the back, flinging rusted nuts and bolts at the wall. "Isn't he the one who stops hearts with poison?"

Reynolds nodded affirmatively. He sighed again, somehow even more heavily than before. "It's a terrible shame to lose an Enthraller so young, but I'm sure we can question Koreath in . . . another twenty years when he re-emerges in another person."

"The circle of demon life," Zale spat.

Badrick didn't comment.

His interest in the topic was over.

And evidently, Reynolds felt the same way about them. Deciding their conversation was done, the tired sergeant briskly saluted the three of them, wishing luck with the Kalik case and ensuring they knew they could call on his aid at any time.

He then abruptly turned away and walked towards the door.

Just before he left, he added with a smile, "Clean this place up when you're done."

"Not bloody likely," Zale scoffed once the door was closed.

chapter
THIRTEEN

Badrick watched, somewhat amused but mostly bored and frustrated, as Zale and Zach argued intensely, refusing to agree on even a single thing. They'd organised a digital evidence wall on a monitor in the corner of the BCR sometime before and were now both rearranging the pieces to emphasise where each thought the other was wrong.

Now and then they'd puff in irritation or throw their hands up disagreeably.

That was the amusing part.

But the moments it occurred were too few and far between to make the situation of any interest, and Badrick was starting to get really irritated. The only time he had any input was when Zale mentioned something about someone controlling the Kalik.

"What?" he snapped angrily. "You never told me about that."

"I'm sorry for withholding that," Zale said sincerely. "I didn't want to consider it was true because the thought is too horrible."

Badrick felt an emotion he recognised immediately; the desire to be angry at someone but being completely unable.

Because, as always, he found that the person's motives just couldn't be ignored.

He *hated* that feeling.

"*Look!*" Zale called after a few more moments of arguing. He lowered his voice so as not to be heard by anyone but Zach and Badrick. "The Kalik have my weapons so yes, someone stole them. But I don't think it was *Lucikefer*." He scoffed at Zach for making what he clearly thought was a stupid suggestion.

"But we saw him with one of them," Zach spat back. "We saw him take it. You yourself fought him with it. Where did that one even go?"

"Badrick's resurrection destroyed it," Zale muttered.

Zach waved his hand dismissively. "Whatever. I reckon he gave them another."

"You're right that Lucikefer is a viable candidate. But I don't think he's our culprit. I mean, for God's sake, he's imprisoned. The Kalik are *clearly* being controlled. There's no way they could fight as a disciplined army like at the Apos base of their own accord. How's Lucikefer supposed to be doing that from the Void?"

"I think he wanted to use them as a fallback plan against Daemnos. Now that he's been defeated, the Kalik have gone back to their usual hunting patterns."

Even Badrick had to sigh at that; it was a stupid thing to say. It seemed like Zach was disagreeing with Zale simply because he hadn't come up with the theory himself.

He was being jealous again.

"Have you not listened to a thing I've said?" Zale groaned. "These aren't usual bloody hunting patterns."

Zach's shoulder rolled in a strange display of contempt. "With your weaponry in the mix, what is usual is no longer what we assume it to be."

Zale sighed, laughing derisively. "Listen to me, Zach. Lucikefer has nothing to do with this. One, he doesn't have the smarts to alter my blades. Two, he wouldn't waste the time adapting my tech for the Kalik. He's a selfish bastard. Why would he do anything for anyone? Three, Lucikefer has *zero* influence over Kalik. They don't fear death and that is all he can threaten them with. He can't control them."

"I disagree," Zach argued once more. "Lucikefer is *very* powerful. He's a Royal."

"You *would* disagree!" Zale hissed furiously. He took a moment to check himself. "Look ... Apparently we can't agree on anything. You think the Kalik *used* to be under control, I think they are *currently*."

"If they aren't, then there's nothing we can do. We've lost.

"But if there *is* someone to catch, we have a chance. Can you just *try* to work on the assumption that there is someone to find?"

It took him a moment, but apparently Zale's words hit home in Zach's consciousness. He finally nodded in reluctant agreement and Badrick sensed they were at long last making progress.

"But I think we should do this separately," Zach said tightly. "I know what Sergeant Reynolds said, but we just can't work together. It gets us nowhere. We'll confer every twenty four hours but otherwise work separately."

"Fine!" Zale exhaled. "But don't involve your team, for God's sake."

"I won't!" Zach snapped. With that he angrily stormed away. "Looks like the race is on."

When the detective was through the doorway, Badrick utilised the silence that followed to ask the question that was on his mind, for once genuinely unsure of the answer. "So what *do* the Kalik fear?"

The answer came without a moment's hesitation. "They fear resurrection."

Badrick blinked; this was definitely not what he'd expected. Unable to find anything in Daemnos' memories, he raised a confused eyebrow and spoke his bewilderment. "They fear being brought back to life?"

Zale chuckled humourlessly. "No, no, they fear those who have been resurrected. And I don't mean you, with your perfect, full-life reconstruction."

Without so much as a warning, Zale spun so suddenly it made Badrick jump. With rapid, nimble fingers he typed onto the nearest keyboard. Badrick watched with popping eyes; Zale moved so fast it was like his life depended on finishing whatever task he'd just started.

Sure enough, within seconds of him beginning there was the cuttingly intrusive sound of a printer.

Zale plucked the sheets from the machine and handed half to Badrick.

"Resurrected," the electric Enthraller read, "a demonically created creature."

"There are two main subgroups," Badrick continued, "regular and Powered."

"When a demon with the right power brings back a human, they become a Resurrected," Zale said, "a half-living creature that lacks a heartbeat and emits waves of toxic energy that can be sensed by any Enthraller."

"'Toxic' meaning it feels awful," Badrick laughed.

"Depending on an element used or cause of death, the

resurrected will return with certain abilities, which brings us to the Powered Resurrected."

"For example," Badrick continued for him, "if a victim dies by cyanide before resurrection, they will acquire the ability to explode people's hearts with a click of their fingers." Badrick blinked in disgusted awe. "Christ!"

"Another example is when a person is exposed to ionic and compound aluminium before death," Zale examined. "They will acquire the ability to protrude an organic metal sword under their wrist."

"Alright, enough," Badrick spat, throwing the sheets aside. He didn't want to read anymore about these revolting creatures. "Your theory is that a Resurrected is controlling the Kalik?"

"It is, yes."

"Did you scan for the 'toxic' energy at the Apos base?"

Zale gave him an annoyed glare. "Yes and I found nothing. But that doesn't mean I'm wrong. We thought that, if someone was using the Kalik as a patsy and creating false evidence, he would have been present. But now we know the Kalik had their own blades. The one controlling them need not have been there."

That made sense to Badrick. Musing on Zale's words, he muttered, "OK, so like you said, that rules out Lucikefer. At no point has he ever died and been resurrected."

"Wouldn't matter anyway," Zale huffed dismissively. "It's human resurrection they don't like." Zale's irritated glare softened and his eyes misted over. "I don't even know if demons *can* be brought back to life."

Badrick knew that Zale could focus on more than one thing. If he were to start musing on something else only a fool would think he'd been distracted from the current topic. But Badrick couldn't think about more than one thing at a time, and so, determined to keep Zale fixed on the here and now, he quickly interrupted that new train of thought with, "Regardless, it isn't Lucikefer."

Zale's eyes resumed functioning and he looked at Badrick. "Right. It isn't."

The electric Enthraller trudged away from his computer and collapsed into a chair. He had the good fortune to find the last swivel seat, so he spent the next few minutes swinging himself left and right.

When he next spoke, it was with tones Badrick instantly recognised; Zale was organising stuff in his head. "There must be a demon or Enthraller that did the resurrecting. So, potentially, we have two culprits. Two people to catch, double the chances of success."

Badrick smiled. "I see. The one who did the resurrecting might be controlling his victim, meaning *he* is controlling the Kalik."

Zale merely bobbed his head to confirm these were his thoughts also.

"We should change our investigation to try and get both of them," Badrick said.

Zale immediately shook his head, regaling Badrick with his past experiences in similar situations. He explained that the Resurrected would *have* to be the one who did the dirty work—the one who always gave the orders to Kalik, even if he/she had their own master—and would therefore be the one who left evidence to find. Any demon or Enthraller using a Resurrected would stay back, hiding in the shadows.

Their best bet would be to find the Resurrected and use him to find the one who brought him back to life.

"If the demon who did it is even involved," Badrick added. "He or she might not be behind their Resurrected's actions."

"Besides," Zale continued as if Badrick hadn't spoken, clearly wanting to finish everything he had to say, "Resurrected are just people, not Enthrallers or demons. They are far easier to find, no matter who they are. They're careless, prideful, and usually completely unaware of just how powerful the Daemonium is, if they're even aware of us at all.

"Even if they know about us, their lack of understanding on our capabilities usually leads to their downfall." Zale leaned back in his chair, smiling triumphantly. "Yep, our best chance is to find the Resurrected and leave the accursed necromantic bastard until a later date."

Badrick nodded, finding Zale's opinion to be sound.

Zale rocked back on forth precariously on his swivel chair, his eyes panning across the BCR, mind lost in thought about the Resurrected and his or her army of Kalik.

The Resurrected is surely only in command of the one clan, his brain whispered, reminding him of his earlier theories. *It isn't possible for a Resurrected to go Hell and recruit other clans, so he'd have to make do with the closest clan on Earth.*

That probably means I'm right in thinking only one clan has my weapons. The Resurrected can't go to Hell and his army wouldn't share my weapon with another clan. They just wouldn't. Even if they would, the Resurrected would have to recruit personally. If he sent his minions to other clans, they'd just get mindlessly slaughtered before they even managed to gift away my inventions because it would be believed they were invading..

And whoever resurrected our bad guy couldn't recruit any other clans himself. Even if it's a demon, and can therefore cross into Hell to find other clans, the Resurrected would have *to be physically present to enslave the clans, and that just isn't happening. Only demons can enter Hell at will.*

So . . . one clan.

That's a certainty.

Zale nodded to nobody but himself, happy with his musings despite more concerns arising right there and then.

What if . . . No. Forget that thought. I highly doubt that the Resurrected has the capability to go to other countries to find new clans. Far too much effort and, having once died, none of their papers would work.

Could the one that brought them back teleport them?

Nope. We'd detect that. Even if a resurrection was never logged on the sensors, which happens more than I care to admit, and we also failed to detect a demon crossing to our world, we would *detect the never-ending teleports between countries. The automated systems would push that to the top of the priorities list, and we haven't seen that.*

The resurrecter is likely as stuck here as his Resurrected.

A question Zale hadn't expected arose right then, causing his forehead to crease with concern.

Are they even in this country?

Are we being attacked from abroad?

Zale tutted aggressively, instantly annoyed with himself; the answer to this question was so obvious it infuriated him that it took so long to figure it out.

Of course not! Our bad guy is here. Their efforts seem focused entirely on this landmass, and it's just not possible that he'd be commanding a foreign clan. Aside from the fact that we'd detect Kalik leaving our world, then reappearing back over into England, the moment they set foot here our native clan would descend upon them with a vicious, territorial rage, which has not happened.

So . . .

One clan.

Native.

Controlled by a Resurrected.

Who is also here.

Understood, he told his brain. *Good work, Zale. You can take a break.* As his mind gratefully powered down, Zale closed his eyes and rubbed his head, groaning with frustration and the effort of having to think so hard.

He hated Resurrected *so* much.

Extremely rare as they were, they were still so troublesome.

Evidently, Badrick agreed, because he quite suddenly tutted and groaned, "What the hell is with the demon world? What's the link between all the stuff that makes Powered Resurrected?"

"Demons experimented with elements from our world," Zale told him, "many millennia ago. Mixing stuff with demonic energy and screwing around with human bodies. Genetic mutations were the result."

Badrick puffed air in amazement, the sound mixed with a hefty element of indignation. "Damn them!" he hollered. "You're gonna have to get me a list of them all."

Zale couldn't help but laugh. "Daemnos doesn't give you the info?"

"Resurrected are one of the few things he has no idea about," Badrick informed him. "He hasn't met many."

"I suppose even Royals don't know everything," Zale muttered absently.

He would have said more, but at that very moment a huge group of agents and operatives barged into the BCR, chattering loudly and disturbing what had been a relative peacefulness. Deciding it would be wise to no longer speak so openly about their own affairs, Zale closed his mouth and chose not to continue.

As he watched the group mill about, conversing on one thing or another, he set to work considering what their next step should be. Zale wanted to find out exactly how someone could have modified his weapons for their purposes.

Thankfully, they'd eventually found a defunct model in *Antiquated Storage* and he would be working on this issue when night fell.

There was absolutely no way a Kalik could perform such

dedicated science—such complicated engineering. The idea of them being able to comprehend even the most menial of tasks in this area of expertise was laughable.

No . . . Everything Zale had feared the moment he saw that first corpse was true.

Someone stole his weapons.

They had forged their own versions.

They'd given them to the Kalik (but only specific Kalik, it seemed—not every beast in the country's clan was using them).

And this person—because the Kalik wouldn't allow *anything* else to order them around—was a Resurrected.

With their accursed bad luck, their suspect would even be a Powered Resurrected.

All of this, he was certain of, despite his ever growing headache and the uncharacteristic doubts plaguing his consciousness.

But there was one thing he had no doubt on. No matter how bad he felt, no matter how much he questioned himself, he did not question his belief that the thief could not mass produce the swords themselves.

And if this theory was correct, the Resurrected would have to somehow siphon the electricity from one model to another.

When building a sword, Zale could charge the weapon up with fresh power.

The Resurrected could not.

This could only mean one thing—there was a finite number of the Kalik weapons out there.

This was exceptionally good news. They were *not* dealing with an epidemic. Any guilt Zale felt over keeping the secret could be forgotten knowing that the world was not under threat of falling under a mass of Kalik that could kill without effort.

Or at least that's what he told himself.

At the very least, it perhaps meant that they had a chance to confiscate all of the damn things one day.

Zale quickly took a deep breath before he got ahead of himself. First thing first; they had to find out exactly when the swords were stolen.

No report was ever logged. They'd never heard of a reported theft and they definitely would have. If they were aware of the theft the Council would put the Daemonium into red alert the moment they detected the breach.

Zale was also sure that the thief had a modern sword. When he saw the Kalik murder the agent—despite the chaotic design—he instantly recognised details belonging to his most recent sword model.

Meaning no old model sword had been stolen from Antiquated Storage, but a new one from one of the high-security storage facilities. So not only were an indeterminate amount of his greatest invention nicked by an unknown crook, at an indeterminate time, but they had been pinched without the guard's notice.

And the Council hadn't detected the theft.

Fools!

Cursing the pointlessness of their lot, Zale took another deep breath and massaged his burning forehead.

Realising this fact cast doubts over Zale's earlier confidence. There were supposed to be better off hunting the Resurrected because they made mistakes.

They didn't understand the Daemonium.

Pulling off a theft like this either proved they *did* or some other powerful variable was involved.

Cloak, maybe?

Either way, it was worrying.

But Zale refused to allow yet *more* doubts cloud his mind. They were starting to become a nuisance and he wasn't very well equipped to combat misgivings on his capabilities.

His deduction was *still* sound. Even if they knew *everything* about the Daemonium, people made mistakes. The one who produced the Resurrected could be found through his or her creation, so Zale and Badrick *had* to focus on the Kalik controlling bastard.

He was certain.

Or rather he hoped.

Zale allowed a large groan of frustration to escape his mouth; if he'd been allowed to keep his own bloody swords, none of this would have happened.

"If people just kept me in the loop," he said aloud, "I could solve all the world's problems."

His complaining drew the attention of Badrick. Up until that point Zale's partner had been tossing a bullet casing over and over, clearly bored out of his mind. With Zale's outburst having torn him from his reverie, he signalled a desire to know what their next move would be.

Zale gestured to give him a few more moments, then set to work on calming his mind, ignoring the pounding in his head.

He needed to consider everything—muse on every single step of his investigation—despite this simple task becoming more and more difficult with each passing moment.

Nevertheless, he forced himself to start.

The blade the Kalik used on the agent had elements of my current model, he thought to himself slowly, concentrating heavily on his own words. *Though the voltage was far lower—enforcing my belief there was a finite amount of power to distribute among multiple swords—I definitely recognised the electrical pattern in the brief second the blade was out in the open.*

Which means what I thought; a current model was stolen. That helps because not only does it mean I can go through the work of an old model to a current model, but it also narrows down the places to try and detect the theft.

The older versions are still safe in the mess of Antiquated Storage, *with the port-pad scanners as security. Having that or using a key card is the only way to get in. But the heavily guarded storage facilities, the ones where my current babies are stored, require a key card specifically.*

I will study the old model later and follow my own steps of upgrading to see at what point I left it open to meddling.

But for now . . . Zale smiled triumphantly *. . . I have another lead to follow.*

Off the top of his head, Zale calculated that a total of five to six months would be required to make the kind of alterations their suspect had implemented. Without having studied the issue himself as of yet, his own expertise would have to suffice, but he was confident his information was sound.

He created the science, after all.

Frankly, his opinion was the *only* opinion.

Two months would be required to properly siphon out his energy into another design and the meddler would have to be *exceptionally* careful. Any wrong move and the energy would escape and dissipate, possibly electrocuting the culprit on its way out.

But the siphoning wasn't the hardest thing to do. It was simply demonic energy and most beings with demonic connections could absorb the stuff, given time at least.

It was the building of whole new models that worried him. Doing so was no simple feat and it scratched at the panic centres of his brain to even think that there was someone else who understood his art.

Yet another calming sigh and he'd pacified his anxiety and was back on his train of thought.

He estimated three months to build a handful of new models.

And judging that anyone who managed this would have to be smart, Zale approximated that someone with that kind of intelligence would take another month to study how to do any of it at all.

Zale was granting their suspect a lot of consideration. He was assuming the bad guy was intelligent.

But Zale had no doubt their enemy was a very smart foe.

He turned towards a console and placed his hands above it, letting them hover there as he continued to think.

Five to six months was his estimated timeframe—so he would look into the storage facilities five to six months back.

Except . . . what if their thief delayed in gifting his modified swords to the demon subspecies? That would mean he would have to go even further back with no determined timeframe in mind.

Zale pondered on this for a moment before tutting with ire and coming to a decision.

Overloading their minds with more data than they could handle would serve no good purpose. He would go with the plan he'd already formed and if it failed, then—and *only* then—would he look past the six month timeframe.

There was no guarantee the thief had used a key card at all, of course, however the theft had gone unnoticed. That screamed authorised key card usage to Zale, and the screams in his head were often right.

He tapped on Badrick's knee to make sure he knew they were no longer just sitting around. His partner's eyes lit up, awakening from their bored stupor, and he swivelled around on his own chair, eagerly leaning forward in anticipation of their next move.

Zale didn't attempt to speak. The massive group was still bothering the place. Instead he typed up instructions and attached them to the data he now transferred to Badrick's port-pad. Once his partner understood what they were doing, Zale sat back and got to work.

Thus, the pair of them spent the next twenty minutes sifting through the list of Enthrallers who had entered any storage facility in which a sword model was kept during the time Zale estimated they were nicked.

Neither of them spoke.

They simply worked in silence.

Around them, BCR life continued. Agents and operatives were sent on missions, weapons and tools were brought in and out and the commanders issued orders and demands. Soldiers ran in at periodic intervals, relaying information they'd divined during battles that might belong in the agents' jurisdiction.

It got very noisy at one point; an argument between two soldiers and an operative erupted, coming very close to physical violence.

Badrick and Zale ignored them all, even when Badrick's chair was violently kicked by a restrained soldier being forced out of the room. They never looked away from their port-pads, their focus entirely on their investigation.

On his first look through, Zale noticed nothing amiss. There were plenty of names in the list, but none really jumped out at him. He detected no discrepancies and no evidence of hacking appeared present.

He huffed with irritation when he got to the bottom, thoroughly frustrated now.

It didn't look like he was going to get a vital clue from this.

But Zale refused to give up. Taking a deep breath to clear his head and ensure he didn't skip past anything out of impatience, he returned to the top and went through it again.

Before he even thought about giving way to resignation, he was going to double check.

And then triple-check.

Just to be certain.

You never know what you might miss if you don't always *double check,* he reminded himself, forcing his eyes to go through each and every name another two times.

Going through details more than once was a rule he lived by.

This time, it paid off.

Zale had to make a double-take when he first laid eyes upon the name. He didn't believe it at first—refused to accept that it could be true—but reconsidered when he remembered what had befallen this person.

Zale kicked Badrick on the foot to get his attention and turned his port-pad so his partner could see.

He'd highlighted the name for Badrick's convenience.

Mawr Burakka.

chapter
FOURTEEN

Lucikefer trembled as he approached the one who awaited him.

It was ridiculous, his fear.

But he couldn't help it.

The power... like nothing he ever sensed before... It emanated from the figure before him, rolling from his tall form in waves.

However, the energy didn't belong to him.

It merely . . . *powered* him.

But the one who gave this man life was stronger than any other power in existence.

Stronger than Daemnos.

Stronger than Lucikefer.

Stronger than the *Devil*.

"Have you got it?" the figure spoke, his voice deep and dangerous, laced with malice and excitement at the thought of Lucikefer's delivery.

"I acquired it," Lucikefer mumbled. "I kept it safe . . . just like you wanted me to—"

The figured reached out a hand and plucked the object from his fingers. He studied it for a long while, grinning from ear to ear and letting the sunshine reflect on the clear surface of the key card in his hand.

But even the light of the far away star couldn't brighten the dark, dead eyes the reflection struck.

"Good work, Lucikefer," he drawled darkly. "Good work, indeed."

Trembling still, Lucikefer muttered, "Am I free to go?"

"Ah, ah, ah," the figure spoke, wiggling a finger in his direction. "What are you going to do now, chap? Still on your hunt for Daemnos?"

Lucikefer nodded rapidly, almost too scared to speak. "Yes," he muttered, almost squeaking pitifully.

"Fine," the figure chuckled. "Be on your way," He pocketed the object. "Oh," he added as Lucikefer attempted to amble away, "and Lucikefer . . . *good luck!*"

chapter
FIFTEEN

The light in Zale's room was too bright after the duller glow of the BCR. It hurt Badrick's eyes, even when he didn't stare directly into the bulb. He wished he could turn it off, but it would have been ridiculous to work in the dark.

Zale was rifling aggressively through the files they'd printed and smuggled up here, his eagerness causing him to almost throw sheets across the room. Some even ended up under his bed and Badrick had to scramble to retrieve them.

After an intense silence, Zale swatted away a large pile of paper from his desk, allowing it to cascade to the floor. Ignoring the mess, he shoved a lone sheet in Badrick's face.

Badrick took it hastily and read what was written upon its

surface.

Read it, but didn't understand its relevance. He glanced up at his partner, an eyebrow raised questioningly. "Mawr was afflicted with septicaemia?"

"The only reason he wasn't dying was because of his demon," Zale smirked. "That's what the report says." He rolled his eyes and added, "Though it won't tell me what his demon's powers are. They're classified!" With a sudden rush of anger, Zale punched the arm of his chair so hard it made a horrible cracking sound. *"Balderdashery!"*

"This is important?" Badrick prompted him.

"This is another recipe for a Powered Resurrected."

Badrick's heart sank to his stomach, giving him a horrendous feeling of nausea. "The record you found said Mawr's card was used a *week* after his death." He gave Zale a worrisome look. "I hate to ask but does this mean Mawr is now a suspect?"

Zale didn't respond at first and this only served to immediately convince Badrick he was right. Why else would Zale fall into a sombre silence right now?

But then movement caught his attention and Badrick saw Zale raising his hand to the level of his eye line.

"No," Zale finally said. "Mawr is not our suspect."

Utterly confused now, Badrick asked, "Why not? It looks pretty clear to me."

"One," Zale started, extending a finger and quietening Badrick with a look, "just because Mawr has the capability to be a Powered Resurrected doesn't mean he's *our* Resurrected. That's a ridiculous leap to make.

"Two, even as a Resurrected, why would Mawr rebel against the Daemonium? Becoming a Resurrected doesn't change who you are. You met him, he was vigorously professional.

"Three . . . Tell me something, Badrick. If you wanted to steal something from this facility, which of these two options would you pick?

"Would you die, be resurrected, *then* grab the sword? Or would you grab the swords, then die and be resurrected?"

It annoyed Badrick that it took him so very long to figure out which of these plans was the better option. Eventually, though, he was able to say with some confidence, "I would do the second one."

"Why?"

"Because I'm known here. If I turned up to steal something after I was reported dead, I'd not only be noticed but our scanners would go haywire. Even if I could dodge the cameras, my toxic energy would light the place up like a Christmas tree."

"Right," Zale said. "Mawr's card was used *after* his death and he's not been seen here whatsoever. I reckon that whoever killed him stole the key card and used it to nab my swords."

"Ah," Badrick finally sighed. "I getcha." He threw up a hand to indicate he wasn't finished. "Though you're making it sound like the Resurrected planned all this. Like he made sure to die and get brought back."

Zale shook his head dismissively. "Hypothetical situation. We don't know what the Resurrected planned or didn't plan. But the deduction is still sound."

Badrick wanted to agree but he couldn't help his desire to ensure they'd considered everything. It was completely probable that Zale had come up with several different theories, crosschecked them in his head, and finally come up with the real answer already.

But Badrick hadn't.

"How do we know Mawr *isn't* the Resurrected?" he asked, trying his best to get on the same wavelength as Zale. "I don't think he'd betray the Daemonium but what if the demon or

Enthraller that brought him back can control minds? Maybe he killed Mawr, brought him back and now they're working together?"

Zale chuckled at that, lowering his head and rubbing his eyes. "You really don't know much about Resurrected, do you?"

Badrick bristled a little, incensed at the unfortunately true accusation. "What do you mean?"

"Resurrected are like Enthrallers," Zale told him. "They can't be mind-controlled."

"What?" Badrick exclaimed. "Enthrallers have demons to protect us. How do—"

"Mind-control requires brainwaves to control," Zale said slowly, as if talking to a small child. He held up his hand once more, flicking his fingers up one at a time as he spoke. "What do Resurrected lack? Heartbeat, organ function, blood flow and . . . "

"Brainwaves?" Badrick guessed sulkily.

"Right."

It made sense to Badrick now. There was no way Mawr would betray the Daemonium, whether on his own accord or at the demand of a demon. Just because he was suddenly a Resurrected didn't mean he would turn on them. In all likelihood he'd have barged back here months ago demanding to be put down.

And if his creator was planning to use him to control Kalik, Mawr would warn the Council. Not go along with the plan.

Mind-control didn't work on Resurrected *or* Enthrallers. Even if it *did*, the theft occurred after Mawr's death. If Mawr was their man, he wouldn't have dared attempt a robbery, knowing that he'd never get away with it unless he was alive and well.

Badrick had to concede; setting aside the soldier's unwavering loyalty, the simple fact that the theft occurred *after* he died meant Mawr did not steal the swords.

Badrick had hoped the culprit of the resurrection had no

involvement. That it was just some random act of cruelty, leaving the victim to wander the Earth as a monster. But the more they got into this investigation, the more it seemed the necromancer-wannabe was in the thick of it.

The Resurrected could *not* have stolen the swords, so unless they had other allies, a demon or Enthraller had somehow broken in here.

Zale shared this idea. "Either a demon powerful enough to exist here on our world *and* hide from the sensors, or an Enthraller who tricked the sensors into thinking he . . . or she . . . was one of us."

"Or a human collaborator," Badrick added, "who wouldn't have set off the sensors at all."

"Christ," Zale sighed. "I'd thought of it but didn't want to think it possible until you said it. Perhaps it *is* a possibility despite the implications of major failings in our detection systems. I'd actually prefer that. Humans are easy to find."

"We could find the real bad guys by interrogating their human allies," Badrick agreed. He sighed wistfully, thinking on how easy that would be. "Shame though," he added into the ensuing silence. "Would be so much better for us if it turned out this was nothing more than Mawr."

"Weird sentence," Zale muttered.

Ignoring him, Badrick asked, "How possible do *you* think it is that someone with powers broke in here without being detected?"

Zale clicked his tongue. "They would have to be someone close to the Daemonium. Someone who knew about this place. Intimately. Someone who knew where all the cameras and sensors were and had figured out a way around them."

Badrick couldn't stop the burst of laughter that escaped his lungs. "Who would know all that?" he exclaimed. *Someone like Mawr*, he thought bitterly, again finding himself wishing the soldier *was* their bad guy.

A shrug was all Badrick got in response to his question.

Badrick gave his partner the gift of a fierce glare. "So we're back to the beginning again. No leads and nowhere to go." He scoffed. "Good job."

"Not completely," Zale said a little icily. "We've upped the percentage that the Resurrected has a master who is actually getting his hands dirty."

"Do we go after *him* now?"

Zale instantly shook his head. "I still think it wise to focus our efforts on finding the Resurrected. They are the more easily detectable and, apart from this theft, the one doing all the work."

"They're the ones leaving evidence behind," Badrick parroted Zale from earlier that day. "Mostly."

Badrick didn't have the kind of brainpower equal to Zale's so he couldn't see the logic that his partner could in focusing all efforts on the Resurrected. But he trusted Zale. The man knew what he was doing.

They fell into a tranquil silence. The pressure of their predicament continued to linger above them like a cloud of anxiety and fear, but at least for now they were surrounded by a calming silence. The tumult of the Daemonium could not bother them here.

Badrick appreciated it, as it would not last forever.

Especially when he knew he had to break it.

"So what now?" he asked for what was quite possibly the eight millionth time—he'd have to stop saying it before someone branded it as his catchphrase.

Zale freed the pages stuck to his limbs from the static he'd generated in his leathery chair, chucking them to the floor. After, he rolled his chair away from the desk, allowed it to crash into the bed and used the impact to throw himself upon its mattress.

"With no new leads, I now work all night in the lab to see if I can discern anything from my wonderful invention."

"Sounds fun."

"Pfft!" Zale huffed. He picked up his pillow and lay on his back, lifting it above his head. As he began to throw it up and down, he said, "There's nothing you can do to help with the research, so get some rest tonight."

Badrick wasn't offended. This was the truth of it, and there was no point being angry about the truth.

*

Zale tutted as the lab automatically cycled into the night shift, the lights dimming to simulate the darkness of night. He stood up, using his legs to push his chair out from under the desk and wandered up to the closest switch. Jamming it back on with the unnecessary venom borne from hours of fruitless work, he stomped back to his workspace and picked up the advanced multi-tool.

It wasn't a regular multi-tool; the instrument was a specialised piece of equipment designed specifically to work on his inventions.

It pained him to think of someone so easily altering his babies when it took him years to simply design and build the tools to make a sword in the first place. He literally had to invent the science himself; the theory, the technology *and* the construction.

Muttering darkly about thieves and their uncanny ability to piggyback great men, he resumed his work, prodding the subject of his irritation with impatience.

The light of his laptop illuminated his face as he went from step to step of his previous upgrades. He was thankful for the notes; the only way to accomplish what he wanted was to literally build a new sword.

This would have taken several days, but with the extra equipment afforded to him by the old model and the data from his notes, he was able to construct a new sword with relative ease, the whole time studying each step of progression with insane concentration.

He'd been here for hours now and was starting to feel the drag of fatigue, dreading the thought of being stuck here for what could be another six hours. The feeling was unfamiliar. He often worked for days without sleep and *never* felt this bad, but the last few days had tired him. He wasn't as spry as he used to be.

He was getting old.

Grinning at the ludicrous idea that he was getting old at age twenty—and thankful for the good feeling of amusement—he took apart a power pack and allowed the electricity to shoot into the air and dissipate. Using his super powered eyesight and his own powers of intelligence, he studied the voltage as it flashed and vanished.

And with a jolt of success he murmured, "Oh ... I see you now."

It looked like he wouldn't have to be here for another eternity after all.

He was immensely thankful for that—

"Three days!"

Zale twirled on the spot, knocking his chair to the floor and almost dislodging the equipment he'd set up. Scanning his surroundings with anxious fervour, his eyes flitted over the entire lab, his mind suddenly much more awake.

What the hell was that?

Zale couldn't see anyone else in the room. Apart from the technician he knew was working on an old Kalik corpse in the decontamination chamber, he was alone.

So who the hell had spoken?

A twinge in his stomach made Zale twitch uncomfortably; a pang borne from what was quickly becoming intense anxiousness. His skin was now tingling with cold and his heart was punching his ribs painfully. When Zale next opened his mouth, a deep fearful exhale warmed the air in front of his face.

The reason for this dramatic change from calm to agitated was simple—the words spoken had not sounded like a voice.

They had sounded like a thought.

As if someone unseen had not issued words at him, but inputted them straight into his head, aggressively forcing them in where they didn't belong.

But it wasn't just this jarring experience that scared him.

No . . .

What sent waves of inexplicable terror shooting into his heart was the fact the voice sounded just like him.

chapter
SIXTEEN

Zale smiled at Badrick's moan of frustration as Carla's powerful legs launched her past him, resulting in an impressive slam dunk. The basketball bounced away and, with a cocky arse-smack in their direction, she hurried to fetch it.

It was good watching them manage to scrape at least five minutes of fun. Like a worried father, Zale would thank whatever gods may be out there for giving the ones he loved some manner of reprieve, even if it was only a moment.

Besides, their laughter eased his own worries. Stopped him ruminating on what he'd *'heard'* in the lab last week and the fear that followed. Their presence helped him remember that it was nothing but stress, and to fret over what occurred would simply be feeding the anxiety. He had to focus on what was truly important.

At the sight of Badrick cursing loudly, Zale felt a smile pull at his mouth. "You truly suck, dude!" he called.

"Shut it!" was the reply. Badrick wiped his mouth and gestured to Carla to try him again.

It only took her ten seconds to wipe the floor with him for what was now the fifth time. As the ball fell through the circle, kicking up the net in its wake, she threw her hands to the air and danced sexily—triumphantly—on the spot, infuriating Badrick further.

"You're too smug," he hissed.

Carla bounced the ball a few times, smiling far too widely for her own good. She glanced at Zale and winked.

"Anyway," she laughed, "as I was saying before Badrick started shouting at his own *suckage*, every single mission John and I are given turns out to be a Kalik. They're everywhere.

"But not a single one has got a modified sword." She sighed, throwing the ball through the net once again. "Or even a normal one. It's all regular Kalik blades."

"Where are they all?" Badrick asked, retrieving the ball. He moaned as Carla managed to get it out of his hands yet again.

"I don't know," she shrugged in answer. "But we were right, the Kalik are a lot more active now."

"It's like they're *trying* to get our attention," Zale muttered, interrupting the both of them. He glanced down at his port-pad, checking the readings in the software he'd activated earlier.

This software was using several satellites to keep watch on Kalik crossings. Coupled with Daemnos' knowledge of the most favoured Kalik crossing sites in the country, they'd been keeping track of as many of the beasts as possible.

It wasn't working as well as Zale wished it would. As always, the beasts kept changing their points of crossing.

It was quiet on his screen at that moment when he'd rather

hoped it would be blaring alarms from the start. But as he'd told Badrick, there was no way to track a Kalik after it crossed unless the satellites sighted the beast by accident, and then you could follow its physical movements.

Keeping up with its energy signature just wasn't possible.

And with the increased activity, the Kalik weren't using the sites Daemnos identified as much as they would have before this situation.

Sighing, Zale continued his thought. "Screaming at us. Trying to get us to listen. But for what purpose? What do they want?"

"Who knows?" Badrick scoffed. "Monsters, all of them."

"Maybe," Zale whispered. He couldn't help but mean it; recently the subspecies was displaying an increased intelligence behind their actions. No longer were they coming across as the overly violent, causeless beings they once appeared to be.

Was it just because they were being controlled by an intelligent Resurrected?

Or were they truly smarter than they'd all been led to believe?

"I don't understand why they're not using the swords," Carla said. "It doesn't make sense. If you had access to such powerful weaponry, surely as many of you as possible would use it."

"Here we thought it was only a matter of time before an agent saw the Kalik using one," Badrick said, his angry tone almost suggesting he wished that had occurred. Zale understood his reasons; consequences of discovery aside, the case would be far less frustrating if the damn beasts used the devices with impunity.

But they just weren't.

"As far as I can tell, only *we* have witnessed it," Zale told him. "Only when we were present, or were going to be, has it happened."

Badrick stopped bouncing the ball and turned to face Zale properly. "That's significant, isn't it?"

"It's so obviously significant, it hurts my head to think about it," Zale snapped. "Whoever is controlling them is clever. He's messing with us. Only allowing certain Kalik to use the weapon. Only the ones *we* deal with."

"Somehow he knows when you'll be the ones out in the field," Carla said. "Considering that, he must have inside information."

"Very fast, up-to-date information," Badrick noted.

"Almost prophetic information."

Stop saying 'information', Zale's mind spat at them secretly. Deciding to keep his irritation to himself, out-loud he growled, "But why? Why bother? Does the Resurrected know that it'd be best to keep the weapon a secret from the Council? How does he even know *we'd* keep it a secret? How does he know we didn't tell everyone?"

There was a long period of silence following this tirade of questions.

In the end, Carla was the one to break it.

"Only way possible is if he or she knows you personally."

Carla was completely right, and it was certainly a worrying possibility. But who the hell in Zale's five year career at the Daemonium had he pissed off so much for them to desire revenge in such a way?

Who the hell *died* and *then* came back for vengeance?

There wasn't anyone in Zale's past who would be capable or willing to go to this much trouble—no Enthrallers or humans and, apart from Lucikefer and his white mate, Zale had met one demon in his life: Horas.

He really didn't like that Carla's theory pointed all the evidence at Mawr, because it collided with his own substantiation against that very point. They'd only known Mawr for a day, but it was true that he was the *only* viable suspect correlating to Carla's theory.

Zale gruffly shook his head before doubts could cloud his

mind. He'd already decided it *couldn't* be Mawr. To doubt his powers of deduction now would only be self-destructive.

But he couldn't help but wonder what other suspects that actually left him.

"What about the swords?" Carla tried taking the conversation in a similar but different direction. "Have you figured out how they could have been changed yet?"

Realising he'd forgotten to apprise Carla on his progression, Zale sat up straighter and nodded. "Aye. I figured out how they would've altered the design." He decided to leave it at that, figuring neither Badrick nor Carla would understand a word if he delved into the actual science. "I didn't even notice this opening when I made it. Major oversight on my part.

"But I've made my own Kalik blade the same way I suspect our thief had to. I see now how he or she did it."

"But you still don't know why?" Carla said insightfully when he fell into silence. She laughed a little and brushed his hair on her way past with the ball. She bounced it over Badrick and achieved another perfect slam-dunk.

"No," he pouted. "Not yet," he added under his breath. *Because I will!*

"We will," Badrick said confidently—pointlessly. "It's only a matter of time."

"Oh, Badrick, you're so stoic," Carla cooed with a wide grin. She promptly outmanoeuvred him on the field and scored another basket. "Shame you can't live up to your hype."

"You're lucky you're hot, Carla," Badrick scowled, which only served to make her laugh harder.

Zale watched them as they continued to duke it out on the court for another half an hour, though his concentration on the game was minimal. His focus was too deep inside his own mind for him to pay attention to the real world.

So much so that he didn't even notice when his port-pad beeped aggressively until Carla and Badrick rushed over, shouting in alarm. He blinked in surprise and glanced down, shocked to see the red warning labels blinking brightly.

"Holy—" he called. His eyes wide and fearful, he answered Carla and Badrick's urgent questions as fast as he could. "A massive crossing. Not where the satellites are pointing. This is being relayed from Command."

"Kalik?" Badrick asked a little pointlessly—the answer was obvious.

As such, Zale didn't bother responding. Instead he swivelled on the balls of his feet and pegged it across the grounds, heading for the Gate.

Moments later he burst into the HQ with his friends hot on his heels. The instant they were across the threshold, they were forced to brake and slow down. The facility was so chaotic, with people running left and right, that Zale was jostled by four different agents before he was halfway in.

He pushed his way through a group of panicked operatives. Badrick and Carla darted around them.

But he got no further; a familiar commanding voice hollered over the din created by the ruckus. "Where's Badrick!?"

Zale's eyes darted up and he sighted Reynolds disappearing across a walkway. Zale bawled to him, raising a hand. A second later, the sergeant's stony face appeared over the railing and, upon sighting the three of them, he launched himself over the side, coming to a neat landing beside Zale.

He immediately turned to Badrick. "Varner, we have a situation."

Clearly surprised at being personally addressed instead of Zale, Badrick stupidly responded with, "What's wrong?"

Zale rolled his eyes. His partner was having a slow day today.

"A massive crossing of Kalik is attacking a human military base," the sergeant told him hurriedly.

"Christ!" Carla's hand went to her mouth.

"What the hell!?" Badrick roared disbelievingly.

"They're attacking a human base?" Carla snapped. "They risk exposure if they do that. Kalik *never* risk exposure! They never attack as an army."

Zale couldn't believe what he was hearing, and he agreed with his friends' shock whole-heartedly.

Carla was correct; the Kalik didn't do stuff like this.

It was entirely against their nature.

But not against the nature of a Resurrected. Zale cursed silently. The damn fool was risking everything.

"Where?" he demanded loudly—louder than he meant to.

"North of England, close to the border of Scotland."

"We can't get *there* in time!" Zale gasped, aghast.

Reynolds rounded on him, his eyes wide and irritated, and bawled sarcastically, "*Thanks for the update, Hood!*" He turned back to Badrick. "We're gathering any soldiers who have a long distance teleport power. Badrick, we need Daemnos. We need the power of a Royal."

"Got it!"

"Can you piggyback other people when you teleport?"

Badrick took a moment to think. "Some. Maybe ten."

Reynolds sighed with evident frustration, but nevertheless nodded affirmatively. "Alright, do it. Teleport to that site ASAP. Take Zale and nine others with you. Gear up, Operative!"

"Yessir!" Badrick hurried away.

"I'm going too!" Carla demanded.

"No, Carla," Reynolds quickly denied her. "This is an army matter. You must remain in the facility."

Carla huffed angrily, but they all knew there was nothing she could do but begrudgingly obey. She grabbed Zale's hand as he made his way past her, communicating with her eyes for him to be careful.

Zale's heart pounded angrily against the inside of his chest all the way to his room, so much so that it made the journey feel like it took an eternity. For the first time ever he contemplated ignoring his prideful nature and moving his armour to the armoury where he was supposed to keep it.

No more of this stomping all the way up the Quarters Tower every time he needed to suit up

Finally, after giving himself a stitch, he was zipped up in his under-suit with his armour adorning his body. He attached the last part—an arm piece, slotting into place on the magnetic clip on his forearm—and hefted his auto-rifle.

Minutes later he was back in the frenzied HQ. He rapidly glanced around for Badrick and saw him organising his weapons alongside nine tall, red figures.

"Ready!" he declared as he approached, for once forgoing any sort of ramble.

There was no time to waste.

They had to go.

Now!

"OK," Badrick announced. "You—" he pointed at the nearest soldier, "and you—" he pointed at another, "grab my shoulders. The rest of you grab hands with each other. Link up. Zale—" he took a hold of Zale's fingers, "take my hand," he finally said redundantly. "This is going to make you feel very sick. So prepare yourselves."

One of the soldiers, clearly the commander of the squad, spoke up, "We'll be portin' into the hottest zone of your careers, privates. Be ready to fight the moment we arrive."

There was a chorus of, "Yessir!"

Badrick faced Zale, his emotionless visor betraying nothing of how he might have felt right then. "Ready?"

Zale nodded.

Badrick took a breath, readying himself to transport so many people.

Zale felt a zap of energy go through his hand and up his arm.

Everything went fuzzy as Badrick's *'flash teleport'* sucked them all out of the space they occupied. The sensation of being squeezed assaulted Zale's bones and for a brief second, everything went quiet.

It was strangely peaceful.

It didn't last.

The world flashed back into existence. The coldness of the outside attacked Zale's body before his under-suit could move to counteract the effect.

The equipment went into overdrive to compensate. As his body warmed, Zale finally tuned in to the dreadful racket that was echoing across the land; screams and gunshots and the sound of the dying.

He set his feet firmly into the ground and glanced around, taking in the situation.

They had arrived at the base, standing on some kind of airfield next to a mangled warplane. To his right, multiple large hangers blocked out the late afternoon sun.

Ahead of him, tanks and armoured cars and fighter jets lay in pieces or aflame, making the place hotter than the winter weather could. The searing heat from the fires was so intense that Zale could feel it through his armour. He put up his arm to block the nearest blaze.

The British military presence in this area lay dead or dying. The few remaining alive had hefted weapons and were firing futilely at their attackers. The regular, human made bullets bothered the monstrous Kalik that feasted on their flesh very little. The creatures swarmed over them—tearing, ripping, slashing—and would do so until nothing but corpses remained.

A Daemonium soldier beside Zale almost doubled over in his effort to keep at bay the bile that threatened to shoot up his throat. His commander slapped him on the back to help him recover from his travel sickness and led the charge towards the Kalik, opening fire with his shotgun. His comrades did the same, volleying endless rounds into their foes.

Many dropped dead from horrendous bullet wounds . . . But now the demons were aware of their presence, and their focus shifted onto the new arrivals. Around them, other soldiers and operatives teleported in—flashing, energising, shimmering—opening fire almost before they had fully materialised.

Deciding he had dawdled long enough, Zale darted into the fray. He took position on top of one of the few tanks that wasn't on fire. From up there he would have a good view of anything trying to charge him.

This wasn't like a battle against the Apos, where each army took a side and shot at each other from a distance. There was no cover to be had here. The Kalik would come at him like velociraptors.

Cover only worked when you were under fire.

He let loose with his auto-rifle, aiming each burst of rounds into his enemies' heads with expert precision. His success gained him the notice of several Kalik, forcing him to rapidly abandon his elevated position.

The claws of one of the monsters narrowly missed his leg, instead digging into the metal of the tank and tearing right through it. Zale rolled out of his fall and produced a dagger, sinking it into the neck of the closest demon. He pulled away, jumping back and putting down the other two that rushed him with short bursts from his rifle.

In the distance he saw Badrick blasting Kalik with his powers. Several of the beasts flailed in agony as flames stripped away their tough flesh, others falling to the ground in bits as red lasers smashed into their chests.

Now and then he would shoot one with his single-rifle, dropping Kalik with a single round.

Zale tried to hurry to his side so they could regroup the scattered mess that was their forces, but he was accosted by another group of Kalik.

Larger this time.

Five of them.

He dug his feet into the gravel and skidded to a halt.

He didn't wait to see if they would attack first.

One burst. One dropped.

Another. The second fell.

The other three charged.

Zale dived into a roll, ducking under their swiping claws. Finding his feet, he used his momentum to launch his body into the air, twisting it mid-flight to shoot them in their spines.

One.

Two.

Three.

All dead.

He landed on his back, skidding across the ground. The paint of his armour scratched away from the friction.

On his feet once again.

Breathing heavily, he darted in the direction of Badrick.

He cursed when he realised his partner had moved on. Zale no longer had a visual on him.

The sound of rapid firing and terrified shouting assailed his ears and a British soldier appeared from out of the smoke, his uniform ripped and his face grubby. In his panic, he almost backed into Zale, but that very same alarm tripped him before they made contact.

Before Zale could drop to his knees to help up the terrified and confused man, a Kalik pushed him to the ground and crushed the soldier beneath its foot. Zale's helmet banged painfully off a smashed up vehicle as he fell.

Raising its hand, the Kalik clenched a fist and extended its blade.

Zale's heart dropped when he saw the blue glow of electricity in his peripheral.

The man's gurgling death groan stopped as the Kalik pulled the weapon from his chest, having plunged it deep into his body. Roaring furiously, Zale jumped onto its back and murdered the monster with a knife to the neck.

A terrible rage overcame him and he yanked the knife out, only to sink it back in. Over and over again, he stabbed the Kalik. Blood spurted everywhere as he screamed with anger.

When his frenzy had subsided and the Kalik lay dead, he stood, breathing heavily.

He holstered the dagger, clenching his fists.

That was when he spotted a Daemonium soldier standing stock still, staring at them.

Zale could not see his face through the helmet.

But from the way the soldier wasn't moving, Zale knew . . .

The soldier had seen the Kalik's weapon.

Zale stared back as the Enthraller's golden visor seemed to glare accusingly at him, a sense of dread rumbling in the pit of his stomach.

It was over.

The secret was out.

chapter
SEVENTEEN

When the red armoured Enthraller spoke, it was with clear anger. "What the f—"

Zale jumped with fright as a massive hulk darted out of nowhere and whipped the soldier off his feet. There was a single cry of alarm as the life was struck from him and his body was unceremoniously thrown to the tarmac.

With the attacker now descending upon him, Zale had no choice but to snap out of his surprise and take it on. As the Kalik dropped to the floor from its new wounds, Zale cast his eyes over the slain soldier, intense remorse coursing through his stiff body.

This guy saw the truth. He'd known.

And Zale was painfully aware that the wanton death was beneficial to him.

He cursed angrily; the soldier hadn't deserved to befall a fate like this.

It was horrible.

But, as much as he wanted to, Zale could not spend the rest of his time mourning the loss. Around him the battle raged on, furious combat rattling noisily across the ruined base. The terrible sight of downed Daemonium soldiers met Zale's eyes, however he was thankful to see the Kalik casualties vastly outnumbered theirs.

Wishing to avoid as many deaths as possible, Zale charged back into the fray, seeking out demons wherever he could find them. He slaughtered endlessly, shooting them, knifing them, electrocuting them until their blood cells burst.

Now and then amongst the chaos, he would sight Badrick darting about, killing Kalik as he went.

Dozens upon dozens were slain already, but still a large force remained and Zale felt the beginnings of fear scratch at his consciousness. An army of Kalik such as this was what he'd feared the most.

Was this what it had been like at the Apos base during the time of the attack? From what he could see the Kalik weren't blindly swinging away, but sticking together and teaming up on their prey like small sophisticated packs of wolves.

Had the Apos befallen this very same fate?

Had they been mercilessly slaughtered, or systematically killed by a strategically thinking force?

And what the hell was the cause for this siege? Attacking a human military base? What was the point?

The sound of something cutting the air interrupted his train of thought, though it took him a second to recognise what it was.

Behind him was an attack helicopter, still intact, its rotors just starting to turn. Why such a powerful weapon was *here*, of all places, Zale didn't know.

Nor did he really care; he had much bigger problems to worry about. The Kalik were swarming closer, surrounding the vehicle as the engine rotated the blades faster and faster.

Someone was trying to escape by aircraft, but Zale could see that the Kalik were far too close for them to escape. The demons would pile on before it could even achieve lift off, smashing the glass and pulling out the pilot.

They were snarling at it now, watching the rotors turn . . .

No wait . . . they were snarling at each other . . . and not with any kind of aggression.

It was a though they were . . . *communicating.*

And to Zale's astonishment, he realised they were moving to form a protective circle around the helicopter. Metallic wrist blades flashed in the sunlight, ready for any prey they might plunge into.

As the aircraft began to pick up, hovering ever so slightly off the ground, several important observations coursed through Zale's head.

The Kalik were guarding a helicopter.

It was taking off.

The Kalik were *allowing* it to take off.

They wouldn't do that for anyone.

Not a single person.

Except . . .

There was only one final—terrible—conclusion Zale could possibly arrive at.

The Resurrected was inside the helicopter.

The aircraft began to lift higher, clearing the tops of the Kalik heads. With no time at all to make a smart decision, Zale darted forward, knowing how stupid he was being but unwilling to allow their culprit to escape.

The Kalik saw him coming. They roared deafeningly, turning in his direction and raising their arm blades. But Zale didn't stop to meet their challenge.

Calculating at a rapid pace, he judged the positions of every organism present. Raising his gun, he fired a single burst of rounds, killing the Kalik he knew would be able to cut him off.

He slung his rifle as the demon crashed to the tarmac, then leapt, pulling out his dagger in the same moment. With a thump, his feet landed on a surprised Kalik's shoulders. The impact made the demon stumble, adding to Zale's momentum. Not waiting for its impressive reaction time to catch up, he plunged the dagger deep into the neck beneath his feet.

As it fell, he used his own impetus, as well as the Kalik's fall, to leap even higher. Zale soared into the air, using every muscle in his legs to launch himself towards the helicopter as it rose into the sky.

His fingers reached out as far as they possibly could, the skin stretching painfully. Drawing close to the bars that served as the landing gear, his momentum began to fail, and he worried he'd only manage to flail stupidly before falling back to earth.

But then to his great elation his fingers met metal and he managed to get a tight grip, keeping himself aloft as the helicopter rose further. Zale breathed a sigh of relief as he swung dangerously beneath the aircraft, but roaring with the struggle of bringing his other arm up to strengthen his grip.

The pain was worth the added safety.

Now he was here there was only one way to go; he would have to try to climb the outside of the helicopter to get in and apprehend the Resurrected.

He hoped beyond belief that his actions didn't result in a violent, fiery crash, but if the Resurrected put up a fight . . .

Ignoring the dread in his stomach, he focused on the task ahead of him.

Zale wasn't afraid of heights, but even he had some alarm at the altitude they were now attaining. He cursed as the first cloud layer engulfed him and obstructed his view. His own hands weren't even visible anymore and his armour and under-suit were now thoroughly soaked.

The pilot seemed to just be flying straight up. To what purpose, Zale did not know.

Of course, he quickly found out.

The craziness of whoever held the sticks was demonstrated as the aircraft tilted, slowly at first, then faster until they were pointing more at the earth than the sky.

Zale then cried aloud as the engine kicked and the pilot threw them towards the ground.

They plummeted for a few seconds, the wind whistling loudly in Zale's ears as he hung on for dear life.

The fall was unforgiving. As they plunged faster and faster the rotors seemed unable to recover from the drop. The only thing they served to achieve was to make the journey far bumpier.

But Zale quickly realised this was the whole point; without warning, having attained the right speed and pull, the helicopter shuddered back under the pilot's control. With a push of the sticks, the aircraft spun fast, the force of its descent throwing the aircraft to the side.

The suddenness of this spin coupled with the speed gifted to it made Zale's fingers lose their grip.

He felt a sense of dire panic as the tip of his middle finger left the metal and he was thrown into the empty space above the Earth. The helicopter continued to spin for a few more seconds, at least just enough for the tail to smash into Zale—he narrowly missed the rotors—and send him spinning violently.

At first, apart from the searing pain of the impact, Zale wasn't too worried. As long as he landed on his feet, Zale could survive any fall, just like every other Enthraller.

And he would always land on his feet.

But then a true unkindness was forced upon him by the treacherous will of fate. The impact from the helicopter smacked him so hard that his auto-rifle went mental. It was knocked about the place, flipping over and around his body, until it finally fell from his shoulders.

The strap skidded down until it found his foot, upon which it hooked. The kinetic energy was transferred to the weight of the weapon and it spun around his legs until it had tightly tied them together.

"Are you kidding me?" he screamed to the sky. Yet again, Zale felt panic rise in his heart. His feet were strapped together so awkwardly that he wouldn't have been able to land even the smallest leap, let alone a fall from this kind of height.

He spluttered as he fell back through the clouds and dampness made its way into his helmet. Truly freaked out now, and horribly aware of the ground rushing to meet him, he tried to arc his body to get his hands to the straps so he could untie them.

He couldn't help but think just how handy his dagger would be right now . . . if only he hadn't left it in the neck of a Kalik guard.

Thinking fast, Zale activated a private conversation with Badrick. He spent three seconds praying for an answer before he gave up on the idea. Badrick *would* have been able to save him but the Enthraller must have been too busy fighting the Kalik down on the ground to get any time to answer.

Accursed person! Zale screamed in his head.

He had seconds left. The ground was horrifyingly close now. Any minute he would smash into the Earth and become nothing more than a blue, grey and red smear.

He ignored such horrible thoughts and forced himself to think calmly. A dozen ridiculous ideas flitted through his mind, all useless and unhelpful.

But then something truly insane popped into the forefront of his mind. Even Zale couldn't believe he would ever consider doing this.

But he had nothing to lose.

Do nothing and he would die.

He spun his body until he was falling face-first. Then, with a roar of effort, he charged his hands with electricity, increasing the voltage as much as he dared, and fired the blast at the ground.

He didn't allow the flow of power to stop.

The voltage crashed into the ground, demolishing the tarmac. The immediate area shone with electricity as the Kalik nearby— the guards who until now remained unbothered where he'd left them—were violently electrocuted.

As the power built up and up, the opposing force of such energy combated the gravity pulling him to Earth, acting like a makeshift thruster, just as he'd hoped it would.

He could already feel his body slowing, his rate of descent gratifyingly decreasing.

But he wasn't sure if it would be enough; he wasn't slowing sufficiently.

Crying with distress, he forced his reluctant body to generate more electricity. It groaned in protest but he aggressively ignored its demands as his bones and muscles shook and tensed with anguish.

His descent slowed even further.

And roaring from the distress of not knowing what would happen when he hit the ground, he stopped the flow of electricity.

A split second later he hit the tarmac.

The impact shuddered his bones and bent his armour plates. His rifle fired off a burst of shots upon impact—which ricocheted off a hanger wall—before smashing apart.

The muscles in his right leg were hurting so much that his breathing had become ragged from the effort of crying out in pain. His left leg had tensed to a degree that he could no longer move it, and the bones in his right arm felt like they had shattered.

Shaken and scraped, he moaned tiredly, cursing the Kalik and all who stood with them, but thanking the Gods that he was alive, promising them many sexy virgin sacrifices for years to come.

"I sure hope you're joking," a voice sounded above him. He strained to look and saw his partner standing over his prone form, his helmet removed and his face slapped with an amused expression.

"Wasn't aware I'd said it aloud," Zale replied hoarsely.

Around them, Zale saw that the battle was finally dying down. The Kalik had obviously been defeated in his absence, but a few stubborn stragglers refused to retreat, as Kalik always did.

With tender hands, Badrick helped him to his feet and led him to sit upon a set of disembodied tank treads, examining his broken body as they walked.

"You're lucky," Badrick said. "You're banged up and your arm is swollen like a bitch, but you don't have any broken bones."

"Damn those swollen bitches," Zale muttered offhandedly, a little dazed from the sudden release of stress in his body. With calm stroking his overwrought insides, and the adrenaline fading slowly, he just felt strangely high.

The last of the gunfire died away, making way for the reign of crackling fire, the sound of vehicles burning and Kalik melting from Badrick's onslaught was all that was left.

Now it was time for the Daemonium to clean up.

This had been a major attack and the risk of exposure was *way* too high for everyone involved.

They had to act fast.

Soldiers began teleporting out, travelling back to the facility to pick up the agents that would take care of the clean-up operation. Badrick saw them arrive only moments later, a sea of blue mixing with the collection of red.

He was surprised to see Carla and Reynolds among them, materialising on the arms of a purple-armoured SpecOps operative.

From the way she turned her head away from the older man, Badrick surmised they'd just finished arguing on whether or not she was allowed to come. Badrick smiled; he knew Reynolds would have been outmatched now that the agents were *supposed* to be here. Carla would have used that argument to her advantage.

And Carla often got what she wanted.

It took her only seconds to locate them, once again suggesting that she had some weird kind of personal Zale-tracking power. Her hair flowed behind her helmetless head as she dashed towards them, crashing into Zale to hug him tightly.

After a few minutes of ignoring his pained howls, she detached herself and moved to Badrick to embrace him as well.

"I'm so glad you two are alright," she sighed, relief heavy in her voice.

Before anyone could reply, Reynolds approached, looking tired and overworked. He wasn't wearing his armour, but still adorned his uniform, though it's regular pristine appearance was trashed. Already the fiery smoke had stained it black.

"Are you alright?" he asked the pair of them.

"Just about," Badrick chuckled.

Reynolds sighed sadly, gazing around at the destruction and death that surrounded them. "Was a blade involved?"

Zale nodded sombrely, wishing he didn't have to.

"But," Badrick stopped Reynolds' reaction, "none of the others had one."

"Still," Reynolds grimaced, "this is the third occurrence. I can't, in good conscience, keep hiding this from Command if it happens again. If you want to keep this a secret until the time is right, you need to work faster."

"But only *one* Kalik, Reynolds," Badrick argued. "It's not an epidemic yet."

"I know, Badrick," Reynolds sighed again. "I know." Now the sergeant faced Carla, lifting something in his hand and Badrick realised it was Carla's helmet. "You forgot this in your hurry."

Muttering darkly, she took it and placed it upon her head, obstructing her heavenly gorgeous face and hair from view. "I'll get to work," she said, hefting her auto-rifle.

Badrick watched her go.

"If you're done perving on my longest friend," Zale's voice cut the silence left by Reynolds' departure—he'd removed himself after giving Carla her helmet, "we need to talk."

Figuring this had to do with the blade Zale saw, Badrick sat beside him on the tank treads and listened as Zale relayed everything he had experienced during the battle, learning of the soldier that witnessed its use.

He felt tension flicker to life in his body when he heard Zale says these words, but it instantly died out when Zale assured him they were safe—the soldier had been killed before he could tell anyone.

"We're lucky," Badrick said.

"It wasn't luck," Zale seemed to snap. "It was terrible." He removed his helmet and treated Badrick to a dirty scowl he wasn't entirely sure he deserved.

Why was Zale angry with him?

"Either way," Badrick replied softly, feeling as though he was carefully treading over an ice field that had weak spots in places he didn't understand, "we're safe."

"Yes," Zale half sighed, half spat. "I suppose we are." He glanced around, rubbing his bottom lip with his leathery thumb. "Did you really not see any other Kalik with the weapon?"

"No," Badrick said. "Trust me. There was only the one you saw."

"Do you think anyone else saw one you missed?"

Zale's voice was thick with worry, but Badrick was happy to know he could calm him with, "If they did, I'm sure we would have heard about it by now. Trust me, we're still safe. The secret's still secret."

"What about our satellites? For sure, they would have been watching."

"No way they saw through the fire and smoke. If they sensed anything they probably thought it was you blasting things."

Zale didn't look entirely convinced and Badrick knew the veteran would've considered variables he hadn't. But he was certain it didn't matter. Zale was too clever for his own good, and despite his playful arrogance he often forgot that most people weren't as smart as him. Anything he thought of, the Daemonium probably wouldn't.

Nevertheless Zale said no more on the matter, instead moving on with the conversation. He informed Badrick on what happened with the helicopter, as well his theory behind its operator, explaining his reasons for this assumption for Badrick's convenience.

As Badrick listened, he tried to think like Zale would. He mused on everything that his partner said, concentrating as hard as he was able. He had to admit that nothing really came from this effort except a resolute opinion that Zale's evidence could not be refuted.

As far as Badrick could tell, Zale was right. The Resurrected had been present. And for some reason had stolen a helicopter.

Badrick saw it flying away after noticing the massive disturbance that was Zale's crash landing, but hadn't thought anything of it. As far as he was aware at the time the only enemies nearby were Kalik, and the subspecies did not use vehicles.

He'd assumed some lucky British soldiers were fleeing the scene. That didn't worry him; the Daemonium would surely waylay any survivors so that the news of what caused this destruction would stay secret from the human governments.

Even now he knew countless satellites above them were being messed with and people who *might* have witnessed this occurrence one way or another were being hunted down, with Enthrallers capable of mind-controlling or mind-wiping standing at the ready.

All evidence of the Kalik would be gathered, burned, disposed of.

Though he *knew* it wouldn't be that simple this time. This was a military base—a government facility. With no culprit known, the British government would probably assume they suffered an attack from a foreign nation.

The Daemonium wouldn't be able follow protocol this time around; clean the site then leave it for the local authorities to comb through and surmise they had no idea *who* or what had been the cause, then—after three months of the cold case lying on desks—allow it to be forgotten.

This time it wouldn't go down that way.

This attack could lead to severe repercussions.

He wasn't sure how the Daemonium would sort this, though he suspected a massive mind-control operation might be in order. Bigger than any he'd ever heard of before.

He hoped he wouldn't be called in to help—Badrick wasn't mentally equipped for such a complex operation—though he knew he'd be called to repel the Kalik again if another raid happened.

They needed the power of a Royal.

It was just a shame he was the one with the power.

Discarding these moody musings for another day, he returned his focus to his dialogue with Zale. Chewing his lip, Badrick said irately, "Can't believe he was bold enough to steal a military vehicle."

"Care to take a guess as to exactly *why* he or she wants one?" Zale tried.

"No way," Badrick laughed. "I don't *feckin'* know." He thought for a moment. "Can we track the helicopter? It's military, it must have . . . stuff inside it to track."

"I'm sure the Daemonium will give it a go," Zale confirmed. "I will too, just in case. But don't get your hopes up. Like we've observed, our enemy is clever. He might have thought of that and taken steps to avoid the eventuality that we follow him."

Badrick sighed and cursed under his breath. But then his face brightened and he shouted, "But we *can* track him. His *stank*," he laughed. "His toxic radiation. We can now follow it."

Zale smiled a small smile. "Yes, I think you're right." He straightened to stretch his spine, wincing painfully. "We should go back and do exactly that. What say you?"

Feeling better than he had in a long time, Badrick jumped to his feet. "Let's do it."

chapter
EIGHTEEN

Zale did his best to ignore the impatient Badrick, who was annoying him immensely as Zale tapped on his keyboard. Badrick kept ushering him to move faster, to which Zale responded with false blitheness. "I can only go as fast as the computer."

Truthfully, Zale was working as fast as absolutely possible, and he too was getting extremely anxious. With his patience at an all time low, what felt like 'fifty eternities'—as Carla used to say— passed before the damn satellite relayed the information from the battle.

"Right, finally!" Badrick exclaimed when Zale indicated that they were ready. "Get that scanner working!"

"We'll be able to follow the taint trail from this," Zale told him, a smile now playing at the corners of his lips. A kind of relief he never knew existed was flooding through him. "We can find our thief and solve this whole thing."

He struck the keyboard furiously, getting more and more impatient by the second as he cycled through the types of scans the system was able to perform. Finally, after much banging on the keys, he managed to open the correct setting to detect Resurrected.

With the excitement and anticipation building quickly, the pair of them gazed eagerly at the screen as the scanners processed the battlefield.

And then their faces dropped when a big fat nothing was revealed.

Neither said anything for a moment.

Then, with what sounded like forced calm, Badrick muttered, "It looks normal. There's nothing. Do you have the right timestamp?"

"Of course I do," Zale snapped, a lot less composed. "Maybe it's broken." He reset the scanner to look for Kalik energy readings. When he pressed enter the screen lit up like a firework display, the power sparked from the numerous murders culminating into a huge amount of residue. Grumbling irately, Zale then switched to Enthraller energy, only to find it working perfectly once again.

One more time, he tried searching for both and the results came in clear as crystal.

"OK, so now . . . " He wiped the entire system of his changes and reverted back to the Resurrected setting.

Once again, nothing emerged. No Resurrected taint spread across the screen and the recording of the helicopter lifting out of the fog with a tiny Zale swinging underneath was completely clear of what should have been a sickly green gas-like glow.

"Are you serious!?" Badrick practically screamed, his

composure gone completely. "Nothing!?" He threw his hands into the air and stepped back, repeatedly bawling curses and startling a gaggle of Agent Commanders.

Zale didn't say anything. He simply stared at the screen in disbelief.

Eventually he could no longer look and swivelled his chair around to face away from the consoles. If he could have seen his face in a mirror, he suspected it would have been white as a sheet with an expression of defeated disbelief tinged with bitter disappointment.

"I must have been wrong," he muttered. "There's no Resurrected. There can't be."

Somehow, above his own shouting, Badrick heard his mutter and stopped throwing his body around with rage. He sighed apologetically to the closest agents and came back to sit next to Zale.

Placing a hand on Zale's shoulder, he said, "Don't do that. Don't start doubting yourself."

Déjà vu struck Zale quite hard at that moment; he remembered Horas telling him something somewhat similar only a week ago.

"I was wrong," he said quietly.

"No," Badrick stopped him with a sharp swipe of a hand. "What you said about Resurrected makes sense. I think you're still right. But maybe we were also right about there being a human ally. Maybe our bad guy has more help than we hoped."

Zale had forgotten about that theory. He was surprised; usually he never forgot about *anything*.

What the hell was wrong with him?

Overlooking this concern, Badrick was correct. What if the Resurrected hadn't been present, instead using a human accomplice to steal that helicopter? That would ensure his toxic radiation wasn't at the scene but also that he achieved his goal.

Because Zale was *sure* the helicopter was the objective of the raid. It was the only possible benefit that occurred during that whole ordeal.

What else could have possibly been achieved by attacking a human base?

Beside him, Badrick appeared to take a deep breath. "We need to keep a level head," he said softly. "We need to focus on our next step."

Again, he was right.

And at the very least they *did* have a next step.

"Alright," he said. "I need the bodies of the British military. I need to perform autopsies on each and every one."

"Every single body? By yourself?"

"*You're goddamn right!*"

Badrick cracked a smile and patted him on the shoulder. "You got it, buddy. Want me to put the orders in?"

Zale nodded and allowed Badrick to turn away and work on his port-pad.

It was hard to believe the battle had only been an hour ago. It felt like months had already passed. A headache was forming at the front of Zale's skull but he did his best to ignore it, not wanting to give in to such a trivial pain when the rest of his body was in so much agony.

He cast his eyes back to the screen, which still displayed the scene of the battle. Groaning irritably he reached over to turn it off—

And he stopped so fast his weary muscles groaned angrily. Ignoring them he retracted his hand and leaned into the screen, squinting heavily.

Zale stared for ten whole seconds before finally saying aloud, "What is that?"

Badrick looked up from his port-pad inquisitively. "What's

what?"

Thinking quickly—would it still be there?—Zale jumped to his feet and demanded that Badrick teleport them back to the battlefield.

"But the agents are still cleaning up," his partner argued.

"I know!" Zale snapped impatiently, waving his hands spastically. "That's why we've got to go *now*. Come on! Comeoncomeoncomeoncomeoncome—"

"Alright!" Badrick roared to shut him up. "Goddamn it!" Wasting no time being gentle, he grabbed a hold of Zale's arm. The next thing Zale knew demonic energy was flowing through him and a flash of light had removed his capacity to see.

Fresh cold air struck his lungs. Stumbling from the shock of it, he forced himself to take deep breaths, wishing he'd taken the time to recollect his helmet. Without it, the whole armour system became useless at keeping him warm.

What was the point of a toasty body when your face was numb?

He did his best to disregard the cold, casting his gaze left and right, trying to determine where they were.

"What are yo—"

Badrick never got to finish. Zale had found his bearings and was now charging across the base, weaving between bodies and vehicles, agents and soldiers, most shouting in anger as he almost bowled half of them to the ground.

Zale could hear Badrick following him from far behind, but didn't slow to allow him to keep up. It was paramount that he got to the third hangar before the clean-up crew got in the way.

He pushed past one last annoyed agent and ground to a halt near the entrance. Rapidly scanning the area for his target, he caterwauled victoriously and dashed further on.

Arriving at his destination, he bent down and picked up the

strange, mysterious object his electric eyes had picked up on the screen.

The thing looked a lot like a torch—a big torch—except it was covered in what he recognised as green demonic symbols. Which was odd in itself; demonic symbols were *never* green. They were always orange/yellow with black.

This object defied all common demonic design behaviour.

Considering these facts, Zale was instantly forced to conclude that whatever this thing was it hadn't actually been made by demonic hands, despite the creator obviously trying to craft that illusion.

But it definitely wasn't constructed by human hands. The simple fact that the symbols were at all present was evident of that.

On the side of the odd object was a little black button. Zale chewed his lip, contemplating how dangerous what he was gripping might actually be. For a second, he was wary, before deciding to throw all caution to the wind. Facing the end which should have housed a little bulb away from himself, he held his breath and pressed the button.

He jumped as there was a loud *zing* sound and a quarter metre spike protruded out, shining dangerously in the white winter sunlight. Zale waited for it to do something else before studying it cautiously, doing his best to avoid touching the spiked protrusion.

Better safe than sorry.

"What is that?" Badrick asked him, quite suddenly appearing from behind.

"I have absolutely no idea," he answered truthfully.

He pressed the button again, hoping it would retract the blade and was greatly relieved when the spike disappeared into the object. He glared at it for some time. wondering what on earth this thing could be and what its purpose was.

Nothing nice, he was sure.

"I'll take it to the lab," he finally told Badrick. "Maybe I can glean some info out of it."

*

With a moan of effort, Badrick got back to his feet. His strained face appeared from behind the corpse, cresting over the top of the bloody, open chest. He wiped his forehead with his forearm and picked at his green lab sheet irritably, throwing the tool he now held back upon the table.

"Would you stop fidgeting?" Zale groaned for the eighth time. For the last half hour all he'd been able to hear and see was Badrick's moans of discomfort and his endless scratching.

Even when he was handing tools to Zale he was clawing his skin and pulling at the sheet with his gloved hands. It was the only reason he'd dropped that bone saw at all.

"This goddamn stuff is itchy as hell!" Badrick argued.

"Well, your accursed scratching is putting me off!"

With yet another plucking of his sheet, Badrick apologised for the disturbance he was causing.

"Its fine," Zale sighed. "You should take a break, friend."

Badrick *pffted* dubiously, but Zale nodded with encouragement, causing Badrick to ask, "Are you sure?"

"Yeah," Zale smiled. "We've been working for seven hours already and we've cut open four dead people. I think you deserve a break."

"What about you?"

"I'm not stopping," Zale shook his head. "Not yet. But you go rest. I can work faster on my own, anyway."

Badrick puffed air gratefully and started to pull his sheet from his person. "Thank God—"

"Ah!" Zale snapped, a finger darting into the air. "What are you doing?"

For a moment Badrick simply stared, nonplussed. It actually took several seconds before his eyes flickered to the body, then to his sheet, and he cried, "Oh, sorry! Don't take this off in the lab. Right, gotcha."

Fool, Zale laughed in his head as Badrick disappeared through the automatic door. As it shut behind him, silence fell once again and Zale returned to his unceremonious reorganising of the dead man's interior decorating.

Only a few minutes after Badrick's departure, Zale determined he would learn nothing new from this poor man's remains. It was clear he was murdered by the claws of a Kalik and not a blade.

There weren't even any signs of a wound caused by a *regular* Kalik blade.

The claws of the demon had literally gutted him, clawing out parts of his ribs and leaving the shattered remains to cause more damage to the vital organs. He took a second to utter a prayer for the soldier before returning his organs to his chest cavity. Sewing his body back up as best he could, Zale organised a small group of medics to retrieve the corpse and return it to the morgue.

They arrived with a new body, helping Zale place it on the operating table before leaving with the original.

Zale sighed as they departed, picking up his tools once more and preparing to cut into yet another decaying corpse. Pausing before acting, he took a moment to look at the face of the female lieutenant he was about to desecrate. She was pretty for someone trained in rugged human warfare. Even though she had opted for shaving her hair into a buzz-cut, it didn't detract from her fairness.

It was such a waste for him to have to do this. This woman, and all her friends, shouldn't have died.

But the accursed Kalik—the evil, mutated, demonic bastards—

had ripped her life away. It was terrible. The worst—

Zale shook his head. There was no time for him to get sorrowful. He had a job to do and he had to get on with it.

However his task was further delayed by the reopening of the door. He glanced up, expecting to find someone whose presence would only annoy him. But to his delight, he found it was Carla strutting through the open archway, already suited up in her own sickly green sheet with gloves tightly covering the skin of her hands.

"Greetings, Zale!" she hissed, her tongue slithering strangely.

Without pausing his work, Zale said, "You're a bloody creep."

She decided to ignore him. Hurrying up to his side, she took a look at what he was doing. "I ran into Badrick out there," she informed him. "He told me you were faster on your own." She gave him an amused look. "Seeing as that's crap, want some help?"

Zale put up a fake irritated stance, acting as if her presence was annoying but he would live with it. "Fine!"

"Funny guy." She pushed him playfully. "Come on. Cut this miss open."

Badrick closed his door behind him, loving the strange buzz that descended over his ears briefly as all ambient noise ceased, his soundproof walls doing their job perfectly. Once he'd gotten used to the silence and he could hear absolutely nothing, he sighed, content.

He liked the quiet.

It helped him relax.

He smiled at that thought.

It had never been that way before. Back in the day—before his 'death'—he'd *needed* noise to stay calm. He needed to be doing something. He needed to distract himself.

Music, loud people, school . . . whatever.

Anything to stop himself from remembering. The presence of silence would offer no distraction from his memories of the past and at the time he couldn't handle that.

Silence was the worst back then.

But since his revival he was different. It was an irrefutable fact—he knew that—though he felt like it had been a good alteration. Badrick was better off the way he was now; strong and powerful.

The past no longer bothered him.

The prospect of his future no longer scared him.

The silence no longer distressed him.

Although, standing here now, in the peace and quiet and with his mind cast back into the past for the first time since his rebirth, he felt a strange sense of unease. He could remember all that he was before—all that he used to be—but it wasn't right. His body felt strangely void of . . . *anything at all.*

The memories of who he was were perfect, but it felt like something was missing.

He could have sworn that—at a very simple, base level of sensations—when his mind worked he should have felt something in the rest of him.

Badrick scowled at his wall angrily; he was *sure* that was a thing.

What was the word for that?

He couldn't even explain it to himself eloquently . . . it was as though he was so far removed from what he was missing that he couldn't describe it, like a child attempting to explain the theory of relativity.

It was frustrating, to say the least.

But in the end he simply shrugged, letting go of the matter with fantastic ease. There was no point dwelling on stuff he couldn't even recall accurately.

Not when he had all this silence to enjoy.

chapter
NINETEEN

Zale caught the water bottle before it hit him in the face. Carla laughed at his clumsiness, sitting in the chair opposite the one he now found himself nestled within. She popped the cap off her own bottle with expert ease and took a huge swig.

"Tired?" she asked. "You're never clumsy. Maybe you're losing your touch."

"Quiet," he chuckled, sipping his water. He quickly decided it wasn't entering his body fast enough and downed the whole bottle.

"Cutting up bodies for two days obviously works up a sweat," Carla noted.

"Well, don't you feel the same way?"

"Yeah, I do," she smirked, wiping her forehead with her arm.

She was certainly right; two days spent working endlessly, with barely any sleep, performing autopsies upon nearly twenty corpses had tuckered Zale out. Carla—having spent that time wasting her days off helping him—clearly felt as sweaty and worn out as he did.

She chugged her water as Zale gazed around, his eyes falling upon the corpse they'd worked on last. He could see the medics preparing it for transport through the glass that separated the autopsy room from the offices they were relaxing within.

He felt a sense of dread knowing just how many more he had to get through. He wished he was done ... although at the same time that would have been worse. It would have left him frustrated that his search had revealed—*yet again*—absolutely nothing.

With yet more to go, there was still a chance of locating something helpful.

"How are you?" Carla asked him, cutting him from his reverie. He faced her, instantly knowing from her expression that she could practically read his mind and knew exactly how he felt.

"There are no words for the impatience I feel," he sighed.

"It getting you down?"

"This whole thing is driving me insane," Zale confirmed a little more aggressively than he meant to. He took a mental step back and breathed carefully. When he was sure he was calmer, Zale opened his mouth to apologise.

Thankfully, Carla knew him well. She nodded her head pointedly, understanding that he wasn't shouting at her.

"My head hurts, like, all the time!" He grabbed his forehead, squinting in pain.

Zale felt a rubbing sensation on his shoulder and realised Carla was now settled on the arm of his chair. "Need a painkiller?" she asked softly.

"No," he rejected the offer, but smiled gratefully. "I just need to get this over with. It's stressing me right out."

"Yeah, I can see that," Carla almost laughed. "I know you. The simple fact that there is so little evidence is killing you."

Zale absolutely loved it when she was this insightful. It meant he didn't have to explain *everything*.

"Plus I feel like I'm missing something," he told her. "I feel like the answer is obvious, like what I have to do next is clear as day but I just can't see it. It's maddening. I'm not working at optimum efficiency. It's this accursed headache!"

"You *have* been a little off recently," Carla said, rubbing his head carefully. His eyelids flickered with delight at the glorious sensation. "But I don't think your smarts have been affected. You've seemed as sharp as ever."

"Well, maybe," he sighed. "I hope." He let her stroke his head for a little longer, saying nothing for a few minutes. When he did next speak, it was because his head felt immensely better. *Praise Carla and her sexy, magic hands.* "Doesn't it feel like we're getting nowhere though?"

"I hate to admit it, but our bad guy *is* fooling us a lot," she agreed.

"We haven't found anything, really," Zale grumbled. "A few bits and pieces here and there, but nothing definitive. We don't even have anyone to question. No witnesses, no accomplices, nobody.

"That's not how it's supposed to work. People are easy. People you can crack." His newly growing frustration fuelled the muscles in his legs and he stood sharply, pacing around the room. "It is so easy to solve a case when people are involved. They're so easy to read." He turned to Carla, right arm pointing at her. "You interrogate a man. One minute he says he always tells the truth, and then he says he always lies. Which is right?"

Carla didn't hesitate. She smiled and said, "He always lies, because one of those statements will always be a lie."

"Exactly!" Zale exclaimed. "And see how quickly you figured that out. People are so easy to figure out. People say stupid things. Contradictory things. Not as conveniently simplistic as that riddle, obviously, but it's the same principle. People are the easiest factor to work with.

"But now say you have a knife. It was either used to kill a man, or it wasn't. Which is right?"

Carla shrugged. "There's no way to know off hand."

"Right!" He sighed and moved back to sit next to her. "That's what I'm dealing with now. I have nobody to question. Nobody to trick into telling me the answers. I have no dialogue to remember and cross reference with our evidence."

"This isn't usually a problem for you," Carla noted, stroking his head softly. "I've seen you solve cases with nothing but your gut feeling to go on."

"And that's also why I feel like I've missed something. I'm supposed to be some kind of super genius. A super detective." He tutted and punched himself in the chest. "Look at me now. A *feckin'* Resurrected of all things has got me stumped."

His friend *'awwwed'* sympathetically. "You put too much pressure on yourself."

"I have to," Zale sighed. "I have to otherwise these people get away scot-free."

Carla didn't appear to have an answer for that, so she simply went back to stroking his hair in silence. He smiled as the strands fell over his eyes and gazed up to look at her, their eyes meeting.

He felt a strange motion in his chest—as if his heart had just skipped a beat—as their eyes bore into each other's. He noticed the glint of her golden hair under the light of the room. Watched as it fell over her shoulder when she moved her arm to touch his cheek.

Her expression was soft. Softer than usual. Her regular provocative demeanour was gone. In its place she even looked a little vulnerable. For a moment his eyes darted to her lips and he wondered if today was the day he should—

The both of them jumped up as the door *zipped* open and in walked the most unwelcome figure at that moment in time.

Badrick.

He stopped when he saw them suspiciously further apart from the one another than was normal.

He grinned at them. "Whatcha doin'?" he asked purposefully slow, and a little sing-song-like.

"Nothing," Zale spluttered awkwardly.

At the same time Carla said something more articulate. "Working on the case."

She glared at him for being so unhelpful.

Badrick's grin didn't vanish. "How's it going?" he queried in that same irritating voice, and Zale wondered if anyone would truly blame him if he punched his partner in the face.

"It *was* going great!" he snapped, finding his words. "We almost had the answers to solving the case, curing cancer and the secret to immortality and then *you* walked in and now we can't remember what we were going to say. Shame on you!"

This just served to make Badrick laugh harder.

And *that* served to aggravate Zale even more so.

"I should go," Carla said, cementing the fact that the moment they *might* have shared truly was over.

Zale sighed with irritation.

So close.

"I'll see you tomorrow night?" she asked him.

"Aye," he confirmed, giving her a quick awkward hug. Carla returned it, just as gracelessly. She quickly left after that, walking past the still smirking Badrick. The door zipped shut behind her, the noise that drifted through the open archway cutting off instantly.

"You two crack me up," Badrick said without hesitation.

"What is *that* supposed to mean?"

"You know what it means." He walked further into the room and punched Zale lightly on the shoulder. "You guys really need to hurry up."

Ridiculously flustered at these accusations, all Zale could say without spluttering saliva everywhere was a repeat of, "What is *that* supposed to mean?" He tried to laugh dismissively, though he could tell Badrick could see the nervousness behind the chuckles. Badrick presented him with a shake of his head before saying, "Zale . . . look, our jobs are dangerous. We could die at any time. Before you know it, you're going to run out of time. Stop beating about the bush and just . . . admit what you want."

For what was probably the first time ever, Zale was at a total loss for what to say. His mouth opened and closed unhelpfully as he stood there in unsure silence. Badrick didn't seem to mind. In fact, he appeared to take Zale's quiet as proof he'd gotten his point across.

He gave Zale another arm punch, then turned and confusingly walked back out the door. Zale stared after him, utterly baffled.

"But . . . " he spoke aloud indignantly, "why did you even come in here!?"

He chose not to pursue this bewildering subject. Badrick's actions were a mystery—probably, even to himself. Zale couldn't be bothered to question it, especially seeing as he still had work to do.

He made his way back towards the autopsy room where, thankfully, the next corpse already awaited him. Pulling on his sheet, gloves and face mask, he waltzed in and quickly got to work.

Zale took a moment to activate the nearby microphones so that he could speak his findings aloud. It would be far better than having to take two minute breaks every ten seconds in order to type the details of his autopsy.

Before making the first incision, he examined the skin of the body, checking for wounds and the like. "Male," he said robotically, "Caucasian, late twenties, maybe early thirties. Appears to have suffered immense blood loss." He turned to the computer to confirm this. "Aye," he mumbled quietly. "Reports concur."

He stepped around the table, checking the man's other side. "Appears to have died from exsanguination caused by deep claw wounds to the throat. There is also a large amount of tissue loss on the right shoulder. A Kalik bite, though quite small."

A gnawing from a Kalik was usually so vastly damaging it could tear away more than half a person's torso. This wound was horrible, sure, but it was nothing compared. The demon responsible must have snapped at its victim and only caught the flesh in the front few fangs.

This was still enough to mortally wound the man, but Zale was sure the cause of death was the violent removal of the man's oesophagus, and so with his hypothesis in place, he pulled back the sheet covering the man's body and made for his tools.

But he never even bothered to reach for his scalpel.

As the man's full body came into view, a third, truly gruesome wound assailed Zale's eyes. Taking an involuntary step back, he blinked, surprised, staring at the gaping hole in the man's ribs.

"What the hell?"

Within seconds, he deduced this hadn't been inflicted by a Kalik. It was too . . . uncommon for that. Sure, it was as messy and chaotic as any other injury caused by the subspecies, but . . . there was just something off with this.

The wound was gaping, a bloody, massive, perfectly round

hole. It was so big that Zale could see right into it, and had no difficulty spotting just how odd it was. The shape of it suggested to him that someone with great strength had rammed a traffic cone into this man's chest. Obviously, that wasn't strictly realistic, but if he hadn't known better he would have accepted this as a genuine theory.

He didn't bother checking for an exit wound; he could already see there wasn't one.

Pushing the body around, he checked that there were no more similar wounds, but everything else turned out to be nothing but small scratches.

Zale let the body fall back into place and chewed his lip, eyeing the bloody cavity with unease. Not a single weapon in existence created a wound like this. This had been inflicted with purpose, perhaps with some kind of blade.

He did a quick check; yep, he could see the scratches and carvings in the walls of the injury. Someone had literally 'whittled' this giant . . . *fissure* with a dagger.

Zale felt disgust bubble up inside him as questions lit up his mind like a Christmas tree.

Who had done this?

Why had they done this?

Had this man been alive when they'd done this?

Why had they done this?

What kind of sick bastard would do this?

And above all . . .

Before anything else . . .

Why the *hell* had they done this!?!

The act was sick, perverted, disgusting. This wasn't the Kalik. There was too much malice displayed here. Those brutes were evil and monstrous but they were still *just* beasts.

The Kalik weren't capable of such wanton malevolence.

Zale took a step back in order to get some distance between him and the body, removing his facemask and breathing in cool, recycled air.

Gory wounds never fazed him, but this time it was just a little too much. It wasn't necessarily what he could see, but the implications behind it . . . the kind of person who would be capable of doing this . . .

It horrified him.

Taking a deep breath, he stepped closer once again, further inspecting the wound. There was no doubt in his mind that the Resurrected had inflicted this ghastly lesion and he was determined to figure out why.

So far this was the only body to sport this kind of wound.

Why had the Resurrected chosen this man to do it to?

The outer circle was very neat, but it was incredibly messy on the inside. Organs, bones and strips of flesh were shredded and splattered every which way. The Resurrected would have lost his ability to carve cleanly the further in he got. That fact was easily visible.

And now that he was looking in deep, Zale could swear he spotted an abnormality. If he wasn't mistaken he could see something inside, lodged between two pieces of bone.

"What is that?" he asked the air.

His lower lip ached as his teeth bit at it with agitation. A disturbing sense of dread was kicking his stomach but he did his best to ignore it. Despite his best efforts, it continued to bother him as he leaned forward to gaze directly into the wound.

No good . . . Zale needed a closer look.

Getting his bearings on the exact location of the abnormality, he pulled back his head and carefully—blindly—reached inside in an attempt to remove it.

He cringed as the pieces of the man's broken body moved and

crumbled under his touch. Zale actually felt his own body tremble with revulsion.

But at least he was close. He could feel the pieces of bone now. A little more fumbling, feeling around, prying and he would have it out—

"Ow!"

He snapped his hand back, withdrawing from the wound with speed. He brought his fingers to his eye and was met with exactly what he'd feared the moment he felt the sting on his flesh.

The red of his blood stained his punctured glove.

Zale felt his stomach plummet.

"Crap!"

Badrick slapped his palm to his forehead, yelling incomprehensibly. It had taken him nearly an hour to remember why he'd gone back into the lab and now that his memory had caught up he couldn't believe he'd forgotten at all.

If only it wasn't for Zale and Carla's ineptitude, he wouldn't have left the lab without his sidearm, which he'd lost on the first day of the autopsies.

Badrick spent two days searching for that goddamn thing and when he'd finally recalled where he'd left it, Carla and Zale made him forget he'd been in the lab for any reason at all.

Damning them to a lifetime of coughing—the least cruel curse he could think of—he about faced and made his way back to the labs . . .

Managing only two steps before he was interrupted by a loud klaxon. The shrill alarm deafened him as the facility turned red with warning lights. Badrick didn't need to ask to know what was happening. These days, there was only one reason the klaxon would go off that loudly.

"Oh no!"

He about-faced once more and darted in the direction of the RCR, hoping to find Reynolds there. Badrick was sure the sergeant would want him to intervene.

However, when he arrived, the man was nowhere in sight. Badrick searched high and low, checking both floors of the RCR but failed to locate him.

Reynolds wasn't here.

In the end it didn't matter; a red uniformed man Badrick didn't know accosted him on his way back down the staircase. "Badrick?"

"Yes?"

"Thank God I've found you," the man said in a heavily American accent. "My name is Kevin. I assume you're looking for Reynolds?"

"Yes," Badrick sighed happily. "Have you seen him?"

The man shook his head sadly. "He's offsite, inspecting an outpost facility."

"Damn it!" Without the sergeant, Badrick didn't know what to do. "What are the alarms for?" he asked, just making sure he was right. "Kalik?"

"Affirmative." Kevin put his hand on Badrick's back and led him down the stairs. "Reynolds left Council orders for you to be found if another attack is detected. He wants you to stop them."

"I know," Badrick nodded. "We need Daemnos."

"Glad you're on board," Kevin cheered. He handed Badrick a folder. "They're attacking one of our production facilities."

"How many?" Badrick sifted through the pages, using Daemnos' powers to speed read as fast as he could.

"Not certain. Too many for the base to fight off, at least."

Badrick nodded and said, "I'll grab my partner and teleport over. Do you want me to round up some soldiers?"

"No time." Kevin shook his head. "It's much smaller than the last attack force. With the backup of our men at the facility, you and your partner should be able to fight them off."

"Understood," Badrick said. "I'll suit up."

chapter
TWENTY

The sting of the needle made Zale wince and grind his teeth. With his arm now bleeding, he dropped the injector on the table and waited for the readouts to update. The computer fuzzed, evaluating the information the little chip that now rested in his forearm was transferring to the machine.

Before he could survey it, a voice spoke behind him. "You are clean. No infection."

He didn't need to turn to know Horas was standing at his back, peering at the computer over his shoulder.

"No," Zale said. "No infections . . . apart from—"

"That was not your fault," Horas interrupted him. "Stop thinking what you are thinking. You were not careless. You are not stupid. There was no way you could have predicted what would be in that monstrous wound." He waved towards the corpse that still lay on the table.

"I should've known," Zale argued.

"No." Horas shook his head. "You could not have known there would be a . . . " he appeared to struggle to find the right words, "*non-dissolved* one in the man's body. They are never utilised in such a fashion. No one, not the Daemonium nor demon-kind, has ever seen them used this way."

"So what do you think I should have done?" Zale almost snapped.

"Nothing different than what you did." Zale sensed Horas placed a hand on his shoulder, though physically he felt nothing. This wasn't strange; Horas was just a vision generated by the wavelength of energy that was the real Horas lurking within Zale's soul.

Physical contact wasn't possible.

"You should tell Reynolds," the vision said.

Zale puffed air and shook his head. "I have two hours before it takes effect and it's already irreversible. I'm not going to waste the time I have left worrying everybody. I have work to do."

"What do you hope to change in that little time?" Horas asked as Zale traipsed moodily across the lab. "You should tell your friends."

"No!" Zale hadn't meant to snap and he immediately felt bad after. "There's no point upsetting everyone. Now . . . shush. I have work to do."

He approached a separate desk, tapping quickly on a console and summoning the medics to come pick up the last body. Then, when the orders were sent, he set to work on his next task.

"What are you doing?" Horas asked him, stepping up for a closer look at what Zale was now removing from a glass container. "What is that?"

"Something I found at the scene," Zale told him, revealing the strange torch-shaped device. "Take a gander." He lifted it higher so as to give Horas a good look. "I had a few hours to study it the other day and what I found is . . . interesting, to say the least."

"What is it?"

Zale smiled, pressing the button on the side. Horas jumped when the spike protruded out of the top, shining evilly in the light.

"What does it do?"

"How many questions do you have?" Zale queried impatiently. Nevertheless, he answered, "You plunge the pointy end into someone and it injects your intended target with the contents inside. It's some kind of toxic gas that causes the victim to suffer a fatal heart attack.

"But it doesn't do it straight away. The gas harmlessly resides in the body, but there's a button on the bottom that acts like a detonator. It sends a small electrical charge that activates the gas and then . . . *whumph*. Victim drops dead.

"But here is the part that fascinates me—the wound caused by the stabby part heals completely. Not only that, but the gas dissipates without a trace. It leaves literally no evidence.

"It's a remarkable piece of machinery, don't you think? I haven't seen demonic experiments this extensive since the eighteen hundreds. Well . . . not me personally, but you get my meaning."

Horas looked appalled. Zale could sense the intense distaste practically irradiating his soul as the demon's feelings vibrated against his own.

And then the demon said, "I have seen this before." Zale looked up, surprised, though he realised he shouldn't be. This was obviously of demonic origin and Horas had experience and knowledge of most things demonic.

His life before the Enthrallers was the cause of that.

"Well, what is it?" Zale prompted him when the demon failed to go on.

Horas hesitated at first. Even though Zale couldn't see his face he could tell the demon was greatly unsettled.

"Do you remember what Reynolds told you about Koreath?" he finally asked.

Zale nodded affirmatively. "The gas demon— Oh." Understanding kicked him like an angry horse.

Horas pointed at the device angrily, his loathing towards its existence so very evident. "This is Koreath's power trapped in a vile machine. It was not just his Enthraller that was murdered. Someone has killed Koreath and harvested his power to put it into that device."

Zale now shared his demon's dismay. What he was hearing was absolutely horrifying. Zale himself was guilty of harnessing demonic powers into technology, but he'd never heard of power *harvesting* before. It sounded horrific.

"How do you harvest a power?"

"Some demons can absorb the powers of others, but that is not what this is." Horas shook his head, bowing sadly. "If you are a demon with a physical power, one that is organic and not supernatural, then your power can be harvested. Koreath was such a demon. The gas was produced in his body. His power was being able to use it."

"Does this mean the device has a finite quantity of the gas?"

Horas actually shrugged, an action he had never before resorted to in all the years Zale had known him. "I could not tell you."

Cursing, Zale turned back to the device, regarding it with new hatred. Even knowing that demons were evil—bar his own—he still didn't approve of the merciless slaughter and brutal harvesting of anything living.

Even a demon.

"I need to tell Reynolds."

To his irritation, Horas disagreed. "No. What you need to do is tell him about the—"

"I already told you, Horas," Zale growled. "No!"

He would have said more. He *would* have made a stronger argument than just a childish *'No'.* But before he could even try to formulate one in his head, the overhead lights shut off and the alarm lights flickered on, bathing the lab in thick red light. The sudden change in ambience was accompanied by a piercing alarm.

"What is that?" Horas asked snappily; the sudden noise had made the demon jump.

"The alarms," Zale said redundantly. He caught himself and elaborated, "There must be another attack."

He spun on the spot and dashed to the storage containers. Opening his private unit, he deposited the artefact inside, slotting it between a prototype pistol he'd once half created but never finished and a hard drive that contained the digital blueprints of his swords.

Locking it up under the protection of his own personal key codes, he stepped away from the units and made his way to the door, intending to find Badrick.

No sooner had he taken his first step that the very person he aimed to locate randomly flashed into existence in front of him. Zale dug his feet into the floor and ground to a halt, eyeing Badrick with surprise.

"What the . . ."

In a voice that sounded somewhat robotic, Badrick echoed, "Meet me at the armoury. We're teleporting into battle."

Without so much as a goodbye, Badrick flashed into nonexistence. Zale blinked, stunned.

"Astral projection," Horas informed him. "The power of

Singularis Isa. As a Royal, Daemnos has every power in existence."

"Yeah, I know." Zale rolled his eyes. He rather hated being told something he already understood but instead of commenting, he simply eyed up Horas' visage and said, "Ready yourself. I'll need unrestricted access to your powers."

"Of course," Horas nodded. "But Zale, I still believe you should tell them about—"

Zale flapped an intolerant arm. "God, there's no time, Horas! We have to go now."

"Denying what has happened to you has no benefit," his demon chided him.

But Zale wasn't listening; he was already out the door and away.

Five minutes later he was suited up—in record time—and blasting through the HQ in the direction of the armoury, thankfully finding Badrick in no time at all. His partner was just slotting his helmet upon his head, the rest of his equipment already prepared.

Apparently being able to sense that Zale was behind him, Badrick's hand shot out blindly and he grabbed Zale's arm without even looking. Zale felt the familiar horrible sense of supernatural transportation and seconds later he felt his feet hit soft dirt.

He immediately familiarised himself with his surroundings— they were at one of their production facilities.

More specifically, it was the site that constructed heavy weapons for the primary Daemonium base.

The location of this siege did not go unnoticed by Zale—once again they were defending an English location. He felt some elation at this. It seemed his theory of only the English-based Kalik being involved had survived another day.

But what was the point of *this* attack?

What did the Resurrected want from here?

Zale still had no idea why the toxic being stole a helicopter, but at least *that* attack had a clear objective.

So what was the goal now?

Whatever it was, Zale had no time to think about it. Their explosive arrival caught the notice of every single Kalik in the vicinity and none of them wasted any time in rushing over them like a destructive wave of claws and fangs and blades.

Beside Zale, Badrick raised his weapon and chuckled, "Now this is what I live for."

*

Badrick felt hard metal meet the soles of his boots and the relative quiet of the Daemonium HQ replaced the buzz of combat. At that moment, he was overcome with disappointment from the realisation that the high-octane action was done and he couldn't help but hope another battle opportunity presented itself sooner rather than later.

On his left Zale stumbled as he landed, looking a little worse for wear. "You alright, buddy?" Badrick asked him. Even the first time Zale piggybacked Badrick on a teleport, he managed to keep his feet on the ground and his stomach inside his body.

So it was odd—after having done it so many more times since—that he fell over now.

Zale simply held up a finger in response, nodding slowly.

Taking his word for it, Badrick stepped ahead of him, checking out the state of the HQ. Everything seemed calm now; the agents were no longer running around every which way and the soldiers had resumed their regular patrols.

He couldn't see any operatives, but he was certain the rest of his kin were lurking about somewhere.

They always were.

Trekking through the facility, he hoped to locate Reynolds. The sergeant would need to be appraised on the situation. However, just as before, he couldn't find him anywhere and Badrick figured the man had yet to return from his own assignment.

And so, resigning himself to what was probably a long and boring wait, he searched for a bench to rest on.

But before he could retire to one of the nearby seats, the easily recognisable sound of helicopter rotors hit his ears.

"I hope that's the sarge," he muttered to himself.

Wanting to get to him as soon as possible if Reynolds was indeed the one who had just arrived by helicopter, he about-faced and rushed towards the exit.

He was stopped by a fierce, incredibly loud scream of incomprehensible nonsense from the other side of the HQ.

Badrick ground to a halt and gazed in confusion at his partner, who was now throwing his arms around like a mental patient at the furthest end of the hall. Lifting his head to the ceiling, he bawled again, spouting nothing but gibberish.

Along with everybody else in the vicinity, Badrick stared at him in bewilderment. For several awkward moments there was just silence; not a single one of them knew how to respond.

But then understanding dawned on Badrick, something which would probably elude all others; the stress of the past few days was probably getting to Zale by now.

He was pretty odd at the best of times. So, with everything that was going on, this was probably normal for him.

Laughing at his eccentric partner, he continued on his way in search of Reynolds.

To his delight he found the sergeant already breezing through the Gate. Badrick breathed a sigh of relief, almost breaking professionalism and hugging Reynolds, but catching himself just in time.

"I am so glad to see you," he told Reynolds.

"Why?" Reynolds asked suspiciously. "What did you do?"

Badrick chuckled at that, though truth be told he wasn't sure where to start.

He decided to begin with the most important matter; the latest attack.

"Another one?" Reynolds exhaled with exhaustion. "Blades?"

Badrick was happy to be able to shake his head.

"Alright, so what was the reason this time?"

Badrick could only shrug as they walked back to the HQ together. "I have no idea. I thought Zale would have figured that out but I didn't get much out of him on the way back. I think he might be ill or something.

"The last time the objective was apparently a helicopter, but this time . . . " He shrugged again, sighing.

Leaving behind the general dark ambience of the Gate, they re-emerged into the bluish brightness of the HQ.

Reynolds continued their conversation with, "What is your next mov—"

"REYNOLDS!"

The sergeant physically jumped as a heavily armoured figure almost bowled him over in its attempt to give him a tight bear hug. Only the man's physical prowess kept him from crumbling beneath the impact.

"Reynolds!" the armoured figure roared. "I am so glad to see you!"

Reynolds wheezed as the bear hug grew tighter. "Hood, get off me this instant!"

Zale slunk away, taking several stumbling steps back. "Sir, guess what! We had a fight. There was guns. And knives. And monsters that went *blaaauergh!*"

Zale reached up and roughly smacked at his helmet once, twice, three times until it finally flew off his head and landed on the floor with a metallic smack. Badrick bent to pick it up, checking its surface for damage. Thankfully everything seemed to be in working order and the visor wasn't cracked.

"Zale, what the hell?" He pulled off his own helmet and gave his partner a bewildered, questioning look.

"Hood, what is wrong with you?"

"Mawr was there!" the electric Enthraller bawled, completely ignoring their enquiries. "He was all like, 'I'm back, bitches', and we were all like, 'Oh my God, Mawr's back', and he was like, 'Yes, I am', and we were like, 'OH NO ZOMBIE!'"

"HOOD!" Reynolds screamed over Zale's continuous ramblings. "What are you babbling about? Mawr hasn't come back. He's dead."

"That's not what happened at all," Badrick spluttered at him.

"It so did, you big liar!"

With a shocked cry of alarm, Badrick was only just able to dodge the swinging fist that Zale sent his way, but his surprise made him stumble, leaving him vulnerable to Zale's next attack.

Thankfully, Reynolds was on the ball; he took Zale's arm hostage and trapped him in a tight body-lock. Not a second later Zale started wrestling so violently he came very close to smacking the sergeant in the face several times. His struggle was accompanied by an incredibly high-pitched scream, as though he were a child being restrained by an impatient parent.

"Christ, Reynolds!" Badrick roared over the din. "Let him go before my eardrums burst!"

Reynolds obeyed, letting Zale fall to the floor. Badrick's partner didn't waste any time; he darted away on his hands and knees, vanishing behind one of the ground floor benches.

Reynolds raised his hands and exclaimed, "What . . . the . . .

f—"

"I think Zale's finally lost it!" Badrick announced.

Zale reappeared once again, crawling creepily towards two agents that were sitting on one of the other benches. He was staring at them intently, as if he was engrossed in what the pair was saying.

In case it was truly important, Badrick used his powers to hone in on the conversation.

For a few seconds he heard only static. He winced at the grating noise that filled his ears before it finally lifted and he was able to hear their voices.

" . . . feel awful about those who died in the battle."

The second nodded in apparent agreement. "It's alright, lad. We'll say a prayer for them tonight. But the important thing is we keep on moving forward. It's in the past now. We have to keep on fighting in their memo—"

He got no further. Suddenly incapable of speech, the agent could only cry out in pain and alarm as Zale jumped up without warning and smacked him hard on the side of the head.

The agent's hand went to his ear and he spun around to see who had struck him. His confusion at seeing Zale was all too easily readable.

Badrick shared his mystification.

"Hood? Why the hell did you do that?"

"You had a crab on your head!" The look on Zale's face suggested he believed he was being completely helpful and couldn't understand his victim's anger.

And then he was gone, darting between alarmed agents and soldiers, the operative vanishing from sight, climbing the ramp towards the BCR.

For a few seconds there was only quiet, the usual hubbub of the Daemonium stunned into silence for a second time.

"I think we need to find out what's going on," Badrick's voice cut into the hush.

"Agreed," said the obviously concerned sergeant. He moved ahead, following in Zale's footsteps. Badrick trotted after him, hoping they'd actually be able to find his partner after he'd bolted to God only knew where.

It took them several minutes, but eventually they located him curled up under a staircase on the third floor.

Badrick peeked under the stairs, eyeing his partner's huddled form. "Dude, what the hell are you doing?"

Reynolds bent down beside him. "Hood, are you alright? Why are you—"

"Wait! Shhh!" Zale stuck his fingers on both of their lips with expert aim. "Do you hear that?"

Badrick did his best to—utterly strained his ears to listen.

Even utilised powers.

But he heard nothing at all out of the ordinary.

"What? What do you hear?"

Zale presented them with a cheerful smile. "This: *Bleeeeeeeeeeurgh!*"

"What the hell is that supposed to mean, Hood?" Reynolds snapped, his patience obviously failing.

"It means you . . . are Zale Hood . . . and I'm not!"

"You've got that completely wrong," Badrick argued. "Are you sick, man? Do you have a fever?"

"I think it's possible," Reynolds addressed him, ignoring Zale completely now as he started to sing out of tune. "We should take him to the Medical Wing. He could be seriously ill."

"Agreed."

Horas watched from the other end of the hallway as Reynolds and

Badrick tried their best to prise Zale's body out from beneath the staircase. He frowned at their failed attempts, wishing he could help.

A brief moment later, Horas felt a surge of demonic energy pulse through his metaphysical body. He turned and grimaced at the sight of a very angry looking Zale, as pointless as this action was.

Zale huffed indignantly and glared at his body. "How long do you think it'll take these idiots to figure out what's actually wrong with me?"

Horas took a moment to think. "I would say . . . about . . . a year."

chapter
TWENTY ONE

The Daemonium felt calmer than it had for what seemed like years; the chaos of the last few days had had everyone—agents, soldiers and operatives alike—on edge. But with another victory achieved over the Kalik, the men and women of the facility seemed able to relax a little more.

Many of them now felt that no matter how bad the situation got, the Daemonium would always triumph.

Unfortunately, a most perturbed Zale Hood did not share their enthusiasm.

How could he when his life had just ended?

He sat irritably upon a bench, unseen by anyone who wandered past, his body wreaking havoc in the distance as Reynolds, Badrick and Carla tried to restrain it.

Horas sat next to him, watching the proceedings.

"I've brought this on myself," Zale sighed, shocked to hear the defeat in his voice.

He'd never heard tones like that from his own mouth before.

"I am sorry, Zale," Horas said, and Zale believed him.

Zale nodded absently, his eyes barely focused. "It's alright," he mumbled. "It's not your fault."

"It was not yours either," said Horas. "I have told you this."

A particularly screechy wail from Zale's flailing body vibrated the walls and it whizzed past them at an impressive speed, its feet padding faster than a baby deer galloping across a field.

Reynolds, Badrick and Carla gave frantic chase.

If Zale had been a physical person, Badrick would have stepped on his foot, crushing it under his heavily armoured boot.

Thankfully, just this one time, Zale was *not* physical.

"Explain it to me again." He faced Horas. "What *is* this? What happened to me? Explain literally everything."

Horas appeared to be surprised. "You have never needed anything repeated before. Are you alright?"

"You're really asking me that right now?"

Horas didn't respond to that. Instead he rolled his shoulders and sighed heavily, readying himself to explain what he'd already gone through.

Zale felt a little guilty, but under the circumstances he figured he was due *some* leeway.

"Your suspect is a Powered Resurrected. You know this because you found a Resurrected splinter in the last corpse you studied. It pricked you and you have succumbed to the illness."

Zale had to repress the urge to tell him to skip this part; he was already getting impatient. But he *had* asked Horas to include everything. It would have been incredibly contradictory to complain now.

"As best as I can understand it, your mind has split in two.

You have managed to separate yourself from the damaged part of your mind. This part of you is the logical half of your brain. The half that is over there is the half that has been affected by demonic insanity."

"But why is there a sane half?" Zale asked. "That doesn't make any sense. Why am I here? How is this possible? And why aren't *I* the one in control of the body?"

"I am not the expert on this matter, Zale," Horas told him, "despite my extensive knowledge. I have never seen this before. I can only offer you conjecture. I believe that your status as an Enthraller has rendered you . . . *half* immune.

"Demons can appear on a spiritual plane of existence within their Enthrallers. I think that because you are an Enthraller, your lucid mind can appear to your crazy mind in the same way that I appear to you.

"Somehow you have tapped into my ability and are doing that right this second. You are appearing to Zale Hood as a sane part of the brain, spawned by my presence in your soul. He can see you at this very moment. He can see both of us. Unfortunately, he is not in any state to recognise either of us."

Zale scoffed angrily. "Well, that's just mental."

"I have to agree with you on that one. It would be better if you were completely afflicted. Having to watch as your body runs amok, life over, with your friends unable to aid you? It must be soul wrenching."

Zale gave him the mother of all scowls. *"Thank you, Horas!"* he hissed icily. "What would I do without your wonderful support?"

Horas visibly winced. "I apologise, Zale."

He could barely hear himself think over Carla's gut-wrenching sobs, her hands cradling Zale's head as he slumbered under the hypnosis a helpful agent had used. A small child-like smile of innocence played on the veteran's face as he breathed slowly, his chest rising gently with each intake of air.

Badrick could barely stand to look.

Something strange was happening in his own chest.

He wasn't sure what it was; he recognised it, but couldn't remember the name of it.

It was annoyingly uncomfortable.

Not to mention distracting. They had to face the situation that stood before them and this sensation now spreading to his stomach was not helping in any way.

He cleared his throat, doing his best to ignore the complaints of his body, and exhaled breathlessly. "We're in agreement, then? Zale has demonic insanity."

His words seemed to echo around him, almost as if the air itself had become hollow with the anguish that now flooded the room. In the space of a few minutes, Carla had broken down, and Reynolds had gone from the strong, powerful figure he'd always been to a broken shell of a man. He stared at Zale's calm face with distress, his body limp and on its knees, his hands resting uselessly by his sides.

"I can't believe this," he whispered. "When did this happen?"

"I don't know," Badrick said truthfully. "He seemed fine before the fight."

"Then it was before that time," Reynolds stated. "It takes two hours for the poison to spread." Reynolds shrugged pathetically. "But who knows? The splinter would have dissolved by now."

"It would have dissolved straight away," Badrick elaborated.

Carla's cries of sorrow grew louder as she unburied her face from Zale's shoulder. "Isn't there . . . something . . . we can do?" she stammered.

Reynolds was the one who answered. He shook his head in

great upset, his tone suggesting he was in mourning over the death of someone close to him—to tell the truth, Badrick figured demonic insanity wasn't too far from dying.

"There's no way to reverse it," the sergeant mumbled. "The fate that has befallen Hood is permanent."

"No!" Carla moaned, stroking Zale's face. "No! No, no, no, no!"

Reynolds reached out and gently put his hand on her shoulder. "I am so sorry, Carla . . . "

". . . but there's no known cure."

Zale walked up behind the kneeling Reynolds and glared at the back of his head with an anger he couldn't help but allow to overcome him. "You suck, Reynolds!"

At that very moment, his body's eyes flashed open and out from the mouth came, *WHEEEEEEE!*"

Zale turned his glare upon himself and snapped, "Shut up . . . *me!*"

"At least we know that our bad guy is a Powered Resurrected," Badrick said, his voice worryingly smooth and calm. "This proves it. He's been messing with Zale since the first day. It was him. I'm sure of it."

Zale scoffed at his partner's matter-of-fact tone; trust broken little Badrick to be commonsensical at a time like this! He *should* have been emotional and worried, not smooth and *pissing* logical!

Zale tried cuffing him over the head, but his hand just phased through Badrick's skull. He roared with rage at his sudden and unfair inability to hit idiots when they deserved it.

"We should try to determine when it happened," Reynolds said. "How it happened."

Fresh annoyance lit up Zale's emotions and he turned his steely gaze back upon the sergeant. "Oh, come on!" he shouted at their unhearing ears. "The autopsies! Think about how long the accursed sickness takes to manifest! God damn it, it's not hard!"

Horas' visage manifested next to him. Even though he could not see the demon's face, he could feel his disapproval. "Zale, I do not think shouting at them is going to hel—"

"You shush!" Zale snapped, cutting him off.

Unaware of their brief argument, Carla turned to Reynolds. She tried to wipe her tears away but ultimately failed. "It has to have been in the labs," she announced. "Like you said—two hours. Maybe there was a splinter hidden in one of the bodies."

Carla had always been beautiful, but all of a sudden Zale regarded her stunning person with an appreciation he had until that moment failed to achieve. He saw her brightness and flawlessness in a way he had never witnessed before. Even with her face wet and red she looked absolutely irresistible.

"My Carla!" he shouted, smirking proudly. "See? My woman can always be trusted to *not* be stupid."

"As far as I am aware, she is not *your* woman. Not yet." Horas received such a look of disdain from his Enthraller for this comment that he took several steps back.

When he was sure he was at a safe distance—not that the distance made any difference—he tried speaking again. "Zale, listen to me. You are just upsetting yourself by listening to them. Come over here. Sit with me."

He plonked himself silently upon a bench and tapped the plastic beside him.

Zale wanted to argue. He wanted to stay and take out his anger on his friends.

But . . . Horas was right.

There were only two options the Daemonium could choose from now; put him out of his misery or care for him until the day of his death.

For some strange reason, he had been gifted—or cursed—with some form of lucidity at what was probably the end of his life. Zale should have been grateful; he wasn't alone during his final moments. If he was to be put down, Horas would be there for him. If he was destined to watch a crazy version of himself wither, age and die with none of the ones he loved able to comfort him, let alone see him, then at least he wouldn't be alone through that.

Horas would be by his side forever.

Sighing with resignation, Zale obeyed the wisdom of his demon and wandered over to the bench, his movements sluggish and his shoulders sagged.

He fell through the bench on his first attempt to sit, phasing through the plastic and almost sinking beneath the floor, much to Horas' delight. But after righting himself and taking a moment to calm his frantic, emotional mind, he made a second attempt, and this time managed to make contact with the bench.

"Seems to work differently for you," Horas muttered, studying Zale with interest.

"What do you mean?"

Horas cleared his throat. "Well, my image—" he indicated to himself, "—is nothing more than a projection. My mind and soul are in *your* soul. This that you see is a controlled hologram. I simply tell it what to do as I look through its eyes. Everything it does is fake. Breathing is unnecessary. Physical actions are pointless. I cleared my throat because it is a habit from when I had a form in Hell. But I did not actually need to. I have no throat.

"But this image of you right here appears to literally be *you*. You are not a hologram, you are like a ghost. That is why you fell through the bench. That would never happen to a demon because our images are *not* us."

"Fascinating," Zale breathed disinterestedly.

He was just being moody; he actually *did* find that incredibly interesting. If there was any chance of getting out of this horrible situation he would definitely be adding it to his list of future studies.

"It would be an interesting study," Horas confirmed. "I am sure you would have done it admirably."

Zale smiled without warmth, his mood too dark for that. "Thanks, but I would probably have buggered it up." He shook his head sadly. "Like I've buggered up everything else."

For a moment there was silence between them. Neither of them spoke.

Then, Horas muttered, "You are right. Everything you touch goes wrong. You do everything incorrectly. You have made everything worse." He turned his blue visor upon Zale and he felt the demon's amused grin from somewhere deep within. "Never doubt yourself, Zale. I have told you that before.

"You are an incredible, remarkable, amazingly trustworthy human being." He shifted closer. "I would not have told the secret of why demons are creating Enthrallers to someone I did not trust."

Zale felt something pull at the edge of his lips. With a shock he realised it was pride, accompanied by the beginnings of a good mood.

It was true. Horas trusted no one.

Absolutely no one.

And becoming a person he even liked was the most strenuous task known to mankind, demon-kind and the Universe as it existed. To have achieved both of those was no mediocre achievement and Zale couldn't help but be cheered up by this knowledge—despite the secret Horas was referring to now playing at the corners of his mind.

Witnessing as well as sensing his Enthraller's emotional

improvement, Horas *'patted'* him comfortingly on the knee.

"It will be alright, Zale," he said softly. "I will always be here."

chapter
TWENTY TWO

The Medical Wing had always been one of Badrick's favourite places. When you were in this sector of the facility, you knew you were safe. The white walls and the pristine, comfortable beds had always been a place of comfort for many of the agents and soldiers who passed through here.

Everybody knew that if you arrived at the Medical Wing then you would be alright.

The familiar Melody would see to that, even if her colleagues failed to. Badrick knew her medical expertise was incredible, having been under her care himself once or twice.

Not to mention she was very pretty, and Badrick tried to laugh at the thought of men being defibrillated because of a simple glance at a beautiful woman. But he couldn't. His mouth was locked in a thin line borne out of anger and a weird . . . *cloud* he could only describe as melancholy.

It had been a long time since he'd felt like this.

It felt weird.

It felt . . . wrong.

He watched Melody insert the drip into Zale, whom they had *finally* managed to calm for the second time, thankfully this time without hypnosis. He was staring around at his surroundings, a child-like look of wonder on his face.

He squeaked humourlessly when she placed the cold metal of her stethoscope against his chest but otherwise didn't react. The medic studied his reaction sombrely as she listened to his heartbeat, a frown creasing her perfect features.

Badrick sensed that there was something irregular in Zale's situation. He could tell from the worry that emanated from her whole body. In a hurry, she removed the stethoscope and placed it beside her, swapping it for a strange looking device that was more of a machine than a tool.

Placing the headphones attached onto her head, she pressed the device against Zale's chest. A small screen flickered on when she activated it and Badrick's eyebrows rose when the screen showed nothing but a bright white light, tinted slightly green from the low quality.

"Oh my God," she murmured.

"What's wrong, Melody?" asked Reynolds, heavy worry tainting his usually authoritative tones.

Melody removed the device and turned her concerned gaze their way. "His heart is beating very fast," she said. "That's not usually what happens. Nothing but the mind was affected in any of the other cases we've seen."

"What about that device thing?" Badrick asked. "What was that?"

"I was checking on the health of his soul," Melody sighed. "Just a hunch, but I was correct. It's exuding a vast amount of energy. It's like its working overtime to accomplish something. Or maybe to maintain something."

"What does that mean?" Carla chimed in for the first time in a few hours. She'd spent a long time just staring at Zale as much as she could, taking in every little detail, not speaking nor listening, nor even averting her gaze.

Melody shook her head. "I can't say. I've never seen this before."

Reynolds rubbed his chin, an action Badrick had seen Zale himself perform many times. Now a small smile played on Badrick's lips; he found it nice to see that the pair shared habits such as this. It was proof of the deeper father/son relationship they clearly shared.

"Is he alright?" Badrick asked.

Melody's expression told him everything he needed to know. "His heart cannot keep this up. In a few days it'll give out. It'll shut down and Zale will die. We'll lose him forever."

A dull thud hit Badrick's ears and he turned inquisitively, only to see Carla on her knees, having lost the strength in her legs. Reynolds bent down and wrapped his arms around the agent, hugging her tightly.

After a moment her shaking arms appeared around his back.

Badrick stared at them, his eyes unseeing, his concentration inside his head. The feeling in his chest was really starting to hurt now. A pressure inside his ribcage, pounding at his bones and cartilage. He felt like he'd fallen into a sci-fi movie and a wriggly organism was chewing its way out of his body, it hurt so much.

He punched his chest aggressively, willing the sensation to go away.

It didn't work.

Anger was flooding his head now, so much so that his vision was fogging and he was starting to see red.

"What would you suggest, Melody?" Reynolds asked her.

"He's not in pain," the medic told them. "So I wouldn't suggest drastic action. Let him live his final days. Spend them with him. It's the best you can do."

"Alright," Reynolds nodded. "Carla, take the next week off, got it? I don't care what the Agent Commanders tell you. I'm on the Council. I have the authorisation to issue these orders." He turned to Badrick. "Badrick, I . . . "

"It's alright," he said, knowing what the sergeant would say. With the Kalik attacks growing more and more frequent there was absolutely no chance of him having any break in the action whatsoever. If and when the Kalik raided another location, they needed the power of Daemnos. "I know what's needed of me."

"Take what time you can get," Reynolds said stubbornly. "I plan to."

"You're a Council Member, Reynolds," Melody said softly. "You're needed. The rest of them probably won't let you."

Reynolds roared—with uncharacteristic malice—multiple swear words describing exactly what he thought of the Council. Badrick jumped out of his skin, as did the medic. As her ears were so close to his mouth when he bellowed, Carla flinched dramatically and tightly squeezed her eyes, her eardrums probably ringing with agony.

"I don't care what those useless idiots have to say," the sergeant uttered a little more calmly. "As far as I'm concerned, they're responsible for this. They've forced Zale to keep everything secret even though they are to blame. If he hadn't felt like he had to keep everything hushed he might have had the confidence to tell us he'd been pricked by a splinter."

"You think that's why he didn't mention it?" Badrick asked,

nonplussed; he hadn't even thought about the fact that Zale said nothing about it.

"I reckon so," Reynolds hissed murderously. "It's the Council's goddamn fault."

"And now he has some kind of heart problem," Carla snarled just as darkly. "This wouldn't have happened if the Council were competent enough to prevent thefts of deadly weaponry.

"And now he's going to die."

*

Standing beneath the sergeant's stern gaze was unbelievably uncomfortable. Badrick had almost forgotten what it was like feeling subservient to someone.

Great power could make anyone overly confident and Badrick was no exception.

So it was a testament to Reynolds' sheer influence that beads of sweat now trickled down Badrick's forehead.

He waited, swaying nervously, for Reynolds to answer the question he'd put forward three minutes before. Wishing the man would speak already, he found his concentration coasting to Zale's current predicament. Thinking of his partner drifting in and out of consciousness—if you could refer to Zale's current state as that— was painful in ways Badrick couldn't discern.

This . . . *feeling* in his chest was still as unbearable as ever. Yet a*gain*, he got the niggling feeling he was missing something.

Something so very important.

Badrick got no further chance to brood on the subject, as Reynolds had quite suddenly slammed his hands against the desk so violently it made the legs buckle.

"Damn it, Varner!" he sighed. "I can't say I'm entirely fond of this idea."

Badrick didn't say anything. He was too nervous.

"I would rather spend these next few days comforting Carla and visiting Zale before we no longer can." The sergeant clenched a fist tightly, communicating his fury and sadness. But then he took a breath and relaxed his fingers, placing his hand gently upon the table. "But you are right. If I can say I'm happy to ignore my Council duties to spend time with Zale then I can say the same to help you."

Reynolds placed himself in his office chair, feeling up the arms as he stretched his legs under his desk. "You want me to help you come up with what to do next," he voiced the request that had started this whole thing.

"We've lost Zale," Badrick said matter-of-factly. "But we still have a Resurrected running around and killing people. I can't do this on my own. I need your help."

"What exactly do you want from me, Badrick?"

Badrick took the opportunity to seat himself opposite Reynolds. As he fell into the chair's cushion, the memory of the last time he sat here jumped into his head.

That had been a very different situation.

Quite frankly, it had been far less stressful.

"You know Zale better than anyone," he said. "What do you think he would do now? I've read his reports on the autopsies and there's nothing. He never even got to finish them and I can't do it."

"Are you asking me to finally allow other agents on the case?"

"No, we can't do that. I just need help."

Reynolds tapped his finger against his chin in thought, nodding his head slowly. When he next spoke it was with a dull, resigned tone. "I can't say I know what Zale planned to do next."

"I'm not so sure *he* knew what to do next," Badrick corrected him. "What I'm asking is for help thinking like him."

"Thinking like him?"

"Yeah." Badrick nodded himself. "If we want to catch this Resurrected, we need to think like Zale."

It was the worst feeling in the whole world.

To see the one you loved—the only one to own your heart completely—in such a hopeless situation was like having someone tear into your chest with a kitchen grater.

Zale had always looked so majestic to Carla.

So beautiful.

So powerful.

Whenever he walked into a room everything would light up. His natural aura was awe-inspiring, as though angels cast light over him at all times of the day.

To know how he was, how he should be, and to see him reduced to nothing but pale ash in comparison . . .

It broke Carla's heart.

Once those eyes had looked at her with such brightness that a part of her truly believed her feelings were reciprocated. That Zale's heart belonged to her as hers belonged to him.

But she always held back. Always too scared to discover that he did not care for her the same way.

She'd spent her life at the Daemonium wondering, wasting time with hopeful flirting and occasional forays into a physical relationship.

And now it was too late. She'd left it too long.

When he looked at her now, he did not see her.

With unrecognising eyes, his gaze would cast over her face and onto something else more interesting to him.

There was nothing worse.

Softly, she took his head in her hands and stroked his cheek as his eyes fluttered gently, his mind clouded by the drugs the nurse gave him in an attempt to calm his raging heart. Carla wished she could gaze into those eyes she loved so much.

Revel in their otherworldly blueness.

There was nothing more beautiful than his eyes when they saw her enter a room. Nothing made her heart race faster than when he looked at her.

But he would never see her again.

The blackness that filled her stomach at this realisation was sharp. Darkness clouded her mind and heart. All happiness—all *potential* for happiness—was gone, dragged away kicking and choking by the black cloud.

The only thing that stopped it spreading forever was the overwhelming sorrow lurking within her heart; pounding, screaming, fitting crazily.

Tears jumped from her eyes as she blinked in an effort to hold them back. A pressure pressed down on her shoulder; the nurse was holding her in comfort. After the woman retracted her hand, she left the Medical Wing altogether, giving Carla privacy with the damned Zale.

Damned.

No exaggeration. That was what he was. He'd dedicated his life to the service of the Daemonium and this was what he'd received as reward.

Carla fought to stop her grip from tightening on Zale's face, not wishing to cause him any pain. As she fought her feelings, the corner of her eye picked up something unnatural standing awkwardly in the corner of the Medical Wing.

She didn't need to check to know it was Acro. The hellspawn was watching her in confusion, unable to comprehend the emotions coursing through her body. The pointless being was broken; she'd always thought so. Just like the rest of his kind.

But his presence did serve one purpose.

She remembered what she had forgotten in the face of her beloved's impending passing. She remembered what Acro told her only hours before.

It was a memory that made her feel all the more worse, yet somehow hopeful in that strange human way that denied all possible logic. Her eyes found Zale's face once again—she had closed them before—and she leaned in to speak in his ear.

"You listen to me," she whispered, her words breaking from the strain of keeping her voice calm. His eyes fluttered more violently as her tones hit his eardrums. "You have to get over this. You have to.

"You can't leave yet.

"You have to stay.

"I need you," she whispered finally, placing a shaking hand on her lower abdomen, her fingers spreading over her uniform. "*We need you.*"

Never before had Badrick seen Reynolds looking so nonplussed. It was disconcerting to see a man of his confidence and calibre this ineffectual.

If Reynolds couldn't do what he'd asked, then Badrick didn't have a hope.

Thirty minutes.

That was how long they'd dedicated to this task with no result in sight.

"I don't know what to say to that, Varner," Reynolds said. "I don't think that plan would work."

"But if we cornered the Resurrected," Badrick insisted. "If we found a way to lure him out of his hole we could—"

"And how would we do that?"

Badrick's voice stuck in his throat. He had absolutely no idea how to answer.

Think like Zale, he said.

Reynolds could do it, he said.

With the sergeant's help, I could do it, he said.

But the more they tried the more Badrick realised how sincerely stupid he was. How could he have been so vain to think *he* could do this? How could he have dared to ask Reynolds to do this?

The irrefutable fact was that no one but *Zale* could think like Zale.

And they weren't bright enough to come anywhere near.

Not even close.

The rage he felt at this realisation made Badrick feel uncomfortable. The anger was now building to a point where he could no longer handle it. Exhaling roughly, he slammed his hands onto the table, staring wide-eyed at the wood, breathing heavily.

They needed Zale.

That was the truth.

But Zale was going to die.

Zale . . .

Dead.

Against his will, Badrick's fingers tightened, scratching the wood as they became claws, then tight fists.

Zale was going to die?

No.

Not if he had anything to say about it.

Reynolds called after him as Badrick violently sprung to his feet and stormed out the office, almost crashing into two agents as they passed the door. Badrick ignored their snappy comments, pushing his way through the corridor.

He didn't stop, barging uncaringly through agents and soldiers alike, until he reached the very bottom of the HQ. Once there, he looked up. The walkways loomed over him, blocking the cold winter sunlight that shone through the window high up on the wall and casting dark shadows over the ground floor.

He closed his eyes, taking deep breaths, staying that way for several minutes. Badrick didn't even open them when Reynolds finally caught up, demanding an explanation.

"I'm not going to just sit there and let him die."

Reynolds' expression softened and he reached out a hand to Badrick's shoulder. "It's OK, Badrick."

Badrick shrugged him off.

Then immediately felt guilty; Reynolds didn't deserve his anger.

"I'm sorry, sir," Badrick said, finally looking the man in the eye. "But I'm not accepting it. I'm going to do something about it."

"What do you expect to be able to do, Varner?" the sergeant asked him, now attempting to use logic in his argument. "You don't have the power to stop this. You're not a god."

"No, but I have a demon Royal in my soul," Badrick said, "and I *know* he can do something. He has every demonic power the Universe has ever invented."

"Which means *you* have every power. If you can't do it, then logic dictates Daemnos can't either."

"I have all Daemnos' powers, Reynolds," Badrick sighed, "but not his every skill. I *know* he can help!"

"*How* can you know?"

"Because!" Badrick caught himself, forcing himself to calm down. "Otherwise there's no hope."

Zale wandered over to Badrick, eyeing him as he sat in the very middle of the Main Hall. Around him, Reynolds and Carla ushered everyone out, moving them into the smaller rooms attached. The

BCR, RCR, recreational rooms, library, armoury, generator room and other facilities became packed with hundreds and hundreds of Enthrallers.

Those with more sense headed off to the Quarters Tower or other parts of the Daemonium.

"What's going on, Reynolds," an Agent Commander demanded.

"Operative Varner wants to try something," Reynolds said. "You've heard of the Zale Hood issue?"

"I have." The Agent Commander seemed genuinely upset. "I am very sorry, Reynolds. I know you were close."

"Well, don't offer your sympathies just yet. Badrick thinks he can help him."

Many were surprised but hopeful after hearing this and wished them luck, most not questioning the determination of the Enthraller who boasted Daemnos as a demon.

Others were not so gracious. Zale was as unpopular as he was praised and a worrying number of people refused to give them the space Badrick required. These hatreds towards him were borne out of obvious jealousy, Zale felt; he never did anything to offend anyone apart from being naturally better than them.

Zale knew he was being arrogant, but watching these people act and speak so callously in the face of his predicament angered him so much that he felt they deserved to be reminded of how crap they were.

However, Reynolds did not need to shame anyone to make them subservient. As a Council Member, he exerted his authority over them, forcing these fools out of the way.

"We have work to do!" one of the agents argued.

"You don't need to do it in the Main Hall, do you!?" Reynolds shut her down instantly. "So shut it and get back to work."

Zale could see Reynolds was putting all his hope into whatever

Badrick was planning, despite his training and own wit, which would be instructing him not to. Reynolds wasn't usually this unreasonable with other members of the Daemonium, no matter how annoying they were.

He felt a strong sense of kinship with Reynolds right then, knowing this was all for him.

Many of the Council Members attempted to resist Reynolds as well, the higher-ups trying to exert their own command over Reynolds, but he managed to combat them with a cunning combination of logic and intimidation.

Reynolds was too smart to be defeated in a verbal debate.

Finally, Badrick, Reynolds and Carla were alone on the Main Hall's ground floor with Zale and Horas observing invisibly on the sidelines. However they weren't the only watchers; dozens upon dozens of Enthrallers were crowded on the walkways above, gazing down inquisitively.

Zale craned his neck to look up at them. "What in God's name is Badrick doing?" he asked.

"I have no idea," Horas answered.

Zale couldn't blame him for having no clue. The pair of them had done nothing for quite a while, just sitting calmly on the bench Horas directed him to some time before. As instructed, Zale hadn't followed his friends, hadn't listened to what they said.

They only picked up on anything strange when Badrick stormed into the HQ, shouting at people.

Neither of them could possibly know what was occurring here.

"OK, Badrick, we've done as you requested," Reynolds declared. "I've stretched my reputation to its limit. This is the last time I'm ever going to fulfil one of your ridiculous requests. Will you please now tell us why?"

"Yeah, right," Zale scoffed. "Reynolds will always let us ask for crazy things."

Badrick didn't answer for a moment. He stared straight ahead, his eyes glazed over, chewing his lip and obviously in deep thought.

"Let's face it, Sarge. We can't do anything without Zale. We need him for this Kalik problem."

"Is that how you're justifying whatever it is you're doing?" Reynolds deadpanned. "Why do you need to justify it at all? I'm not going to like it, am I?"

"We don't have Zale right now," said Badrick, ignoring the question. "We have a pathetic excuse for a Zale."

"Hey!" Zale couldn't help but exclaim indignantly.

"I have one of the most powerful demons inside me. I *know* Daemnos can help." Badrick's expression turned to one of anger. "But he doesn't talk to me. He has the unique ability to whisper to me from inside my soul but he never appears and talks." Badrick aimed his gaze at Reynolds. "So I'm going to force him to talk."

Horas visibly jumped as Zale suddenly shouted, "No! No, don't do that!"

However, the demon seemed to share his panic, as he also hollered, "Is he an idiot?"

"No," Zale sighed. "He's just desperate."

"I'm not going to leave Zale to die," Badrick continued.

"Don't do this!" Zale stepped closer to Badrick, trying to kick him on the leg. Just as before, his limb just phased straight through it. "This is exceptionally dangerous. He shouldn't do this. I'm not worth it."

"Yes, you are."

Zale stopped flailing. "What?"

Horas stopped spluttering. "What?"

Reynolds stared at Badrick in confusion. "What?"

"Did he just . . ." murmured Horas. "Did he just hear you?"

Badrick blinked, looking quite lost. His eyes were misted over and he swayed where he sat. He blinked a second time, clearing his vision, then said, "Sorry . . . Nothing. I had a weird moment."

Zale saw him glance around as if looking for the source of a noise he might have heard. Zale waved his hands in front of his partner's face, wondering if Badrick actually had the power to communicate with entities such as Zale's current form.

When nothing came from it—Badrick's eyes as unseeing as always—he bitterly gave up.

"This is a risky ritual," Horas said. "If he is doing what I think he is doing."

"Oh, he is," Zale tutted.

"Does he not know how dangerous it is?"

"Of course he does."

"Still," Horas said. "Despite that . . . This is not wise."

"No," Zale breathed. He glanced at his demon tensely, thoughts of everything that could go wrong darting through his head. "No, it isn't."

Meanwhile, Badrick wasn't letting Reynolds ask any more questions. He requested that Reynolds go with Carla and head back to the Medical Wing to be with Zale. Apparently, when Zale woke up he would need his friends around him.

Badrick closed his eyes, his legs crossed tightly and his hands on his knees. He took five very deep breaths.

Then he began to chant.

Voavar hukta vi yta wovas T' k' Sola alk ista wo dak mon ym upa loc

T' . . .

"Is that not the Banishment Ritual?" Horas enquired. "This is not the ritual I believed him to be planning." That was clear as day; Zale could tell through his tone of voice that Horas had no idea what Badrick was up to, which would be worrying the demon.

Horas was supposed to understand everything regarding demonology.

Zale strained his ears to listen, similarly confused as to what Badrick was doing. From what he could hear Horas was right; Badrick *was* using the words of the Banishment Ritual.

. . . Voltr qe kam ormant iltrruk qe an selek vi ak, milm ot iu . . .

"He's saying it backwards!" Zale exclaimed, understanding dawning on him. He grinned, laughing at Badrick's daring.

"What is so funny?"

"He's chanting backwards. A ritual to trap a demon chanted backwards will . . . " He hesitated to go over it once more in his head. "I think Badrick is . . . The Banishment Ritual spoken backwards will have the opposite effect. I think . . . maybe . . . I'm not really sure."

"Tell me, Zale," Horas said. "Tell me what you think is happening."

. . . osteruk w oak dolke vi pol sah . . .

Zale hesitated before answering, unsure of whether or not he had deduced this correctly. He didn't want to speak if he was incorrect . . . If Horas didn't understand, then how could he possibly . . .

Deciding to throw caution to the winds, he told Horas what he had concluded, even if it sounded ridiculous to the demon.

"I think the chant is going to have the opposite effect, but because Badrick is using the ritual on himself it won't summon Daemnos. The effect won't be that Daemnos is released rather than banished. That would be impossible until Badrick dies. But I think it will drag him to the surface so that Badrick can force him into some kind of conference inside his head.

"He's doing this because summoning Daemnos wouldn't be enough. He needs to use the Royal's own crazy power against him by morphing a different one for his own uses.

"As long as it works, the energies will be chaotic because it's not what it's supposed to do, but they will be strong as a result.

"No other demon could do it, but Daemnos' power can." Zale eyed Horas nervously. "Does that sound ridiculous?"

Horas actually tutted. "Stop doubting yourself!" he exclaimed uncharacteristically. "If you really require validation of your skills, then yes I believe you are right. Your deductions ring true to me."

Zale felt relieved, though a little embarrassed.

. . . ak est yokr Monkavil kam gultr oe!

A ferocious force of power exploded from Badrick's body, knocking back anything that was unlucky enough to be in its way. Even Zale and Horas were thrown away by its unforgiving onslaught.

It knocked him so hard that his concentration slipped and he phased right through the ground.

Struggling in the dark, confined, alone and a little scared, he focused heavily on floating back up to the surface. After a few terrifying moments of blackness the reassuring halo of sunlight reappeared as he crested over the metal floor. He pulled himself up, glancing around to ensure that Horas was well.

He found him in the corner, standing back up. Horas gave him a shaky thumbs up—shaky because of his unfamiliarity with the human gesture—and indicated for Zale to look at Badrick.

The operative's eyes were wide open, his head bent back slightly as though he were looking up at something above him.

His eyes were blood red.

Zale nodded knowingly, more to himself than anything.

Badrick had achieved his goal.

He'd summoned Daemnos.

chapter
TWENTY THREE

Badrick's eyes shot open.

Reynolds was gone.

Carla was gone.

The spectators above him were gone.

He was alone.

A little confused, Badrick stumbled to his feet. He felt quite weak, though he had expected that to happen. The power he'd just called upon was immense. Forcing a Royal to do anything was no easy feat.

Having said that, he wasn't so sure he had succeeded.

Daemnos didn't appear to be anywhere in sight.

Badrick glanced around, desperately hoping that he would catch a glimpse of the manic demon prince. But all he could see was a strange, greyish tinge to the space around him.

He frowned; what was with this weird colouration?

He didn't have the answer.

And he didn't even get a chance to rack his brains to find one.

Before he could make another move a terrifying sound hit his ears.

Creepy, echoing, childish laughter.

He spun on his heel, desperately trying to find the source.

The echoing giggles grew louder.

Until it was all he could hear.

Drowning out all other noises.

He slammed his hands against his ears, squinting in pain.

He spun once more—

AAAAAARGH!

Badrick coughed in surprise as Daemnos' helmeted head came into view, so close to his face that his nose almost brushed on the visor and that familiar—yet no less horrifying—scream filled his ears. He fell back, landing heavily on the metal floor.

Daemnos' threw back his head and laughed in that same manic cackle he always used. Only . . . there was something wrong with his voice. It wasn't how it was supposed to sound. It didn't sound like Daemnos talking.

"We're in your head, ickle bickle Badrick!" the demon caterwauled shrilly.

Badrick grumbled angrily, pushing himself to his feet. "You sound—"

"Different?" Daemnos cackled.

"More than different," scowled Badrick. He glared at the demon. "You're using Zale's voice. Why?"

Until that point, Daemnos had been cackling incessantly, never stopping, never quietening. But after Badrick spoke he abruptly stopped.

He lowered his head to face Badrick properly. Badrick glared back; he got the distinct impression that the demon was trying to intimidate him and he refused to give Daemnos the satisfaction of knowing he'd succeeded.

"The link," Daemnos said suddenly, far more serious than he'd ever sounded before.

"The link?" Badrick took a moment to remember what he was talking about. "Do you mean the link between Horas and you? The one Lucikefer made?"

"Yes. It's still active."

"I'm aware."

"You are aware of nothing!" Daemnos snapped, still with Zale's voice. "This is more than your average supernatural link, Baddy Badrick. I don't like it. But I now have to live with it until one of you dies."

Badrick rolled his eyes. "What are you talking about, you dramatic idiot? A link between demons is a link. They're all the same."

Daemnos returned to laughing. "You speak as if you know anything but even the Daemonium doesn't understand it."

"I know what you know," Badrick reminded him. "Demons used to link all the time back during your reign in Hell."

"Not like this," Daemnos argued. "Not this link. There's an unseen variable to it. Somewhere. Somewhere hidden. Deep inside. Woven into its strands. Even I can't locate it. That angers me!" He spread his hands and screamed, "A LOT!!!!"

Badrick took a step back, wary of Daemnos' exceedingly erratic behaviour. He'd always been mental but he seemed to have entered an all time high level of insanity.

Daemnos didn't let up. "The link connected me to all of your friend's memories and thoughts. I know everything he knows." Daemnos paused, breathing heavily. "At least, I think I do. Only up to the point we connected. I don't have instant access to current events inside that egg of his."

"How is that possible?"

Another burst of grating laughter, then, "I don't know, Badrick. I don't know. I don't know. I don't know. I don't know.

"But it allows me to adopt his voice. Better and more focused than simple mimicry. Strange, isn't it? Amazingly fun, though. *Peter picked a puck of pickle peppers.*"

Badrick ignored the demon's error.

He couldn't have cared less.

Because something had just occurred to him.

Something so large that it literally turned his world upside down.

"You don't sound like me."

Daemnos stopped rambling and turned his focus back to Badrick. "What's that?"

"You don't sound like me. I never thought so, but you're supposed to sound like me. All demons are supposed to sound like their Enthraller's a little bit." Badrick glared at Daemnos, wondering if he had orchestrated this himself. "But you don't sound like me at all. Now you're using his voice, I can finally hear it properly. All this time . . . it's been Zale."

Daemnos' screams of laughter were louder and more screechy than ever before. "He finally notices!"

"I knew I recognised Zale's voice from somewhere," Badrick sighed. "I *knew* it. I thought it was from when he drove past me in the time travel mess that Lucikefer caused. But it's from *you*."

"Are you done rambling?" Daemnos snapped. "Now *you* sound like Zale. Quiet!"

Anger bubbled up inside him, but Badrick didn't act upon it. As much as he hated to admit it, Daemnos was right. He had come here—into his *own* damn head—for a purpose.

They had dawdled enough. *He* had dawdled enough. Zale couldn't wait any longer.

"You have come here to ask me to revive your friend," Daemnos stated before he got a chance to speak.

"Can you do it?"

"Badrick!" he laughed. "Don't dance the ignorant dance. You know I can."

"Alright!" Badrick snapped. "Then let me rephrase the question. *Will* you do it?"

"Maybe."

A terribly nauseating sense of desperation welled up in Badrick's stomach—it was odd; he hadn't felt like this in a long time. It made him feel incredibly sick. "Please, Daemnos. We need him!"

"That's true, you do," Daemnos agreed. He threw his finger into the air and wiggled it slowly. "But, Badrick, do not grovel. No one ever gets anything by grovelling. You're the Enthraller of the most powerful demon alive! What are you grovelling for? Besides . . . Makes me look as pathetic as you . . . through association."

"I . . . " Badrick didn't know what to say.

What was wrong with him?

For over a week now, Badrick had been strong. He was confident and powerful. He always had a voice. People listened and obeyed him.

But Daemnos had left him speechless and Badrick had no idea how to respond. In the face of this dark and psychologically deranged creature, he was abruptly aware of how small and insignificant he was.

"How about this?" the Royal spoke up. "If you let me take over your body for two hours so that I can ravage the angelic Carla Hunter, then I'll do it."

"What!?" Badrick screeched. "I'm not letting you kill Carla."

Again, Daemnos' irritating laugh bounced off the walls like a series of tennis balls. "You innocent little freak. I said *ravage*, not savage." His delighted grin was evident in his voice.

Understanding eluded Badrick for a few seconds. He frowned at Daemnos, not understanding the difference.

And then it hit him.

"Urgh, God, no!" He threw his arm to his mouth in a display of revulsion. "I'm not letting you do that."

"Oh, you prissy little bitch!" Daemnos chuckled delightedly.

When Badrick heard that laugh he realised that Daemnos had not been serious in his request; he just wanted to entice an entertaining reaction from him. Badrick grumbled darkly and lowered his hand.

"If I do this for you, child," Daemnos started, "then you will do something for me."

Sensing progress, Badrick stepped forward. "Anything," he stated. "Except . . . that other request," he added sickly.

"You make sure Zale catches your bad guy," Daemnos demanded. "The next time you have an encounter, you will scan for link energy at the site. Do you understand? Scan for demonic link energy.

"Why?"

"Because I said so!" the demon screamed, his supernaturally augmented voice reverberating the fake walls of Badrick's mind's construct of the HQ. "Your baddie, Baddie Badrick, has his own link. Make sure you catch him. He is the biggest thorn in my side since Cera."

Sarah, Badrick echoed in his head. *Who the hell is Sarah?*

"And after that, you watch out for Zale, Badrick. He knows things. Important things. And he can do things too." Daemnos chuckled one last time. "You watch out for him."

"Wha . . . what?" Badrick stammered, confused and wary. "What do you mean?"

The Royal did not answer him. He stepped closer, each step made with cruel purpose.

He approached.

Intimidating

Daunting.

He drew in unnervingly close, his visor now only inches from Badrick's face.

Despite the strength he had . . .

Despite all the power and the confidence he'd achieved in the last few weeks . . .

Despite it all Badrick felt terrified at the demon's proximity.

Feelings such as these were so alien to him that his head began to pound with the stress of it all.

Daemnos reached up and grabbed hold of his black uniform, pulling him closer against his will.

"We have a deal," he hissed.

A flash of light blinded Badrick. A ringing started in his ears. And before he knew it, a solidity he hadn't realised he was missing returned to his aching body. In a rush of noise, the clamour from the onlookers above him returned.

But he ignored it.

He was too busy trying to control his breathing to care about their tumult.

Despite his ragged gasps, he managed to open his mouth and speak out to the room, "Did it work?"

"Did it work?" Badrick repeated through pained breathing.

Zale looked down at him sadly, wishing he could provide his partner with some kind of comfort.

"No, man," he whispered. "It didn't wor—"

A searing flash of red light engulfed him, obscuring his vision. His skin stretched agonisingly. He screamed in torture as the wispy material that made up his current form was dispelled and replaced by corporeal matter.

On a soft, clean bed in the Medical Wing, Zale gasped cool, fresh air.

chapter
TWENTY FOUR

Zale did his best to breathe through the clump of golden, curly hair that slinked down his throat. Carla didn't let up, not caring that she was suffocating her best friend. As long as she could touch and grip every inch of a living, healthy Zale she didn't seem to care what else happened.

Badrick smiled at the sight of them.

A feeling of relief flowed soothingly through his body, cooling and relaxing his sore muscles. He knew he'd be alright in a moment, but for now the sensation was a good substitute for actual health.

"You're welcome."

He turned to Daemnos, who was watching the pair next to him.

"Thank you, Daemnos."

"Like I said." The Royal presented him with a mock bow, then turned and walked away. Badrick couldn't help but laugh. This was a pointless action—Daemnos just wanted to make a cool exit.

"Daemnos!" Badrick stopped him.

"What, human?"

"Why haven't you helped us before this?"

"I don't like talking," Daemnos laughed. "I'm shy."

Badrick scowled a little aggressively. "And here I thought you were on our side. Was I wrong?"

"*Of course* I'm on your side, Badrick. I simply live by the philosophy of the late Mawr Burakka."

His eyebrow rising, Badrick asked, "Which is?"

Daemnos chuckled and recited, "*Doesn't mean I'm going to do it for you.*"

And with that, he vanished, returning to the recesses of Badrick's soul. Badrick gazed at the empty space the demon left in his absence, chewing his lip thoughtfully. He was more than certain that, even if he was given a thousand years to do so, he would never determine the enigmatic motives of Daemnos.

He was broken out of his thoughts by the sound of Zale muttering with a shaky voice, "Really? Are you sure?"

He turned back just in time to see Carla nodding. "Acro told me."

Zale stared at Carla for moment, and Badrick frowned, suddenly dying to know what they were talking about.

"What—"

He was interrupted by Zale pulling Carla even closer than before. She buried her face into his neck, holding him just as tight.

"That's the best news I've ever heard," Zale whispered in her ear, further agitating Badrick. "We'll figure it out."

Carla nodded from inside the mess of her hair.

Badrick was going to use the silence that ensued after that to get appraised, but he entirely missed his chance when Zale pried the red-faced Carla from his body and immediately proceeded to tell them everything that had happened from his point of view. What it was like to be afflicted by the insanity, what Horas had told him about his experience, what he'd seen them do.

Resigning himself to finding out what the exchange had entailed later, Badrick allowed the conversation to continue.

"Seriously?" Reynolds asked him. "You were conscious the whole time?"

Reynolds had a wide grin on his face. He was clearly happy to see Zale well, sane and alive.

"Aye, I was," Zale coughed, still recovering from the crushing he'd received at the hands of Carla. "It wasn't all that bad, to be honest. The worst part was watching you guys make so many stupid mistakes."

Badrick laughed at that. "How many mistakes did we make?"

"*About fifty!*" Zale screeched.

An agent laughed as he brushed past Reynolds, looking back to grin in their direction.

"Yeah!?" Badrick shouted after him indignantly. "You keep laughing . . . *Chuckles.*"

"I'm so glad you're OK," Carla said, hugging Zale again. "I was so worried."

"I know," Badrick heard Zale whisper into her hair. Smiling himself, he reached forward and tapped Zale on the shoulder, unable to express his relief any other way. He gazed back at Reynolds, expecting to see the same look on his face.

But Reynolds was no longer smiling.

"What's wrong?" he asked the sergeant.

Reynolds ground his teeth with a troubled look shadowing his features. "I was just thinking . . . What if all the victims of demonic insanity go through what Zale did? That means they watched us kill them. That's . . . horrible."

"Horas said it was only because I was an Enthraller," said Zale. "So I wouldn't worry about it."

Reynolds scoffed. "Then the infected Enthrallers saw us. That doesn't make it any better."

No one had an answer to that, and Reynolds' worries had totally sobered the mood. Eventually, it was Badrick who broke the silence. "Well, either way, we can thank Daemnos for his help. He really pulled through."

Everyone murmured in agreement, nodding and pointing at each other.

Though Reynolds mumbled, "Still don't trust him."

"You don't?" Badrick queried, surprised. "But you voted for me and him to stay when I came back."

"He's still a Royal," Reynolds scowled in his direction. Badrick got the feeling the look was directed at Daemnos himself, who was probably watching through Badrick's eyes.

"Speaking of Daemnos," Zale said softly, "I'd like a private word with Badrick, if that's alright."

The other two agreed, giving him warm smiles and once more welcoming him back to a life of sanity. Before he left, Reynolds shook his hand. Carla got in one more hug.

For a moment, Badrick thought that the two of them would kiss.

Finally.

They stared at one another, eyes boring deep into the other's. Time seemed to stretch endlessly. Seemed to slow . . . Almost stopped. Badrick really thought that they might finally get it over with and admit how they both really felt.

But then the two of them appeared to remember he was there, and they simply smiled. Their hands refused to part as they moved from each other, but eventually Carla slid her fingers from Zale's and she left the Medical Wing.

"You two," Badrick sighed tiredly, though he couldn't stop grinning. "What did I tell you earlier?"

"Forget that," Zale huffed. "I have something I want to talk to you about."

"What's up?"

Badrick's partner regarded him for a moment or two, his fingers playing with themselves almost nervously. It took him a while to speak, but he finally did so, beginning with, "Over the last few days I've noticed a change in you."

"What do you mean?" Badrick asked, unsure as to what Zale was referring to. The only change Badrick was aware of in himself was his growing confidence, strength and power.

But Zale's tone of voice suggested this change was bad. Badrick was surprised. He didn't consider an increase in confidence a bad thing.

"I mean you're broken, friend," Zale said bluntly. "Your morality is totally screwed. You don't seem to care about anyone. In fact I would even go so far as to say that you can't feel emotions properly any more. That they've been damaged."

"That's ridiculous," Badrick chuckled.

Fully aware that he was lying to himself.

The moment Zale said the words an instant panic rose in his chest and—so suddenly it was nauseating—he understood the pain that had plagued his chest for so long.

His body had tried to *feel*.

But it couldn't.

He *was* broken.

"You've fallen into the trap you so desperately wanted to avoid," Zale continued, "except you're much worse than the other Enthrallers. But I think now I understand.

"I got a little glimpse into you when I was crazy. When Daemnos touched me I saw into his head, and my journeys back and forth through matter and corporealness have opened my eyes to a greater understanding of what you really went through.

"You died, Badrick, and then you were brought back to life, ready for service and battle. Daemnos saw to that. You were overloaded with knowledge and power in one big go. You didn't get to experience the *process* of learning all your skills and powers.

"You weren't exposed *gradually* to the horrors of our world; it was thrust upon you in one moment. You didn't have the benefit of a gradual increase. You never got to build a defence against the allure of demonic apathy.

"Not to mention the whole ordeal you experienced . . . I don't think anyone could survive that emotionally. Daemnos may have been able to rebuild your body to his specifications but demons are powerless against emotions.

"Daemnos said it was because of your emotional power, but I think he lied to you. In truth, he couldn't bring you back to life without your mind breaking from the stress and leaving you a vegetable. So instead he simply denied you real emotions at all."

Badrick stared at Zale, unable to fully believe what he was being told. Sure, he'd realised that his feelings had been a little messed up, but was he seriously lacking in morality? Badrick didn't believe that. Just because he didn't well up at every death or put the needs of the one before his duty did not mean he was morally reprehensible.

He opened his mouth to argue, but he never got the chance.

Zale stopped him, having not noticed he was about speak. "You have to remember how you felt. How you used to think before your death. Before you came back to life." Smiling kindly, he added, "You should find someone to hold on to. Someone to keep you good and on the right path." Zale allowed his hands to fall by his sides and his gazed averted to the window nearby, where they could see Carla standing on the walkway just outside with Reynolds. "That's what I do."

Badrick wasn't sure what to say. He had no words.

He *wanted* to say something.

He *wanted* to dispute Zale theories.

But he couldn't.

He was completely unable to formulate an effective argument.

So instead he said the only thing that came to his head.

"We have to get back to the investigation." Badrick winced, painfully aware of how pathetic that sounded.

Zale gave him the mother of all scowls and crossed his arms moodily. "Any other time," he said slowly, "I would have a go at you for changing the subject." His expression softened and he sighed tiredly. "But you're right."

Elated that Zale was playing ball with his subject-change, Badrick seized upon the opportunity with an iron grip. Grinning, he told Zale about what Daemnos had said about the link their demons shared.

"He wants us to scan for demonic link energy," Zale recited, speaking each word pointedly, "because . . . why?"

Badrick shrugged; an act that perfectly communicated his feelings on the situation. "I guess he thinks it will help. He said the guy has his own link and for whatever reason Daemnos really wants us to catch this guy."

"Or girl," Zale said.

"Or girl."

"Alright, fine," his partner agreed. "We'll check the original attack sites. The energy would have dissipated by now, but we have recordings of the areas, especially the hangar base. You never know."

"Good idea."

With a plan of action in mind, Zale jumped from the bed the medic had kept him on and headed for the door. Badrick followed, overjoyed at the idea that they might *finally* be getting somewhere.

Moving through the hallway, they emerged onto the walkway their friends had perched themselves upon. Badrick stumbled in his steps when he realised there was a third person with them—a person he recognised.

He hadn't expected to see Zale's rival, Zach, especially after having forgotten that he even existed.

The stress of the past few days had removed Zach from Badrick's consciousness entirely.

The detective smiled warmly as the pair of them approached. That *also* astonished Badrick. Not only did he never see the man smile even a little bit, but he never expected to see such a kind gesture towards his so-called hated rival.

"Zale, Badrick, I'm glad you're here," Zach said. In the split second before he next spoke, two things happened.

One; Reynolds turned to them.

Two; Badrick saw the look of irritation on his face.

Then Zach finished talking and Badrick understood why. "I have figured out who our perp is. I know who it is."

And Badrick realised that this was not a warm smile. It was a smug, victorious grin. Zach's teeth were glinting at Zale, not with kindness, but in a cocky display of conceitedness.

Wow, Badrick thought to himself. *I must be off if I can't tell the difference between kindness and a grin that arrogant.*

"Oh," Zale grinned back, though his voice was heavy with humour, "you do, *do you?*"

Bristling at Zale's mocking, Zach aggressively pointed at him and said, "I have deduced that Mawr is our culprit."

Reynolds puffed air, his eyes wide. His face was turned away from Zach, probably so that the agent wouldn't see his derision.

"You're wrong, Zach." Zale shook his head.

"I found his key card access on a storage facility," Zach snapped. "The timeline is correct. He must have been exposed to carbon monoxide and killed. It *has* to be him."

"Zach," Zale murmured, his voice less scathing and far friendlier, "I'm sorry, but you've got that all wrong." He tried to tell Zach the theories he'd shared with Badrick only a few days before, but the agent cut him off, causing Zale to visibly seethe with rage.

"I *know* we have the right suspect. Now, if you'll excuse me, I have to organise my team. We're going to find Mawr." Before anyone could stop him, Zach about-faced and charged away, vanishing through an arch.

"Idiot!" Carla snapped.

"Now now, Carla," Zale sighed. "He's just doing the best he can."

"His best isn't good enough," Badrick growled, annoyed at Zach's uncooperative attitude. "We don't have time to mess around with half baked theories. We have to—"

AAAAARGH!

Badrick's hands smashed into his ears and his eyes clenched at the pain of having the familiar scream obliterate his drums. He roared along with the noise as his friends grabbed at various parts of his body, demanding to know what was wrong.

Something spurred him to turn and he did so, spinning on his heel.

His vision now rapidly faded; his eyes might as well have not worked at all. Badrick blinked, trying to clear them, hating the impairment. He felt vulnerable without his vision.

But when he opened them, he wondered if he shouldn't clench them shut again.

He was no longer in the Daemonium.

Badrick didn't have a clue where he was; he was standing in an unfamiliar building.

And before he could even get a chance to focus, his surroundings melted impossibly, merging together like runny paint.

FLASH!

A blinding light and the setting changed. He was somewhere new and again Badrick had no idea where he now stood.

No . . . that wasn't strictly true . . . With a gasp, he realised he recognised exactly where he was.

Blazing smoke obscured his vision. Fire burned hot on his skin. Vast aircraft hangars loomed before him.

Badrick was at the military base.

Why was he—

FLASH!

With shocking suddenness, his surroundings altered *again*.

Rust.

Dirt.

Blood.

The mining facility!

FLASH!

Analogous greyness greeted him . . . Walls of concrete . . . covered in black, dried gore that peeled off the surfaces like old, decaying wallpaper.

Badrick was back at the Apostaticus base.

It looked exactly how the Daemonium had left it.

Except for one thing . . .

Though it was very reminiscent of a certain dream Badrick used to have, the presence of the figure standing before him was most unfitting.

Bloody Daemnos.

The demon vibrated, as though he was incredibly excited. And in an ecstatic whisper, he hissed, "It's starting!"

chapter
TWENTY FIVE

Without warning, the vision ended, faster and more sudden than it had appeared. Dizziness took over and Badrick almost stumbled right over the rail, saved only by the quick reflexes of Zale and Reynolds.

He placed his hand upon his head and blinked purposefully as they pulled him back, bombarding him with questions. In an effort to shut them up, he raised a hand and waved it gently. Thankfully, they got the message and provided him with the room to breathe.

He took several deep breaths before reopening his eyes and doing his best to explain the reason behind his momentary freak-out.

"I saw Daemnos," he said. "I had a vision."

"Which grade?" Zale asked instantly.

"One," he stated. "I saw a vision of a place. Many places"

"What places?" Reynolds demanded.

Badrick took another deep breath, then explained, "First, it was the Daemonium base we defended from the Kalik." Once the pattern had become obvious, Badrick's earlier confusion lifted and he'd recognised the grey/blue walls he'd first seen. "Then the military base, then the mining facility, then the Apos Base. But like I said, Daemnos was there. He said, 'It's starting'." Badrick looked at them questioningly, hoping they would have a clue as to what the Royal meant.

Zale's brow creased. "Well, what does that mean?"

Badrick could only shrug.

And then he could only scream as Reynolds issued a loud cry of alarm, reaching forward with his balled up fist and punching Badrick's arm out of its socket. He felt a responding surge of energy course from Daemnos into his body, stabilising him against the force of the strike. It was the only thing that stopped him flying off the walkway and into the wall forty metres away.

He glanced at Reynolds, who was looking intensely shocked at what he'd just done.

And then Zale broke the silence that had ensued. "I'm sorry, does he owe you money?"

"I apologise," Reynolds spluttered as, with a grunt, Badrick snapped his dislocated shoulder back into place and poured power into it in an attempt to dim the pain and heal the bone. "I don't know wha—YOW!"

Reynolds' hand glowed white and his fist shot out once more, this time at Zale's face. With the reflexes of a panther, Zale ducked the blow, bending his athletic body like someone straight out of the *Matrix*.

"God, my back," he groaned, righting himself. He quickly returned his attention to the sergeant. "What the hell, Reynolds!?"

"My speed-fist!" was the responding cry of alarm. "I can't—" Reynolds' whole body jerked as it happened again. This time the energised fist smashed into the railing, obliterating it and raining glass and metal upon those below. "I can't control it."

"What's wrong with it?"

Zale never got an answer.

This was because, with a yelp of distress, Badrick felt his arm rise of its own accord. Demonic power charged in his palm and exploded from his fingers with such speed he could barely keep up. The resulting purple charge cracked Zale on the back of the head and the electric Enthraller was thrown from his feet, right through the gap Reynolds had created with his fist.

Thankfully the charge had been weak—not even strong enough to break skin or singe his blonde hair—and Zale still had enough sense to throw his hand out and grab the walkway before he completely fell to his death.

"Zale!" Carla cried, bending down and grabbing for his hands as he dangled precariously below.

"I'm alright!" he cried.

Badrick didn't share his notion of wellbeing. Before he had a chance to react to his actions he felt his eyes heat up—a devastating beam of green fire shot from the globes and smashed into the wall, leaving angry black scorch marks upon the originally untarnished material.

"What the hell are you two doing!?" Carla screamed as Reynolds' fist smacked his own shoulder. He cried out, but thankfully appeared to be more or less unwounded. The angle of the self-inflicted blow had been awkward. He hadn't been able to do much damage to himself.

Once again someone's question went unanswered as a series of panicked shouts erupted below them.

Zale glanced down as the floor beneath lit up with a variety of vivid colours. He could see terrified agents and soldiers taking cover as their colleagues unwillingly blasted their powers left and right.

Carla was next.

Her hand lit up blue as she tried to pull Zale back to the walkway.

Thinking quickly, he allowed himself to drop just before her energy ball took his head off.

Landing on his feet, he joined the unaffected in taking cover behind the various benches and ramps. However the numbers of this group continued to dwindle as more and more of them were affected by whatever force was now taking them hostage.

It continued until only Zale was left hiding behind a bench, glancing around with a mix of wonder and anxiety as the Main Hall was continuously smashed to pieces. With a deafening crash, the walkway his friends were standing on was carved in two by a humungous energy missile. The lot of them were only saved by Badrick's Royal reflexes; he grabbed both Reynolds and Carla and leapt from the walkway moments before its destruction.

Enthrallers dived out of the path of the plummeting debris. Zale did a quick check; no one had been hurt.

"What! Is! Going! On!?" he bawled over the din.

"Our powers are messing up!" Reynolds screamed in response as his white fist dragged him across the floor. "It has to be a Energy—Agh!—Energy Disrupter Pulse."

A roar of anger erupted from Badrick's mouth.

Apparently he knew what an Energy Disrupter Pulse was.

Zale did too; an E.D.P was a demonic power similar to an E.M.P that, instead of affecting electrical equipment, disrupted the powers of other hellspawn, sometimes to chaotic effects.

"Who set one off?" Badrick's infuriated voice hollered over the ruckus.

"There are no Enthrallers in our employ who have that power," Reynolds told them. He bawled furiously as his fist ruined a perfectly good bench. "God damn it! That was where I liked to relax! Whoever did this is going to suffer!"

"Be glad it isn't an Organics Disrupter Pulse," Zale almost laughed, ducking an energy ball from Badrick. "Otherwise your hearts would stop."

A scream of a higher pitch attracted his attention, but he was forced to cover his eyes as a flash of green/blue light shone so brightly it was painful. Instantly recognising the harrowing signs of an explosive take-over, he knew exactly what to expect when he next looked.

The demon that now stood in the soldier's place appeared ecstatic to find himself standing in the physical plane, glancing around and laughing excitedly. The now very real material of his manifested armour echoed noisily as he banged his fists together.

Zale jumped up, blasting the hellspawn with a powerful surge of electricity as quickly as he could. The demon cried out in agony, falling to the floor upon which he convulsed violently, electricity coursing through his form. Zale wasn't proud of having done this, but he had to ensure the demon knew who was boss. If it thought it could get away scot-free, the thing would try to cause havoc.

Maybe even hurt people.

Begging for mercy, the thankfully weak-willed creature allowed itself to be escorted away by two agents who had managed to gain some semblance of control over themselves. Still, as they exited the Main Hall in the direction of the prison, one of them would jerk violently and an energy ball would fly at someone. Nonetheless they were only weak blasts and luckily it only happened once or twice.

Around Zale, the rest of the Enthrallers went either way; with effort, some managed to force their bodies under their control, but many more lost themselves further to explosive take-overs, creating loud bangs and filling the Main Hall with blue smoke.

The demons were quickly restrained by those in control, many simply raising their hands and allowing the agents to escort them away. Zale stood at the ready, the only Enthraller unaffected by the S.D.P, keeping watch on the people around him.

He felt himself relax when he realised that the situation was slowly ending and the local area was beginning to calm down.

The most dangerous of them all had, at some point, dropped to the floor and was now sitting on his hands, shouting curses at them, threatening to chop them off if they continued to misbehave. Laughing at his partner's comical rage, Zale approached the flustered Badrick.

That was when Reynolds emitted a brief scream and exploded, puffing fresh blue smoke every which way. When the intensity of the smoke had finally lessened, Zale saw a bright green figure standing where Reynolds had once been.

"Oh my God!" the demon Lora shouted. "This feels so good." She held her hands up to the agents that tried to storm her. "No need, gentlemen. I have no quarrel with any of you."

Her voice was just the way Zale remembered.

Just as strange

With the exception of his own, male demons sounded like copies of their Enthrallers but with a smoking problem. That was the way it was.

However, this was not the case with the female demons.

No … the she-demons followed a similar rule, but with an exception. They did not growl their way through life, instead speaking with an almost lyrical voice. However, they *did* still sound a bit like their Enthrallers, *but* as if they were women.

If a female Enthraller had a she-demon, this was not so bad . . . but in the case of a male Enthraller, sometimes it got downright weird.

As was the case with Lora.

It was like someone had recorded Reynolds speaking, morphed it to resemble a sexy woman, and then promptly jammed it into the hellspawn's voice box.

Lamenting her sudden physicality, the demon's head turned and her visor found Carla, who was tightly holding her wrist in an attempt to keep her powers under control, making the flesh of her hand slightly purple. "Carla, you sexy bitch! How are you?"

"Lora," Carla said in greeting. "Looking good."

A laugh . . . and then Lora's gaze fell upon Zale.

"Zale Hood," she uttered slowly. Lora began taking slow, meaningful steps towards him. A suggestive hum sounded from beneath her helmet as she approached. Reaching up, Lora removed the equipment adorning her head, revealing a gorgeous face and long, dark brown hair.

As she continued to move towards him, she persisted in discarding her armour piece by piece until only her under-suit was left.

And then she removed that.

"Oh . . . " Zale stammered. "Er . . . "

Sidling up into his personal space and wrapping her bare arms around his neck, Lora pressed her slender yet curvaceous body against his. Zale was only numbly aware that his jaw had dropped as his eyes immediately darted to her chest.

"I was hoping to see you again one day," she purred. "You know, you'd make a phenomenal king. We could use a new leader, what with ours being killed by my Daniel.

"You should take me as your queen, my prince. *This* body could be *yours*." She stroked his face and grinned excitedly. "You know the best thing the Devil ever gave demon-kind? The power of sex." Her expression darkened. "Do you know the worst thing to ever happen to demon-kind? The inability to ever have it again. It's been centuries, my prince, since I last . . . "

"Dear God," Zale found himself saying, his eyes wide and staring, the goings-on of his surroundings no longer even registering in his brain.

"I have such pent up energy, I'd be Godlike. Don't pretend that doesn't entice you—"

"OK!" Carla suddenly shouted, grabbing hold of Lora's arm and dragging her away. "This is a PG thirteen show. Enough of *that!*"

Lora simply laughed. "You could join in if you like, beautiful!"

"Can someone please take this bitch to the prison?" Carla threw out to the hall. Her request was met by two agents who threw Lora's under-suit back to her and dragged her away, laughing and winking as she went.

"What the hell was she talking about?" Zale spoke, eyebrow raised.

"Weirdo!" Carla growled in her direction, glaring after the she-demon.

There was no time to continue the conversation. Now that the Enthrallers had more or less regained control of themselves, a Daemonium-wide operation to discern what occurred went under way, almost everyone on the site pitching in.

Zale, Badrick and Carla remained in the corner, conversing in their own little bubble. No one bothered them; the Enthrallers were all too busy to care what the youngest of their number were up to.

"What could have caused it?" Badrick queried quietly, watching the surge of activity sombrely. "Maybe a new recruit we haven't heard about lost control."

Carla disputed that theory quickly. "No, I keep track of all new recruits in case there's hot guys to have my way with." She winked playfully at Zale. "Honestly though, I like to see who comes in and there have been no new recruits with the S.D.P power."

"Maybe someone in the dungeons decided to get revenge?"

"That isn't a completely stupid theory," Zale said, "but Malcolm's power blocks everything, and besides, why would they take so long?"

"It could be someone recently imprisoned," Badrick suggested, clearly picking up steam now that his new theory hadn't been completely passed over. "Or maybe someone waiting for the right moment to attack?"

"What?" Carla said. "Like as part of a bigger conspiracy."

"No," Zale stopped them. "I can't handle another massive conspiracy. Let's stay with the one we have, shall we?"

Badrick's eyes widened. "Could the Resurrected have had something to do with this?"

"That would suggest he has powers of his own," Carla winced.

"God, I hope not!" Zale screamed shrilly.

But none of them could refute it, and this new potential revelation stunned them all into silence.

Badrick eventually broke the uncomfortable quiet. "What I don't understand," he frowned, "is why you didn't get affected." His words were directed at Zale. "You didn't lose control at all."

Zale smiled and shrugged. "What can I say? I'm lucky."

"How do you mean?"

"His powers aren't affected by S.D.Ps," Carla told him. "You need an E.M.P for that."

They were strange, the next few seconds. At first everyone just nodded, all musing on this answer.

But, slowly, one by one, their faces dropped.

Then, at the exact same time, all three of them burst out

yelling, running in three different directions.

A few agents tried to ignore them, telling them to shush. But those more open minded to the competence of these three kids immediately stopped what they were doing, joining in with the yelling.

As fast as they could they spread the word of the potential danger of an impending E.M.P.

There was clearly no doubt in Zale or Carla's mind that there *was* one about to go off, and Badrick trusted them without exception. If they thought the threat was real, then so did he. He helped them spread the word, recruiting other now panicked Enthrallers in the search. The group, ever growing, darted about the place, covering every inch of the facility.

Zale dashed in the direction of the RCR.

Carla, the BCR.

So Badrick decided he would take the Gate, making for the HQ exit as fast as he could. There was no time to waste; an E.M.P wouldn't just damage Zale, it could take out the entire base. He didn't know if the Daemonium had supernatural protection against that possibility, but he definitely didn't care to find out.

The HQ exit zipped open and he stepped through.

He instantly doubled back when he heard a woman shout, "I've found it!"

Acting quickly, he searched for the owner of the voice. Locating her, he used his powers to leap to the third floor.

As he drew level and landed perfectly on his feet, he saw Zale already ahead of him, barging through agents and soldiers alike. The woman slapped Badrick on the shoulder and indicated for him to follow.

They passed through two doors and an archway before they

rediscovered Badrick's partner. He was standing over a large object that definitely didn't belong. It was half as high as Badrick, just reaching the height of his waistline and it looked like it had been constructed by a mental patient with only a mediocre knowledge of explosive devices.

Nevertheless, he had no doubt that it worked perfectly.

Zale clearly thought so too, as he didn't waste time conferring with anyone on how to disarm it. Before Badrick and an assortment of agents could do anything else, he spread his hands over the device and zapped it with voltage.

The device sparked and fizzled violently before the countdown display finally darkened and the numbers gratifyingly vanished.

To his great relief, Badrick heard the distinct sound of machinery powering down.

He laughed, slapping Zale on the back. "How did you know that would work?"

Zale's exhausted face turned in his direction. "I didn't," he breathed. "I hoped."

Badrick decided not to comment and he was saved being forced to by the arrival of a very welcome face.

"Reynolds!" he cried happily. "Are you OK?"

Zipping up his under-suit so tight only his vividly red angry face was visible, the sergeant nodded. "I'm alright, thank you." He glared at Zale.

The Enthraller threw his hands into the air. "I didn't do anything! She came onto me!"

With one last glower, Reynolds began talking very fast. "Listen, the alarm system was tripped. Someone just escaped the facility."

"The person who left this, I imagine," Badrick commented darkly, kicking the E.M.P.

Zale put his hands between him and the device. "Don't do that," he laughed nervously. "It might still go off."

Badrick apologised as the sergeant clicked his fingers impatiently. "Operatives, this is a major problem. Someone waltzed in here carrying a bloody great bomb and then escaped without being seen *at all!*"

"More than one person," Zale said. "No one carried this thing on their own."

Reynolds glanced at the E.M.P, his expression freezing in place. In his eyes, Badrick saw true anxiety and felt his own stomach drop at the sight of it. "We only detected one person leaving."

Zale was the one to answer. "So there's still someone he—"

He choked as something dark and huge pushed him to the floor, knocking the air from his lungs. Badrick roared in genuine panic as he recognised the grotesque face of a hulking Kalik demon. The dark eyes glinted cruelly as it regarded Badrick with both hatred and hunger.

Unarmed and without his armour, Reynolds jumped away from the demon. A split second later he regained his wits and lunged at the creature, his fist glowing white with the energy of his speed-fist power.

But the Kalik dodged the strike, moving impossibly fast for something so bulky, and knocked Reynolds away.

Badrick whipped out his pistol and took aim.

Seeing the weapon, the Kalik made the choice to retreat. It bowled over the other Enthrallers and vanished through the door.

Confusion tore apart Badrick's mind; Kalik *never* ran away.

But then a rare stroke of intelligence poked at his brain, and Badrick quickly surmised the Resurrected had to currently be in direct control of the monster. Whoever their enemy may be was commanding it to flee.

"Come on!" Badrick shouted, pulling Zale to his feet.

Zale was faster than him and so pulled ahead as they followed in the Kalik's wake. They passed stunned agents and soldiers—none of whom were wounded—jumping over and around them in pursuit of the Kalik.

They emerged into the Main Hall, glancing left and right, looking up and down.

"There!" Zale shouted, pointing up at a walkway.

Badrick didn't look fast enough; the creature was already plummeting to the ground floor. It landed heavily, knocking over Badrick's colleagues and roaring in their faces.

It took a breadth of a second to check its surroundings before flitting away, dodging the Enthrallers that tried to take it down with a success none of its brethren had ever managed.

Anxiety coursed through Badrick's stomach.

This thing was outwitting them!

Zale leapt over the railing in chase. Badrick followed.

And that was when he saw Carla coming out of an archway. Judging from the speed she'd appeared, it was clear she'd heard the commotion and had come out to see what was happening.

Except she was looking the wrong way.

And the Kalik was charging straight at her.

"Carla!" Zale's voice echoed through the Main Hall, and Badrick felt his very bones shudder at the sound of genuine, heart-wrenching terror in Zale's voice. "Watch out!"

Carla swivelled, but it was already too late. Within seconds the demon was upon her. Before even she could stop it, the Kalik raised its hand, summoned a blade of electricity and thrust it towards her abdomen.

She threw her arms up in an effort to stop it—her hand lit up with demonic energy. But the Energy Disrupter Pulse was clearly still having some level of effect on her and the energy failed to release.

With a sickening zap, Carla was lifted into the air by the Kalik's strong arms.

The blade sunk deep into her stomach.

chapter
TWENTY SIX

Zale's cry of distress drowned out anything that might have made a sound.

Carla's responding choke was strained and agonised as she was suspended in midair, gripping the Kalik's arm as it held her body up off the floor.

In a panic, Badrick rushed forward to pry the Kalik away.

Zale beat him to it. He jumped upon its back and gripped both halves of its mouth. At the lack of mercy and the unbelievable strength only sorrow and fear could bring, the Kalik's head split appallingly as Zale tore it in two, spattering black blood onto the floor.

Its grip failed and the blade sputtered out of existence.

Carla fell heavily to the floor, rolling along the metal. Her body convulsed and Badrick grimaced with dismay as an unnatural horrid black mist starting seeping from her wound. She coughed abominably as the smoke spewed out of her chest.

Out of nowhere, a massive quantity erupted from her body and rocketed to a spot several metres away like some kind of smoky missile. The smoke vanished, only to be replaced by a blue armoured figure that was now writhing inhumanly on the floor, wailing a monstrous screech of torture.

The true, corporeal form of the demon Acro rolled in and over himself as his own body convulsed, black blood spewing from his torso in an appalling torrent of ichor. Then, with a deafening crack, he exploded, black gunk splattering the wall and floor nearby.

Over by the Kalik, Carla fell still.

"No!" Zale screamed. "No, no, no, no, no!" He continued to shout these words as he stepped over the savaged Kalik and hurried to her side.

Badrick couldn't move as he watched Zale roll her over and lift her body from the floor, cradling her on his lap and repeating the same cry of anguish over and over again. Around him, all was still; everyone was watching Zale and Carla. Many had their hands over their mouths as they stared, just as horrified as Badrick was.

"It's OK," Zale was now telling her. He ran his hands over her wound, inspecting it. "It's going to be OK. Oh God!" he cried when he saw the damage. "Oh God! You'll be fine. I promise. I'm going to help you."

He cradled her tightly, rocking back and forth as she continued to cough and splutter in agony.

"Oh God, someone help!" Zale cried, the beginnings of tears flicking from his eyelashes. "Get a medic." He looked up at the stunned onlookers and screamed at them, *"Someone do something!"*

A few people left, bolting out of sight.

Maybe to find a medic.

Maybe to just get away.

Either way, it didn't matter.

It was too late.

There was nothing anybody could do.

"Carla, I'm sorry," Zale sobbed, rocking her again. "I'm so sorry. I'm sorry. I'm sorry."

Carla stared up at him, her usually bright eyes already whiter than they should have been. Her lips trembled as she tried to speak, but all Carla could do was cough in agony.

Her left hand shuddered up to the level of Zale's face. With an arm shaking so much it suggested this was taking all her strength, her fingers found his cheek.

They brushed his skin softly as she stared into his wide, blurry blue eyes and on her face played a smile so full of love the likes of which Badrick had never seen before.

A terrible rattling sound interrupted Zale's cries as Carla strained to make words form through her gasping breaths.

Then, with great effort, she managed to cough out, "My . . . Zale . . . "

That was all she had.

The smile slipped from her face.

Her eyes misted over.

Her arm fell to her side.

And Carla's body went still.

"*Oh God!*" Zale's face lost all colour, a deathly pallor dominating his stricken features. "*Oh God!*" he repeated. "No!" He shook her gently. "Why!?" Zale gripped her tight. "*WHY!?!*"

Around them, a mournful silence had fallen. Several of the onlookers' eyes wetted. Even those who knew them little or had never met the couple welled up at the sight of Zale—usually so charismatic and powerful—crouched over his dead would-be lover with tears streaming down his face and incoherent screams erupting from his lungs.

"*Please get up!*" he squeaked. Tears dripped onto her face, which he didn't wipe away.

When Zale realised that she would not respond, his face creased even more. Clearly in conflict inside his own head, his emotions drowning out anything else that made up his consciousness, Zale did the only thing he could do.

He opened his mouth and screamed unintelligibly.

Badrick felt someone hurry past him and saw that Reynolds was rushing to his partner's side. Bending down, he tried placing his hand upon Zale's shoulder in an effort to pull him away.

Zale lost his hold of Carla and she slid to the floor.

The Enthraller struggled against Reynolds' grip, wrestling violently and roaring so loudly Badrick's ears stung. Badrick felt his hands go to his mouth, dismayed by the sight of Zale pushing Reynolds away and scrambling back to Carla's side with none of his usual finesse. The sensation of his eyes getting wet surprised him. Thick globules of salty water ran down his cheek.

The pain of the agonising emotion inside his chest was overwhelming. He felt like he himself was going to scream from the sheer woe of it.

Still, there was no movement. Nobody in the Main Hall could tear themselves away. All they could do was watch.

Finally Reynolds managed to overpower Zale and pull him into a tight hug away from Carla's body. He sobbed into the sergeant's under-suit, screaming her name over and over. Badrick looked into Carla's face; the sight of her lying there, broken, was truly awful. Her perfect skin was white as death and her eyes—once so full of life—stared back at them, unseeing.

And yet, despite her violent death and dead eyes, she looked strangely peaceful.

Too peaceful.

It was horrible. Cut down so quickly. Dispatched as though she was nothing. Her life extinguished so fast it was as though she had never been here.

It seemed wrong. There was nothing *calming* about this.

Still nobody stirred. Despite the fact that there could be more Kalik in the building, no one seemed to care.

Badrick understood why; he couldn't bring himself to move either.

What was the point?

Carla was gone.

Badrick wanted to lie down and go to sleep.

Never do anything again.

Get away from the pain that seemed to stem from his very soul.

But then a small group of bright colours moving towards Reynolds and Zale caught his notice, and with a start he recognised several faces among them.

They were members of the Command Council.

Badrick's face creased with fury. A red mist descended upon him at the sight of them. If it wasn't for *them* none of this would have happened. The Kalik would not have gotten their evil hands on powerful weapons. The Resurrected would not have had such success.

Carla would still be alive.

In the recesses of the darkness clouding his mind, he heard the mocking whisper of Daemnos.

Do 'em, he pushed. *Do 'em. Go on!*

Shut up! Badrick snapped, pounding on him with metaphysical fists until the Royal fell into submission.

Meanwhile, the Council reached Reynolds and Zale, looming over them like a dark beast, blotting out the light. Reynolds eyed them warily, the same anxiety clearly flowing through his mind as it coursed through Badrick's.

There was no denying it now.

The Council had seen what killed Carla.

The secret truly was out.

The group of Council Members parted and out stepped a grey-haired man, somewhat older than the rest of them. Fresh deadly ire shot into Badrick's heart when he realised it was none other than goddamn Jonathon Carver.

The bastard had a small smile on his face—a confident, victorious sneer—and his eyes were wide with vicious glee at the sight of the distraught Zale.

"Operative Zale Hood," he spoke, his voice echoing cleanly in the silence of the Main Hall, "you are under arrest."

"What?" Reynolds glared up at Carver hatefully. "What are you talking about?"

Shaking with the excitement at this opportunity to make more inexcusable statements, Carver simpered, "Do not think we are blind, Reynolds. We all saw what killed Agent Hunter.

"That technology comes from only one place: Operative Hood's weapons. You have been on the Kalik case for days and you did not inform the Council that you let the demons steal your tech.

"We are now forced to come to the conclusion that you lied because *you* were the one to supply our enemies with such deadly weaponry."

The sheer injustice of this statement was so intense that it spurred Badrick to finally move. He jumped to his feet, relieving his knees from the stress of his weight, and stormed towards the Council.

But he was too slow. With no sound at all—not a scream, not a whimper, not a curse—Zale sprung to his feet and converged on

Carver. The agent cried out as Zale's fist met his face. Badrick heard the crunching of bone even from this distance and his mouth fell open in genuine shock as Zale followed Carver as he fell to the floor.

He leapt upon the Council Member and began laying into his jaw line.

Over and over and over.

For a brief moment, as Carver roared in pain, Badrick had to double check what he thought he'd just seen.

Zale's eyes . . .

He believed he'd seen them go deathly black.

But then one of Zale's hands obscured his face as he brought it back to pound Carver anew, and when Zale's features were next visible the irregularity was gone.

As Badrick frowned in confusion at what he'd just witnessed, pandemonium erupted.

The rest of the Council started shouting unintelligibly, their voices merging with each other and making it impossible to hear what any one of them was saying. When they realised that this was achieving nothing, more than half of them reached for their side-arms.

Yanking them out and aiming at Zale's head.

Reynolds was next to leap to his feet. He smacked one of the guns down before grabbing Zale by the shoulder and tearing him away from Carver.

His face bloody, his nose broken and probably missing a few teeth by now, the Council Member scrabbled behind the protection of his fellows.

"Zale, enough!" Reynolds roared at the Enthraller, placing his palm in front of his face. He then turned to the Council, screaming even louder. "Back off! *BACK OFF!*"

Badrick was by his side in an instant. In a flash of heat he ignited his arms—using another power to protect his clothing—and mixed his roars with that of the sergeant's, flailing his arms threateningly in their direction.

At the sight of the searing fire licking the air every armed man and woman faltered, backing away, trembling. However, they did not lower their weapons. Reynolds continued to shout. He smacked a man's pistol from his hands so hard it skidded across the floor.

Badrick became aware of two soldiers, armed and armoured, sneaking up from behind. It only took a quick study to see that this pair was loyal to the Council. From the way they converged upon Zale, it was too obvious.

One grabbed the walking conduit, trying to secure both of his arms.

The other made the incredible mistake of trying to restrain Reynolds.

He paid for it dearly; the sergeant smacked his hands away, gripped the man's single-rifle and pushed it against the soldier's chest. His grip on the weapon failed and Reynolds yanked it away, repaying the soldier's efforts by smashing the butt into his visor.

The man toppled back as Badrick dealt with the second, using powers of telekinesis to launch him far, far away from Zale and allowing him to hit the wall for good measure.

"Reynolds!" One of the Council finally bellowed louder than his colleagues and was heard over their racket. "You are out of line!"

"*No, you are out of line!*" Reynolds answered with equal wrath. "Look around you! Don't you see what you are doing? You're splitting us down the middle, forcing us to choose sides which should not exist. We are on the same side here. We're all comrades.

"This is exactly what our enemies want. If we fail from within they can destroy us. They'll wipe us out in seconds and the world will have no one to protect them. Is that what you want?"

Nobody answered.

"If you weren't always looking for an excuse to punish Enthrallers you didn't like, this would never have happened. We would have come to you for help!"

A woman bristled. "You knew about this?"

"*Of course I bloody knew about this!*" Reynolds shrieked.

"You're out of line, Reynolds!" the woman roared, repeating her colleague's earlier statement.

"Probably, yes," Reynolds scowled. "But so are the lot of you!"

Carver was the next to speak. Empowered by the backing of his colleagues, he stood sharply, nose still streaming, eyes glaring. With renewed confidence—though Badrick noticed he did not step away from the protection of the men and women that stood between him and the raging Zale—he snarled, "It is time to answer for your insubordination. Sergeant, you have abused your privileges for far too long. Operative Hood has—"

"*I will kill you!*" Zale's shriek of sheer hatred deafened Badrick. He was forced to allow the fire on his arms to die out so that he could stop his partner from lunging at Carver once again.

Reynolds also turned his attention to Zale. "Come on, Zale, calm down. Don't lower yourself to Carver's standards. We can sort this calmly—"

"No, to Hell with all of you!" Zale roared. He cast his eyes over Carla's still corpse one more time—looked as though he was about to walk back up to her body—before pushing Badrick from himself and storming away across the Main Hall.

Badrick went to follow him, to try and calm Zale down.

Or at the very least be there for him.

But as he took a step in Zale's direction, a commanding hand gripped his shoulder. He immediately rounded on Reynolds, ready to argue.

But Reynolds shook his head. "Let him go, Badrick." Badrick immediately relented; the terrible sadness in Reynolds' eyes completely disarmed him. "Let him be on his own."

Relaxing his muscles, he fell back onto the soles of his feet, obeying Reynolds' advice and gazing after Zale as he vanished through an archway.

The Council, however, were far less negotiable. As one, they opened their mouths and started to shout, their words unintelligible in the mix of their incessant voices.

It was so aggravating—so *infuriating*—such a display of injustice that Badrick felt disgusted by their behaviour. He made to shout back, planning on using his powers to augment his voice and intimidate them into silence.

But before he could every one of them shut up.

The silence was deafening after the racket, and for quite some time every one of them simply gaped. But then their mouths snapped shut as they stared at one another and Badrick was surprised to see a rather hefty element of disquiet now spreading throughout their ranks.

"What . . . " he began, turning to Reynolds for answers. He blinked with surprise to see that Reynolds shared the same expression as his fellows. "What's going on?"

Reynolds didn't answer for a moment. He continued to stare at the rest of the Council, all hostility between them now gone. Badrick wasn't great at reading body language but he sensed that the whole group had just been united by something he hadn't been aware even occurred.

When Reynolds *did* speak, it was with a hoarse whisper. "All Council Members are connected to the Hierarch upon joining the Council." Reynolds played with his chin worriedly. "When he needs us we can hear his summons."

"It's been months," a Councilwoman murmured. "What does he want now? Of all times?"

"He hasn't taken charge in so long."

"Why now?"

Badrick could see every single one of the Council Members was deeply unsettled by this new development. Their uneasiness served to worry him as well; why were they *this* disconcerted?

Badrick felt Reynolds hand return to his shoulder. "Badrick," he whispered, the fretfulness in his voice so readable Badrick felt his body squirm uncomfortably, "help take Carla to the labs. We'll need to prepare a burial detail."

"But—"

"Please, Varner," Reynolds stopped him, his face stony and pleading all at the same time. "Do as I ask. Just this once."

Looking into his face now, Badrick could not deny him his request. He relented and nodded affirmatively, turning sadly away to wander in the direction of Carla. He clicked at two of the closest agents, communicating with his hand what he wanted them to do. As for the rest of them, the Council ordered the Enthrallers to return to their duties, a little more harshly than was necessary.

Badrick helped the two agents lift Carla from the floor, hefting her to waist height.

He got a horribly good view of her calm face as they cradled her away.

Again, he felt anger go through him; it wasn't right that she looked so calm when she had been robbed from them so violently.

It was right then that Badrick remembered why he hated death so much.

chapter
TWENTY SEVEN

The Daemonium medics took charge of Carla's body, handling her prone form with great care and respect. At Badrick's request, they agreed not to perform an autopsy and so simply took her away to arrange her funeral.

He couldn't bear the thought of them cutting his friend to pieces to determine a cause of death they already knew.

His mind was alight with thoughts. They shot through him, electrifying his charged synapses and denying him his one wish; to be able to wind down.

But he was so wired it practically hurt.

Through the glass, he watched the medics lay Carla upon a table and begin prepping her body for burial. Badrick could see the horrific hole in her chest where the Kalik's blade had pierced her body.

At the sight of it, Badrick felt his fingers curl his hands into fists.

The Resurrected had done all of this.

The E.D.P.

The E.M.P.

The Kalik.

Everything inflicted upon them was the Resurrected's doing.

The rage he felt at realising this undeniable truth was indescribable. It burned his heart with a red hot flame and his mind started to fog.

His vision blurred as his face and neck flushed red from his anger.

His hands tightened even more, the nails digging into his palms and drawing blood. His chest hurt so much . . . He felt like he was going to explode and cry all at the same time. *Nothing* could have prepared Badrick for this.

Zale had been right on the money.

He wasn't perfect.

He wasn't powerful.

He was broken.

Someone he cared about had died and whatever bubble impeding his ability to feel and act with moral judgement burst with explosive results. Badrick could see it all now. Everything he'd done and said since coming back. All the . . . wrong.

All this time, from the moment of his rebirth, Badrick was *wrong.*

A tear escaped his eye as the overwhelming rush of emotions clawed at his heart and stomach. He allowed it to fall onto his cheek, refusing to wipe it away. Badrick wanted to feel the warmth of the tear on his face. He needed to feel like he was no longer broken.

As he focused on the drop slowly creeping along his skin, the thought of eyes and tears made Badrick's mind involuntarily poke at the memory of seeing Zale's change, and fresh worry scratched at his insides at the thought of what that had been.

Many terrible theories coursed through his head.

Was it Zale's soul? Had Badrick witnessed it corrupting under the strain of such sorrow? No . . . that sounded ridiculous.

Maybe Zale was becoming a Forsaken. He'd looked monstrous enough.

Perhaps Horas was taking over, using Zale's body to hurt Carver. It had looked demonic, for sure.

That didn't sound *too* farfetched.

However, Badrick quickly abolished all these stupid ideas and did his best to assure himself all was fine.

Horas was the only demon in recorded history to affect a physical attribute of his Enthrallers; their eyes were permanently electric blue, with voltage sparking and brightening the colours to beautiful vividness.

With Horas apparently being kinder than most patron saints, Badrick figured the demon was enraged at the death of his Enthraller's lover as much as his Enthraller. Surely, that was all it was. Their combined anger—that dark and monstrous grief that Badrick could now also feel—briefly altered the augmentation of Zale's eyes before returning to what was normal for them.

If anything could do such a thing to his partner, it was Carla's death, for sure.

Sounds legit, a creepy voice whispered in his head.

Not entirely sure if he should trust Daemnos' opinion on his demonological accuracy, Badrick nevertheless felt better having come to this conclusion.

At the very moment he felt his worry ebb, the door to his right zipped open. Instinctively—unwillingly—Badrick's hand shot up and dashed away the tear, leaving his face dry as could be. Although his anger remained, with great effort he managed to regain control of his stricken face and return a calm expression to his features, not wanting anyone to see him cry.

In the corner of his eye he glimpsed blue and black; an agent had just walked in.

But he didn't quite realise who it was until the new arrival said, "Hey."

"Zach?" Badrick hadn't expected to see the detective here. He assumed Zach was busy trying to find the non-existent Mawr.

"I came to pay my respects," Zach said softly, stepping up beside him and gazing through the glass at Carla's whitening body. "A terrible thing."

Badrick didn't reply; he couldn't.

Thankfully he was saved having to by the very welcome, very much needed reappearance of Sergeant Reynolds.

Back in his pristine red and black uniform, the man stopped in the doorway before he could completely step over the threshold. The door whined at him to remove himself so that it could close, but the sergeant ignored the complaints.

He stood stock still, his face one of pure incredulity.

As though he'd just been told something he couldn't quite believe.

"What happened?" Badrick asked, his inquisitiveness getting the better of him.

Reynolds' mouth opened slightly.

No sound came out.

When he continued to remain silent, Zach cleared his throat and prompted him on. "Sir?"

Reynolds did the same, his rough coughs awfully loud in the quiet of the lab. "The Hierarch is . . . *displeased.*"

"In what way?" Zach asked.

"He is upset with the Council's administration ... or something like that. He's disappointed with the methods they have employed. He is appalled by their inability to handle the *'Kalik Crisis'* efficiently.

"He's taking action."

"Is he going to come down here and tell us this himself?" Badrick asked, a little sarcastically.

"No."

Unable to think of a response, Badrick just went, "Oh."

"The Hierarch has taken *drastic* action," Reynolds continued. This was where he finally moved. Stepping properly into the room, he allowed the door to close. It whined long and shrill as the metal slid shut, its gears and mechanics worn out from the repeated half in/half out position it had been forced to adopt for several minutes.

Badrick likened the whining to the kind of sound a person made when relieving themselves of a heavy object.

Reynolds paid no attention to the door. Instead he opted for telling them something that shocked and surprised them. "He's disbanded the Council."

"He's done what!?" Zach practically screeched.

"We're disbanded," Reynolds said. "Nada. No more."

"What the hell does he plan to do instead!?" Zach began bawling questions at an impressive rate. "Is he going for a dictatorship now? What happens to the old Council? Are they demoted? What will happen to those of us who work for them directly?"

Reynolds put his hand in the air to quieten him, but the detective continued to rattle away. In the end it took the combined efforts of Badrick and Reynolds' voices to shut him up.

"He's going to form a new Council," the sergeant told them, "and ... "

Badrick frowned when Reynolds trailed off. From the look of it the man didn't quite know how to continue. "What's up, Sergeant?" he pressed, dying to know now that they'd started.

Reynolds cleared his throat once again and coughed, "In light of recent events, the Hierarch has elected me as the Council Dominus. He says he is impressed with my judgement and wishes me to lead the new order."

For a moment, Badrick stared with confusion and it was only when Reynolds elaborated that he understood the magnitude of what had truly occurred. "The Dominus," Reynolds said quietly, "is in charge of the Daemonium."

If not for the fact that one of his best friends was lying dead only ten feet away, Badrick would have screamed with glee. As it was, he at least managed a small smile. "Wow," he whispered. "That's great, isn't it?"

Reynolds returned his smile with one of his own, though it looked very strained.

"*Hold on!*" Zach interrupted their moment with another bellow. "Daemonium laws dictate you cannot be Dominus if you are a sergeant. You have to be an Agent Commander or a—"

"That's right," Reynolds interrupted him once again. "You . . . apparently . . . are now looking at General Daniel Reynolds."

"Goddamn what?" Badrick managed to exclaim. "That's awesome!"

Zach clearly did not share his enthusiasm; "The Hierarch cannot just take matters into his own hands like this."

Reynolds scoffed at him, a little rudely. "It may have been a while since he has, but you forget the Council had very little power up until a few years ago, and it wasn't until only last year that he resigned his post as Dominus and left the running of the place up to us entirely.

"He's the Hierarch, Zach. Dominus or not, he can do what he

wants."

"But he can't—"

"Enough!" Badrick rebuked the agent coldly. "Please let it go. Is now really the time to defend the Council after everything that's happened?"

Zach fell into an angry silence, clearly unable to think of a suitable riposte.

"Although," Badrick continued on his own, "I do share Zach's concern a little bit. Don't get me wrong, Sergeant—I mean, *General* . . . " Reynolds winced when he heard his new title spoken aloud—clearly it hadn't sunk in all that well yet. "Don't get me wrong, it's great someone finally beat those sons of bitches down to the ground.

"But why here? Why now? At this point in time. Doesn't it seem . . . well placed?"

"How do you mean?" Reynolds squinted.

Unable to dispute these concerns in his head, Badrick said aloud, "He could have done this ages ago. I can't help but feel like he only took action when there was no way out for Zale . . . don't you think?"

"A lot has happened," Zach hissed; a reminder of his anger at being cut off. "Zale's been in trouble a lot recently. The Hierarch never helped him out then. This is coincidence."

"Yes, but there was always a way out," Badrick insisted. "We always managed to scrape out of the danger. Don't you agree that after this the Council wouldn't have been swayed? They would have locked him up."

Reynolds' head bobbed agreeably. "Yes, they would have taken him to the prisons."

"OK," Badrick sighed. "So why did the Hierarch do it? It seems too convenient. He had plenty of chances to do this major reset. Plenty of excuses." He rolled his eyes, thinking back on all the things the Council had said and done—*tried to do*—even in the short time he'd been around.

Reynolds' responding expression to Badrick's words was deeply worrying. He hadn't *really* expected anyone to back him up on this, but Reynolds appeared to have taken him completely seriously.

"The Hierarch is a mystery," the sergeant murmured. "I don't *want* to think that the only reason the Hierarch has done this is because of Zale but . . . He *was* always fond of him."

"Now you tell me," Badrick spluttered.

Reynolds' irked expression deepened. "He often spent a few moments a week conversing with Zale. He never did that with anyone else he wasn't forced to work with." Reynolds shook his head and closed the final few metres between them, drawing up to the glass and laying his eyes upon the medics working on Carla. "Like I said, he's a mystery. The Hierarch has led the Daemonium for hundreds of years. Longer than anyone can remember so no one really knows him." At Badrick's surprised huff, he elaborated, "For some reason the Hierarch is connected to his demon's longevity. He will never die of old age.

"Anyway, as for the right here, right now," Reynolds sighed, "I'm sure the old man's motives will reveal themselves soon enough.

"They always do."

He fell silent after that, saying nothing, doing nothing . . . probably thinking nothing. He just stared at Carla.

Badrick was completely content to allow the newly appointed general to stand there in utter silence and observe with him the visage of their lost friend.

Unfortunately, the visage wasn't exactly pretty. All Badrick could see was that horrific black tear in her chest.

The sight of it forced him to recall the moment she died over and over again. He could see, in his mind's eye, her body writhing on the floor, black smoke pouring out of her chest.

"Jeez," he found himself saying, remembering the entity that exploded.

That smoke had been Acro.

A poor, weak, atrocious imitation of Zale's swords may have take her life but still, it wasn't a regular weapon. It was a weapon of pure demonic energy. When the blade entered Carla's body, it also touched the metaphysical energy that existed inside her, the weapon being of the same nature *as* that energy.

And that energy inside Carla was Acro.

The blade not only stabbed Carla, it had stabbed the demon.

"The love of Zale's life was not the only death today."

Prompted by Badrick's choice of words about what she really was to his partner, Reynolds spoke up, cutting the sombre silence that had ensued after Badrick's explanation. "I wish . . . " He stopped and Badrick felt a tinge of sorrow when he noticed that the Serg—*General*—had started crying. "I wish they had just told each other. Everybody else knew, for God's sake."

"They screwed around a lot," Badrick informed him, "if you know what I mean."

"That's not the same. Carla . . . she loved Zale more than life. And he can pretend otherwise all he likes, but he felt exactly the same. But they were never brave enough to actually tell each other for fear that the feelings were not reciprocated.

"It's ridiculous. Of course they were. Everyone knew it." Reynolds put his hand to his face. Thick, warm tears fell from between his fingers and splattered on the floor by their feet. "But they couldn't see it. Carla wasn't exactly Christian, and if there was ever a guy she wanted, then she had him. But after a while she just stopped. Eventually she never touched another person. She always kept herself for him."

Badrick felt a small unwelcome laugh fighting its way up his throat and was powerless to stop it. "Zale humps everything he comes across," he found himself saying.

At that Reynolds actually joined in with the laughter. "Yes, he does." He flicked his finger in the direction of Carla, his motions sharp and uncomfortable with his sadness. "The difference between men and women, right there. Guys hide their feelings with actions, females hide them with inaction. If you know what I mean."

Badrick *did* know what he meant, despite Reynolds' uncharacteristically gauche manner. Carla pretended she didn't have love for Zale but did not touch another guy. Zale, on the other hand, hid his true feelings by sluttin' about the place.

Badrick didn't think Carla ever minded. Not in the way most people might have in their situation.

But that was just it.

There was no similar situation. Theirs had been a completely unique set of circumstances.

"Men and women," Zach uttered. "Sometimes worlds apart."

Badrick couldn't help but agree.

The computer that had failed him met its demise at the hands of his devastating electrical power. Exploding from the voltage, the machine parts flew every which way, smashing into even smaller pieces on the walls, ceiling and floor.

Fortunately, there was no one nearby to berate him. The BCR was devoid of people apart from himself, recent events having torn every Agent Commander into action within the HQ.

Zale breathed heavily as smoke rose from what remained of the computer, his fingers still sparking with voltage.

He didn't understand it.

Not one bit.

An S.D.P was not something a Kalik could do; the beasts didn't have any abilities like that. Only the main breed of hellspawn could manifest demonic energy into their deadly powers.

A Resurrected shouldn't have possessed that power either.

But a Kalik *had* been present, meaning the foul zombie was behind this attack. Not only that, but he obviously had his own set of demonic powers.

He or she set off the S.D.P to stop the Daemonium being able to fight the Kalik infiltrator.

Zale thought back to something Badrick mentioned to him since his rebirth; *"If an Enthraller is resurrected then their demon is dragged back."*

It was clear.

The Resurrected had a demon.

In life, their target was an Enthraller.

Zale was certain, and all of this proved that the scumbag had been *inside* their facility not an hour before.

That should have made everything simple.

It should have helped him end this disaster.

But here was where he failed; the computer had been unsuccessful in detecting . . . *anything*. There was no Resurrected taint anywhere to be found in the Daemonium facility. There was no footage *anywhere* of the Kalik entering the base.

And what Zale fancied might be footage of their villain was far too blurry and *far too* quick for him to prove anything.

For all he knew, it was just Enthrallers moving about.

Even though whoever he kept glimpsing was moving with purpose, and definitely appeared to be placing himself/herself as far out of the way of the cameras as possible, he couldn't stop these doubts now clouding his judgement.

Once again, the Resurrected had outwitted him.

Once again, he had been defeated.

And this time Carla paid the price for his incompetence.

This was why the computer had met with an untimely end.

Zale now stood there, breathing heavily, his anger practically seeping from his pores as he glared at the consoles.

What the hell was he supposed to do?

Carla trusted him and he failed her.

She lost her life because of him!

There was nothing more he could think of.

He could achieve nothing with these feeble, fruitless attempts to put his investigation to rest.

He should have given up and taken Carla to safety years ago—

Badrick's disembodied voice suddenly struck his consciousness. It wasn't really his partner, but rather a memory of him. Zale's eyes snapped closed as the voice recited to him something Badrick had said not two hours before; *'Daemnos told me to tell you to scan for demonic link energy.'*

His lids flew open and he stared unseeingly into the distance, his mind working overtime, thoughts and theories and plans hitching lifts on the electric charges zapping across his brain at an impressive rate.

Could the Royal be trusted?

"Who cares?" Zale snapped at himself; what else could he try now? What did he have to lose anymore?

Wasting no more time, he kicked a chair aside and brushed up to a fresh computer. He tapped away on it, his fingers dancing across the keyboard with expert ease.

There was no real software for detecting link energy in their systems. What they *did* have was extremely limited.

Link energy was not the kind that could be detected, not as easily as other types of radiation, not to mention it had been seen only once before since scanners came into the game. Because of this, the system couldn't alert them when it cropped up. It just didn't understand the energy without help.

Zale would need to do some inspired programming in order to succeed.

Finalising his command prompts, with a kicking in his chest as his heart played a samba against his ribs, he straightened up, flexed his fingers, then pressed the Enter key.

A split second later the computer shrilled.

The blue lights of his monitor winked off to be replaced by the flashing red warning lights.

On his screen, a bright blue/white flash dominated all else. Nothing could be seen past the glow of demonic energy.

"Holy!" Zale cried in disbelief, staring wide-eyed at the console.

Link energy.

It was everywhere.

All over the base.

As though it had irradiated every surface of their facility.

Zale had studied the link energy connecting Horas to Daemnos only a few times since arriving at the Daemonium all those years ago and he knew that the sensors registered it as a rope of energy, linking out of his chest.

When he'd studied it before Badrick's arrival to the Daemonium, the camera had always displayed the rope stretching endlessly, past the range of the cameras.

But once Badrick became a part of the Daemonium, the monitors clearly displayed a beam of energy connecting both Zale and Badrick no matter where they were in the facility.

For the first time Zale had been able to see the other end of the rope.

It was a perfectly crafted beam.

Thick and powerful, but sleek and clean.

Not like this.

Not like what he saw now.

The recording of the energy practically erupted out of his computer, the readings were so *massive*. The waves and layers of the powerful force were shredded, all over the place, as if torn or corrupted.

Zale had no doubt. This link energy belonged to the Resurrected. How, he had no idea. With who it was connected, he didn't know.

The answer to that would lie with his or her demon.

What interested Zale the most was the abnormally unstable structure of the link. He'd noticed the moment he saw it that it looked like it was minutes from unravelling. The Daemonium didn't understand much in the supernatural science of link energy, but if he had to hazard a guess he would have said it was because of the simple fact that the Enthraller was a Resurrected.

His or her death, as far as Zale was aware, would have destroyed the link. The demon then being dragged back into the Enthraller's body, returning to their original state, however flawed, could have messed the stable structure completely. The link must have tried to rebuild and failed to do so correctly.

Not that Zale cared; what did it matter if it was chaotically constructed? With this recording he finally—*finally*—had something to track the Resurrected.

A smile played on his lips.

It wasn't a kind smile.

With vengeful anticipation, he set to work. First Zale reopened his old files, bringing up satellite recordings of every evidence site they had.

The Apos base.

The hangar base.

The production facility.

There was nothing whatsoever at the home of the slaughtered Apostaticus, but Zale had expected that. There was never any evidence to say the Resurrected had been present at all, so he wasn't surprised to see nothing show up on his screen.

The production facility was the same—the Resurrected had not made an appearance there either.

However, the hangar base was an entirely different story. After a few inspired rewrites into the software, the chaotic glow of shredded power obscured everything else, even Zale and Badrick's own presence.

"Gotcha!"

Now that Zale possessed two recordings of broken link energy, he had enough data to identify it no matter when or where it reappeared, once he'd scrutinized the power and identified its unique make-up. Praising the Daemonium satellites, and their penchant for recording a site with every single type of scanner they possessed, he tapped on the keyboard one more time, scanning the energy as thoroughly as he could so that he would have a sample ready and waiting. With that in his possession, he would be able to instantly match it to any link he found further down the line.

This would help.

Grinning savagely, he completed the scan and readied the data for transfer to his files.

But then he saw the little alert in the bottom right hand corner of the screen.

He found himself frowning with irritation; what was this? Why was there an alert bothering him *now* of all times?

Desperate to get it out of the way, he double clicked it.

Instantly the display on the screen altered.

It flashed once.

Then again . . .

And again.

Until it was blinking red at him endlessly.

Zale lost control of the computer as the machine took over.

And a computerised voice began to speak.

"Demonic link energy detected," it droned. *"Signature identified as the Horas/Daemnos link."*

Unable to comprehend what he'd just heard, Zale stood stock still, staring at the flashing warning display in perplexity.

The Horas/Daemnos link?

That wasn't true.

How could a third person share a two-demon link?

Besides, their link was completely different to the Resurrected's.

The computer was wrong.

It had to be.

But then, almost as if it wished to dispute his claims, the display changed once again. A rendered image of the Horas/Daemnos link appeared next to the image of the Resurrected's.

To the naked eye, they looked completely different; one smooth and strong, the other falling apart.

The machine compared them right in front of him, the automated software taking over as it was apparently programmed to.

"Link pattern confirmed," the machine spoke once more. *"Signature identified as the Horas/Daemnos link."*

"That's impossible!" Zale hollered. But he was just lying to himself; though feeble, there was no disputing what the software was telling him. What the software *could* do, it was perfect at doing.

So it was the simple truth . . .

The Resurrected shared Zale and Badrick's link energy.

The Resurrected shared their link!

At that very moment, the Agent Commanders returned, demanding to know what the noise was. They'd brought Badrick with them; likely they'd already been bringing him to strong-arm Zale out of the BCR.

Zale shushed them all immediately, his mind working fast.

As it did so, he could feel genuine panic rising in his chest.

Because everything was becoming god-awfully clear . . .

To have a link, his mind spoke, *you have to have a demon or* be *a demon.*

He is a Resurrected, so he isn't a demon.

To share our link energy, the Resurrected would have had to have been present when the link was made.

Unless someone was hiding in the bushes next to Badrick when I passed him . . .

"Oh . . . My . . . God!"

Someone who died.

Was turned into a Powered Resurrected with the ability to create those *accursed* splinters.

To make that happen, they would have had to have come into contact with carbon monoxide.

Otherwise commonly known as exhaust fumes.

Just before they died.

But, said an unhelpfully thorough voice in Zale's head, *what if the puppet-master of the Resurrected is the one with the link? That would be a totally different demon or Enthraller. That would mean it couldn't be who I think it is . . . That would mean the Resurrected is still someone we don't know.*

Zale hated to admit it . . . but that threw a wrench in his . . .

No! Daemnos was very specific about scanning for link energy in relation to the Resurrected.

It had to be the man whose face was now grinning ear to ear

inside Zale's head.

As Badrick clamoured for answers, Zale fancied his heart had actually, genuinely stopped beating.

"No . . . " He heard sound come out of his mouth, faint as though he were a million miles away. "No . . . No way . . . "

"What's wrong, Zale?" Badrick cried. "Tell me!"

His heart still and cold, his body tense and stiff, his mind stunned silent . . . Zale turned and said, "I know who it is."

chapter
TWENTY EIGHT

(Five to six months earlier)

Lucikefer spun on the spot, panic rising in his chest. He couldn't see the one who distressed him, but he could sense his suffocating presence. Stretching his own senses out into his surroundings, Lucikefer did his best to detect his assailant. When that failed, he tried goading him into the open with words.

"What do you expect to achieve with this pathetic display of intimidation?" he asked the air. "Don't you have any idea who *I* am!?" Lucikefer spread his hands and used his powers to explode the earth on either side of him, erupting dirt, rocks and water into the air.

It was a powerful display of supremacy.

And it didn't work in the slightest.

With a shout of pain, Lucikefer crumbled from a strike to the back of his helmeted head. It was such a strong blow that he felt the metal dent and his head explode. Falling to the sand of the beach he'd been cornered on, he writhed on the minute stones, attempting to regain his footing. Before he could do so a heavy weight pushed him back down. His attacker grabbed the back of his now dented helmet and forced his visor into the sand.

"Get off me immediately!"

"Why?" was the mocking, laughing reply.

"Because I—"

Lucikefer shut up.

Fear the likes of which he'd never known struck his very soul when he felt the surge of energy exuding from the one who pinned him.

It did not belong to him.

But it was . . . *attached.*

And Lucikefer realised that this one had a master.

Someone more powerful than the Royal had *ever* encountered.

"You are going to do something for me, Lucikefer," his attacker crooned. "You are going to do as you are told."

Lucikefer was so scared that he could only say, "Alright."

In what was a purposefully posh tone of voice, the assailant said, "We will leave you alone. We will come near you not." He laughed at his own words. "We will not interfere with your plans whatsoever and we hope to see you in our ranks when all the Universes belong to us.

"But first you will do something."

"I already told you I would!" Lucikefer bawled like a pathetic newborn human.

His attacker laughed gleefully and leaned in close, ensuring the added weight of his action dug into Lucikefer as much as possible. "You are going to kill the Enthraller Mawr Burakka."

"Why do you—"

"You are going to kill him. You are going to do it quietly. And then you are going to find his access key card.

"You will bring the key card to me. Do you understand?"

Lucikefer was too terrified to ask any more questions. He nodded vigorously, communicating his obedience.

"Good show, chap!"

The weight lifted from his form and Lucikefer scrambled to stand. He backed away as fast as he could, keeping the figure in sight; he was laughing now, mostly at the sight of Lucikefer's fear.

The Royal trembled to his feet, his metal boots digging deep footprints in the beach's sand.

But then a smidgen of bravery, fuelled by intense curiosity, returned to his blackened heart and Lucikefer asked a question he instantly wished he hadn't.

"Who are you?"

The figure laughed ecstatically, starkly reminding Lucikefer of his uncle Daemnos.

"Don't you remember, Lucikefer? It's me. The one you had murdered in cold blood." He took a mocking bow, his grin wider than ever.

And in barely a mutter, he said, "The Resurrected formerly known as Charles, reporting for duty."

chapter
TWENTY NINE

"Charles?" Badrick eyed him with scepticism. "Your *friend* Charles?"

"Yes," Zale nodded.

"The one who rode past me on a motorbike, with you at the handlebars . . . *Charles?*"

Zale tutted with impatience, turning on his heel and giving Badrick the most intense evil-eye. "Why is this so hard for you to comprehend?"

"Because, man, it's so . . . " Badrick waved his hands in the air, struggling to find the right word, " . . . unlikely."

Zale continued his barrage with the evil-eye, unrelenting in his glare, until Badrick finally sighed, saying, "It's gotta be someone else, man. Someone else could've been there when the link was made."

Zale almost laughed at that. "Who exactly are you suggesting?"

Badrick thought for a moment, his finger on his chin. Eventually, he muttered, "Well, Reynolds was there too, wasn't he?"

"Not in the right time-zone," Zale tutted, glancing at the console which now displayed the criminal record of his old friend. "He was in London. The link was crafted four years in the future in your town." He turned an accusatory eye upon Badrick. "Besides, Reynolds doesn't radiate taint! There's no toxic energy surrounding him."

Badrick clicked his fingers at him. "But we haven't found any toxic stuff at any of the scenes, so maybe he can hide it."

"He's got a heartbeat!" Zale hollered. "Badrick . . . do you *want* Reynolds to be our bad guy?"

Badrick immediately blanched, waving his hands and shaking his head. "No, no, no . . . sorry. I just . . . Charles? It's insane. It can't be."

"If he had a demon without us knowing . . . " Zale muttered. "If he was an Enthraller all along, then he could have been caught in the middle of the link. He was there, and besides the white demon's powers weren't very well aimed." He nodded, his mind made up; he was certain this was right. "We all got caught up in it. It's a three way link. We're all connected."

"Oh crap!" Badrick suddenly exclaimed, his hands going to his mouth. "If an Enthraller is resurrected their demon is dragged back to them." From the look that now spread across Badrick's face like an unwelcome mask, Zale figured his partner was now on board with his theory. Badrick didn't speak for a moment, simply staring at the metal floor.

Eventually, he glanced up, his lips warped by the pull of his fingers on his face, and muttered, "Why have we never known about this?" he asked. "How have we never detected the presence of another person?"

Zale could only shrug, but he did his best to offer an explanation. "It could be because of the toxic energy warping his signature. He's a Resurrected, after all. His demon left him shortly after the link was made, which would have cut him off from the connection completely until recently, when he was resurrected. And then he was dragged back in and apparently the link was too."

Zale initiated a scan of the BCR and found the visual aid he wanted; the consoles now displayed a live feed of both him and Badrick, and cleanly showed the blue/white energy connecting the two of them.

"The scanners don't even register there is another person attached to us," he said, pointing to the screen. It was true; logically there should have been another connection heading off into the distance from both he and Badrick, but there was nothing. "It's been corrupted, Charles' connection. Our scanners aren't equipped to consider it as a factor when looking at our perfect link so it doesn't even show. That's why we never knew about it, not until we scanned for raw link energy."

He turned to Badrick just as his partner uttered, in a tone of voice that parroted his own, "How unhelpful."

Zale felt himself laugh. "Isn't it just?"

Badrick studied Zale as he mused on the discovery of their suspect's identity.

He didn't like what he could see.

It was clear Zale was putting all his focus into the Charles matter, and that was *very* bad. Badrick wasn't an expert on emotional therapy—*Jesus*, he had only recently figured out *how* to feel again—but he suspected that Zale's concentration was doing him more harm than good.

He'd been angry.

He'd raged beyond belief.

But he wasn't grieving.

Badrick could see it with his own eyes; something about Zale's current body language just screamed a refusal to cry.

He wanted to find Charles. *Needed* to get revenge. He *probably* wanted to kill him.

Badrick desired to say something. Wanted to stop this stupidity right this instant.

But he had no idea what to say.

Nothing—sophisticated or otherwise—even popped into his head.

Heck, Badrick didn't even know what to do with his *own* feelings.

Zale closed the gap between them in a flash, causing Badrick to jump a little.

"Badrick," he said quickly as his partner tried to speak. "Listen to me." He rubbed his hands together, a little nervous now that he was about to speak the rest of his thoughts out loud. "We have no more time."

"What do you mean?"

"Charles attacked the Daemonium," Zale sighed. "Whatever he wants, whatever he's after, this screams endgame to me."

Badrick's face went grey as stone. "You think he's close to getting what he wants?"

Zale nodded. "I do." He stepped away again, returning to the consoles and his feverish typing.

"We can stop him, right?" Badrick queried.

"Are you kidding me?" Zale cackled. "Now that we know what to look for, there's no place Charles can hide. I'll find that scum, even if it takes me years."

He was tapping the keys so hard that his fingers were starting to hurt. But he ignored the dull pains, his hands moving so fast and so stubbornly the keyboard was likely to erode away to nothing at any moment.

Thankfully, it was saved this brutal fate as Zale's task was completed within only moments of him starting.

"What are you doing?" Badrick queried as the displays began to light up with results.

"Scanning for link energy," Zale said. "Now that I've identified the makeup of Charles' link I can search for it. I'm going to do a country-wide scan until I find the bastard."

"How long could that take?"

Zale couldn't give his partner a definitive answer. "Any time between right now and days from now. It depends on where he is. I'll do the UK first. Unless he can teleport, he can't have gotten far in so little time. If I get nothing, I'll move onto Europe. Then the Americas. If I still get nothing I will scour the rest of the world until I find Charles.

"Badrick . . . " His gaze once again met his partner's, "I need you to tell Reynolds what I'm doing. He's going to want to know about it."

"Got it." With that he vanished, the BCR falling into silence as Badrick departed with speed.

It took some time to get Reynolds to pay attention; his day had become far busier than he'd expected and a whole load of important duties had befallen him. Badrick understood this but it didn't change the fact that what he had to say was just as imperative.

Reynolds reached out and shook hands with the commander he'd just recruited to be part of the new Council. The newly appointed Council Member appeared resistant to the idea, but also extremely honoured, as could be told by the small appreciative smile pulling at his mouth.

Badrick agreed; Commander Quill was a good choice. Badrick never truly met him, but he knew that Quill green-lit their early mission into the Kalik investigation. Not to mention, Zale spoke highly of the man. His respect for Quill was the whole reason Zale had chosen him, of all the other commanders, to implore for help.

Finally, Quill left the Main Hall, heading towards the Council's lair to receive some kind of badge or whatever; Badrick wasn't really paying attention. He was too busy trying to waylay Reynolds before he moved on to his next order of business.

"Right," Reynolds sighed heavily, blowing air hot into Badrick's face. "Yes. Hello, Badrick. What do you want?"

He proceeded to relay what Zale had told him. Speaking quickly, he explained who the electric Enthraller believed to be their bad guy, as well as providing the evidence to back it up.

Reynolds' look of revulsion was all too clear. "Charles?" he squirmed. "Really? That low-life? *That's* who's been behind this the whole time?"

"I had difficulty believing it too."

"Don't get me wrong, I believe it one hundred percent," Reynolds said. "But I'm appalled by the idea that after all this time it turns out our culprit is Zale's old friend, of all people."

"What do you want us to do?" Badrick moved the conversation on. A horrible pressure had started to constrict his mind and he was desperate to move ahead and catch the bastard before he did any more damage.

"Exactly what you are doing," Reynolds said. "I can't do anything to help right now. I've been charged with finding replacement Council Members." He leaned in closer, tutting with irritation. "If I'm honest, it's more stressful than you could ever imagine."

"Oh, I *can* imagine," Badrick sighed.

"But I don't want to leave Zale on his own," Reynolds continued. "Not now. Not after . . . *everything*."

Badrick certainly agreed with that. Zale needed his friends more than ever.

Reynolds rolled his shoulders in a manly display of authority. "Once I'm done with this, I'll find him and offer my assistance. We should—"

His hands slapped to his ears and he winced in agony. Badrick did the same. All around him, Enthrallers went from mildly alert to outright jumpy as the most piercing and deafening alarm blocked out all other noise.

"Jesus Christ!" Reynolds exclaimed, momentarily forgetting himself. "What is that?"

"The scanners?" Badrick guessed, thinking Zale might have already succeeded in his task.

"That wasn't the scanners," Reynolds argued. His fingers were twitching now, his expression one of severe stress. "That was something else entirely."

His claim was further reinforced as the alarms were cut silent and a voice he didn't recognise bawled for Reynolds' presence in the Red Control Room. Obeying the disembodied voice, the pair of them ran, side by side, in the direction of the Army's headquarters.

Badrick listened intently as the generals began filling Reynolds in upon their arrival.

"Sir, we detected a massive surge of energy near the border of

Wales."

"What was it?" Reynolds asked.

"You sure ain't gonna like this," one of them hesitated.

"Just tell me, Kevin."

Kevin sighed, exchanged glances with the woman opposite, then said, "Kalik, sir. A whole army of them."

This news hit Reynolds so hard that he stumbled, the strength in his legs weakening.

Badrick understood why; Kalik barely registered at all on the Daemonium's equipment, their signatures were too weak. The only time was when they crossed or killed, and even then it was pretty dismal.

To generate the kind of energy that would make the alarms go this mental would take . . . Christ . . . It would take *thousands* of the things. More than even at the last few attacks.

Reynolds appeared to regain control of his legs. He stared at the other general, licked his lips and asked, "How near to the closest city are they?"

"Close enough to pose a major threat, but far enough to stay out of sight." The General summoned a hologram from the machinery and Badrick stepped up for a closer look. The image was of a lightly forested network of fields. It looked calm and beautiful, a great place to relax, Badrick thought.

At least it would have if not for the light of hundreds upon hundreds of heat signatures warping the image and making it near impossible to properly discern anything.

"This is bigger than anything before," Reynolds said. "Do you think they plan to attack a major population centre?"

"If they do, all hell will break loose."

"You're telling me," Reynolds sighed. His eyes were so wide and so transfixed on the hologram Badrick was surprised he didn't wear them out. "If those Kalik swarm over a city, everything comes undone. That's too big to cover up. The sheer amount of cameras that will capture their image . . . We'd never find them all before the news was all over the internet."

"We could eliminate the websites and internet videos," Kevin suggested.

"Not before the damage is done." Reynolds shook his head. "Not before they get downloaded." He straightened his back and chewed his lip, having earlier put his hands on the table in order to study the hologram more carefully. "But if they stay there . . . " he murmured. "If they don't go near the city then we *can* keep this quiet. Look, they aren't near any populated areas."

"Are you suggestin' an attack?"

Kevin's stunned question didn't get answered.

This was because an out of breath Zale Hood had just barged into the RCR and distracted everyone from their conversation. Kevin himself jumped in fright as Zale almost collided with the hologram desk, his head phasing through the image and disappearing into a clump of trees.

When he was back in view, he raised a hand, only two fingers straightened.

"Two things," he said. "One; what the hell was that alarm?"

Badrick was the one to tell him, redirecting his gaze to the hologram.

Zale's reaction was much like Reynolds' and Badrick had to steady him as his partner's muscles decided to quit working.

His face white and his fingers twitching, the electric Enthraller fought to regain his composure. With a voice that was slightly shaky, Zale whispered, "It's a distraction."

"How do you mean?" Reynolds asked.

"Charles wants us off his back," Zale growled, the anger that had been so badly hidden no longer even trying to remain masked. It spread through his handsome features like a warped disease.

"He must have known his actions would lead to us discovering him so now he's trying to scare us. He wants us to deal with this threat and forget about him."

"Bastard!" Badrick exclaimed.

"Reynolds," Zale shouted. "Please, let me go after Charles myself." When Reynolds opened his mouth, his expression suggesting he was about to argue, Zale stopped him with, "Sir, it *is* part of my case. The plan was for Badrick and I to take down the Resurrected. Just because of this new development doesn't mean the plan has changed."

The logic in this statement definitely hit home in Reynolds intelligent, rational mind. His mouth snapped shut and he gave Zale a most pleading expression. "Don't put me in this position, Zale," he said. "Again!"

Zale spread his hands to the air and shrugged. "As I hear, you're in charge now. So it's up to you. But Charles was my friend. He's my responsibility. No one is going after him but me."

Reynolds appeared to have momentarily forgotten that he had been appointed as the head honcho. He coughed, embarrassed, glancing around as though he hoped no one had witnessed this forgetfulness.

But even so, he didn't look like he was going to green light Zale's mission request. His face was stony, his head slowly shaking from left to right and back again.

Badrick steeled himself for a denial.

But then Reynolds' tightened muscles relaxed and the near angry expression on his face softened. The man's shoulders also calmed, dropping quite a distance, and in a defeated voice, Reynolds said, "Your logic is sound. By Council order, you were given jurisdiction over anything to do with Kalik. I cannot revoke it.

"Or, more accurately, I won't revoke it. The Council may be

gone, and to Hell with the lot of them and their reign, but I won't allow the few decent procedures they enforced to go with them. My first act as Dominus will not be a petty revolution against the old ways that made sense.

"Besides . . . your partner has a Royal inside him. Nothing is more powerful than that." Reynolds rolled his eyes, his old self shining through the mist of mixed emotions. "You have my blessing."

Despite the warped feelings that had tied his heart since Carla's vicious murder, Badrick felt a smile tug at his mouth. *This* was why the Hierarch had made Reynolds Dominus. The man was an incredibly fair and intelligent leader.

He pivoted, expecting Zale to be as relieved as he was.

But his partner was staring at his right hand, flexing the fingers, as though something was wrong with it.

And the look on his face . . . If Badrick hadn't known better, he would have said it was fear.

"What of the Kalik?" a soldier asked the generals. "This . . . Charles or whatever is hardly a problem compared to this."

"*This Charles*," Reynolds said, "is the reason the Kalik have amassed. He is our priority." His hand went into the air, stopping the argumentative soldier from snapping back. "But you are right, the Kalik are a serious problem."

"We can't let them move from their current position," Kevin piped up.

"We have to keep them there," a woman concurred. "If they move, we have to stop them."

"What do you suggest, Kate?" Reynolds sighed.

"I say we fight them," Kate said sharply. "Badrick would be extremely helpful here. Daemnos' power would be a valuable asset. He could kick their arses on his own, probably."

Reynolds immediately shot that idea down. "No, Badrick will

find Charles with Zale. We cannot run the risk of their leader getting away. If he does then this will just happen again. We need to cut the head off the snake. Without their leader, the Kalik will return to a manageable level."

"It's true," said Kevin. "They're too simple to stay organised without a leader. I'm amazed to find out they had one, but at least it all finally makes sense."

Zale looked quite offended to hear that Reynolds considered Charles' escape a possibility without Badrick, but he chose not to speak up. Badrick would have said something to make him feel better, but he couldn't help agreeing with Reynolds.

They would need the power of Daemnos for this.

"We have to manage our assets cleverly," said Reynolds. "The army will deal with the Kalik. That's our job."

"Pretty sure that's what Charles wants," Zale mumbled darkly, still glowering. "For us to engage the Kalik in battle."

"That fact has not escaped my notice, and I hate to play into our enemy's hands." Reynolds glared at the hologram hatefully. "But at the moment we have no choice. The only way we can stop those Kalik from moving is if we distract them. They have yet to move anywhere, yes?"

A woman at a console nodded and hollered, "They're holding position, sir."

"An army this big will require a massive response force," Kevin told Reynolds. "Unless we want to drive there in a hundred cars or use a thousand helicopters, we'll need the drop-ships."

Reynolds sighed and banged his fist against the desk. "Goddamn it!" he exclaimed angrily. "Covering up the use of those damn things is always so difficult."

"It'll be fifty times easier than covering up a Kalik attack on a city," Kevin argued.

Reynolds burst out laughing right then, but Badrick could tell it was humourless. "No kidding," he snapped, though his anger wasn't directed at Kevin. For a moment he simply stared, blinking slowly and barely breathing. His face was whiter than snow, his eyes like glass as they reflected his attempt to remove himself from his emotions.

"What are you thinking, sir?" Kevin asked.

"I'm thinking you're right," Reynolds eventually sighed. "Trying to cover up a Kalik invasion wouldn't be possible."

"I'm sure y'all could do it," Kevin said quietly, "but . . . "

"We can't risk it," Reynolds continued, nodding in agreement at Kevin's unspoken words. "We have to engage them in battle. Stop them from moving on. Slaughter them all if we have to."

"Any idea how we're going to do that?" Kevin smiled apologetically. "It's an army. Not a hunting party. How are we going to beat them?

"There's so many," a woman muttered; Badrick only just heard her over the clamour of the RCR, but he could sense the wavering fear in her voice without difficulty.

"That there is." Kevin tapped his hands on the desk, chewing his lip. "We'll need a plan of attack. A sound strategy. This isn't the Apos. We'll need to think this through."

Reynolds didn't need to voice his worries for Badrick to figure them out. From the way they always talked, the Daemonium had never faced anything like this before. Even the best of them had hardly an idea on how to deal with the Kalik army.

It must have been like being a mathematician and finding an area of maths you'd never heard of before; your knowledge and experience would just abandon you if you let the uncertainty take hold.

Badrick had experienced that issue in maths class more times than he cared to admit.

And he had no idea how to help at this moment either. When

it came to battle strategy, he was less than adequate.

He was the brute force.

Not the brains.

Reynolds interrupted the quiet at that moment. He opened his mouth, paused, then said, "I don't think we need an elaborate strategy." Having been saved from admitting his inadequacy, Badrick raised an eyebrow and asked the General what he meant.

"I think . . . " Reynolds said. "It's radical . . . but I think there might be a way."

chapter
THIRTY

The General moved his hands over a keyboard and tapped in a number of commands, manipulating the hologram.

When he was done, he said, "Think about it. Kalik are extremely simple creatures. They live to kill. That is *it!* So what do you think they would do if we presented them with a hundred meals? Two hundred? Three hundred?"

"They'd freak the hell out," Zale answered. "It'd be like Christmas."

"Exactly!" Reynolds pointed at him. "All reasoning would go out the window. All strategy. I doubt even Charles could keep complete control of them if we charged an army into their ranks."

"That would mean a lotta deaths," Kevin commented. "Of our guys."

"That's why it's radical," Reynolds sighed sadly.

"What's the point of the strategy?" Kevin asked. "Is that it? Charge headlong?"

"No," Zale said. "Have a little more trust in your Dominus." He approached a keyboard and worked on the hologram himself. Among the assorted projections of Kalik and Daemonium soldiers Reynolds had placed appeared thin white lines, carving into the Kalik formation. "Let me guess," he said, "you're thinking we distract them with a tasty meal of soldiers. They lose all control of their senses and that's when we pick them off with strategically placed snipers."

Badrick realised the white lines were projections of rifle shots. He nodded, happy that the hologram now made sense to him; he'd been embarrassingly clueless ever since Reynolds altered the image.

"You read my mind," Reynolds said. "It's the only way I can see. Please . . . " he pleaded, "if you can think of a strategy that doesn't involve hundreds of our friends dying, speak up."

To the General's great dismay, no one was able to provide one.

"Any other strategy invites the possibility of the Kalik organising against us," Zale murmured. "Either with their new tendency to be more intelligent than we can predict or with Charles directing them."

"We have to eliminate that possibility," Kevin nodded, though he appeared highly hateful of the plan. "We have to cloud their minds."

"It'll be to our advantage if we can distract Charles from the battle," Reynolds said. "Leave the Kalik abandoned." His piercing gaze found Zale. "Please tell me good news."

For a moment, Zale didn't say anything in response. His eyes did not move from the hologram, his body remaining stock still.

As he continued to remain unresponsive, Badrick decided to

speak up. "I don't know if we can promise that. It could take ages to find—"

"I've already found him."

Anyone who may have wanted to speak instantly decided against it as all eyes turned towards Zale.

"Already?" Badrick spluttered incredulously.

"Where is he?" Reynolds queried, wasting absolutely no time.

"It's what I was on my way to tell you when the alarm sounded." He raised a hand and lifted a second finger. "I decided to scan places the Kalik have been as well as the local area," Zale told them. "I found link energy at the Apos base."

"Excellent. We shall—"

"*And* the Forsaken's cave."

Reynolds blinked with disbelief. "The Forsaken—"

"The cave where Badrick opened the fourth fissure," Zale nodded in confirmation.

"How is that possible?" Badrick asked. "Two locations?"

Zale shrugged apologetically. "I don't know. Maybe he dumped the energy."

"Not possible," Reynolds shook his head. "You can't dump link energy like demonic energy."

Zale shrugged a second time. "I'm sorry. I can't explain. I have no idea how he did it."

Reynolds shared a worried glance with Kevin, who appeared just as unsettled as the General.

But then Reynolds shook his head and deactivated the hologram. "OK!" he hollered. "We don't have *any* time to bang about theories and slack off shooting the breeze like we always do."

He indicated to Badrick and Zale. "As you asked, you're on Charles duty. You find him. You stop him helping the Kalik and you bring him in. Got it?"

The pair of them nodded their understanding.

"Gear up," the General ordered.

As Badrick hurried away, he heard Reynolds addressing Kevin. "Your work has always impressed me, Kevin. Ever thought about joining the Council?"

*

Badrick followed Zale through the Gate, slinging his single-rifle over his shoulder and pulling on his gloves. Fully equipped and his body safely secured inside his armour, he felt ready to do what was required.

Having said that, he was not without some trepidation.

The evil they were facing was immense. Its power was more than he'd ever seen, bar his own demon's.

Even Lucikefer hadn't been able to do this much damage.

Compared to Charles' reign of terror, the threat of the Royal seemed pitiful.

Badrick could hardly believe he'd ever considered the petulant child of Satan a danger.

Being in his own thoughts so much, Badrick was unaware his partner was going to grind to a halt until they almost collided.

Thankfully, he was able to divert his own momentum and slip past Zale's shoulder without crashing into his back.

When he'd regained his balance, he stared into the blue visor in question, already wishing he could read his partner's expression.

In the end he didn't need to ask why he had stopped; an armoured General Reynolds was beckoning to them and Zale was already in the process of changing direction. Badrick hurried to keep up, reaching within earshot just as Reynolds held out his hand to Zale, presenting him with an object Badrick didn't recognise at first.

"As Dominus, I return this device to you," the General said, his arm still held forward. "I don't deny the Council had the right to chide you for its creation, but its removal from your possession served no purpose."

With a speed that suggested he was more than excited, Zale snatched the device from Reynolds hand and activated it. A curved, bright blue blade of electricity zapped into existence. Zale held the sword before him, possibly familiarising himself with its heft.

"Thank you, Reynolds," Zale muttered, barely audible over the ruckus the Enthrallers were making. Badrick could see hundreds upon hundreds of soldiers, geared up and looking powerful in their armour, their equipment ready in their tightly gripping hands.

"Reynolds, I want you to take the other swords," Badrick heard his partner saying.

"No, Zale," Reynolds shot him down. "They were locked up for a reason."

Zale puffed derisively. "The enemy already has the technology, Reynolds. With it, they have an advantage. You're outnumbered as it is." He removed his helmet, possibly so he could stare at Reynolds in the eye. "Kalik are dangerous. With my weapons, they're near unstoppable. Take my swords."

Reynolds glared at him with an anger Badrick had never seen on his face before. "Goddamn it, Hood. I hate it when your logic makes sense. There's never anything I can say to argue." He threw his hands up in the air. "*Fine!* Broken every other rule the last few weeks, might as well smash the last one and call it a day."

If Zale wanted to answer, he never got the chance to speak.

As Reynolds finished talking, a horrendous grinding sound erupted around them, drowning out all other noise. For a while, Badrick could not determine the source, but then picked up on the shouts, and he realised what was happening.

His jaw fell and his eyes flew wide open. If he'd been holding his rifle in his hands he'd have dropped it to the gravel.

The ground was moving.

Literally *moving*.

A massive crevice had appeared in the middle of the grounds in front of the Gate, splitting the earth in half. The two sides slowly rumbled apart, spreading the gap further and further and further. Badrick gingerly stepped closer to the edge, his legs shaking as he caught sight of what lay through the newly formed fissure.

Absolutely massive gears—the size of his old house—lining the walls of the metal cavern below cranked slowly, creakingly, as though they hadn't been used in centuries.

His eyes popped when it dawned on him just how deep this hole was.

And in it, firmly secured on metal cranes and locks, were aircraft.

Big.

Sleek.

Thrusters the size of cars.

Dozens of them.

Maybe hundreds.

A never ending number packed in tight, as far down into the ground as was possible to see.

As Badrick gazed into the depths of the earth, the two aircraft closest to the surface suddenly lit up with activity. The thrusters roared to life, the darkness beneath the windshields flickered as people moved behind the glass, and the doors slammed shut.

With a burst of fire and exhaust, the two vast vehicles disconnected from the metal arms that secured them. Then they rose, faster than Badrick had expected, cresting over the edges of the crevice and lifting into the air.

Badrick craned his neck, gazing up at them as they lifted higher and the second pair down beneath his feet lit up with activity.

"Oh . . . my . . . God!" was all he could say.

Beside him, Zale managed a small smile. "Now you know why we didn't build *our* base underground."

"Amazing," Badrick said. "Absolutely bloody amazing."

To his disappointment, Badrick didn't get much more time to awe at the Daemonium's military power, obviously far more superior than he'd imagined.

The part he had to play in the events that would come next was of dire importance.

They were the key.

Without them, everything would fall apart.

As Badrick followed him to the vehicle depot, he could almost hear his partner's voice in his ears; "We can't kill Charles. We have to capture him alive. Acquiring him so that we can interrogate him is of utmost importance."

Badrick couldn't help but agree; as much as he wanted to tear Charles limb from limb, he knew that the Resurrected could be only *part* of some bigger conspiracy. If the demon that brought him back to life was involved in these horrendous events, then they needed to discover him or her just as badly as they needed to stop Charles.

Badrick *hoped* whatever power was responsible had nothing to do with the Kalik attacks. If that was the case, then it would all end with Charles.

Of course it didn't matter if he or she was or wasn't; the simple fact that they had dabbled in such necromantic powers meant the Daemonium would need to intervene in their activities.

Badrick shook his head with despair as he clambered inside Zale's car, his mind alight with apprehension and the desire for it all to be over right then and there.

There was so much stacked against them.

So many enemies to fight.

So much to do.

It all seemed too much.

Unfortunately, Zale didn't seem available for consoling at that moment; he was so determined to finish the job that he'd not stopped since the attack on the HQ.

Hadn't rested.

Hadn't grieved.

Badrick gripped the chair, his heart pounding his ribs to splinters as Zale implemented his customary driving habits. Filled with such impatience, the electric Enthraller did not wait for the ground to glue itself back together, swerving their car around the vast circular opening and almost plummeting the vehicle straight into the hole.

Badrick's heart skipped a beat as the car only just managed to *not* topple them to their demise and breathed a sigh of relief as they approached the Wall Gate. The guards opened it for them, allowing them to exit.

Without waiting for it to even finish opening, Zale slammed his foot down on the pedal and they rocketed forward once more. It was such a tight fit that Badrick's side of the car scraped against the metal of the gate, scratching the paint from the vehicle and making him cringe.

"Jesus," he muttered, sneaking a glance at Zale before fitting his helmet back upon his head.

He hoped his partner calmed before they reached their destination. Zale's agitation could become a hindrance if it continued.

*

It took Zale nearly half an hour to convince Badrick that the plan he'd formed was wise. He was annoyingly resistant, not as willing to accept Zale's judgment as he usually was.

But Zale kept on him.

Over and over.

There were two places to go. Two places that burned with link energy.

They didn't have time to waste. They had to find Charles *now!*

So it only made sense for them to split up.

Divide and conquer.

Storm both locations at once.

But Badrick refused to see the sense in his plan. Utterly repudiated his suggestions.

"We should stay together," Badrick said firmly. "Splitting up won't help us."

Aggravated but unwavering, Zale never stopped trying to force him to agree to his scheme, even though his own head blared in agreement with Badrick. Annoyingly, the host of Daemnos had a point, because it was true that Zale had not formed this plan with any kind of strategy.

On better days, whenever his emotional mind formulated tactics, his logic stamped them out of existence. He was far too wary and too clever to listen to his emotional judgement, no matter what it said.

But he couldn't do that now.

Not today.

Too much had happened.

Too much had been lost.

His anger—nay, his *rage*—was uncontrollable and he couldn't disregard it.

It was controlling him.

To hell with logic.

To hell with reasoning.

Charles was his.

And he wanted Badrick out of the way.

They would split up.

Whether his partner liked it or not.

chapter
THIRTY ONE

Like a thunder of dragons, the fleet of dropships moved over the countryside, the intense heat from their thrusters roasting the air particles as they soared through the clouds. Glancing at the four dozen ships that followed his, Reynolds felt a potent sense of pride and strength.

As though he was part of a collective power.

An unstoppable force.

He knew it wasn't strictly true; they were nowhere near undefeatable and believing they were would lead to their downfall.

But it was an intoxicating notion, nevertheless.

He stepped away from the open deployment hatch and turned to the thirty nine other soldiers packed into the transport with him. Reynolds studied them, focusing on their limbs, hands and feet to determine their emotional state.

Twitchy. Irritable. Not one calm and collected.

Most were agitated. All were afraid.

These men and women may have been soldiers of the Daemonium—powerful, strong and disciplined, they would fight to the last—but that didn't stop them from being scared, and Reynolds knew that the level of fear within an army determined the ferocity of their fight. Fear was useful, yes—in some situations it was like a super power; those who feared could run faster, fight fiercer, jump higher.

But right now?

No—the men and women of the Daemonium Army needed to be fearless. They needed their strength and power. Any fear would weaken their might. Weaken their resolve.

To the last they would fight, but to the last they would die if they feared their enemy.

They needed to be angry.

They needed morale.

It was this thought—this belief—that inspired Reynolds to open a fleet wide channel on his comm.

"Listen up," he spoke. He noticed every visor in his transport (bar the pilots) turn his way and knew that every other soldier flying in the dropships was now focused on his voice. "This is Serg—General Reynolds." He winced at his mistake, took a moment, and then tried again.

"I'm not going to lie about what we're flying into. Many of you have never fought a Kalik before—our agents usually deal with their hunting parties—but trust me when I tell you that they are a force of nature.

"These Kalik have formed an army. Bigger than we've ever seen, even during the last few days, and I'm not going to pretend that this is going to be easy. We're going into a battle unlike anything we've ever faced.

"But face it we will." He took a second to breathe and calm the anxiety coursing through his own veins; he was certain this speech was only making matters worse.

But he felt like he should keep on going.

"Some of us won't make it," he said. "That's a hard fact. The only strategy available to us calls for great losses. You all know this.

"But I'm not asking you to fight on your own. I'm not sending you to your deaths from the safety of the base like the aristocrats of the old Council. As your General, and your Dominus, it is my duty to fight *with* you.

"The same danger now looms over me. I can and probably will die with you. No matter what the Hierarch says, I will always be Daniel Reynolds, your comrade.

"I can't ask you to forget your fear. I feel it too. But remember . . . what we do here today determines the fate of the world. If we fail here I have no doubt the Kalik will swarm over a city and everything we've worked for since the dawn of time will be destroyed.

"Tel me; will you have that happen on your watch, soldiers!?!"

Within the confines of his transport, he heard a chorus of voices roar, "Sir, no, sir!"

"That's what I thought!" he hollered back, hoping beyond hope that the rest of his army was just as confident. "Will you follow me, comrades? One last time? As your leader?"

Once again soldiers bawled, "Sir, yes, sir!" and followed up with a volley of sharp salutes. He heard a chorus of chatter over the comm. and was relieved to learn that his terrible, improvised speech had resonated with the rest of his force.

"We're approaching the site, sir," the pilot interrupted the bellows. "ETA, five minutes to drop point. I suggest you look outside."

Crap!

He turned his back on his soldiers and averted his gaze to the ground beneath their craft.

Behind him, he heard a man mutter, "Oh, my God."

Reynolds could see them now.

Camped down there as if they belonged.

As if they were a part of this world and *not* a disgusting abomination of demon-kind.

Hundreds of them.

"Christ!" Reynolds couldn't help but exclaim. All the scans and all the holographic lights in the world could not have prepared him for the sight of the monsters scarring the landscape with their mere presence.

"ETA, one minute," the pilots announced. "Prepare for drop."

Reynolds pounced on the opportunity and called, "Alright, this is it! Are you ready!?!"

A choir of confident *booyahs* reverberated across the comm. in response.

Confident his soldiers would do their jobs, Reynolds slung his weapon over his shoulder, tensed his legs, grabbed hold of the side of the aircraft, nodded to the woman to his right . . .

Then he jumped.

Reynolds was the first to go. He knew it would have to be that way. The soldiers would follow him but only if he set the example. They had to know he was prepared to fight and die.

He heard soldiers shouting commands over the comm. as he plummeted to the earth, his arms and legs wide to slow his descent. Not that it mattered; he would survive no matter the speed as long as he landed on his feet.

He became aware of confident calls from his headset, and turned as much as he could just in time to witness hundreds of red bodies filling the skies.

Below, the Kalik noticed their presence for the first time, finally catching their scents, and, just as Reynolds predicted, the sight of so many fresh bodies to perforate, tear and feast upon sent them into a gibbering rage. A wave of ecstasy and shaking desire to kill visibly spread across their ranks, and they flailed their hands and jaws in the direction of the falling soldiers.

Reynolds straightened his body as the dirt rushed to meet him. His feet shuddered as he met with the earth, the soil exploding outwards from the impact.

Behind him, two thousand pairs of boots hit the ground, one after the other. An endless series of thuds as dust and dirt erupted into the air.

The Kalik's exhilaration increased tenfold. They fell over and under each other in their glee, many pulling out their wrist blades despite their strict traditions, others flexing their claws and gnashing their jaws noisily. Reynolds felt disgusted at the sight of them. He'd never had much time for hating demons—there was no point despising something for what was simply in their nature—but even he wasn't mighty enough to look upon the Kalik and stay professionally detached from abhorrence.

"Load!" he roared. Countless weapon clicks answered his call. "I'll see you on the other side, comrades!"

And with that, he pushed his feet into the ground and propelled himself in the direction of the Kalik. A resounding battle cry of approval rocked the world behind him and he knew his army was hot on his heels.

Red bodies flashed into the air, various soldiers flying ahead and smashing into the Kalik hordes as they too charged in their direction. Others teleported, dashing in and out and thinning the herd with rapid, calculated strikes. Many jumped over their comrades, weapons firing from above, their bullets tearing the enemy to shreds.

Reynolds reached for his belt as the main bulk of their force drew closer. He flicked twice the object he now gripped and felt a sensation of great power as Zale's invention responded to his actions.

He swung the electric blade as the two armies came to a dizzying crash. The Kalik's roars filled his ears as he thrashed the weapon left and right, disembowelling demons by the dozens.

He was in the thick of it now with Kalik on every side.

But he wasn't alone.

Clearly he'd done something right; with a ferocity he hadn't expected, his forces lay into the opposing army, beating them back, hammering them down and using the beasts' careless excitement as a battle advantage.

If there was only time, Reynolds would have felt pride.

A bird landed on the car while Zale waited for Badrick to do as he was told. The animal pecked at the armour, testing for weaknesses in the hope of locating food. Badrick watched as it assaulted their vehicle before flying away, its little wings carrying it into the sky with insane speed.

"I don't like this," he said when he could find no other distraction.

Zale wanted to smack him, but instead resigned himself to simply grinding his teeth to dust. "Dude, come on now!" he almost growled.

"Fine!" Badrick opened the door and stepped out, slamming it behind him. "Be careful, you goddamn idiot. Promise me."

"I assure you I'll be careful!" Zale sighed, rolling his eyes secretly behind his helmet.

His partner turned his back and faced the forest that lay

beyond. Somewhere through there he would find his target.

Seeing this accursed forest again sent shockwaves of nostalgia through Zale's body; it'd been a long time since they'd first set foot here. Despite his hatred for this place, Zale couldn't help but wish he could go back to that time.

Things were so much easier then. He'd been a fool to say they'd suffered.

Then again that was the way, wasn't it? Twenty years from now something bad could happen and he would scold himself for feeling the pressure at *this* point in time.

"Stay on the radio," Badrick told him.

"Yessir," Zale drawled back. He didn't let Badrick say anymore. Zale slammed his foot on the pedal and felt the thrust as his vehicle darted forward. The car spun a full one hundred and eighty degrees, kicking up the dirt and stones into the forest.

In the rear-view mirror he noticed Badrick watching him drive back up the path before hefting his weapon and trudging into the trees.

The journey to Zale's own destination didn't take very long. He drove like a bat out of hell, never stopping, never slowing. Not until the savaged Apos base rose up in the distance, blocking out the grey winter sky with its shadowy structure.

He parked quite a distance away, jumping from the vehicle and locating a decent scouting site. He wasn't going to walk blindly into a trap. First, he had to ensure Charles wasn't lurking somewhere outside or had some Kalik guards defending the entrance.

Because he had no doubt that Charles would be *here*.

It was the whole reason behind Zale's choice of location. Zale hadn't told Badrick that he'd known all along that their enemy would be situated here—he wanted his partner out of the way, dealing with whatever Charles had left at the Forsaken's cave.

This had been the site of Charles' first attack. The first time the bastard had messed with them. The Forsaken's cave was just another trick, just another mockery. There was no way Charles would be there. Whatever link energy resided in that spot was something else.

Maybe Charles *had* exuded it, as impossible as that was.

Some demons were able to dump their energy to lay traps or divert their enemy's attentions. It was a neat trick, rare in its usage, but maybe that was what Charles did. Perhaps the instability of his link allowed him to siphon bits off.

From his perch, Zale checked the place out, lying in the grass for nearly ten minutes. After determining that there was nothing outside, he threw a rock as hard as he could at the wall, then ducked back down.

When no one and nothing came outside, he decided it was at the very least marginally safe. Picking up his weapon, he rose to his feet and proceeded towards the front door.

The place was just as the Daemonium left it. Furniture remained in pieces, equipment was scattered every which way, machines sparked dangerously and blood caked nearly every surface.

He kicked aside a computer, briefly wondering when the Daemonium's decommissioning effort would begin. They couldn't let this facility remain to be found by an unlucky hiker, or worse, some kind of law enforcement.

Or worse yet, the Apostaticus could retake it, and even if they didn't they might try to salvage the place.

There was a lot to take here, obvious by the sheer size of the underground structure.

But although the size of the place might be beneficial to the Apos, it was starting to annoy Zale immensely. He wasn't sure exactly where Charles might be and it really *was* a bloody huge facility, so Zale was forced to prepare for a long and boring search.

He quickly learned it was highly unnecessary.

This was because, as he passed a set of double doors, a voice pierced the quiet.

A voice that rang the bells of recognition so loud it hurt his head.

"Hello, lad."

Zale ground to a halt and took a breath, his heart having leapt into his throat. Taking a second to flex the fingers of his right hand, he breathed a second time, then backtracked.

Slowly, he pushed open the double doors and walked into the room beyond.

There he was.

Standing directly in the middle of what appeared to have once been a kitchen.

He looked exactly as Zale remembered; with his dirty blonde hair and lanky limbs, his rugged face and dark brown eyes.

He smiled widely when Zale walked into view.

Zale did not.

And he couldn't stop himself from exclaiming, "Jesus!"

"Not quite, chap," Charles chuckled. "It's good to see you." He grinned wider, gesturing towards Zale with energetic enthusiasm. "Look at you. As tall as me and everything."

Zale let the door swing shut behind him, taking three steps into the room. It banged loudly as he came to a stop and glared at the young man who used to be his friend.

"Good to see me," Zale muttered mockingly. "Is it, now? I *would* say the same but your minions have tried to kill me several times."

Charles clapped his hands together, saying, "I had to make it hard for you."

"Make what hard for me?"

Charles didn't listen to him. He ignored the question entirely, laughing at Zale and grinning like a man who hadn't seen his brother in years. "You look awesome! That armour. I *wish* I had me one of those suits.

"How *do* you run around in those things? They look heavy as hell!"

Zale glared pointlessly at Charles, hating him for ignoring his question. He wanted to smash Charles' face against the wall for his disrespect.

But something inside of him instead made him say, "Demonic metals. The elements are light beyond scientific understanding."

Still grinning the cocky grin that Zale remembered all too well, Charles laughed, "Fascinating. Of course, I actually knew all that."

Zale frowned. "How, exactly?"

Charles just sniggered at him.

"OK!" Zale bawled. "Enough! I'm here for answers! It's time for you to explain everything. I don't care if you don't want to. You're going to talk."

At these words Charles immediately sobered, though a ghost of a smile still lingered on his lips. "Of course I am. Why wouldn't I?"

Zale hadn't expected him to say that at all.

But he didn't waste time questioning it, beginning with the queries he wanted answered before the Daemonium's agents got in the way. "What came first?"

"Getting Lucikefer to kill Mawr Burakka and take his key card."

Zale felt his eyes close and a sad breath of air escape his lungs. "*You* had Mawr killed?"

"It was necessary."

"Why?"

Charles spread his hands and looked around, as if he could see through the walls to the outside world. "Why . . . to equip my army, of course."

"But *why* Mawr?"

When Charles only continued to grin, Zale ground his teeth with barely suppressed rage, and exclaimed, "I should have asked *how!*" It was getting harder and harder to look at Charles' face without raising his gun and blowing it away. His head was starting to hurt for reasons unknown and all he could think of was Carla.

Her body.

Broken.

Bloody.

Dead.

All because of this man in front of him.

"Elaborate?" Charles grinned.

"How do you even know about the Daemonium?" Zale asked him. "How did you rope Lucikefer into obeying you? Did the one who resurrected you tell you everything? It doesn't seem possible. How did you know so much?"

Charles didn't answer for a moment. He simply leered at Zale, rocking slightly as he bounced his left leg up and down, up and down.

But then he finally opened his mouth and murmured, "The link."

When it appeared Charles would say no more without more prompting, Zale continued, "OK, fine. So you're an Enthraller. Yes, that's right! Stop grinning. I figured it out. Your demon was linked to mine and Badrick's. But that doesn't explain—"

"My demon," Charles interrupted him, "is Orlan. He has the power to generate an Energy Disrupter Pulse—"

This time Zale cut him off with, "Irrelavant! Tell me how—"

"—and mind-reading."

Zale felt the breath catch in his throat and his mind light up with a thousand different thoughts.

In his peripheral, Horas materialised and joined Zale in staring disbelievingly at Charles.

"I never believed it possible!" the demon exclaimed.

Zale knew exactly what Horas was thinking and he shared his incredulity.

However, he did not disbelieve the credibility of Charles' claim.

Finally, after everything that had occurred, Zale understood how Charles pulled everything off.

Finally, he figured out how they'd always been one step behind.

Finally, he could see how Charles knew so much about the Daemonium.

The answer was simple; he'd gotten it all from Zale and Badrick.

Charles had combined Orlan's power of telepathy with his link to the pair of them, running the power across the rope and right into their minds, seeing and hearing everything they could, and knowing everything they did.

That was how Charles knew how to alter his swords. He studied the science in Zale's thoughts.

He knew where they would be, when they would be there, what they were doing there.

Understood where every Daemonium camera was and stole Zale's secret methods of avoiding their gazes.

And now that Zale's brain was busy working things out, something else finally dawned on him.

Something that he should have figured out hours before.

The S.D.P power was how they could never track Charles' Resurrected taint!

With its ability to disrupt demonic energy, the power masked the readings.

No . . . It didn't mask it . . . The S.D.P cancelled it out.

Suppressed it completely.

His head alight and his senses sharp from the adrenaline now coursing through his veins, Zale closed his eyes nodded his head. "I see."

"Good."

"But it wasn't as clean an infiltration as you thought," Zale said, more theories and thoughts pouring into his head. He raised a finger and waved it at Charles. "Your actions warped our link. That's why Daemnos sounds like me instead of Badrick. He involuntarily channelled into me because of the telepathic energies embedded all over the link thanks to you."

"Perhaps," Charles bobbed his head agreeably. But then he stopped mid-nod, staring at Zale intensely, a small grin playing on his lips. And then he said, "Or maybe it's more than that."

Something clicked in Zale's head. For reasons he could not fathom, a sense of dire dread filled his heart. If he had been a weaker man, panic would have overridden his senses.

Out of his open mouth came the simple question of, "What?"

Charles' cocky grin returned and he lowered his head to leer at Zale through his eyelashes. "How do you think I was brought back?"

"How would I know?" Zale roared.

"*Oh come oooon!*" Charles drawled mockingly. "You must have some clue, lad."

Through his dread, writhing anger boiled to the surface. Baring his teeth, Zale snarled, "Don't be an idiot. I have *no* idea! Now tell me! Tell me who did thi—"

With a cruel smile, Charles' quiet voice cut through the air like a knife.

"It was you, Zale.

"You resurrected me."

chapter

THIRTY TWO

Reynolds ducked the swiping blow of a viciously sharp claw, using his momentum to swivel on the spot and plunge his blade into the Kalik's side. The powerful weapon sliced clean through the demon and the two parts tumbled away from each other.

His victory offered him no respite. He didn't even have a chance to straighten.

Several feet away, he saw another of the beasts stretch its arm to the sky, an electric blade already extended. With the reflexes his twenty plus years in the Daemonium army had gifted him, he deactivated his weapon, let it drop to the ground and then reached for his single-rifle.

One bullet was all it took to save his nearby comrade from death. The soldier turned just in time to see the demon drop. He glanced around for his saviour and raised a hand of thanks once he'd found him.

Reynolds returned the gesture, retrieving his sword from the grass and returning to the battle.

Before he could engage another demon, he heard three sharp cracks.

A relieved smile spread across his face as he realised that the snipers had *finally* moved into position. Four more cracks pierced the din of combat and over the heads of warring bodies he saw four Kalik tumble to the ground.

Their kin didn't even notice; they were too busy giving in to the insane bloodlust that gripped their kind in the face of so much fresh meat.

The plan was working. If the main bulk of their army could keep the beasts distracted long enough, then the snipers would be able to pick the rest of them off and save the soldiers' arses.

Reynolds hoped he'd be alive to witness the victory.

Badrick snuck noiselessly through the cave entrance. Even with his metal armour, Badrick was quieter than a soft wind; Daemnos had imparted the physical skill to accomplish this with great ease.

He crept through the lower floor tunnel which he knew would lead to the flooded hall that once served as the Forsaken's bed/bath/living room/toilet.

He felt sick at the simple thought of it.

With great care he strode into the water, half expecting something evil to jump out and plunge its teeth into his calf. As the water cascaded at his disruption, he scanned every inch of his surroundings with his eyes, using a sight-enhancement power to aid his efforts.

As he did so, Badrick also stroked the upper level with his

demonic senses, teasing out any secrets that might lurk up there. It didn't take him long to search the entire interior, and when he finally concluded that there was absolutely nothing to be found, he relaxed his abilities.

Badrick frowned, staring around angrily.

"What's going on?" he asked the cave.

There really was *nothing*.

No Kalik.

No Charles.

And according to his port-pad, not even any link energy.

It had vanished.

"How dare you say that!" Zale roared so loudly his eardrums threatened to burst. "What a stupid lie!"

"What if it's not a lie?" Charles appeared to be getting a lot of enjoyment out of Zale's rage and he had to fight harder than ever to stop himself from killing the Resurrected. "You brought me back to life. You created *this* Powered Resurrected."

"I don't even have that power!" Zale argued aggressively, combating the lie at its most basic level.

"It was you who resurrected me," Charles repeated.

Zale slammed his lips together several times, gaping like a fish as his brain failed to provide a suitable response to Charles' words.

What the Resurrected was claiming was preposterous.

Completely untrue!

How could Charles possibly have thought his lies would be believed? Aside from the fact that Zale had no such power, the only way he could have been the culprit and not been aware was if he'd experienced lost time.

Zale had lost no time. He could account for almost every single second of his entire life and had never experienced a black out that wasn't caused by someone's fist or bullet.

"How dare you," he finally repeated. He felt his fingers tighten on the trigger of his gun and had to fight his own body to prevent the weapon discharging. "How *dare* you accuse me of being the one who brought all this on! Your actions have led to *hundreds* of deaths." He took a quick breath, then screamed, "Your slaves killed my Carla! How *dare* you pin *that* on me!"

For the first time since Zale laid eyes on his former friend, Charles' smile slipped from his features completely.

"I admit I wasn't fond of that order. But it was for the best. She was in the way. She had to be removed from the equation."

"Excuse me!?"

That was all Zale had to say. For what had to be the first time in his memory, he was speechless. He had no idea how to respond to such a claim.

The smile instantly reappeared, flashing darkly in Zale's direction. "Ah, Zale," Charles crooned. "You truly are a magnificent being. Far more powerful than you realise. I'm glad I was ordered to make it as hard for you as I could. It gave me a chance to see what you can really do."

Zale jumped on the opportunity Charles presented him with these new words, desperate to regain control of his thoughts. If he could find things to question then his brain might get the kick-start it needed and begin working properly once more.

"That's the second time you've mentioned being ordered around," he hissed. "What—"

Infuriatingly, Charles cut him off with, "I serve a higher power."

Zale felt his stomach drop miles further than he believed possible; so it was true that the demon or Enthraller who *had* resurrected Charles was involved in these horrendous affairs. It was the only person Charles would possibly obey. He had no loyalty to anyone else.

They had discovered their Resurrected's identity.

It was time to discover the resurrecter.

"Who is it?" he asked, only warming up, expecting a dodge and getting exactly that.

"Now, now," Charles giggled. "Spoilers."

Zale was in the middle of shouting yet again when Charles managed to silence him with a sharp wave of his hand.

"Sorry, dude, but that's enough for now." His hand went to his belt and he detached some kind of object. "We must move things along."

With a razor-sharp jab of panic, Zale easily recognised what Charles was now fiddling with; a detonator.

Makeshift.

Crude in its design.

But very real.

It had barely any casing, and even from this distance Zale could see the wiring. Within two seconds his mind had studied the creation and he knew that it would work if activated.

"What are you doing!?" he roared, taking a nervous step back. "You're going to blow us up?"

"Not us," Charles cackled, laughing rudely in Zale's direction. "I wasn't sure if you were going to bring your new best bud with you, but just in case you acted as irrationally as I hoped, I lined the Forsaken's cave with explosives."

"*WHAT!?!*"

With barely hidden amusement, Charles feigned surprise, widening his eyes and placing a dainty hand on his chest. "Oh . . . didn't I mention? Badrick's gonna be buried in rock."

And without hesitation, he slammed his thumb upon the detonator.

The water splashed across the wall as a horrendously loud crashing sound caused Badrick to jump back in fright. His eyes shot to the ceiling only for him to find it no longer existed.

A roar of fear escaped his mouth and he stumbled backward even further, his eyes glued to the remains of the cave as they appeared to tumble towards him in slow motion.

Badrick tried to escape.

And had he not allowed panic to override his senses, he would have been able to. But he failed to act quickly enough and, before he knew it, the rocks had reached him and he was forced beneath the water by their profound weight.

"*NO!*" Zale turned on his heel, darting for the door, intending to bolt out of the Apos base and get to his car as fast as possible. Behind him he could hear Charles' laughter. It rang in his ears, piercing the drums as he reached for the door.

But as his hand touched metal, Zale felt something strange happen.

A spark.

A demonic ember.

Time seemed to slow as he made the effort to alter his focus to the swift sensation in his chest in order to identify it. He had less than half a second before something powerful gripped him by the back of the neck and he felt the ground leave his feet, his hand pulling at the doorknob and tearing it clean off.

Everything decolourised, as though his vision had become damaged. Colours were now impossibly inverted and Zale instantly squeezed his eyes shut against the glare.

He was spinning now, his body weightless, as though gravity no longer existed. Like space debris, he tumbled, feeling nothing but freezing cold.

And then it ended.

Without warning, his feet hit solid ground and he tumbled from the impact, the sudden presence of something beneath him throwing him completely off balance.

He greedily gulped the cold, fresh air that leaked into his helmet, not having recognised the lack of it until he'd fallen to the floor. Fighting the urge to be sick, he wrestled to his feet, determined to get away from Charles and get to Badrick as quickly as he could.

He didn't care what had just overcome him.

It wasn't important.

Weak as he felt, he was back on his feet. He gritted his teeth and pushed forward—

And that was when he finally clocked it.

Cold, fresh air.

There was no cold, fresh air to be had in the Apos base. It was underground and filled to the brim with blood and decay.

It was nothing but rotten inside.

This realisation forced his eyes to refocus. Blinking several times, he pushed the blurriness out.

He did not see what he expected.

Instead of soulless concrete walls and bloody floors, a cold, grey sky greeted him, half obscured by a blockade of trees and a tall, beautiful mountain.

He swivelled, stunned out of his mind, facing the base of the mountain.

The entrance to the Forsaken's cave lay before him.

"What—" A deafening crash suspended his words and he instinctively threw his hand in front of his visor as a thick plume of dust billowed from the opening.

"Badrick!" Zale screamed. "No!"

Within seconds he was at the cave entrance, hitting away the dust that lingered in the air. He didn't manage to get very far; the opening was blocked by a wall of humungous, solid boulders.

"Not again!" he cried, plunging his fingers between the cracks and straining to part the rocks. "Badrick!"

Demonic energy flashed behind him, and a cruel voice crowed, "Call, call, call all you want. It won't make a difference, Zale." Charles appeared over his shoulder, placing one hand upon it and the other against the cave wall. "He's dead and he'll be staying that way. You won't resurrect him like you did me."

"That wasn't me!" Zale screeched. He threw himself at Charles, charging his fist with electricity as he thrust it into his stomach. The impact, coupled with the force of his powers, sent Charles flying back, tumbling down the slanted dirt floor.

He came to rest beside a cluster of rocks, banging into them with a crack.

But the knock to his side didn't seem to faze him. He was coughing from Zale's powered strike, but Charles merely sneered at his smashing into the solid stone. Struggling to his feet, Charles gave him a look that suggested he was proud of Zale.

Which only served to make Zale even angrier.

He threw a blast of electricity at Charles, intending to scare as opposed to actually injure. A chunk of the rock beside the Resurrected's head separated from the rest as it exploded into pieces.

Charles leaned against what remained unaffected, *infuriatingly* laughing his head off.

"Shut up!" Zale roared, anger flooding his senses. "Shut up and stay there," he tried a little more calmly. "I'm getting him out!"

At that Charles cracked up louder than ever, as if Zale had just told him the funniest joke he'd ever heard. "No, you won't. You don't even want to." Zale ignored him. He returned to the fallen rocks, once again struggling against their weight.

"You don't need him anymore. He is a nothing." Charles stood straighter, rubbing his chest and wincing slightly. "You can join us, instead. Stand above the rest.

"We have the special powers, my friend. We are Singularis Enthrallers. Two sunflowers in a sea of orchids. You are an . . . electrical marvel, Zale. You are powerful and you don't need that demon of yours to realise it.

"You will be magnificent, Zale. I can't wait to see the *new* kind of *evil* you could bring to this world."

Zale roared over his shoulder, "Would you shut up!?!"

"What you just did . . . Horas can't teleport, Zale." He felt a squirming in his stomach and desperately tried to ignore it. Something pressed down on his left shoulder once again and he realised Charles was standing directly behind him. "Something else did it for you."

Charles ducked with incredible speed as Zale swung for him, this time aiming for his head.

"That's it!" Charles screeched, his face twisting madly, ecstatically. "Get angry! Strike me down. I won't dodge the next one."

Zale tensed the muscles in his arm in preparation for wiping away that cruel, smug grin.

He was ready to beat him into submission . . .

When something grey appeared in his peripheral, touching against Charles' temple.

"Dodge this, you motherfu—"

The owner of the pistol didn't manage to finish his God awful movie quip; the gun went off and Charles' head exploded in a splash of black and red and brain matter.

Zale felt his muscles tense and relax in quick succession as his whole body jerked in surprise at the suddenness of the bang. It was such a fright that his body began to ache from the strain the wrenching put on his limbs.

But the dull pain was nothing to the shock of seeing Badrick spinning the pistol and holstering it with the cockiness of John bloody Wayne.

"You should be dead," Zale whispered, stunned. "No one can survive the amount of rocks that would have crushed you."

Badrick clicked his tongue and pointed a finger at Zale. Taking a quick second to laugh with amusement, he sobered and said, "It was Daemnos. When the rocks fell he spun some kind of cocoon of energy around me. The rocks knocked me out for a minute but the water was so cold it woke me up." He laughed again. "I teleported out after that and found you and . . . Charles, I assume."

Zale was trying to figure out whether or not he should hug Badrick; he'd been truly afraid that his partner was dead.

Again.

And after what happened to Carla, he wouldn't have been able to handle another loss.

He'd been ready to collapse.

So seeing Badrick alive and well made him want to leap upon his partner and suffocate him with bear hugs.

But a small part of his brain spoke up and prevented his body from acting so unprofessionally.

In truth it was probably time he stopped mourning Badrick every time he 'died'.

The bugger would probably just come back.

And so, overcoming his euphoria, he stepped forward and simply made do with shaking his partner's hand. "Good to see you're alright."

"Thanks."

With the pleasantries out of the way, the reality of their

situation came rushing back so fast it made Zale feel a little nauseous. "Wish you hadn't shot Charles in the head, though," he sighed, looking for the body. "Now we have no way of finding the de—"

Charles wasn't there.

The body was gone.

"What!?" Badrick shrieked angrily, stepping forward and spreading his arms wide with incredulity. "How!? I got him in the head. I saw his brain hit the goddamn rocks!"

Zale didn't bother expressing his fresh surprise and antagonism. Didn't bother mentioning that the aforementioned brains had also vanished along with their owner.

Instead, he resigned himself to just sighing and murmuring, "Any chance the demon who brought him back resurrected him again?"

"Right in front of us and we didn't even notice." Badrick scoffed with frustration. "How crap are we?"

"I doubt the demon actually came here." Zale almost laughed, though it would have been a cold, humourless chuckle as he wasn't capable of genuine laughter right now.

He didn't think he ever would be again.

"The demon did it from a distance," Badrick nodded. "That sucks! Now we have to find him again."

Thankfully, that wasn't going to be hard. Zale had already figured out how to track Charles' link energy; the one thing his S.D.P didn't seem to be able to hide. Using his port-pad, he rapidly connected to the Daemonium's systems and downloaded the software required.

Within minutes—thanks to their Godlike internet system—he was booting the software and typing in what he required.

"Got it," he said, showing Badrick the trail of bright blue energy on his screen. "Can you track that mid-flash?" he asked, referring to his partner's method of teleportation.

Badrick nodded his confirmation and reached out his hand to Zale.

chapter
THIRTY THREE

Reynolds removed the blade from the Kalik that collapsed beneath his strength and stood on its neck to ensure it was dead. Around him, the last of the demons also fell, decapitated by a Lieutenant wielding another of Zale's remarkable inventions.

Assorted gun sounds disturbed the air as the soldiers fired bullets into any of the Kalik that were still twitching, and with a sigh of relief Reynolds realised that the battle was finally over.

His alleviation didn't last long however, as without the distraction of a hundred Kalik trying to open him up he was now able to focus on the world around him.

The smell hit him first.

Then he saw the bodies.

He felt like it should have made him feel better that there were obviously hundreds more dead Kalik than their own troops, but looking at the carnage it was hard to convince himself of that.

Red dead bodies—made all the more vibrant by the blood spattered across their armours—lay everywhere, standing out far more vividly than the dark brown of the Kalik. The sight of them warped Reynolds' vision. Individual Kalik blurred together, becoming one big indistinguishable mass, until all he could see were his slaughtered comrades.

And all of a sudden it didn't feel like much of a victory.

He felt a jolt on his shoulder, marking the presence of a person behind him.

"We did it, sir," Kevin said. "We won."

"But lost so many," Reynolds uttered morosely, still gazing around at all the death.

In a voice just as sad, Kevin sighed, "I know, sir. But they died for *you*. You led us and they fought and died for you."

"No," Reynolds said. "They died for humanity, and that's the truth." He turned his gaze upon Kevin, studying the new Council Member's shattered visor. He could see right through the gap left behind; there was a nasty gash above Kevin's eye where the pieces cut him. "They died in defence of the world. They're heroes. All of them."

Kevin nodded. "Damn right, they are!"

Zale wasn't sure if Charles was truly mad or just enjoyed messing with them way too much, but frankly, he couldn't lie and claim to care.

All that mattered to him was catching the Resurrected and fixing *everything* he had destroyed.

Badrick, of course, *did* seem to care, evident from the way he next said, "Why the hell has he led us back here?"

Zale couldn't answer that.

He didn't know what mental plan involved running back to the human military base that had been savaged by Charles' Kalik followers and making camp until Zale and Badrick arrived.

Charles hadn't moved in five minutes. Clearly with his master's help, the Resurrected had teleported to this location and surrounded himself with his minions.

Zale could see them now, barely able to keep still due to their natural desire to hunt and kill.

But stay they did, because of their fear of the one commanding them.

Zale couldn't help but be a little impressed.

If they could recruit a Resurrected one day . . . they'd never have to fear the Kalik ever again.

They could even use them against the Apos.

An idea with some merit, but one to consider later.

They had a job to do right now.

"They haven't seen us yet," Zale told Badrick. "Let's keep it that way in regards to you." He pointed to the roof of one of the nearby hangars. "I want you to take position up there. Keep Charles in your sights but train your powers on the Kalik around him. When I give the word you kill them, got it? But don't kill Charles." He paused, remembering Badrick's bullet. "Not that you could make it stick."

"What're you going to do?" Badrick queried.

Zale growled, grinding his teeth, "We need to finish our chat."

With that he stepped forward, keeping his auto-rifle in his hands, moving in the direction of Charles' position.

Badrick wasted no time; he leapt high into the sky, coming to rest on the metal roof of the hangar. He did his best to make it silent but this time failed to completely hide the muffled clang of his boots against the steel.

Grimacing, he tiptoed along, moving quickly, only stopping when he reached the edge of the roof and was able to monitor the scene below.

From this vantage point he could see Charles and his retinue of Kalik without obstruction.

He saw Zale reach them, the anger in his body language crystal clear. If Charles was able to read it, he didn't expose his awareness. Even from this distance, Badrick could see the massive, cruel grin twisting his features.

"Zale!" the Resurrected cooed. "Welcome." He rubbed his chin and face. "I scrub up well after a bullet to the head, don't I?" Then he indicated to one of his guards. "Sic 'em!"

The demon charged, roaring with vicious delight.

But its enthusiasm did nothing to bolster its attack effort; like a living oxymoron Zale sidestepped with a strange calm-like rage and grabbed the largest spike on the demon's shoulder.

Then, with a roar of pure wrath, he jammed his auto-rifle into its side and opened fire. The demon screamed in agony as its body was torn to shreds. Zale did not ease off the trigger until his clip was empty, and when the click echoed across the base, Zale slung the weapon, reached in with his other hand and tore the remains of the Kalik in two.

When the halves spattered wetly onto the tarmac, he lowered his hands, breathing heavily. With enhanced hearing, Badrick could hear the raggedness of the breaths.

"Jesus!" Badrick muttered.

Badrick didn't feel any kind of admiration of himself at the thought that he'd been right all along; Zale had refused to grieve and now he was losing control of his anger.

Charles was clapping like a mental now. "Bravo, you awesome

thing!" he was bawling. "I'm very impressed."

Zale didn't respond. Still breathing heavily, he stepped closer, his every step communicating menace.

"You look tired, Zale," Charles commented. When Zale didn't respond—simply panted and glared—Charles chewed his lip, and changed the subject with a chuckle, "This was my favourite of all my days out." He glanced around the base with a wide leer. "You know, I stole that helicopter just for the fun of it. I learned how to fly it through your mind and it was so fun watching you struggle to figure out why I would attack a human place.

"For the hell of it," Charles said matter-of-factly. "But it had a purpose. Leave clues here and there. Let you figure things out. Do things for you."

"Enough of your accursed lies!" Zale suddenly hollered, and Badrick wondered what Zale meant. To him, it sounded as though Charles was suggesting he *wanted* to get caught. "Charles, I'm bringing you back to the Daemonium. You will answer for what you have done."

"I really don't think that I will," Charles giggled ridiculously. "I think I'll con—"

Without warning, Charles stopped talking. His expression froze in place and his eyes misted, as though he was listening to someone speak only to him.

And in the corner of his eye, Badrick saw Zale stumble dizzily. His gaze darted to him in concern, but was relieved to see Zale straightening.

Relieved, yet still worried and wondering what had just affected his partner, Badrick did his best to keep an eye on him as well as Charles. Gripping his weapon tighter, Badrick returned his sights back upon the Resurrected.

Charles' face had fallen dramatically. The cruel grin completely vanished to be replaced with what appeared to be shock and disbelief.

His eyes widening, Charles murmured, "Oh . . . I will?" He spoke without direction, aiming his voice at nothing. "That's not . . . That's not what you promised. You said I—"

Giving the distinct impression that he'd just been threatened with intense pain, Charles jerked backwards and sharply bowed his head.

Within seconds, his original confident aura was gone.

Now he looked simply pitiful.

The fear that spread across his face was such a contrast to his previous expressions that Badrick was shocked to see it.

"Yes . . . Yes, I'm sorry," Charles stammered. He was shaking now, every single finger twitching independently of the others, his limbs jerking like maracas. "I obey."

And to Badrick's surprise, Charles shuddered to his knees, bowing his head further and saying no more.

Zale appeared to be just as shocked as Badrick was.

Badrick didn't know what to do. Surely this was some kind of trap. Should he go in for the arrest? Should he stay where he was?

Or should he just blast everything in sight and remove all need for concern?

Badrick greatly wished he could go with that third option, but he'd messed up once already in the last hour and only through the actions of what had to be a very powerful demon had his rashness not cost them dearly.

Besides, his question of whether or not this was a legit surrender was quickly answered without his prompting.

The demons swivelled and stared at Charles, an expression as close to incredulity as they could manage spread across their monstrous faces. With roars of disapproval, they bound away from the Resurrected. One even darted in the direction of Zale.

Badrick jumped to his feet as Zale raised his gun. With rapidity he charged energy in his hands and let rip with a flurry of red blasts. The projectiles each struck a Kalik before Zale even had a chance to open fire. Not that he could have done; in his rage, he'd failed to remember that he had yet to reload his weapon. A mistake a rational Zale would *never* have made.

Heck, even an *irrational* Zale was too smart to make that sort of error.

Knowing this, Badrick recognised the familiar feelings of worry rise up in his stomach. He was scared for his partner. Something was so very wrong.

Because he refused to grieve, Zale wasn't himself at all.

From down below, Zale waved his thanks, indicating for Badrick to descend. Not bothered to clamber down or even teleport, Badrick simply let himself drop.

Landing heavily, he hurried up to Charles as Zale did the same. Reloading his auto-rifle, Zale roughly jammed the barrel into the Resurrected's head. Charles winced at the pain but otherwise didn't react.

"OK, Zale," Badrick said, gently pushing the gun down. He couldn't help but worry that Zale was going to put a bullet in their suspect purely on principle. Knowing that this man had been the one who killed Carla, Zale was surely conflicted right now. "Come on. Don't bash our bad guy around. You check there aren't any more Kalik. I'll keep an eye on him."

After a moment's hesitation, Zale nodded his agreement. He turned his back and hurried away, looking left and right and watching the fleeing Kalik disappear into the distance.

And as Badrick trained his gun on Charles, he couldn't help but think . . . *Is that it?*

"This is a trap," he said. "What are you planning?"

"No trap," Charles spat, bitterness lacing his voice. "I have been abandoned by my master."

"Who's your master?" Badrick asked.

But Charles only laughed again. "Nice try."

Angered, but still in command of his emotions, Badrick tutted and said, "Fine. We still got you, you son of a bitch! Be unhelpful, for all I care. We'll get everything out of you back at base."

"Ah, the Daemonium," Charles sang sadly. "Not looking forward to getting there."

Badrick checked behind him to see where Zale had gotten to. He found him some distance away, standing stock still, his hand to his head.

With a quick surge of energy to his ears, Badrick realised he was in contact with Reynolds, communicating their victory. Reynolds was happy; he was promising the arrival of a dropship as soon as possible and giving orders for them to keep Charles secured until then.

"You'll be there soon enough, like it or not," Badrick told Charles, taking enjoyment out of being able to tell him this.

"Before I go," the Resurrected muttered, "one last thing."

Upon his face was an expression that Badrick recognised all too well.

Fear radiated from him. A terror fuelled by the simple thought of what he was about to do. Rebelliousness could be seen in his eyes, but it was almost completely overshadowed by his dread.

Badrick was only able to recognise this because he himself had worn that expression so many times before; when Badrick lived with his abusive uncle, he'd occasionally be inspired to fight back, but his fear of the man would send tidal waves of terror shooting through him even as he acted.

It was clear to Badrick; Charles' abandonment was inspiring him to say something. He was scared, sure, but now he was angry.

Badrick was sure of it.

Therefore he thought he was ready for what would be said

when Charles opened his mouth.

But in the end all that came out was, "Don't trust Zale."

And then he laughed.

Frustration boiled the blood in Badrick's veins. He was sure he'd seen what he thought he saw in Charles' eyes.

Had it been a trick?

It couldn't have been.

No way was this idiot *that* good of an actor that he could portray such complex emotions so convincingly.

Was he?

Whatever the answer, Badrick had no more time to wonder; Zale ran up beside him so fast it was as though he had simply materialised out of thin air.

"They're on their way, Charles," the electric Enthraller snarled. "We're going to get answers out of you. I'll torture you myself if I have to."

Badrick didn't dare say a thing. Though he could not see Zale's face, Badrick understood by the sound of his voice that getting in his partner's way right at that moment was more than a bad idea.

Only a fool would try.

*

Zale watched the dropship shudder to a landing with a heavy heart.

Just because they had *finally* secured their suspect did not mean it was all over. In truth, it was probably just beginning; there was a still a necromantic bastard to locate and by Charles' own admission the demon or Enthraller responsible for his recreation was involved in everything.

He or she had not resurrected Charles in passing.

Charles *served* this unknown higher power.

That was what mattered now; finding the puppet-master.

At least that was what Zale was trying to tell himself, but he wasn't succeeding all that well. He was losing a viciously fought debate in his head on what was more important; finding the resurrecter or worrying on what Charles had said.

About him.

About whom Charles claimed was the resurrecter.

It *had* to be a lie.

It couldn't *not* be.

Charles always did like to play games.

Enjoyed manipulating Zale into doing what he wanted.

Zale shook his head—no longer would he get away with it. Charles was *never* his friend. He had never deserved any of the respect Zale afforded him in the past.

Nothing he said was worth listening to.

Zale needed to—

"Zale!"

Reality came crashing back as Zale clumsily tumbled out of his own head. Shaking it, he tried to refocus his blurred eyes. Something green appeared in his field of vision before he quite managed to, but he didn't need perfect eyesight to recognise it as Badrick.

As the olive figure swam back into focus, he realised Badrick was gesturing for him to board the dropship. In his reverie, Zale had failed to notice that the dropship crew had already detained Charles and escorted him aboard.

"Come on," Badrick said. "We're going home."

*

For reasons he couldn't quite explain, Badrick did not feel happy to emerge into the HQ. He should have been ecstatic; they'd accomplished their mission and were now back under the protection of the facility.

Everything was good.

But Badrick couldn't see it that way.

Coming back here only reminded him of what had occurred. He could see the spot where Carla had been killed, and beside that Acro's remains had yet to be cleaned up.

Zale was also staring at the place her body fell. With his helmet now under his arm, Badrick could see his face, wrought with distress.

Badrick didn't know how to comfort him.

He didn't even know how to comfort himself.

Something strange was happening inside him, prompted by the memories of Carla's death. His heart was beating faster than normal, his mind racing.

A horrendous pressure was straining against his chest.

He felt like he wanted to cry.

It was horrible.

It wasn't right.

He'd cried before. He'd felt sad before. But never like *this*.

No ... This was more like when Daemnos' meddling had finally broken and his emotions had re-emerged in all their splendour.

Badrick put his hand against his chest, fighting desperately against the tears that threatened to seep from his eyes.

And he couldn't help but wonder if he really had fixed himself ... or traded one problem for another.

Zale suggested to his partner that he get showered and fed; it had been a long day and neither of them had eaten in almost twenty four hours. He would do the same, as long as his stomach was fit enough for food. Frankly, Zale suspected his acids were still churning too much for him to eat.

The tension that built in anticipation for the grand conclusion was still there. Even though Charles was finally apprehended, the dread of what would come next was *still there*.

It didn't feel over.

He could see Charles being escorted to the prison and knew that the Resurrected would never escape from within its confines. Not even his master could surely spring him from a cell in the Daemonium.

Zale closed his eyes and sighed tiredly—the master was still out there somewhere. A demonic being of great power caused *all* of this. They'd resurrected Charles and commanded a Kalik army to devastating effect.

And this master now understood them intimately. Either through Charles or somehow even before finding the dead human, he or she learned of the three way link.

Figured out how to use it to their advantage.

Achieved so much destruction with it.

But who the hell was this puppet-master?

Zale couldn't even begin to wonder on that now; his never ending headache was threatening to explode and he could barely concentrate.

Besides, before he could do anything else there was something that needed to be done first.

Someone needed to be honoured . . .

chapter
THIRTY FOUR

The black of the night sky was so deep it was as though the heavens had been snuffed out, replaced by an engulfing void. The only sign that this was not the case was the beautiful glow of the white stars, illuminating the darkness, especially bright this night.

Almost as though they'd come out especially to bear witness Carla's passing from this world.

There were no graves in the Daemonium.

No space.

No time.

No desire to look upon the dead.

Badrick understood the reasoning completely. If he'd had to spend the rest of his life looking at a grave marker with Carla's name on it he would have quit and run away.

Far away.

He was thankful for the funeral pyre tradition the Daemonium practiced.

They were in the middle of one now. Carla lay upon a table of wood and thatch, a hundred agents, soldiers and operatives surrounding her in a circle, heads bowed.

Nothing broke the silence of the night but the guards still on duty atop the Wall. Even from this distance, Badrick could see some of them sneaking glances over, breaking vigilance to pay their respects to the dead agent.

Badrick had seen funeral pyres before.

After the Apos attacked them, primarily.

Of course, small pyres were set alight almost every week. Theirs was a dangerous business. Casualties were to be expected.

But never before had he been to one and *never before* had he seen a procession as big as this. Badrick was aware that many liked Carla but he hadn't known she'd been *this* popular.

Among the mourners were people he recognised; the new Dominus, General Reynolds, accompanied by his favoured colleagues; Kevin, Quill and some others.

His new prisoner safe and secure, Malcolm had also shown up.

Zach stood with his team next to a large flock of soldiers, their blue uniforms a striking contrast to the sea of red.

The sight of the old Command Council angered Badrick greatly. Having shown complete apathy to the agent's death, Badrick felt that Carver had absolutely *no* place here.

But he left them alone.

He wouldn't start a fight.

Not now.

It would be disrespectful to Carla's memory.

Turning his back to them, Badrick returned his attention to the rest of the crowd.

As he gazed around, still amazed at the numbers present, Badrick realised he could not readily identify the face of Carla's partner anywhere in this mass. Though he tried his hardest, pulling the man's face from memory, Badrick could not find him.

Carla's partner was not here.

Despite his concern, Badrick could only assume John just couldn't stand to be present. It wasn't hard to figure out why; if Badrick had to watch Zale burn away to nothing . . . It was completely understandable that John would miss this if he couldn't bear to see Carla as she was now.

And then there was the one who had more right to be here than anyone, standing atop a platform, higher than the rest.

Zale.

His face was stone.

As though he was trying to hide his emotions.

But the attempts to mask his pain only communicated his sorrow more.

It emanated from his form in waves.

Badrick could see his hands shaking.

A man dressed in a priest's uniform suddenly stepped from the masses, climbing the platform and standing near Zale. He turned to the crowd and spoke aloud, calling so everyone could hear him.

"Tonight, we say goodbye to Agent Carla Hunter." The priest hesitated, allowing everyone time to process his words. "A truly magnificent Enthraller, she was taken before her time." He indicated to his left. "Our new Dominus would like to say some words."

Reynolds shook hands with the priest—who departed to the side, watching from a distance—glanced at Zale for a hesitant moment, then began to address the crowd.

"I remember when Carla first came to the Daemonium," he said a little quietly. Coughing, Reynolds made an effort to raise his voice. The next time he spoke he was easily audible. "She was this nervous little thing, fifteen years of age, powers manifested earlier than normal, almost killed her schoolboy lover." A laugh escaped his lips and he said, "She was so nervous she humped every similarly aged Enthraller in sight to keep her mind off what had happened to her. All the good looking ones, of course." He winked at the crowd to an assortment of sad chuckles.

"Like the rest of us, the prurient nature our demons inflict upon us often overtook her. We're all guilty of that. I'm sure many of you can relate." There was another round of soft laughter.

"But Carla . . . she . . . " Reynolds faltered for a moment, looking to the sky for strength. "It takes years to control those urges. It takes years for new Enthrallers to stop sleeping with every pretty person they see.

"That's why it speaks volumes about Carla's strength of will and . . . *sheer* power that she had no trouble burying those instincts when she met the one she ultimately loved."

Behind Reynolds, Zale shifted uncomfortably. With his powerful sight, Badrick spotted a tear finally escaping his left eye.

"She *did* love you, Zale," the General spoke, turning his head to the electric Enthraller. "You should know that."

Zale didn't speak. He simply nodded gently.

"And I don't think I have to remind you just *how* good she was at everything she did," Reynolds addressed the procession once again. "Only twenty years old, only five years part of our organisation, and only one of those years in active service.

"And she was better than most of us. Without a doubt, she could flatten me in hand-to-hand combat. I would even bet that, had my good friend Mawr Burakka survived long enough to meet her, she would have taken even him to school."

There was a combination of laughs, mixed with the disbelief of some of the soldiers; clearly comrades of Mawr who had known him well.

"Carla was . . . No! She *is* and always will be an example to the rest of us. She was a pillar of strength. She was immensely liked. The voice of wisdom to many of us dumb thugs who chose violence over reason. It's amazing just how many of you have come to say goodbye. This is the biggest funeral I've seen within our walls for many years and it fills my heart with joy to know she is getting a proper send-off."

Reynolds closed his eyes and took a moment before continuing on. When he next opened them, they were glistening.

"I will forever remember the time she corrected the Hierarch on his demonology. I will forever remember when she returned home with her partner, having killed nearly twenty Kalik without a scratch on her person. I will forever remember how helpful she was to others.

"I will forever remember Carla."

He raised his right hand high into the air and bowed his head. Around Badrick, the entire crowd did the same, every one of them chanting, "*I will forever remember Carla.*"

Recognising this as some kind of traditional honour to the dead, Badrick hurried to do the same.

Reynolds stepped down from the platform and the priest replaced him. He quickly began with a series of chants, which many of the others joined in with. It took Badrick a moment to recognise what was being said, but he eventually figured out the speakers were chanting various religious rites.

As they continued into the night, he got the feeling that this was actually an established practice within the Daemonium's society.

He was surprised to hear that the Daemonium had a large notion of religion or that they even fell in line with that sort of thing.

But he shouldn't have been; the people around him weren't reciting from any one religion. The chants were clearly from an assortment of many.

Maybe all of them.

Having demons jammed into their souls and knowledge of Hell literally written down, it would have been stupid to assume that the afterlife didn't exist. And with such evil in their souls, with no proper way of discerning which afterlives existed, it shouldn't have surprised Badrick that the Daemonium venerated many of them.

Forgiveness from *any* deity for what they were.

At its core, that's what the Daemonium wanted.

Up on the platform, Zale was handed a torch. The reflection of the fire flickered in his sparkling blue eyes, mixing with the voltage that powered them as he stared into the flames.

Badrick was glad; the duty of lighting Carla's pyre *should* be given to Zale.

There was no other who had earned it.

The flames didn't take long to catch. Within only seconds, the pyre had completely lit up, the fire licking at Carla's flesh and slowly warping her pristine uniform.

Badrick watched as Zale stepped back to his original place and stared as the flames consume the love of his life.

Watched as Zale refused to allow himself to cry *again*.

And that was all it took.

Building faster than he could keep up with, a massive influx of agonising sorrow slammed into Badrick's chest and he almost screamed with the effort of keeping back the tears that threatened to torrent from his eyes.

He gripped his chest tensely, fresh worry sparking his mind.

Something's wrong, his mind told him. *You're broken.*

This thought was so horrible that he was actually glad for the interruption that stepped up from behind, holding a shortwave radio.

"Operative Varner?" the owner of the radio asked.

Badrick immediately stamped on his panic, on his emotions, on his thoughts, and turned his back on Zale, dragging his attention to the agent.

"Yeah, that's me." He glanced at the radio. "What's up?"

"I've . . . " The agent hesitated, licking his lips. "You're friends with him, so I don't think it's that bad but still . . . I feel wrong telling you this before the General . . . " The agent's eyes flickered to Reynolds.

"What's wrong?" Badrick prompted him, a gnawing sense of dread now replacing his sadness.

The agent sighed, giving in, and said, "Do you remember Lucikefer?"

"Unfortunately."

"Well, he had two slaves on Earth. Two Ordinarius. We got one of them a while back but the other has eluded us since."

Badrick nodded, remembering the Ordinarius that had been dragged kicking and screaming into the Daemonium. "Did you find him?"

"No . . . he found us."

Badrick blinked twice. "What?"

"He's on the radio," the agent sighed, shaking the device in his hand. "He says he has information on the demon that created the Resurrected and will only speak to the one who has Daemnos."

Badrick's eyes widened and he instantly beckoned for the radio. After a moment's hesitation, the agent did as he requested.

"Thanks, man," Badrick said, slapping the agent on the arm gratefully and putting the radio to his head.

Before he'd even managed to speak, as if the demon could sense the presence of his ear, a voice sounded from it. "Is that Daemnos?"

"It's the Enthraller of Daemnos."

Badrick was shocked to hear the Ordinarius' voice quavering, his breathing ragged with . . . That was *fear*. Badrick recognised it immediately.

"Good," the demon sighed. "Good."

"You said you have information on the Resurrected's master," Badrick said. "Who is it?"

"No," the demon snapped. "I won't talk until you bring me in. You promise me protection and then I talk."

"Not how it works," Badrick snapped back, instincts kicking in, 'negotiable-Badrick' coming online. "Give me something and then we'll see what we can do."

With an angry demonic curse, the demon muttered, "You cannot stop him. He will kill us all."

"Not good enough," Badrick said. "Who is it?"

"A power unlike anything you've ever seen. Unlike anything anyone has even seen. Stronger than the Devil, Daemnos and Vermiah combined. Stronger than *all* the Royals combined." The demon paused, his breath still shaky. "Nothing can stop him."

"OK." Badrick licked his lips, somewhat unsure of how to proceed. "Tell me who it is."

"Evil is old," the demon rambled, ignoring the question entirely. "Evil is ancient. That's the way it is. That's the way it *should* be."

"Oi!" Badrick stopped him.

"I don't know who it is," the demon stammered. "I only know what I've seen. He will devour not only this existence, but all three. The entire trinity will become blackness.

"He is the end for all of us.

"He is the prophesised king of all demons."

Getting impatient now, Badrick growled, "Enough of the demonic *prophetic* crap. Get on with it."

"He is unique. The first of his kind. The only one of his kind. Young, but more dominant than anything old. In some circles he is called the End of Life," the demon whispered, "but to the rest of us he is known as . . .

"New Evil . . . "

<u>And some final words:</u>

As this book is self published and I lack the advertising and marketing budget of more traditionally published books, my main form of advertising comes from you guys (the readers).

So please, if you liked, loved, hated, despised or felt/thought anything about this book at all, leave me a review and let me and others know what you thought.

For more immediate updates on new releases and works in progress you can follow me on:

http://www.facebook.com/JavscoBooks

or

http://www.wattpad.com/user/Josh_Brookes

CONTINUE THE SERIES:

The Daemonium must now recover after the chaos caused
by the Kalik army, maintaining order despite the
destruction.

But a new evil is rising.

Though the agents have the puppet, the puppeteer still
eludes them. Unseen and unknown, it outwits them at every
turn, and soon it becomes clear that not even Badrick and
Daemnos might be able to stop it . . .

9 781912 663026